TRINITY
STONES

TRINITY STONES

THE ANGELORUM TWELVE CHRONICLES
BOOK 1

L.G. O'CONNOR

SHE WRITES PRESS

Published 2014
Printed in the United States of America
ISBN: 978-1-938314-84-1
Library of Congress Control Number: 2013957211

For information, address:
She Writes Press
1563 Solano Ave #546
Berkeley, CA 94707

This is a work of fiction. Names, characters, places, and incidents portrayed in this novel are either products of the author's imagination or are used fictitiously, and any resemblance to actual persons, living or dead, business establishments, events, or locales is entirely coincidental.

Cover Design: Derek Murphy, Creativindie

To my husband Leo, forever and a day . . . And for the one soul without whom this series never would have existed.

Journey forth in peace and love.

"There is no such thing as chance; and what seems to us mere accident springs from the deepest source of destiny."

 –Friedrich Schiller (German poet and philosopher, 1759–1805)

"The sin, both of men and of angels, was rendered possible by the fact that God gave them free will."

 –C. S. Lewis (Irish novelist and theologian, 1898–1963)

Excerpt from the Book of Human Angels — 5 Enoch (Hidden)
Translation: Essenes Aramaic papyrus text scribed 2nd century BC

"As it was so spoken, and then written, much time has passed since Michael bound the Watchers, led by Semyaza, to the confines of darkness. Wrath has been meted upon the Nephilim spawn. Their bodies and souls ripped from their being, leaving them shades of darkness to wander the corridors between Hell and Earth without peace."

. . .

"A new breed of Watcher has come, three hundred strong, to live among and as man to understand their strife and to empathize with their pain. Protected now by the children of Uriel, these Watchers will balance the evil that has been cast down from Heaven."

. . .

"The forces of darkness unite to battle for their freedom, to reach the key that will deliver them from Judgment Day and remain forever free."

. . .

"It is with the birth of the First of Holy Twelve that the prophecy begins, it is with the battle that the prophecy ends."

Prelude

San Francisco, California

Dr. Sandra Wilson gripped the steering wheel. The rush of air from the defroster did little to keep her awake. Her eyelids fluttered shut from the glare of the overhead street lamps and the rhythmic slap of the wiper blades. Flexing the muscles in her face to keep her eyes open, she concentrated on the stretch of road illuminated by her headlights while shadowy figures of parked cars and low industrial buildings sped by in her peripheral vision.

Ten more minutes and her head could rest safely on her pillow.

She had slept barely ten hours in the last thirty-six. Her covert work with Dr. Tom Peyton, on top of her busy schedule at Stanford University, had her working eighty-hour weeks for the past month. This week was worse. They'd accelerated their schedule, trying to complete the project. They were so close. She was sure it was only a matter of days until they finalized the vaccine protocol. Their success would ultimately save the one life that mattered most to the Angelorum.

But her research wasn't the only thing preventing her from sleeping. Her Guardian had been taken by the Dark Ones three days ago. Her grief over his capture weighed heavily on her heart. Knowing they wouldn't kill him provided her some consolation. He had something they needed.

Out of nowhere, a shadow the size of a large dog darted in front of her car. Sandra reacted on reflex and jerked the wheel to the right, avoiding a parked car. Snapped fully awake, she could feel her heart thump against her rib cage. The car bucked violently, yanking her hard against the seat belt. The thick nylon strap bit into her shoulder. After lurching twice, the car sputtered and coasted to a stop at the side of the road in the Lower Haight district of San Francisco.

Shit. Sandra frowned, hitting the steering wheel with the heel of her hand in frustration. Her mechanic had begged to buy her "classic" car on several occasions. Next time, she would take him up on his offer.

She sat dazed for a moment then sighed and took out her cell phone.

Thank God for modern technology. The phone sprang to life under her touch and displayed the time: 1:30 a.m. Her eyes lit up after a few finger taps. There was a bar within walking distance that stayed open until two. She dialed the nearest cab company and gave the bar's address for a 1:45 a.m. pickup. She'd send a tow truck tomorrow.

Relieved she hadn't swapped the rubber-soled flats she wore in the lab for the heels in her bag, she stepped out into the cool, damp night. Retrieving her rain poncho from the backseat, she slipped it over her head to protect her from the light drizzle, and tucked her long, dark braid under the hood. The coat fell short on her graceful six-foot-tall frame but provided enough length to keep her dry.

With a weary sigh, she grabbed her purse and set off toward the bar. Her mind drifted back to the final anomaly she needed to solve to complete the vaccine formula.

She'd gotten a block away from her car when a ripple of energy sparked her senses and the hairs prickled on the back of her neck. A shudder shot straight through her and she knew. The shadow she'd seen wasn't an animal.

Glancing around the deserted street, she surveyed the area. This wasn't the best part of town. Common criminals didn't worry her as much as the Hunters—the ones who weren't quite human.

No, no, no! This is all wrong. Her mind raced back to the premonition of her own demise; she'd seen a different vision. *Daylight. It's supposed to happen in daylight.* It could only mean one thing . . . something must have changed in the Trinity Stones. Why hadn't the Angelorum contacted her? They could have at least sent a warning.

A streetlight winked out, followed by another, then two more. Then all at once, the remaining lights on the surrounding buildings and down the street in front of her flickered and exploded. Shattered glass tinkled as it rained down and hit the pavement.

Plunged into complete darkness, the silence grew around her, and the black void magnified her exposure with every breath she took.

Sandra's chest tightened and her skin broke out into a cold sweat as the realization gripped her. The Dark Ones had sent something even more powerful than one of their soulless Hunters after her.

Her superior night vision kicked in and she glanced back, spotting the black haze of the disembodied demon heading toward her. Fear and frustration animated her limbs, pumping her legs into action. Her eyes darted between the industrial buildings, looking for an escape route. She'd known this assignment could end as a suicide mission but foolishly thought she could outwit destiny.

The demon would be unstoppable without her Guardian and his angelic weapons. Her only chance would be to outrun it and get someplace with people before it could fully manifest.

A quick glance over her shoulder revealed the black, inky haze gaining on her. Only moments remained before the demon would be close enough to take physical form. She screamed as its energy bore into her head—a hot, searing pain in her skull—ready to take her down like prey. Her legs grew weaker as she sprinted down the dark path between two buildings, hoping to find an exit onto an adjoining street. The looming presence of the demon made her shoulder blades burn where her wings used to be.

Just as she thought she couldn't take another step, an alley opened to her left. Her spirits lifted. Lights a few blocks ahead . . . people not far away. With a burst of adrenaline, she hurled herself around the corner, ripping the sleeve of her poncho on the jagged brick exterior of the building. She ignored her aching lungs and pushed on.

The sound of hooves scraping against the pavement filled her with dread, and hope drained out of her like grains of sand inside an hourglass.

Death can't be cheated, she thought with bitter resignation.

Her legs gave out, and the demon lunged with inhuman force.

Excruciating pain radiated from the center of her back, the blow driving her to the ground. Her hood flew back, and the crunch of her bones echoed in her ears as her cheek met the wet asphalt. She lay paralyzed, in agony, her eyes pinned open. Blood warmed her ear as it fanned out in a puddle underneath her. The demon lowered its red-skinned face. Drool hung in strings from razor-sharp teeth. Its breath heated her hair in rank puffs while air whistled from her mouth in panicked gasps. She knew what was next; it anticipated feeding before destroying her completely.

Sandra said a silent prayer.

A ring of white light spread between the buildings, engulfing her and blowing the demon back. Embryonic warmth seeped into her, filling her with peace. Within the glow, a man dressed in a tunic as white as the wings unfurled behind him appeared before her dying eyes. His hypnotic purple gaze captured hers.

She recognized him.

"Who's going to save him, Jonas?" she asked the angel telepathically. Without her, Tom would surely be next.

The angel's intense purple eyes held compassion and a soothing pull. *"Worry not, Hope,"* he said, using her true angelic name, *"The others will finish your fine work."*

Expelling a final breath, she relaxed. The silver cord severed from her body and released her soul. Floating up and away, she glanced downward at the demon.

Enraged, it stood below, watching its dinner escape unaware she wasn't what she'd appeared. Consuming her soul would have led to its blazing destruction.

Protected underneath the angel's wing, Hope cast away her earthly concerns and gladly returned into the embracing light of Heaven.

Chapter 1

One year later . . .

New York City. Wednesday, March 19, 7:30 a.m. EDT

"HEAL ME," he whispered.

What?

Cara ignored the man with the V-shaped scar on his cheek, who was pressed up against her side in the fast-moving subway car. With her face half hidden behind a curtain of auburn waves, she continued to scroll through the e-mail on her work phone. Taking half a step away, she tried to create some distance between them.

The car banked hard to the left, a metallic squeal of brakes echoing off the tunnel walls as the train barreled around a turn. Cara swayed under the weight of the briefcase slung over her shoulder and shifted back into the man.

"Sorry," Cara mumbled without looking up. Readjusting her grip on the overhead bar, she widened her stance to gain better balance in her high heels. She'd debated wearing her birthday splurge, a pair of Christian Louboutins, but decided if she had to spend another day at her miserable job she could at least be miserable in style.

She crinkled her nose at the man's overpowering cologne. She glimpsed at him and shivered. Even though he was well-dressed, something about the hardness of his black eyes and his long, slicked-back hair made her skin crawl. She made another attempt to shift away, but realized it was impossible to put any more distance between her and the man without rudely pushing her way through the jammed car. But it might be worth it.

Standing just shy of six feet tall in her heels, Cara's eyes surfed over the top of the crowd. She spotted a clearing farther down. Everyone appeared to be packed together in her half of the train, giving wide berth to a muscled hulk of a guy dressed in black with a dark-blond ponytail hanging just below his shoulders. She couldn't understand why—he didn't look particularly dangerous. Granted, he was built like a linebacker. Had he not been slouched over as he stared intently at something inside his massive palm, he would've stood taller than everyone else on the train, somewhere between six and seven feet tall. Her eyes traveled over his chiseled profile, and concluded that, at least from the side, he was handsome in a gladiator sort of way.

As if sensing her eyes on him, he glanced at her. His intense, crystal-blue eyes locked on hers for a split second before he turned around and gave her his back.

A surge of heat coursed through her, and her cheeks reddened. *Make that a Greek god. A big, gorgeous, intimidating one*, she thought, abandoning her plan to move. Too bad he was the kind of guy who'd never look at her twice—or even once, it appeared, for that matter.

Taking a deep breath, she shook her head and turned her attention back to her smartphone. She opened her next e-mail and began to read. Her stomach lurched and she paled as her eyes darted over the paragraph-long rant from one of her best clients: " . . . incompetent . . . scheming . . . pulling my assets . . . illegal trade . . . "

Trade? What trade? Her pulse raced. She hadn't made a trade for this client yesterday or even this week. Her bastard boss, Rick, must be screwing with her portfolio again. She was convinced he was setting her up to get fired, and nervously fingered the diamond solitaire she wore around her neck—her touchstone in times of distress.

Cara's chest grew heavy, and an impending sense of doom gripped her like a riptide about to pull her underwater. It was the calling card of a long-buried and half-forgotten specter rearing its ugly head.

No, not now! Not again after all this time. Her eyes widened in panic, and her breaths came in short bursts. She needed out. The space in the train was suddenly way too small.

Her rusty coping mechanisms churned inside her, trying to kick into gear. She knew there wasn't much time before the panic attack escalated and took over.

Only a few more seconds, she thought, unconsciously tapping her shoe. Chambers Street was the next stop. Instead of changing trains at Wall Street, she'd get to work another way. If she made it to work . . . and didn't end up paying a voluntary visit to the emergency room at New York Downtown Hospital.

Her heartbeat picked up steam, and her chest constricted until her vision narrowed into pinpricks and she viewed her world from deep inside a tunnel.

I won't suffocate . . . I won't suffocate . . . She squeezed her eyes shut, trying to readjust her vision as her hand gravitated to the Xanax inside the emergency kit in her handbag. While she panted in shallow breaths, crazy health stats from years ago came rushing back: six to nine minutes of oxygen deprivation caused irreversible brain damage. Chances were good she wouldn't black out before she made it safely above ground. But if things got worse, she knew the Metropolitan Transit Authority had access to oxygen.

"Heal me." This time the stranger whispered directly into her ear with warm, fetid breath, ripping her out of her thoughts. His voice sent a tremor along her spine.

Consumed by the anxiety attack blooming inside her, Cara barely managed to mumble, "Leave me alone."

The car came to a sudden halt and the doors flew open.

Thank God! Cara shoved past the man. Clawing her way by a girl with blue streaks in her hair and a guy in a Brooks Brothers suit, Cara propelled herself through the door and into the flow of people on the subway platform.

The man with the slicked-back hair and V-shaped scar sunk his fingers into her shoulder in a painful grip and spun her around to face him. Alarm rose inside Cara in a violent wave. An odd heat warmed her shoulder as his black eyes bore into her. She could have sworn she saw light flashing around them. Just as she was about to scream, the man let go and gave her a condescending smile.

Cara turned away from him and blindly bolted through the crowd, her lungs struggling for air.

On the other side of the train, Chamuel's blood raced as he silently cursed the lack of service on his cell phone.

What in hell is Achanelech doing here? The bastard had gotten on at the last stop. Chamuel needed to let Isaac, his friend and the leader of the Tri-State Guardians, know ASAP that a Dark One lieutenant had just swung into town from the West Coast unannounced. Worse, the archdemon was sniffing around Chamuel's new charge.

Chamuel cursed again when he glanced over and saw Cara Collins staring straight at him through the crush of people on the train. He abruptly turned his back on her. Under better circumstances he wouldn't have minded gazing into her lovely green eyes, but he didn't want her to notice him tracking the demonic energy of the man standing next to her. The train car was too full to allow Chamuel to effectively cloak behind a veil of invisibility. The best he'd been able to do was shield his energy from detection, which was good enough. Achanelech's attention seemed fixated on Cara.

Chamuel sensed her discomfort and desire to get away from the archdemon.

Smart woman, he thought. When he suspected she was no longer staring in his direction, he turned back to survey the scene. Had she known the truth about the being standing next to her, he would have understood the sudden panic that consumed her.

Instead, he frowned, puzzled by her strange reaction. It wasn't the archdemon, but something else that drove her fear. He didn't expect Achanelech to break the rules and make any sudden moves, but either way, Chamuel was ready.

The train screeched to a halt at Chambers Street, and Cara scrambled her way to the door. Chamuel blended into the flow of bodies, hanging back to follow her.

Achanelech grabbed her shoulder through the crowd, and she stumbled to a stop. Chamuel growled in his throat and reached for a blade underneath his duster. Cara's eyes were wild, and fear rolled off her, hitting him straight in the gut.

No one in the crowd noticed the sudden burst of light that flashed from the archdemon's hand before he let her go. After giving Cara a mocking smile, Achanelech melted into the crowd. She took off toward the nearest exit like a woman running for her life. Without thinking twice, Chamuel tore off through the crowd after her.

People made way for him as he took the stairs two at a time until he was on the street. His new charge was fast on her feet even when wearing high heels. He watched her long auburn hair swing from side to side ahead of him as she ran, cutting through the horde of pedestrians on the sidewalk along Church Street.

He drew closer, and without warning, she took a ninety-degree turn into a fast food restaurant. Walking in through the glass door behind her, he watched her run down a narrow hallway toward the back of the building alongside the long counter manned by uniformed workers buzzing around fulfilling breakfast orders. Stopping before the end, she disappeared into a door on the right.

Chamuel followed her. The moment he entered the hallway, he glanced back. Ensuring he was out of view, he breathed a sigh of relief and cloaked. His strength flagged for a moment as he disappeared behind a cloak of invisibility. He wished he had eaten more. Cloaking soaked up energy that he preferred not to expend, but even on a good day, his striking appearance made it difficult for him to blend into a crowd. Twice on the streets of New York he'd been mistaken for a well-known NFL player who also stood at six foot seven, shared the same square jaw and blue eyes, and wore his blond hair in a ponytail. Wrap that package in a black duster to conceal his weapons, and Chamuel screamed anything but inconspicuous. And since Cara had already seen him, he didn't have a choice.

He reached the door. She'd disappeared into the ladies' room. For a nanosecond he thought about ducking inside, but wisely rejected the idea. Instead, he posted himself outside and took out his phone. He tapped a text to Isaac: ACHANELECH IN NYC. WTF? CHECK IT OUT. TAILING NEW CHARGE. CALL YOU ASAP. He hit Send and pocketed his cell. Until Cara was safely at work, he wouldn't be going anywhere or talking to anyone.

Crossing his arms over his broad chest, he leaned up against the wall and waited. His mind drifted back her lovely green eyes, and something long forgotten stirred inside him. She was more attractive than he'd expected, not that it should matter. Poor girl didn't know what was about to hit her.

He shook his head. His assignment as her Trinity Guardian didn't officially start until this evening. Together with an Angelorum Messenger, the three of them would, in some way or another, influence the balance of power between good and evil. It was only on a whim that he'd decided to do some early reconnaissance and follow Cara this morning. But he knew better than anyone . . . There are no coincidences.

Then he let out a snide laugh. He could almost hear the whispers of the Trinity Stones fucking with his fate.

His cell phone buzzed in his pocket. He slipped it out to read the text.

CALL ME.

Chapter 2

INHALE. HOLD. EXHALE. Cara repeated the mantra, trying to wrestle her heart rate under control and convince herself she wasn't about to die. The last place she expected to be on her twenty-seventh birthday was crouched down inside a graffiti-covered metal stall in a filthy bathroom. Her coat grazed the grimy floor as she stared at the little blue oval pill in one hand and her cell phone programmed to 911 in the other.

For the first time in five years, anxiety shattered her and made her contemplate taking a drug she'd hoped she'd never need again. Memories of her high school and college years, when she was the victim of severe panic attacks bordering on agoraphobia, flooded back to her. Her former therapist had warned her that the attacks may return during times of extreme stress, but Cara had thought she was safe since so much time had passed.

Anger boiled up alongside of her fear. Her hand tightened around her cell phone until the edge bit into her palm. She didn't want to be that girl again. She had worked hard to become the tough-as-nails investment banker she was today. Despite her issues with her misogynist boss, she was proud of what she'd accomplished and was good at what she did. She wouldn't let the anxiety win. She'd conquered it once, and she'd do it again.

Cara's body started to shake uncontrollably from the excess adrenaline that coursed through her courtesy of the fight-or-flight response—a signal that the panic attack was subsiding.

After a few more minutes, she was able to breathe without gasping. Slowly, she pressed her hands against her thighs and straightened up, the muscles in her arms and legs weak with residual tremors. Relief filled her with the knowledge she would live another day.

Opening her Louis Vuitton handbag, she returned the pill to the plastic container and slipped it back into her emergency kit next to a bottle of water, an inhaler, a list of hospital phone numbers, and caffeine pills for milder attacks.

She left the stall and stopped at the sink. Balancing her briefcase and handbag, she splashed some cold water onto her cheeks, patted them dry, and reapplied some blush. Her eyes, with a mixture of fear and determination, stared back from the mirror.

Now that her attack had abated, her thoughts returned to the man who'd grabbed her. Had she not been half-crazy from the anxiety attack, the whole encounter would have freaked her out more. What could she say?

Only in New York, she thought.

Her pulse almost back to normal, she glanced at her watch. She was late for work.

"Shit!"

Cara pressed End and dropped her cell phone into her purse, relieved her call into work claiming an unavoidable emergency was handled. Her mental state progressively improved as she walked. She wished she could say the same for her physical state. She tried to ignore the ache in her ankles and the balls of her feet. Had she known she'd be walking the last leg of her commute, she would have skipped the stilettos. Traffic was too dense for a cab; even in heels she would get to the office faster on foot. At least the weather was nice for late March, the temperature unseasonably mild.

She passed by Saint Paul's Churchyard and noticed new buds already emerging on the trees; a sweet smell in the air permeated the regular aroma of the city. Cara navigated around a cluster of people stopped in front of her. As she passed, an old homeless woman reached out and grabbed Cara's wrist, jerking her to a stop on the busy sidewalk. Cara tugged her wrist back but was unable to twist out of the woman's grasp.

"Hey!" she cried out.

The woman's eyes locked on hers. "Heal me. I beg you."

Oh God, not again. Cara's eyes darted past her, looking around for the dark-haired man on the subway. Could they be working together? Not finding him in the crowd, she sized up the old crone in front of her. The woman lacked a cart or bags, was unkempt, and the scent of her unwashed body clung to her soiled clothes. Her long, wild gray hair framed eyes full of sharp intelligence within a dirty, creased face.

"I'm sorry. I don't understand," Cara said curtly, wanting to move on without causing a scene. Not that anyone took notice. The flow of commuters continued to move around them unfazed.

Holding Cara's wrist in an iron grip, the woman's eyes traveled from the top of Cara's head down and around her body. She yanked Cara down to eye level with unnatural strength, and her sour breath brushed her cheek. "The light of Heaven surrounds you. I beg you—heal me."

Cara's heart beat faster. The woman's intense stare unnerved her.

Haven't I had a shitty enough morning already? Cara thought, torn between annoyance and fear. She badly wanted to free her hand and get away from the woman's foul breath. She pulled her face back and tried to inject some compassion into her response.

"I have no idea what you're talking about." Not knowing why, Cara stood riveted as the woman's eyes continued to travel the perimeter of her body.

Suddenly, the woman seized Cara's hand and placed it on her shoulder. A powerful surge of energy slammed into Cara. Flowing in through the top of her head, it filled her with intense, tingling warmth as it tunneled down to the center of her chest, blasting out of her hand and into the woman in front of her.

Peace washed over the woman's face until she glowed, lit from within. Tendrils of light radiated outward as energy flowed in a continuous stream through Cara and into the woman.

Cara watched, spellbound, as the lines disappeared on the woman's face and smoothness returned to her skin. Forty years melted away instantly as Cara stared in open-mouthed disbelief.

She smiled at Cara. "You're ready."

Cara stumbled backward, breaking their contact. The light and the blazing heat disappeared instantly. Her heart pounded. "Ready for what?"

Without a word, the woman turned and ran uptown.

"Wait!" Cara yelled. She raced after the woman, darting around the pedestrians on the sidewalk, trying not to shove people as she ran. But the woman picked up speed, somehow traveling with ease at a pace too fast for Cara to follow.

Cara watched her turn left onto Barclay Street toward the Woolworth Building. By the time she rounded the corner, the woman had vanished.

Cara came to a halt on the sidewalk. Stepping out of pedestrian traffic, Cara leaned against the brick building to rest, gulping greedy breaths into her oxygen-starved lungs. She contemplated going home and crawling back into bed.

Without warning, laughter welled up deep inside her. As creepy as the encounter with the crone was, she didn't feel the sense of doom that usually preceded a panic attack. Then again, she'd rarely had attacks when real danger was present. Like the time she went bungee jumping in college to get over her anxiety disorder—she'd discovered that type of fear wasn't a trigger. Yet, the fear of losing a client in combination with the escalating situation at work was enough to unwind her. *Go figure.*

She decided to store this morning in her "weird experience" file and think about it later. In the meantime, she had a boss to deal with and a client to save.

"One disaster at a time," she mumbled.

Chapter 3

CHAMUEL IGNORED THE TEXT from Isaac and followed Cara up Church Street. His senses sharpened the moment he saw the old woman reach out and grab Cara's wrist.

He remained cloaked and moved toward Cara. He watched and listened carefully, closing his distance and preparing to intervene if warranted.

He came to a halt fifteen feet away when the woman seized Cara's hand, placing it on her shoulder. A bright, white light dove from the heavens down into Cara, traveling through her and into the woman. The blast of energy shot outward, hitting him in the face. The tiny sparks tingled as they landed on his skin. No one on the street, other than him, had the ability to notice anything unusual.

"Holy Father," Chamuel muttered in awe. It was rare to see an unawakened Soul Seeker like Cara, who had yet to accept her Calling, wield so much power. There was something else—and it had nothing to do with her power. Her quiet beauty struck him.

Chamuel jerked his head to the left. He sensed another presence similar to his own, another Nephilim. *What the . . .*

He scanned the crowd around him, but there wasn't anyone who matched the presence he sensed. The street looked exactly as it should. Passersby with shopping bags, briefcases, and strollers filled the sidewalk.

Still, a wisp of energy breezed by him, pulsing and pulling at his power. Someone he'd never met before; someone hiding behind a veil of invisibility like him. Cloaking prevented them from being seen or heard from behind the veil, but allowed energy to pass through. Chamuel found the presence of the other Nephilim troubling but didn't sense any immediate danger.

Warily, he returned his attention back to the scene between Cara and the homeless woman.

"You're ready," the woman said, and that's when he knew that she wasn't an ordinary woman.

Sentinel, he thought. He swore under his breath. She worked for the Dark Ones.

Before Chamuel could react, she moved swiftly away from Cara. He jumped into action and gave chase, passing Cara and cutting through the crowd. He shoved past a couple holding hands, and leapt over a large pile of garbage bags at the curb, trying to keep up with the fluttering hem of the homeless woman's skirt as she wove through the people on the sidewalk with ease. He left a strong, invisible breeze and baffled stares in his wake.

The Sentinel smirked at him over her shoulder and picked up speed. A burst of Nephil energy blew past him, and seconds later she vanished into thin air.

Chamuel realized his problems were even greater than he'd originally thought. Once assured of Cara's safe arrival at work, he'd make that call to Isaac.

Could their luck get any worse? An archdemon, a Sentinel, and a rogue Guardian all in one day.

They must all be working together, he thought.

Cara rounded the corner onto Church Street a moment later out of breath with her suit jacket askew. A single wave of hair clung to her ivory cheek. Brushing the errant strand behind her ear, she slumped against the brick exterior next to a storefront window and shifted her briefcase more securely onto her shoulder. She shook her head followed by a short burst of laughter; Chamuel wondered what she found so amusing. He suddenly wished he could ask her, but that was out of the question. Pushing off the building, Cara headed toward the direction of her office, and Chamuel followed unseen behind her.

Fortunately, for both Cara and the Guardianship, he'd listened to his gut this morning. Forewarned was forearmed. Knowing Cara had been spotted would allow them to take the proper precautions. Equally important was the intelligence he'd just gained. The Sentinel had escaped with the help of a Nephil. Since the Dark Ones didn't have any Nephilim in their ranks, it could mean only one thing.

There was a traitor in the Guardianship.

Chamuel shadowed Cara until she entered Cabot Investments. He parked himself outside the entrance, leaning his oversized frame up against the limestone exterior.

Still cloaked, he dialed Isaac, keeping one eye trained on the door.

"What took you so long?" Isaac asked gruffly. Chamuel could picture his old friend—the blond brush cut and the icy blue eyes of a drill sergeant.

"Sorry, but Cara made a detour on her way to work," he replied, opting to leave out the details of her meltdown in the ladies' room. "Then we had a surprise visit from a Sentinel."

Isaac cursed under his breath. "Tell me what happened, and don't leave anything out."

Chamuel recounted what he'd observed.

"I've confirmed that Achanelech flew in this morning," said Isaac, "and his plane is about to depart from Teterboro for the West Coast as we speak. The fact that he could be behind the Sentinel visit is bad enough, but it also begs the question of how he even found out about Cara."

"I've been wondering the same thing," replied Chamuel.

Over the phone he could hear Isaac drumming his fingers on his desk. "This heightens the pressure to protect her while she's being trained and until she receives her Calling. I suspect the Angelorum knows something is up. They called this morning. They're flying in a heavy hitter to mentor her, someone from the High Council."

Chamuel drew his eyebrows together as he pictured the faces of the twelve High Council members of the Angelorum, the governing body of the secret angelic protectorate. With a small shake of his head, he realized who'd be sent. If he was right, that would explain why he'd been chosen so quickly and assigned to this Trinity. "They haven't told you yet?"

Isaac gave him a snide laugh. "When has the Council ever told the Guardianship anything in advance? You know, it's the usual can't-reveal-the-future-because-it-interferes-with-free-will conundrum. As always, we'll get our information on a strictly need-to-know basis, and they don't think we need to know . . . yet."

Isaac was right about the High Council. Bound by two sacred rules, the Council's role was to watch and to orchestrate. They couldn't use their knowledge to interfere with free will or have direct involvement in human affairs. Although they retained some latitude surrounding their activities, they primarily use the Trinities to carry out their work.

Chamuel's frown deepened as he pressed the phone to his ear. "Yeah, but I think we should be more worried about *why*. Can you remember the last time they sent a Council member to mentor a Soul Seeker? I can't."

"Not in the one hundred fifty years I've been alive," Isaac replied.

Chamuel was only a couple of years younger, so not while either of them had been alive. This news troubled him on several levels.

"Let me chew on this one for a while," he said. "In the meantime, what about the traitor in our midst working for the Dark Ones? We need to get a grip on that one fast. Last thing we need is a security breach right here, right now."

"Agreed," Isaac said gravely. "Investigating the whereabouts of all of our people shouldn't take more than an hour. I'll transmit the order to other Guardian Houses around the world and should have a completed report within the next twelve hours. We'll find the traitor, turn him in, and let the Council decide his fate. But, I can't possibly imagine it's one of ours."

Chamuel silently agreed. No way it could be one of theirs. "Will you send me the report?"

"Out of respect, yes, but you turned over the reins, remember?" Isaac chided.

It was true: Chamuel, who was recognized as one of the Guardianship's best strategists, had given Isaac control after reentering the mission rotation a week ago. Being on active duty limited his leadership position to his assigned Trinity, while Isaac's Tri-State Guardians managed the overall security of the region and provided backup to the Trinities.

"I know. Be patient with me. It's not an easy transition." Suddenly restless, Chamuel swept his hand over his face and moved away from the wall to pace.

"Understood, but to serve in a Trinity is the highest honor for any of us." Isaac paused and then lowered his voice. "Hey, Cham, how're you holding up? Are you sure you're ready for this?"

Chamuel shifted uncomfortably and cracked his neck. He'd avoided discussing the tragedy with Isaac, or anyone, for decades. "Ready or not, here I come. I can't hide forever, I," he said, calling Isaac by his nickname.

Isaac blew out a breath. "Okay, I'll take that for now. So, tell me again why you rolled out of bed so early to spy on your new charge?"

"Dunno. Bored, maybe." The best Chamuel could figure was that his decision was somehow tied to his destiny. In reality, he'd been hit with an unexpected bout of loneliness and couldn't handle watching the walls close in on him. He'd just moved back to his SoHo loft from the Connecticut headquarters a little over a week ago. Even though he used to routinely stay in Manhattan a couple of days a week, something about giving up his room at Isaac's Guardian House solidified the change he'd made. He already missed the camaraderie of the Tri-State team and fighting with their cook, Luigi, for control of the kitchen.

"Well, I'm glad that you did," Isaac said.

"Send me the report when you have it." He hung up.

Spotting a food cart, Chamuel's stomach grumbled. *Time to have that break-fast*, he thought, and uncloaked. No one noticed his sudden appearance next to the glass door of Cara's building. Using the glass as a mirror, he stared back at his own vivid blue eyes. He wore the standard, all-black Guardian uniform; his open duster exposed the T-shirt and cargo pants underneath. Even though his hair was still neatly tucked into a ponytail, he couldn't resist smoothing the sides with his hands. Satisfied that he looked presentable, he smiled. The expression softened his face and transformed his image from intimidating to attractive.

Chamuel ambled over to the street vendor to buy an egg sandwich and a cup of coffee. Not exactly gourmet, but it would do. Starting his assignment early, he planted himself outside the building and devoured his breakfast under a veil of invisibility. He wasn't willing to take any chances with Cara's safety after this morning's surprises. He smiled. Maybe it was wrong, but he looked forward to catching a glimpse of his very beautiful new charge.

Chapter 4

Achanelech shifted his weight onto his jewel-topped cane and paced the cabin of his private jet, impatiently waiting for his consort's return so they could take off. He'd gone to take a look at Cara himself and, he must say, he was disappointed. Was this the best the Angelorum had to offer?

He winced as he walked. Unable to retract the claws at the end of his toes, his Armani leather shoes pinched his feet. Although he paraded around in human form most of the time, he couldn't fully transform his feet, or his forked tongue, to the human equivalents. He'd never honed his skills that far.

His leg ached more than usual today as he hobbled back and forth along the aisle. An old battle injury that had never healed followed him across all his forms. All the milling about he'd done earlier in the subway hadn't helped. Then there was the incessant pulsating on the back of his neck under his hairline where his sigil lay hidden under his skin. But even the pain in his leg wasn't enough to quiet the demonic whispers reverberating in his head, calling his name, and making his neck throb.

The hellspeak of his demon children taunted him as he waited. The sound grated on his nerves and nearly drove him to the edge of madness whenever he had no distractions. Their hunger drove their insistence. They needed more souls to keep them satisfied and to prevent a not-so-friendly summoning through the portal into Hell by his Master. Achanelech understood, but they would have to wait. In the meantime, he would do what he could to elude a trip to Hell . . . forever. He'd gladly waste away here on Earth, a dusty chunk of Purgatory, than take his place in the perpetual hierarchy of suffering down there, even for a visit. The only thing worse would be getting thrown into Heaven's prison with Semyaza and his fornicating Watchers to spend an eternity consumed in remorse until Judgment Day.

Speaking of which, he wondered how his pet Nephil had performed on his assignment.

Vile abomination, he thought with disgust. He couldn't even bring himself to acknowledge the Nephil by its gender. That would have bestowed a certain level of dignity Achanelech was unwilling to give it.

Angels breeding with humans. The Watchers deserved to rot in darkness for sullying their bloodline. He may have fallen far and had his wings ripped from his body, but he was once of their essence. How those of his ilk could bear to get caught up in the pathetic little lives of humans, much less breed with them, he didn't know. Humans would be the eternal weakness of his enemies, the Angelorum—a bunch of bleeding liberals blindly protecting His creation. To look at mankind as more than what they were—a mere source of food—was stupidity of the highest order.

The noise level rose to a crescendo in his head.

"Be patient, pets. Sustenance shall be forthcoming," he whispered in their language. The pulsing on the back of his neck receded. He passed his hand through his hair and gave his sigil a good rub.

The door of the plane cracked open and in walked his consort in the guise of a homeless crone. She was followed quietly by a tall, blond Nephil male wearing the loose, white garments of an ancient slave. Achanelech was nothing if not nostalgic. His consort had insisted his pet be bathed, the filth removed from it prior to being brought into her presence for this mission. His Nephil's appearance now fresh, its angelic beauty unable to be contained, churned up feelings of loathing within Achanelech. Had the abomination dared to show its brilliant white plumage, Achanelech would have become violent. They were a reminder of what had been taken from him. Leathery bat wings sprouted from Achanelech's shoulder blades whenever he took demon form now, providing a pale shadow of the beauty he'd lost.

The male hung back with his eyes averted, giving off an air of respect and deference.

"Mission accomplished," Emanelech said before the air shimmered and her shape melted, transforming into that of the tall, raven-haired beauty in a slinky dress, which she knew pleased him. "She's quite powerful, that young Soul Seeker."

He looked at her impatiently. "Yes, but is she the *One*?"

Arching a brow, she gave him a sour look. "Our source believes it to be the case. Regardless, her essence could provide a hearty meal indeed."

"Then let's dispatch her. I was less than impressed," he said, thinking of the hungry mouths he had to feed.

"No need to be hasty. She's still unawakened. And don't you think it would be best to get our facts straight before we send word to the Master?" She gave him a smug smile.

He suppressed a growl deep in his throat, despising the fact that she was right. Instead, he nodded in the male's direction and asked her, "What about this one? How did the halfling do?"

Even as Achanelech looked at the Nephil, he wondered how much he could trust it after the abuse inflicted on it over the last century. Until his minions had started capturing other Nephilim, this one had been their only specimen. The creature standing before him was oblivious to what it was or that more of its kind existed. Achanelech kept it sheltered, under constant watch due to its value. But that value had been diluted recently with a dungeon full of the half-ling's Nephilim brethren kept secretly and securely hidden at another location. If Achanelech could harvest the abomination of its soul, he would. But its Nephilim essence rendered its soul poisonous to the Dark Ones. The same was true for members of the Angelorum; their souls were equally as poisonous. Another one of the galling rules in the battle between good and evil.

God forbid the playing field wasn't level, he thought, using a modern turn of phrase.

Emanelech cast a cold glance in his pet's direction. "Fine. No complaints."

"Mongrel, what say you?"

The Nephil kept its head bowed. "The mission was a success, Father," it responded softly, but not softly enough to mask the rich, melodic tone of its voice.

Achanelech ground his teeth at the sound. If a whip had been handy, he would have used it to add fresh scars to the flesh underneath the halfling's clothes. Nephilim heal fast, but with the right instruments, marks remained. The thought filled him with delight.

Raking his eyes over the Nephil, Achanelech snorted. He was unsure whether he despised the halfling's light coloring more because it reminded him of the Nephil's angelic half or human half. Compared to Achanelech's own dark looks, the male looked soft despite its clear masculinity and large stature. After pos-sessing this Nephil for well over a century, Achanelech found the male a poor substitute for the retribution he'd hoped to exact for the loss of the one who had mattered to him most at the hands of his enemies.

"Acchie, I was thinking . . . " Emanelech said, finger to her lips.

Achanelech's brow shot up, and he gritted his teeth at the nickname. "Oh? That could be a dangerous proposition."

Her ice-blue eyes turned to black. "I understand you're in need of some souls. Unless you'd like to procure them yourself, I'd suggest you rethink your tone."

If she were a less-powerful being, he would have killed her after having lain with her, but she was far too dangerous, and in many ways his perfect match.

Hence, her longevity at his side. Brushing his hand over his face, he released a heavy sigh. "Fine, chérie. What were you about to say?"

Her eyes faded back to blue, and she glanced at his pet. "Maybe we should chat in private."

"Step outside, mongrel," he said, dismissing his pet with a wave of his hand.

Once the door was securely closed behind the male, she continued. "Your Nephil. He'd be the perfect spy to confirm our suspicions about the girl, now that we know she's in New York City."

Achanelech wanted to question her sanity but knew better. "Why him?"

"Simple. He's a Nephilim. He can get close without causing panic. Demons will be hunted, but with him, the worst that could happen is they assume it's a case of mistaken identity with one of the Angelorum Guardians."

"How do I prevent him from running?"

She sniffed. "Like he has anywhere to go. Besides, I thought you implanted him with a tracking device."

He hated to admit it, but she had a point . . . again. He'd tagged the Nephil as a child, and recently embedded a high-tech GPS under its skin. If his pet went rogue, he could always hunt it down and kill it.

"I'll give it some thought."

Emanelech stretched out on the bench seat and kicked off her high heels. "Unless you want him to fly back under his own power, it might make sense to decide before we take off. And for Lucifer's sake, give him some proper clothes."

Achanelech walked over to her, trying to mask his limp. A cold smile touched his lips. "Don't get too smart, or someday I might just have to kill you."

"Give it your best shot, hot lips," she said, grasping his collar in her hands and pulling him down into a kiss.

Chapter 5

France. Angelorum Sanctuary. Thursday, March 19, 4:00 p.m.
GMT + 1 / 10:00 a.m. EDT

CONSTANTINA UNLOCKED THE DOOR to the high-domed Sanctuary. Her hooded velvet cloak swept across the threshold into the warm, white room—the most sacred place within the hidden compound. Unlike the grandeur of the rest of their underground city, the Sanctuary had simple décor. Bench seating circled the walls, enough to accommodate all three hundred members of the Sanctus Angelorum. Light illuminated the room, mimicking natural rays of sunlight and masking the fact that the compound was located deep underground.

She crossed the suspended catwalk that connected the wooden door she'd entered through to the staircase accessing the circular seating. Walking down one level of stairs, she stopped at the twelve seats designated for her and the eleven other High Council members.

Lowering the velvet hood, Constantina released her long, blonde hair and shook it free. She slipped off the ocean-blue cloak to reveal her gray traveling suit, and draped the garment over her chair before proceeding down another level to the ground floor and the Trinity Pool.

She took a deep breath, hoping nothing had changed since her last visit. But with free will, one decision could change the course of her mission and the destinies of those involved. A mixture of disquiet and anticipation had kept her up during the night. She'd been waiting for this day for twenty-seven years. Since the day Cara Collins, the First of the Twelve, was born . . .

Constantina stood at the edge of the shallow, raised enclosure and gazed into the vast, white sand–filled Trinity Pool, searching for the answer to her question. Drawn in by the hypnotic rainbow of colors coursing through the many thousands of Trinity Stones, she listened as they cried out to her their secrets.

Each triangular three-part stone represented a single Trinity of three souls connected to a center stone—a fourth soul—who would play a part either now, or in the future, in an event that could tip the balance between good and evil. Collectively, the stones represented the destinies of each soul within a Trinity and all the events not yet fulfilled. Fueled by the free will of the souls they represented, these eyes and ears of Heaven blazed with the lifeblood of destiny.

As she stared into the Pool, her body felt heavy and she yearned for home. She sighed, thinking of the many obstacles and the high price that lay ahead for them all. For both those she loved now and for those she would love in the future.

"Constantina?" The voice snapped her out of her reflections. Angelis descended the stairs to join her.

"Angelis, do you fare well?" she asked the tall man with bright eyes. His short dark hair was tinged with gray, and he wore the long white robe of the High Council leader. He more closely resembled an accountant than the leader of an angelic protectorate. Constantina looked at him with pride. She knew she'd made the right decision to pass up his post in this lifetime. Angelis made a fine leader in her place.

He smiled warmly. "I fare well, Constantina. Are you ready for your journey?"

She smiled back. "Yes, I'm looking forward to finally meeting our Cara after these twenty-seven years."

He reached up to pull down the large magnification apparatus that overhung the Trinity Pool. "Any more revelations to be gleaned from the cluster?" He peered into the magnifier, looking at the unusual cluster of Trinity Stones representing the Holy Twelve.

Constantina glanced through the glass lens with Angelis and paused. "Only that time is running short, and there's been a slight shift. Danger could be at our doorstep sooner than we'd like." It still worried her that not all the Trinity Stones were whole. The cluster contained several broken ones, a phenomenon that hadn't existed within the Trinity Pool until this cluster had shown up.

"Hmm, our West Coast charges too?"

Constantina listened to the hum of the Trinity Stones and watched as their faces flashed by. Unlike Cara, they hadn't yet fulfilled enough of their destinies to become final members of the Twelve, nor had anyone else. But as possible candidates, they still required protection.

"I'm afraid so. We can't escape the fact that our destinies are all entwined. There are no coincidences."

"Constantina, something still baffles me . . ."

"There's much to be baffled by in this group of stones. Which anomaly are you specifically questioning?"

Taking his attention away from the viewer, he met her eyes. "The one in the Collins Trinity Stone—the uncharacteristic color."

Constantina shrugged. "Yes, that's quite fascinating. But the stone isn't ready to divulge its secret yet." Then she looked up at Angelis. "Have you noticed that at least one-third of the Trinity Stones have disappeared since we last looked?"

He met her gaze. "Yes, I'd noticed. It could mean many things right now."

She shook her head, her lips pressed together tightly. "It could, but more likely we're not the only ones who know the identity of the First of the Holy Twelve."

Angelis frowned and conceded. "Yes, that's a possibility."

Constantina studied the Trinity Stones, watching and waiting for them to reveal more. Like a spinning roulette wheel, images and potential outcomes spun within and across the stones in a kaleidoscope of color, activity, and whispers. Pieces locked into place only as free will decisions collided with destiny to increase the probability of an event to a near certainty.

"How much time do we have?" he asked.

She released a breath. "There's a high probability that the opening salvo will be made by the Dark Ones shortly, a couple of weeks from now. She'll be safe until then." Constantina paused and then gazed at Angelis. "I don't have as much time as I wanted to prepare her."

The stones only hinted at what was to come afterward. Minor skirmish or not, it didn't lessen the danger or probability of defeat.

Constantina pointed into the magnifying glass. "I find this most interesting of all."

"The glow surrounding it?" he asked, pointing to the cluster and outlining it with his finger.

"Yes. Our Holy Twelve are surrounded by more than the usual amount of love, passion, and complexity. This will not be a straightforward journey for many of those involved. We need to accept that a few rules will be broken along the way by them . . . and us. We'll need to walk a fine line in order to maintain our noninterference rule. I daresay, many of us will be tested along the way."

Angelis sighed. "Your insight, as always, is brilliant and correct. Constantina, I'm sorry to have put you in this position."

She lifted her eyes, and wore a look of resignation. "Think nothing of it, and don't worry about me. I'm much less important in this overall equation."

He clasped her shoulder gently. "You'll be vulnerable. The threat of exposure increases with your direct involvement."

"If that is His will, then I accept it. My soul is at peace with my choices."

"You've already sacrificed one of your children . . . "

A pang of sadness touched Constantina. "Hope made her sacrifice willingly. As for me, I accept my destiny, a choice, as you know, that I made long ago."

She knew the many reasons why she was chosen, least of which was who would make the opening salvo for the Dark Ones. She'd seen the face of her old nemesis flash across the Trinity Stones, fiery arrogance and all. Many years had passed since their last encounter . . .

Angelis gave her shoulder a final squeeze and nodded. "Very well, Constantina. I'll inform the rest of the Council of your departure. Thank you . . . from us all. Journey forth in peace and love."

"And you," she said as he left.

Alone again in the Sanctuary, her eyes came to rest on the Trinity Pool, pulled back in by the brilliant kaleidoscope of flashing colors.

Her attention was drawn to another stone in the cluster, a broken one, farther away from the Collins Trinity. She swallowed, knowing more would be revealed over time as free will shaped the destinies involved. Why that Trinity Stone had allowed her a glimpse of its secret but held it from the others, she didn't know. Yet, she remained silent on her discovery, afraid to hope for the impossible.

For all her pragmatism, Constantina wasn't able to prevent the heaviness from settling within her heart. Some things weren't within her power or purview to change. When it came to those she loved, she wished she had no more knowledge than the average human being about events affecting them. But in her world, time didn't travel a linear path; it folded in on itself, revealing events in an order dictated by destinies and decisions. The reason she was here, why all of them were here, was to protect mankind—a choice they'd all made long ago. And sometimes their choice required sacrifice—sometimes, unspeakable sacrifice.

She thought of her daughter Hope, and sadness enveloped her. Hope's death had come to pass, and now Constantina prayed that another of her children wouldn't be sacrificed before this was over.

With calm resolve, she collected her cloak. Closing the door of the Sanctuary behind her, she entrusted her fate to the Trinity Stones and set off to embrace her destiny.

Chapter 6

New York City. Perry Street Apartment. Wednesday, March 19,
10:00 p.m. EDT

CARA'S MIND KEPT LOOPING through the encounter with the crone, but she
didn't understand it any better now than when it first happened. What stayed
with her most was the warmth and brilliance of the light. Even the creepy guy
with the V-shaped scar and the panic attack paled in comparison to the old
woman on the street. After regaining her composure, Cara had managed to
unwind the trade her boss had made behind her back and smooth everything
over with her client.

A static-filled buzz jarred Cara out of her sullen contemplation of the day's
events. She pressed the release for the outer door of her West Village apartment
to let her visitor inside. Her best friend had insisted on stopping by on her way
home from work.

Cara waited patiently for Sienna to make her way to the fourth floor, as her
whippet, Chloe, scampered off with the clatter of doggie toenails across the wood
floor to fetch a toy from her basket behind the sofa. The dog was entirely black
and brown with the exception of a kiss of white on the back of her neck in the
shape of a heart, and the white end of her tail.

Moments later, the elevator dinged and Cara opened the door. Keeping the
chain in place, she peeked out into the gray-walled hallway.

"Senny, is that you?"

A voice came echoing down the hall. "Of course, it's me. Who were you
expecting, Prince Charming?"

Sadly, no.

Sienna came teetering into view in sky-high heels with a designer handbag
dangling off of her arm. She carried a huge box wrapped in colorful paper and
an oversized bow. Only the silken black hair on the top half of Sienna's head was

visible along with her sky-blue eyes, which peeked over the edge of the package. Cara unchained the door to let her in.

"Let me help you with that. You look like you might tip over."

Chloe came rushing over to help, a toy bone in her mouth.

Sienna turned and gave Cara a peck on the cheek, then transferred the box to her. "Happy Birthday, Carissima," she said, using the nickname she coined for Cara back when they were sixteen.

Cara looked at the box and smiled for the first time that day. "Thanks, Senny."

Walking past her, Sienna smirked. "I would have brought you a cake with twenty-seven candles, but I didn't want to set the place on fire."

"Gee, thanks. Don't forget, you'll always be older than me," Cara said, balancing the package and relocking the door behind them.

Sienna batted her eyelashes. "Older by only three months, and don't forget 'wiser.'"

That remains to be seen, Cara thought with a chuckle.

"And here's something for you too, my princess." Reaching into her purse, Sienna pulled out a stuffed squirrel and held it out to Chloe. The dog's soulful brown eyes lit up, and she dropped her bone.

Giving the toy a quick squeak, Sienna tossed it deep into the living room. Chloe raced after the squirrel as quickly as her greyhound-like body would take her and pounced on it. Picking it up, she trotted around the apartment squeaking her new toy with relentless zeal.

Cara rolled her eyes. "Okay, now *that's* going to be annoying."

"Oh, lighten up. Smile for fuck's sake. It's your birthday." Sienna headed for the overstuffed sofa.

Cara followed, putting the massive box down on the coffee table. "You'd make a sailor blush with that mouth, and how the heck can you walk in those shoes?"

Sienna shot her a look. "Who walks? That's what cabs are for." Then she winked and gave Cara a wicked smile. "And for the record, blushing is not all I'd make a sailor do."

Cara shook her head and chuckled. The dark cloud she'd been under all day started to lift.

Sienna worked as a fashion designer for up-and-coming Italian designer Nicolas Alda. Wearing crazy platform shoes could easily have been part of Sienna's job description. A fashionista since high school, it's more likely Sienna's choice in footware was voluntary.

Sienna's brows furrowed, giving Cara an ultracritical once-over. "What's that *shmata* you're wearing?" she asked, her Jewish roots showing.

Cara bristled. But, then again, Sienna had that effect on people. Cara looked down at her oversized T-shirt and yoga pants. "Senny, I'm going to bed after this, not hitting the streets of New York."

Next to Sienna, in her black skinny pants and matching tailored jacket belted at the waist, Cara agreed she looked plain. But even if they'd been dressed identically, Sienna would still attract most of the attention. There were no two ways about it. Sienna was a stunner with her long jet-black hair, blue eyes, and slender build. Cara had the same slender build but her milky Irish complexion, long auburn hair, and green eyes meant that in the summer, Sienna tanned while Cara just freckled and turned the color of dappled shrimp.

"So how was your trip back from Paris? Was Fashion Week amazing or what?"

Sienna shrugged and gave her a blasé look. "I popped a Xanax before takeoff. It made taking a red-eye bearable. As far as Fashion Week, if you call running around like a lunatic with a roll of duct tape and a sewing kit amazing, then I guess it was."

"Well, you're more awake than I expected," Cara said.

"That's what sheer will and five Venti Starbucks lattes will do for you." Sienna kicked off her platform shoes, and tucked her long legs underneath her. She flipped her hair over her shoulder and looked down at the dog waiting to be invited onto the sofa, the new toy temporarily forgotten.

"Come sit next to Aunt Senny," she said, patting the cushion next to her. Chloe jumped up and nestled her little body down next to her.

"Do you want a glass of wine?" Cara asked, rising from the sofa.

"Not until you tell me why you look like someone killed your cat," she said and then kissed the top of the dog's narrow head. "Sorry, girl. I know this is a canine household."

Cara scowled at her. "I'm fine, really." *My life sucks. Who am I trying to kid?* She felt pathetic.

Sienna frowned back at her and threw up her arms. "Lemme guess. Cara's Misery for five hundred dollars, the married loser, or Cara's Misery for one thousand dollars, the prick of a boss. Ding-ding-ding!"

Cara released an exasperated sigh. She hated when Sienna was right.

"Red or white?"

"Huh?"

"Wine. Red or white?"

"Come on, Carissima. Don't be that way."

Cara put her hands on her hips. "What do want me to say? Kai hasn't called to wish me a happy birthday, or that asshole Rick purposely changed one of my client's trades without my knowledge?" *Or that I haven't had sex in five years?*

"Fuck the job. You can always find another one," Sienna said with a cavalier wave of her hand. Then her expression softened. "Listen, if there's one thing that

I wish for your birthday, it's that you find a great guy. You need to let go of Kai. It's time. It's been ten years."

"Nine," Cara said. Nine since they'd broken up. Five since he'd married someone else. But Cara's heart refused to let go or find satisfaction with someone else. No one she'd met could make her feel the way Kai had—and if she couldn't have that, she'd rather be alone.

Sienna rolled her eyes. "Whatever."

Cara rubbed her hands over her face, trying to erase the tortured look she wore. "Senny, I wish I could let go. I really do. I don't know what holds me to Kai, but something does. I can't explain it."

"But, honey, it's so unhealthy. You need to move on." Sienna said and batted her black eyelashes. "Because there's no one I know who needs a night of mind-blowing sex more than you do."

"*Thanks.*" Cara's mind flashed briefly to the huge guy with the blond ponytail before she gave Sienna a sour look. "How about that glass of wine?"

She went to the kitchen without waiting for Sienna's response. Cara knew her close friendship with Kai kept him too connected to her, but the thought of not having him in her life sucked the oxygen right out of her lungs.

"I'm not going to let this go," Sienna yelled from the living room.

What a surprise, Cara thought. She loved Sienna and wished she could at least put on a more cheerful face. But the events of the last few months had beaten her down. She could deal with either her personal life or her professional life being crappy, but dealing with both at the same time drained the energy right out of her. She was convinced that's what had caused the full-blown panic attack she'd had earlier today, and the niggling sense of impending doom still lurked in her psyche, waiting for her to let her guard down again.

Last year, she'd been a rising star at Cabot Investments. She'd interned during college, and then was given a full-time position upon graduation—a highly unusual path for a kid just out of college without a master's degree. Turns out, she was a whiz when it came to derivatives. The senior partner had been her mentor and a close friend of the family, but when he died unexpectedly of a heart attack at the age of fifty-five, everything changed. Her new boss was a horse's ass.

Cara leaned on the sink in the kitchen and took a breath, trying to take solace in her surroundings, which at this point, was the only thing she could control. Her small kitchen with blue painted walls was decorated in a warm, country style. Light-green enamel canisters sat on the counters, and a weathered old cupboard with a chicken-wire front was pushed up against the wall—both flea market finds. She was an avid collector; her things grounded her and provided a coping mechanism when her world threatened to blow apart. Her meticulously organized apartment was warm, chic, and eclectic—it made her happy even when the rest of her life couldn't.

Cara grabbed a corkscrew from the bar in her kitchen and a nice Cabernet she'd been saving. She returned to the living room with wine in one hand and two glasses dangling from the other.

Sienna greeted her with a compassionate smile. "I'm sorry you had such a crummy day. Now, open your present."

"Yes, ma'am." Cara removed the bow first and then the colorful paper. She opened the box and gasped. "It's beautiful."

She pulled out the red cashmere swing coat and slipped it on. She ran her fingers down the sleeve, letting the soft fabric caress her fingertips. Grinning, she twirled in a circle for Sienna; the hem of the coat flared out around her as she spun.

Sienna wore a self-satisfied smile. "Straight from the runways of Paris."

Truly touched by the gift, Cara walked over and gave Sienna a hug, catching the heady aroma of Sienna's jasmine perfume. "Thanks, Senny."

Even though Sienna stood the same height as Cara in flat feet—five feet seven inches—Sienna felt like a delicate bird in Cara's arms. For all their differences, and as brash as Sienna could be, she took good care of her. Cara loved Sienna like a sister and appreciated the fact that she was always there when she needed her, and had been since high school when their bond was forged over their shared anxiety disorder. Cara never forgot hiding in the girl's bathroom, breathing hard as she crouched over the toilet, and hearing similar sounds of anguish in the next stall.

Sienna hugged her harder. "Be happy."

"I'll try," Cara whispered back and opted not to share what had happened earlier—mainly because she would have felt like a reformed alcoholic admitting to having a drink.

The doorbell buzzed and they both jumped.

"Who the hell is ringing your bell at ten thirty at night?" Sienna asked.

Cara gave her a wide-eyed look of surprise and shrugged. She walked over to the door and looked through the peephole before opening it, keeping the chain intact.

A courier stood at her door with a manila envelope. Cara wondered why the buzzer hadn't sounded unless one of her neighbors broke the rules and let him in on their way in or out.

Knitting her brow, she asked, "Can I help you?"

"Cara Collins?"

"Yes."

He held out the package to her, slipping it through the door, and then handed her a clipboard. "Please sign here."

She took the package and scribbled her signature onto the receipt and handed it back to him.

"Good night." He smiled and walked back toward the elevator.

Cara stood dumbfounded, staring at the return address: Watson & Haskins, New York. She'd never heard of the firm before but immediately wondered if her creep of a boss had done something to get her sued or fired. The package lay frozen in her hands as she stared, afraid to open it.

"Well?" Sienna asked impatiently.

"Give me a second." After Cara put her coat back in the box, she sat down and opened the manila envelope. She removed a letter-sized envelope with a note paper-clipped to it. The note was written in neat script on Watson & Haskins letterhead.

"It's an appointment reminder for tomorrow at ten a.m.," Cara said, puzzled.

"Clearly not one you made?"

Cara shook her head and tore open the envelope. Her hand froze when she saw the name at the top of the personalized stationary: Hannah Brunt-Collins.

Sienna's eyes widened. "What's the matter? You look like you just saw a ghost."

Cara's mouth moved but nothing came out. Her eyes darted over the contents of the handwritten letter.

"What?" Sienna pressed. "Don't keep me hanging! What is it?"

Cara pressed a hand to her chest. "I . . . It's . . . from my grandmother," she whispered, brows furrowed as she tried to process the words.

"Huh? Which one?"

"My dad's mother, Grandma Hannah."

Sienna wrinkled her nose. "Wait a minute. Aren't both of your grandmothers dead?"

"Yeah. She died twenty-three years ago."

"Okaayyy . . . What're you waiting for, Christmas? Read it to me!" Sienna leaned forward, ready to rip the letter from Cara's hand.

Cara nodded. She scanned the letter and read the first paragraph out loud.

Dearest Cara,

Happy birthday, my dear. If you are reading this letter, it's your twenty-seventh birthday. I only wish that I could have been with you longer to share the many joys of your life as you grew into the amazing woman I'm sure you are now. I'm so sorry that I left you while you were so young, but these things happen, and that is what was meant to be.

Without missing a beat, Cara skipped down to the last paragraph and continued to read.

If all has gone according to plan, tomorrow you have an appointment to meet with Watson & Haskins. They will provide you with the details. Please know that I loved you dearly. My spirit will be with you.

Love always,
Grandma Hannah

Cara brushed a tear away after she finished reading the letter . . . the parts she could actually share, that is.

Sienna raised her eyebrows. "That's it? It sure doesn't tell you much."

Cara shrugged and refolded the letter, slipping it back inside the envelope. Setting the letter aside, she drew her legs up onto the chair and hugged them to her chest, trying to hide her trembling hands. She'd loved her grandmother and remembered her with great warmth, even though Cara was a young child when she died. One of Cara's earliest memories was when she was three. Sitting on her grandmother's lap, she was presented with a little round purse full of Easter candy. Cara could still picture her grandmother with her snow-white braid and a smile that reached her kind blue eyes.

"Are you, okay?" Sienna asked softly.

Cara released a deep breath. "Yeah, it caught me off guard. A voice from beyond the grave, even in a letter, is a little jarring."

"What do you think it's about? Money? You think she left you something?"

Cara kept her face neutral. "My grandmother led a very modest life. She didn't have much money." Cara eyed the unopened wine on the coffee table. "I think it's time for that drink. Would you mind doing the honors?"

"Sure, no need to ask twice," Sienna said, stifling a yawn. She glanced at her watch. "One drink, and then I have to go. The jet lag is kicking in."

Sienna trimmed the foil on the top and twisted out the cork. With the expertise of a sommelier, she poured them each a glass without losing a drop.

Sienna raised her glass. "To finding a better life and a hot, available man."

"I'll drink to that." Cara gave her a reluctant smile and touched glasses. She wished it could be that easy, but she'd never had that kind of luck. If anything, she'd spent years hiding her heart inside a protective bubble. Her feelings for Kai may be misplaced, but at least they kept her relatively safe.

After finishing their wine, Cara walked Sienna to the door. Sienna smirked as she looked once again at Cara's ensemble. "I've made a reservation for seven o'clock on Saturday at Raphael's. From there, we'll let the games begin. And wear something nice; show some cleavage for once."

Cara narrowed her eyes. "You sure you want the competition?"

Sienna glanced down at her B-cups. "Bring it on. All you need is a perfect handful. Any more is just excess." She winked. "Call me when you find out more about the letter thingie."

"Absolutely." Cara gave Sienna a quick hug, glad that she couldn't see her face.

"Bye, Chlow-Chlow," Sienna called over at the dog balled up on the sofa.

Closing the door behind Sienna, Cara sighed with relief. Her hands once again trembled as she snatched up the letter. She sat down next to Chloe where there was more light.

This time, she read the entire letter, including the part she hadn't read to Sienna. The paper shook in her hands.

Dearest Cara,

Happy birthday, my dear. If you are reading this letter, it's your twenty-seventh birthday. I only wish that I could have been with you longer to share the many joys of your life as you grew into the amazing woman I'm sure you are now. I'm so sorry that I left you while you were so young, but these things happen, and that is what was meant to be.

Cara, what I am about to tell you next must stay secret. I can't emphasize this enough. Otherwise, to put this even more plainly, people you love could die.

My dear, you were born with a gift. From the moment I saw you until now, as I write this letter, you have always given off the signal that you are one of us. This gift doesn't usually run in families, so you can't imagine how thrilled I was when I discovered it in you.

As a result of this gift, and your ultimate mission, you have inherited fifty million dollars. Half, twenty-five million, is for you personally. You'll act as the custodian for the other half, passing it to the next generation when the time is right. Like your sponsor did for you. I'm merely the messenger in this transaction. With this money, comes great responsibility.

I realize that I haven't even begun to answer the questions you must be asking yourself, but someone will come soon to explain more. I don't know who that will be, since much time will pass between the writing of this letter and its delivery.

If all has gone according to plan, tomorrow you have an appointment to meet with Watson & Haskins. They will provide you with the details. Please know that I loved you dearly. My spirit will be with you.

Love always,
Grandma Hannah

This morning, Cara didn't think she was gifted in any particular way. *Can I heal people? Can I make them younger? Is that the gift my grandmother meant?*

Overwhelmed, she hyperventilated, not knowing which part of the fantastical news to process first. Anxiety and loneliness slammed into her with the realization that there was no one she could tell without people she loved potentially dying. What would she tell her family?

She reached for her half-full wineglass, but the wine already in her stomach bubbled angrily, and she put the glass back down. Worry overshadowed her thoughts, digging deep into her brow. Chloe must have sensed her distress; she awoke and licked her hand. Cara petted her and stared into the dog's expressive eyes, grateful for her company.

Even though this news had the potential for a happy ending to her miserable job problem, she couldn't escape the ominous implications of the letter. Inheriting money didn't suck, but putting someone else in danger because they'd found out she'd inherited it more than sucked.

One thing was for sure. Tomorrow couldn't come fast enough.

Chapter 7

HE'S PERFECT, SHE THOUGHT, pausing to drink him in with her eyes and to savor her last seconds of unguarded observation. Cara approached him from across the floor of the art gallery.

She'd never seen him dressed in all white before, but if anyone could pull it off, he could. The sleeves of his linen collared shirt were rolled up to the elbow, revealing the tanned skin of his arms. Against the white walls of the gallery, he appeared luminescent, almost otherworldly. Her eyes traced the fine lines of his profile as he stood, transfixed, near one of the paintings.

She ignored her insecurities this time. He preferred blondes, but made an exception for her. She'd never be mistaken for Miss California, but she could live with that. Her strong physical attraction to him generated a visceral reaction whenever he was near.

He turned toward her and she continued her approach. She watched his face, a face that was almost too pretty, surrounded by blond hair in a conservative cut. His intense blue eyes caught her gaze, and he broke out in a dimpled smile, revealing flawless white teeth. She walked into his arms in one fluid motion. They were well matched for intimate eye contact—he at six feet and her slightly below that when wearing heels. She leaned in to inhale the clean, fresh warmth of his neck and then slowly brushed her lips up to his soft but firm waiting lips. His kiss always reminded her of a cool drink of water, refreshing and life-giving.

Given their normally reserved physical relationship, Cara surprised herself with her boldness. Surprising her more, he didn't pull away and met her kiss fully.

"It's good to see you," he whispered, holding her in a close embrace, the taste of his kiss still on her lips. With some hesitation, they broke apart to walk the gallery. He took her hand in his. The engraved silver ring he wore—a gift from his father—was cool against her finger.

She'd been thrilled when he'd asked her to come. Cara knew this moment was special and equally as fragile. Rarely was Kai this open with her. He usually tried to push her away when she got too close. Maybe he'd finally forgiven her after all these years? But this wasn't the first time she danced on the edge of hope's sword.

She tensed, knowing exactly where this could lead. He would get too close, and then she would watch him retreat, guilt spilling over him as he struggled internally with his feelings. That's usually how it played out, leaving her to deal with the sting of disappointment. She felt like Sisyphus stuck in an infinite loop of rolling the stone up the hill, only to have it roll back down as she neared the top. Would this time be different?

They stopped. He held her hand in his and pulled her closer, gazing into her eyes. She sensed his words. They were just a breath away. Would he finally grant her wish? He'd no more than spoke her name, "*Cara—*"

"*Kai—*" she started, when suddenly the gallery swayed, and something warm and wet on her face penetrated her thoughts. Her hand ripped from Kai's, and her conscious mind dumped her out of her dream with an unceremonious thud.

Cara grudgingly opened her eyes to see Chloe standing over her with her tail wagging while she lapped her cheek. "That was a really good dream you interrupted," Cara said, exasperated.

Chloe paused momentarily at the sound of Cara's voice, ears up and brow crinkled. Determining that Cara had nothing more to say, she resumed dispensing her wet kisses.

"I love you too." Cara surrendered, scratching the dog behind her ears. Finished with her good-morning ritual, Chloe dug her way under the covers and settled comfortably against Cara's leg.

Cara's palm tingled where Kai's hand had rested next to hers, and she swore she could still feel the tender touch of his kiss on her lips. She closed her eyes and sighed, savoring the last echo of his skin on hers. The beauty of the dream mingled with the disappointment of having Kai slip away and out of her reach . . . again. Her heart responded with the all too familiar ache of his absence.

She sat up in bed and yesterday's events came rushing back, waking the butterflies in her stomach. She picked up her iPhone from the nightstand to check for new texts and e-mails—still no Kai.

Frowning, she couldn't decide what upset her more: the anxiety over her grandmother's letter or her disappointment over Kai missing her birthday. She flung the phone onto the bed and huffed.

He better have a good excuse, like being swallowed up by a sinkhole, she thought. She couldn't believe she hadn't heard from him. Or had she through the dream?

Her dreams about Kai were more like premonitions or visions—crystal clear, tactile, and rife with emotions. To hear that he believed she'd never cheated on him all those years ago, if only in her dreams, would be enough.

Though many years had passed since the incident that caused their breakup back in college, the smoldering attraction between them remained, lurking beneath the surface. On occasion, with alcohol as an excuse, they'd slip into a night of heated passion. But that had ended when he married someone else.

She combed her fingers through her sleep-matted hair. She wished she could stop loving him, especially since he was married to that blond fashion plate, Melanie. He'd never cheat on his wife, and she could never be with a married man. Even when she and Kai had tried to take a break, they couldn't go too long without contacting one another. Honestly, she didn't know if it was their attraction to each other or some deeper connection that kept them from straying too far outside of each other's lives. Something would draw them back together—a dream, an event. An eerie and inexplicable bond existed between them that they both accepted, but neither of them understood. As strange as it sounded, she could actually *taste* how much he cared about her. And he didn't need to know her true feelings, or that she would protect him with her life if she had to.

Ironic how fate worked—they couldn't be together, yet they couldn't be apart.

Since she couldn't have him, she longed to find someone like him. But when it came to love, she readily admitted her track record was crap.

Even though Kai lived in California and she hadn't seen him face-to-face in over a year, every Wednesday she looked forward to the sound of her cell phone ringing at eleven in the morning. Just hearing his voice was enough as they traded snippets from their week and sought the other's opinions on various topics. And considering yesterday was Wednesday, he had even less of an excuse for dropping the ball on her birthday. One of the amazing things about Kai was that he legitimately had a photographic memory.

She scowled and threw back the comforter. "He's toast," she mumbled. Stretching her legs over the side of the bed, she tensed as her thoughts returned to the dream. Her dreams involving Kai always came true.

This morning's dream had been one of the most beautiful she'd ever had. As opposed to the last dream she'd had just short of a year ago, which had been the most frightening. Still, it bothered her on so many levels.

In that dream, Kai had been stabbed in the chest and his throat had been slit. Powerless, Cara watched the halo of blood fan out underneath him. The life drained from his eyes as they glazed over in death. She'd woken up hysterical, her pillow soaked with tears, and an empty cavern where her heart was supposed to be.

They rarely spoke about that dream or the events that followed. When Cara had warned Kai of the dream the next day, he'd altered his work schedule for that evening, and his colleague, Dr. Tom Peyton, had been murdered in the employee parking lot.

Cara believed her intervention saved Kai's life, but sacrificed another's in his place. Her shoulders still hung heavy with that karmic burden, and she continued to rack her brain, analyzing whether she could have done anything different to prevent the outcome. More importantly, her sixth sense continued to tingle, and she wondered if she'd stopped the event or only delayed it.

Cara had noticed a reliable pattern with her dreams of Kai. It had to do with the sequence of her dreams—and last night's dream didn't fit the pattern. She paused again and wondered if her dreams could be the gift her grandmother referred to in the letter. But her dreams were tied primarily to Kai.

Still . . . food for thought.

Either way, she needed to set aside her feelings about him missing her birthday and talk to him about the pattern of her dreams. She made a mental note to call him later. Meanwhile, , she retrieved her phone. She had another call to make.

A prerecorded voice answered. "Rick Russo of Cabot Investments, Vice President of Client Relations, leave me a message and make it a great day." Cara rolled her eyes. Someone should tell him that rolling his *R*s makes him sound like an asshat.

"Rick, it's Cara," she croaked roughly. "Sorry to call in sick today. I think I need to see a doctor. See you tomorrow." She hung up, relieved. Not much of a lie. Chances are she would see him tomorrow, and in reality, she probably should see a doctor. He didn't need to know she meant a shrink.

If she expected to make her appointment, she'd better get moving. Leaving her loyal hound in a warm ball under the covers, she walked to her closet to select something to wear.

She laid out a pair of black pants and a cashmere sweater. On her way to the bathroom, she snatched her phone from the bed and dropped it into her purse next to her emergency kit, praying that she wouldn't need the kit anytime soon.

Chapter 8

San Francisco. Solomon Residence. Thursday, March 20,
4:15 a.m. PDT / 7:15 a.m. EDT

"It's good to see you," he whispered, holding her in a close embrace, the taste of her kiss still on his lips. With some hesitation, they broke apart to walk the gallery in comfortable silence. He'd asked her here for a reason, and it was time to tell her why. He stopped and took her hand in his. Pulling her closer, he gazed into her eyes. His words hung in the air, just a breath away. "Cara—"

Kai stirred, awoken by the not-so-subtle movements of his four-year-old daughter, Sara, as she crept up onto the queen-sized bed between him and his wife, Melanie. Undisturbed, Melanie slept on. She'd always been that way. Kai joked that she could sleep through an earthquake. When Sara was a baby, Kai had been the one to do the predawn bottle feedings because Melanie would sleep through her cries.

"Sara, go back to bed. You know you're not allowed in Mommy and Daddy's bed in the middle of the night," he said, without turning toward Sara or moving his head from the pillow. He hoped to jump back into the dream he'd just left, afraid that if he moved he would forget where he'd left off, or worse, forget the dream entirely.

The feel of Cara's kiss lingered on his lips. His guilt was gearing up for a full-frontal assault, but it wasn't enough to make his semiconscious brain forsake the dream. There would be plenty of time for self-recrimination later. He wanted to hear the words he'd planned to utter to Cara, sensing they were vitally important.

"Daddy, I'm scared. I was dreaming about monsters. They were trying to get me," Sara whispered, trying to burrow her way under the covers. "Can't I just stay here for a little while?"

Even though he and Melanie had set a rule that their bedroom was off-limits at night except for extreme emergencies, how could he refuse? In Sara's young mind, scary dreams counted.

"Okay, sweetheart. Just for a minute then we have to put you back into your big-girl bed. I'll check for monsters, and we can leave your door open and the night light on."

He scooped her into his arms and snuggled her into the warmth of his chest. Her silky long hair tickled his arm. She had blond hair like her mother and the bluest eyes—his eyes. He loved her with an intensity that he hadn't thought possible and couldn't imagine life without her. A host of emotions consumed him when it came to Sara—unconditional love, protectiveness, and the fear that someday something unexpected could happen. He found it incomprehensible that a father could leave a child . . . like his own father had left him . . .

"The monsters said they were going to kill you, Daddy, and I didn't know what to do," Sara whispered in a small shaky voice.

"Shh. Don't worry. I won't let any monsters hurt me." *Geez, what kind of television has this child been watching?* He'd check the parental controls on the TV in the morning.

"Luke said he'd protect us, but I'm still scared."

Huh? "Who's Luke, sweetie?" Kai wondered if he should be concerned.

"Our Guardian Angel," she answered and settled into him while Melanie slept like the dead on the other side of the bed. "He came at the end of the dream."

Relieved to hear the angel was part of Sara's dream, Kai stroked her hair and decided to let it pass.

His thoughts drifted back to his own dream. It had been a while since he'd had a romantic dream about Cara. Their connection was something he didn't fully understand, but something he would never willingly give up. They hadn't been romantically involved for years, not that anything could have continued once he married. He believed in his vows and so did she. Melanie accepted his friendship with Cara, and the two women had developed a cordial, even warm, relationship.

He blushed, thinking about the kiss. Guilt always tore at him after thinking of Cara in that way—the way they used to be. Lucky for him, it didn't happen too often. He secretly admitted that Cara was his one true regret and lamented that he'd failed to believe and forgive her when he'd had the chance. But back in college he'd been stubborn and too afraid to let her get close enough to rip his heart out a second time. Instead, they managed to nurture a friendship after their breakup, which had grown exponentially over the years. A couple of times he'd relented, and they'd let it go too far, but distance separated them. During the six years he'd attended MIT to earn both his master's and PhD, she'd been either down at Georgetown finishing the last three years of her undergraduate degree or working in New York City.

He would never tell Cara, but he loved her like no one else. There was something unexplainable about his connection to her; she was a beacon for him. Just knowing she was out there somewhere, he could breathe and go on with his daily life. He expected that people would come and go. But he knew Cara would always be there for him.

Cara didn't know the truth about why he'd married Melanie—that she'd been pregnant. Right or wrong, he thought it best for Cara not to know. Sadly, Melanie miscarried only weeks after the wedding, but they had Sara a year later. Looking back, he would have made different choices, but that time had long passed.

He hugged his little girl tighter and kissed the top of her head. She was the one precious thing he'd never change. Sara snored softly as she lay snuggled against his side. He pulled her closer. Squeezing his eyes closed, he tried to seduce himself back to sleep.

His eyes refused to stay shut. As he stared up at the ceiling, self-loathing swirled around inside him. The truth? He was in love with both women but wouldn't acknowledge it to himself, much less to anyone else.

He turned to look at the clock. The alarm wouldn't ring for another ninety minutes. His mind churned too quickly to fall back asleep. He left Sara in bed with Melanie and quietly slipped away.

His thoughts turned to work as he padded to his office. He clicked on the small desk lamp and fired up his computer to check the nightly lab results, anxious to see if his most recent experiment had worked. He'd made a bold move to try something different and was curious to see if the latest combination of genes spliced into his host cells yielded any change. Full results wouldn't be available yet, but he should be able to determine the viability of the samples—information he needed before the next implantation.

Two months ago the experimentation cycle times had taken much longer, but at Kai's insistence, Forrester funded the switch to a newer class of bioengineered proteins, which allowed targeted mutations to be created in any gene within the genome. The new technology allowed him to be more surgical in his approach to gene editing and get results within two days.

Kai reached for his messenger-bag briefcase and took out two laboratory notebooks marked with the word FIREFLY and a volume number. He set them on the desk. His pulse sped up as he opened the earlier of the two hard-bound books and stared at the numbered pages filled with copious handwritten notes.

Kai had been with Forrester Research for nearly four years but had spent his last twelve months working on Project Firefly, a top-secret genetics project for an unnamed group referred to as the Foundation. One of the leading privately funded research facilities in the world, Forrester had concentrated primarily on medical research for cancer and degenerative and infectious diseases until 2004, when they expanded into genetics research to seize commercial opportunities after the publication of the Human Genome Project results.

Although Kai's primary expertise wasn't in genetics, he had jumped at the chance to continue the research of his deceased colleague and acquaintance, Dr. Tom Peyton. Kai was one of Forrester's senior scientists and recognized as their best resident troubleshooter. He'd been flattered when the division president asked him to take over the research. In the president's opinion, enough progress had been made on Project Firefly to allow Kai to come in and quickly make sense of the work. But Kai hadn't found that to be the case. Many aspects of the project remained shrouded in secrecy, even from him, the lead scientist. The client sponsoring the research drove the level of security, handicapping Kai even on a good day. He'd spent a year crashing and burning in the lab to the point where he'd been ready to leave the project. In addition, the Foundation was losing patience, and every day the situation grew worse.

Until now . . . Kai stared at two scientific notebooks containing notes left behind from the late Dr. Tom Peyton. One notebook Kai had received when he started the project a year ago, and the other he'd found only a few days ago in a locked file cabinet while rummaging through his old work to help pursue a new idea for Firefly. Missing since the beginning of the project, Kai had doubted he'd ever find the notebook that preceded the one he'd been given. A chill shot through him when he found the notebook among his files, not knowing how it had gotten there.

Smuggling both books from the lab, Kai had examined them side by side two nights earlier and noticed something odd. The notations were all wrong between them, raising Kai's suspicion that a section of the documentation had been replaced or, more accurately, had been fabricated. Scientific notebooks used in the lab were all bound with numbered pages specifically for proving chain of custody. Missing pages would be impossible to hide, since ripping out one page caused the adjoining page to fall out. It didn't appear the books had been tampered with, but the scientific notations had stopped matching the contents of the pages at the end of the last notebook.

An outside scientist wouldn't have noticed the anomaly in the notes, but the same senior scientist had trained Tom and Kai when they'd started with Forrester after grad school. Before he passed away, Dr. Lawrence Noble taught them both his personal research and documentation methodology that he'd aptly called the Noble Method, leaving Kai and Tom with the distinction of being the last two scientists trained in this unique method.

Kai had been told the project involved genetic modification for a rare degenerative disease that caused accelerated organ loss. Now he suspected the truth was different. How much different, he didn't know. After this discovery, Kai started at a new point in his research. If what he suspected was true, there was a third set of notes . . . somewhere.

In the dim light of his home office, Kai logged in remotely to the Forrester system. From his laptop, he had visibility into the lab equipment and the last two sets of samples he'd prepared: one before reading the newly found notebook, and one after.

His login successful, the screen on his laptop jumped to life. He opened each file, arranging them side by side until he was looking at ten magnified thumbnail images. Each was labeled with the date and protocol so Kai could distinguish one sample from the next. He hoped to see fat healthy cells.

Kai scanned the five older samples first. None of them showed any modification of the alleles, which would have indicted the gene mutations Kai hoped to see. As he reviewed the latest five, his pulsed quickened. One sample appeared to have some modification.

"Yes!" He punched the air. Repaired at the breaks, the cell seemed to be functioning without the deleted protein. He made the requisite notations in the latest notebook. Later, he would move to the next stage of the experiment with the one, and attempt to replicate his success with some new combinations.

A reminder dinged on his computer, and he looked up.

Oh, crap! Cara's birthday. According to the alarm, he'd missed it by twelve hours. He'd meant to call her yesterday for their weekly chat, but had gotten so caught up in his discovery that he'd forgotten.

What a total shit heel, he scolded himself. No wonder he'd dreamed of her.

Glancing at the clock on his computer, Kai did some quick math and reached for the phone.

Chapter 9

New York City. Perry Street Apartment. Thursday, March 20, 8:00 a.m. EDT

CARA HIT THE OFF SWITCH on her blow-dryer just in time to hear the chorus of "Don't Stop Believin'," her ringtone for Kai. Her heart leapt and she ran for the living room. On the way, her towel loosened and fell to the floor. She stumbled over the wet mound of terry cloth and cursed. If she planned to make it through the day, she'd better get a grip on herself.

Naked, she scooped up the towel and lunged for her cell phone.

"Hey, I'm a terrible friend. I can't believe I missed your birthday."

She smiled at the sound of Kai's voice, and her shoulders relaxed immediately. "You suck. I can't believe you forgot. How long have we known each other?"

"I know. I feel like shit. Forgive me?"

"Depends. I'm open to flowers."

"You hate flowers. Besides, you're allergic to almost all of them."

True, she was allergic to most flowers, but she liked the gesture. Kai could give her a bag of potatoes and she'd love them.

"At least you remembered that."

His voice softened. "I remember a lot of things." The double entendre wasn't lost on her. Her memory zipped back to what it had been like before he'd gotten married. His blue eyes longing for her as he ran his fingers through her hair. His lips coming down to meet hers. Her hands running over the blond hairs of his chest while he made love to her that last time.

She shook the memory away and started to relent, but couldn't help sulking. "You get points for calling at five a.m. your time to beg forgiveness, but for someone with a near photographic memory, it was a pathetic showing. Don't you ever look at your calendar?"

He chuckled. "Not as much as I should. Fine, expect a fruit basket."

She laughed. "You're sending me fruit? Seriously?" The more she thought about the fruit, the funnier it became until she laughed so hard she cried. She just couldn't picture him buying fruit for anyone . . . ever.

"What?" And then his laughter mingled with hers. That happened with them sometimes, one would trigger a laughing fit in the other. The first time it had happened was during an art class they shared in college over something just as innocuous. They were both thrown out for disruption.

She calmed down and grew serious. "Hey, I planned on calling you later anyway. I had another dream last night."

He hesitated for a second. "Yeah . . . I had one too."

Cara tensed. That had never happened before. "You did? What was it about?"

"It wasn't scary like the one you had last year, if that's what you're asking."

"Well, that's good, but that's not why I'm asking."

She could barely hear him whisper, "I kissed you in the dream."

Her skin tingled from his words, and a rush of warmth coursed through her. She hated that he could make her react this way. "Do you remember anything else?"

"No. Sara crawled into bed and woke me up."

Good, she thought. She didn't want to talk about her dream if she could avoid it. After what had happened yesterday, she now questioned the cause of her connection to Kai through her dreams.

"Hmm. You know, it's kind of creepy—the way you show up in my dreams," she said. Luckily, he was the only one. Well, except for Tyler—the very brief and only relationship she'd had since Kai—and it had been years since she'd dreamt of him. Tyler was the only man whose life was in serious jeopardy if she ever crossed paths with him again. "Actually, the reason I wanted to call had something to do with the dream from last year . . . "

"What about it? I've never figured out who Le Feu could be."

In the dream, Kai had yelled a warning at Cara before he'd been stabbed. He'd said, "Le Feu! Run, Cara, run!"

"Me neither, but that's not it. I've figured out something about my dreams, which doesn't seem to make any sense based on last year's events." She took a deep breath and added, "I think you're still in danger."

Apprehension crept into his voice. "Why? What did you figure out?"

"I've noticed a reliable pattern over the years—real life is always one dream behind. The prior dream is fulfilled anywhere from a day to a couple of weeks *after* I've had my next dream. My next dream was the one I had this morning."

Silence.

"Kai, are you still there?"

"Hold on, I'm calculating." She drummed her fingers on her knee, waiting for his analytical brain to spit out its conclusion. A couple of moments later, he said, "Holy shit, you're right."

His confirmation filled her with a mix of relief and anxiety. "Be careful. For all we know this means you're still in jeopardy."

"Thanks for letting me know," he said, concern in his voice. She heard him sigh. "Hey, I have to get ready for work, and I'm sure I've already made you late."

Kai's words plunked her back into reality. Her mouth opened. She wanted to tell him about the letter, but the words died in her throat and she pressed her lips closed. Not being able to tell him filled her with loneliness, but the thought of anything happening to him terrified her more. Instead, she asked, "Before I go, how is everything going with work this week?"

He'd been stressed about it the last time they'd spoken, but he never gave her many details.

"Last thing I want to do is give my favorite investment banker an insider trading tip, but things seem to be progressing." His tone had a forced casualness. She sensed this was his attempt to lighten up the conversation.

She chuckled nervously. "No worries. I don't aspire to prison stripes. Have a good day, and I'll look for that fruit basket."

He laughed. "How about an eCard and we call it even?"

"Deal."

"Okay. I'll call you in a few days to catch up. Sooner if anything weird happens." Then he added softly, "Happy birthday, Car." He hung up.

She smiled again and flushed with warmth, liking it that he called her Car. Wrapping the towel around her more tightly, she headed back to the bathroom to put on her makeup.

Maybe she'd be able to face this day after all.

Chapter 10

WHAT THE HELL is he doing up here? Chamuel wondered as he towered over Zeke on the roof of Cara's apartment building. The sleeping, dark-ponytailed Guardian lay flat on his back on the asphalt with his legs crossed at the ankles and his arms folded across his broad chest. Chamuel stared down at the young Nephil's boyish face, still dressed from his night out in form-fitting slacks and a tight knit shirt with sleeves exposing his tattooed forearms. Chamuel eyed Zeke's street clothes and shook his head, feeling slightly guilty for interfering with Zeke's hopes of a night filled with female companionship.

God, I'm getting old, Chamuel thought as he nudged Zeke with his boot. "Wake up."

Zeke cracked open one eye and groaned. "I'm hatin' on you right now, Cham. I can't believe you called me into service on my night off." He pushed up on one elbow. "Next time, call me before I go clubbing and have a few drinks in me. Hand over the coffee." He held up his hand, waiting.

Chamuel dangled it over him with a sour look on his face.

Zeke rolled his eyes. "Please?"

"It's espresso," he said and handed the cup to Zeke.

"Whatever. I'd drink mud right now if it had caffeine in it."

Chamuel frowned. "And show some respect to your elders. What're you doing up here uncloaked anyway? I thought I told you to wait on the fire escape?"

"I've only been here a few minutes. I didn't have enough energy left to cloak, especially after I saw your charge naked." He stood and smirked. "That was just too much for me to handle."

Chamuel ground his teeth, his hands clenching at his sides. "I'm sorry, what did you say?"

"Keep your knickers on. I wasn't doing a Peeping Tom on her." Zeke brushed asphalt pebbles from his pants with his free hand.

"Then how did you see her naked?" Chamuel asked with a low growl. The thought of anyone seeing her that way made him apoplectic, not to mention . . . jealous.

Zeke released an exasperated sigh. "Will you chill? She must've just gotten out of the shower. She ran to answer her cell phone, and her towel dropped as she lunged for the darn thing. I caught the view from the fire escape through the kitchen doorway."

Chamuel huffed and shook his head. He still wanted to wipe the smug smile off of Zeke's baby face. He and Isaac had taken Zeke under their wings as a small boy, but there were times when Chamuel wanted to kick his young Nephil ass despite knowing that underneath his childish behavior was a reliable and good-hearted Guardian.

"So, you came up here?" he asked gruffly, passing his hand across his chin.

"Yeah, after my eyes nearly popped out of my head." Zeke gulped his espresso, his eyes springing open the rest of the way. "That's some good stuff."

Another growl rumbled up from Chamuel's throat.

Zeke clapped him on the shoulder. "Cham, don't worry. Your charge is safe with me. You have my oath." This time, Zeke's sincerity reached through his words.

Chamuel sighed. "Just don't get any ideas."

"You know I don't mix business with pleasure." Zeke smiled and winked. "She's pretty hot, though."

Chamuel answered with a menacing glare. He didn't need to be reminded of that, nor did he need the thought of her naked body tormenting him all day.

Zeke threw his hands up. "I know. Not going there."

Deciding to remove himself from Zeke's baited hook, Chamuel changed the subject. "Thanks for relieving me. I owe you one. That couple hours of sleep did me good, not to mention the shower."

"Yes, you do owe me one," Zeke said, removing a slip of paper from his pocket and squinting at it. "And her name is Sophia."

Chamuel snorted. "You're unbelievable."

"In more ways than I can count." Zeke grinned then cupped his hand to his ear and looked at his watch. "You better get moving. I just heard her lock the apartment door. She's heading toward the elevator." Zeke drained his cup of espresso and handed it back to him. "I'm outty." He cloaked before jumping to the ground below.

Chamuel looked over the roof's edge just as Zeke reappeared across the street and melted in behind a couple of chattering girls in high heels and work clothes.

A moment later, Chamuel spotted Cara's bouncing, auburn hair and red coat cross the street below him. His face flushed with heat at the thought of her wet from the shower without a towel. Giving himself a mental shake, he cloaked and flew in behind her.

Chapter 11

CARA SUPPRESSED A YAWN and stepped out of the elevator into the warmth of a hall lit by a large, antique crystal chandelier. She'd felt better after speaking with Kai. But other than her early-morning dream of him, she'd barely slept. The caffeine from the pot of coffee she chugged earlier, coupled with adrenaline, barely made up for the deficit.

Mozart played quietly in the background, and the perfume of the spring bouquet on the hallway table filled the air. One whiff of the sweet-smelling lilies and Cara sneezed in rapid succession. She caught her reflection in an oversized antique French mirror suspended over a marble-topped table, and she dabbed her nose with a tissue from her purse. Her hair cascaded in loose waves over her shoulders. Other than the deer-in-headlights glimmer in her green eyes, she could pass for sane.

She couldn't resist taking a second to admire the red swing coat. Somehow, Sienna's present anchored Cara to reality, making her life seem closer to normal.

"Miss Collins?" A Chanel-clad woman interrupted Cara's thoughts.

Cara turned and blushed. "Yes, sorry."

The woman smiled. "Mr. Gladstone will see you now. My name is Claudette. Please, follow me."

Cara guessed Claudette was in her late thirties. Her brown hair was cut in a sleek and smooth bob. Everything about her implied a sense of efficiency as she led Cara down the hallway to a set of ornate cherry doors.

Beyond the double doors was a narrow, wood-paneled hallway covered in plush oriental rugs. The center hallway stretched out in front of them, leading to offices along both walls with many intersecting hallways along the way.

Beautiful oil paintings, illuminated with picture lights, lined the walls. Cara had minored in Art History in college and was passionate about both paintings and sculpture. As she and Claudette navigated their way deeper into the maze of hallways, Cara recognized works from early-seventeenth-century Dutch masters and wished she had more time to appreciate them. One of the more magnificent pieces was a nineteenth-century Hudson River school canvas painted by Thomas Cole. However, Cara's personal favorite was a Guy Wiggins early-twentieth-century New York City street scene during a snowfall. Nice to know she was reaping the benefits of her education and countless trips to the Met.

They finally stopped in front of another set of paneled double doors. Claudette knocked softly before pushing open the door on the right and ushering Cara inside.

"Mr. Gladstone, this is Cara Collins. Please call me if you need anything further."

Cara stepped into the office, a beautiful library with paneled walls on the lower half and built-in bookshelves above. A large partner's desk sat in front of the back wall where a large Italian pre-Raphaelite painting of two angels hung in a gold frame.

A tall, older man in his sixties with a cherubic face and a head of white hair sat behind the desk.

"Hello, Miss Collins. May I take your coat before you sit down?" he asked, easing himself up and out of his chair.

Cara handed her coat to Mr. Gladstone, and he hung it up next to his own on an antique coat rack. Gesturing for Cara to sit down on one of his guest chairs, he moved back to his seat. Her apprehension mixed with her excitement. It wasn't every day she inherited fifty million dollars.

Gladstone's eyes were kind and intelligent. "Please, Miss Collins, take a seat. If there's time later, or if you so desire, we can retreat to the fire." His manner put her more at ease. She glanced to her right toward the fire glowing in the hearth and spotted the two leather Chesterfield-style chairs with an antique tea table between them. The smell of leather, pine, and burning wood tickled her nose.

"Thank you, I'm fine here," she said, putting her purse down next to her chair.

"Should I call you Miss Collins, or do you mind if I call you Cara?"

"Cara, please."

"Cara is such a lovely name." He smiled and repositioned himself in his chair. "I'm sure you're filled with questions."

You have no idea, she thought.

"By way of a quick introduction, my father handled your sponsor's affairs, and that responsibility was passed to me when he retired. The objective of our meeting today is to discuss and transfer certain holdings to you and to describe the continuous process and parameters needed to access those holdings. My instructions are very specific, so let's see how far that gets us, shall we?"

Cara nodded. "That sounds reasonable."

"Very well." Mr. Gladstone put on his reading glasses and pulled a thick, ornate leather folder from his desk. The clasp on the folder was made of a round, gold metal seal. As he pushed down on the center of the clasp, it clicked open. He removed several sheets of creamy-white paper. "Let's start with the real estate holdings."

She tried to control the shock that crossed her face. "I'm sorry, what?"

He smiled kindly. "As a part of this trust you've inherited two real estate properties: a penthouse apartment on Fifth Avenue and a farmhouse outside of Greenwich, Connecticut."

Cara's mouth hung slightly open. That was some high-end property.

He stared over his lowered glasses, concerned. "Are you all right, dear? May I continue?"

She swallowed and nodded.

"In addition, there are two garaged vehicles parked in the lot underneath the Fifth Avenue property." She managed to suppress any additional reaction. She already had a car, a luxury for a Manhattanite. Three cars was just plain overkill. Gladstone paused. "Would you like me to call Claudette for a glass of water or perhaps some nice tea?"

Cara smiled weakly, feeling a bit foolish. "No. Please continue."

He readjusted his glasses. "There are two accounts, one where you are the trustee, and the other is in your name for your use. We administer both accounts. I will provide you with a copy of the investment plans for each account. We can set up a subsequent meeting to discuss any changes in the portfolio mix, if appropriate. Our goal is twofold: growth and income generation. Your accounts have been growing without funds withdrawn for over twenty-five years, so the appreciation has been substantial. The original fifty million dollars has tripled within that time, and is now worth more than one hundred fifty million dollars. We would have outperformed our targets if the last ten years had been better, but I hope you are pleased nonetheless."

Cara's eyes widened, and she shifted in her seat. Watson & Haskins had done very well managing the funds. She wished she'd done as well managing her own clients' portfolios.

If Mr. Gladstone noticed her surprise, he didn't acknowledge it. "Cara, the funds will be distributed in increments of five hundred thousand dollars annually, and taxed at the long-term capital gains rate. The amount will be adjusted for inflation every year. Just call it pin money. The upkeep of the properties and the cars will be paid out of the fund directly by us. Just submit those expenses, and we'll send you a quarterly statement."

Cara breathed a sigh of relief. Maybe it wouldn't be as difficult to upkeep the properties as she'd originally thought.

"My grandmother's letter said this all needs to stay confidential. Can you tell me more about this money?" For the moment, she held back on asking about the part where people could die.

"Some. These are your resources for life, but they revert to the trust when you pass on. At some point in time, you will designate the portion of money you're keeping in trust that's not yours. Someone will explain why you were chosen as a custodian when the time is right. In the meantime, if something happens before then, that portion will be merged with your holdings and the assets will revert to the trustees, with the exception of the original twenty-five million dollars. They will distribute the money again at the appointed time to the next designee."

"What about my husband and children if I get married?" Cara asked, entwining her fingers together.

"It's up to you how you choose to use your annual income, my dear. The original twenty-five million dollars is yours to spend during your lifetime, if that's something you want to do. Just contact us with the request."

"Okay, I understand." Cara pressed her hands into her lap.

"Think of the remaining portion as renting versus owning. The money is available for your use, but at the end of the day, the only difference is you may not be able to choose who inherits it. Is it really so different in life? You can't take it with you when you die, even if you own it."

He had a good point. Weird as it was, Cara was relieved. That much money made her nervous. She was used to a healthy salary, so she could adapt if she ignored the lump sum and focused on the annual disbursement. As a portfolio manager, she knew how to handle money, so watching over the fund statements and the investment growth would be easy.

Then a funny thought struck Cara. "I have a dog," she blurted.

He smiled. "My dear, that's fine. I only used the rental analogy to set you at ease in your understanding. Animals are allowed."

He leaned over the desk and handed her a small stack of papers. "Please sign wherever my secretary put the little clear signature sticky notes."

After looking over the papers, Cara took a deep breath and looked at him in earnest, the pen in her hand hovering over the first signature line. "What do I tell people? How do I explain all this wealth?"

He covered her free hand in his. "No one needs to know the contents of your bank accounts, dear. For the rest, it's always wise not to stray far from the truth. These assets are in your care, so might I suggest that a lucrative caretaker's role has just become available through the firm of Watson & Haskins?" His eyes crinkled in a warm smile and he winked. "The best part is that it wouldn't require you to quit your current position."

Her mood lightened. His suggestion, while unconventional, could work. "For a minute, I thought you were going to suggest an inheritance from a dead relative," she replied, poised to sign.

"Ah. The shortcoming in that excuse would be immediately apparent within your own family."

Her shoulders slumped, and a lump formed in her throat. She'd have to lie to her family. A shiver ran through her with the realization that her life would change. Never had she been so alone. She nodded and lowered the pen. In return, he removed another leather pouch with Hermès impressed on it in gold.

Whoever these people are, they have good taste, she thought.

Gladstone handed her the pouch. "The keys are numbered. Each corresponds to a set of house or car keys." Then he handed her a small envelope. "This one contains the addresses and description of the cars, your ATM card, a checkbook, and my business card. This year's disbursement has already been deposited into your account, and today will be the annual anniversary for the disbursements. In addition, please see Claudette on the way out. We have a warehouse in Brooklyn where we keep a storehouse of furniture. You're free to swap out furniture in either residence. Furnishings are part of your arrangement. We're also happy to dispose of or store any of your current possessions. Claudette will give you the address and all the details. We've had the Manhattan residence fully furnished and the refrigerator stocked. The Connecticut residence is furnished, but not stocked with food."

By the time the man had finally finished his presentation, Cara's head was spinning. She nibbled her lower lip, overwhelmed.

"Cara, dear." Gladstone's voice softened, and his eyes held genuine warmth. "I know this must be overwhelming. There's a car waiting downstairs to take you directly to the Manhattan apartment. I promise you, all will be revealed shortly. In the meantime, I hope you don't mind, but we moved your dog and some of your personal belongings to the apartment. You'll have an opportunity to go back to your old apartment over the next week and decide what else you would like to move, dispose of, or put into storage. Again, just contact Claudette."

Cara eyes widened. "Why would you do that? Why would you move Chloe and my things?" she asked, alarmed.

Gladstone tented his hands on the desk. "Cara, we don't believe you'll be safe in your current apartment, and we want to take every precaution to ensure your safety. The trustees agreed this would be the best course of action. I'm so sorry I can't tell you more." He leaned closer. "One more thing, dear. Don't leave the apartment until you're contacted."

Cara sucked in a breath. *Okay, add "afraid" to my laundry list of emotions.* This was the first time anyone suggested *her* safety was at risk. Her encounter with the woman on the street had been highly unsettling, but not particularly threatening.

"Wait," Cara blurted. She couldn't let the conversation end before she asked the question that weighed most heavily on her mind. "The letter said that people I love could be in jeopardy, even killed. What does that mean?"

He smiled at her benevolently. "As long as you don't share what you've learned here today, it's unlikely you'll put anyone in immediate danger. Try not to worry."

Easy for him to say. She swallowed, her nerves strung tight as piano wire.

Gladstone stood. "It was lovely meeting you, Cara. If I can be of further assistance, you have my card. Just one final item: all our correspondence with you will be sent to the Manhattan apartment. Let us know if that needs to change."

Cara wished someone would pinch her to wake her from this surreal dream. She gathered the pouch and envelope into her purse and went to retrieve her coat from the coat stand. Gladstone stepped around the desk, shook her hand, and opened the door.

Almost on cue, the perfectly coiffed, Chanel-clad Claudette stood waiting on the other side.

"Best of luck to you, Cara," said Gladstone and politely left her with Claudette.

On the way out, Claudette handed her an additional envelope. "This is the name of our contact, your account number, and the location of the Brooklyn warehouse. They'll take good care of you. Now, let me take you down to the driver."

"Thank you," Cara said, accepting the envelope and adding it to her already overstuffed purse. They stepped into the elevator when it arrived, and Claudette pushed a button in the elevator not on the key pad. The elevator descended to an underground parking garage where a Bentley limousine with tinted windows waited with the back door open for her. She shook Claudette's hand and thanked her.

Cara sat in the back of the car and sighed, consumed by a host of unresolved questions. At least she had a semi-plausible story to tell the people she loved about her new living arrangements. What she still didn't know was how much of her old life she would be required to leave behind, or how much danger she and her loved ones were actually in. And what the heck happened on the street yesterday with that homeless woman? She couldn't help but think it was a clue to her gift, if not the gift itself.

At least Cara was hopeful no one would die today, since she didn't plan on telling anyone what she'd learned in Gladstone's office. Then a thought struck her, and a small smile formed on her lips. There was *one* decision she planned on making today as a result of her newfound wealth . . .

Tomorrow she'd quit her miserable job. A small victory, but she'd take it.

The car took a while to emerge at ground level. Cara knit her brow in confusion. They appeared to be several blocks away from the Watson & Haskins offices.

I feel like a spy, she thought. Too bad she didn't have any of the same skills.

They entered another underground lot ten minutes later, which wound around for quite some time before the car stopped in front of an elevator.

She jumped when the driver, hidden behind a dark separation panel, spoke through the intercom. His voice was smooth, with a soothing, unearthly quality. "Miss Collins, you can exit here. You'll need a key to get to the top floor. Just slip it in next to the elevator button. It's the same key that will open the apartment door."

"Okay, thanks." Cara fingered the key in her hand, thankful she wouldn't have to fumble around in front of the elevator. Like a swimmer about to step off a diving board, she took a deep breath before leaving the car, and swan dived into her new life.

Chapter 12

San Francisco. Forrester Research. Thursday, March 20,
7:30 a.m. PDT / 10:30 a.m. EDT

KAI PULLED HIS BLACK AUDI A6 into the Forrester Research facility parking lot. Tucked in among a private, three-hundred-acre tree-filled campus, the facility was located just north of San Francisco. Rather than the telltale chill of March, the day promised to be unseasonably warm and sunny after the fog burned away.

Taking a deep breath of pine-filled air, Kai strolled down the landscaped pathway to his lab, which was housed in an ultramodern building designed to disappear into the landscape. Between the weather, the promise of additional discoveries, and his removal of himself from Cara's shit list, Kai was invigorated and hopeful for the first time in months.

His thoughts shifted to the next samples he planned to prepare. Full results wouldn't be available until Monday morning, but he could wait, knowing he finally had a decent shot at isolating the protein that caused the degeneration.

The anomaly indicated by the lab notebooks niggled at him, compelling him to explore his theory that the hidden results actually existed. The more thought Kai put into it, the more convinced he was that Tom's Noble notations could be a clue. Maybe he was wrong, but what if he wasn't?

Kai slid his badge into the card reader and walked through the turnstile. The hallways buzzed with scientists on their way to their labs, many carrying cups of coffee.

Like one of Pavlov's dogs, Kai suddenly craved a cup.

His young intern walked straight toward him wearing a broad smile. "'Mornin', Dr. Solomon! I got your e-mail and started to prepare the materials you requested," she said with a perky Southern accent. She was a graduate student at the University of California and worked for him two mornings a week.

Kai stopped and smiled. "Thanks, Kristi." Her ponytail and freckles made her look about fourteen. *I must be getting old*, he thought.

Giving him a conspiratorial smirk, she reached out to touch his elbow and moved close enough to whisper in his ear, "Triple W called out of the office today."

Kai's smile broadened. Wicked Witch of the West was the code name for Emily, his overly efficient project manager. He knew he shouldn't encourage Kristi, but sometimes he couldn't resist. They both shared the same distaste for Emily.

"Thanks. You just made my day." He winked at her. "I'll meet you in the lab in fifteen."

"See you then," she said, flouncing off in the opposite direction.

The lure of coffee set him on a course for the cafeteria. Elated to be without Emily's prying eyes, he would make a few phone calls and poke around.

Emily had been assigned to the project shortly before Tom's death. An attractive woman in her early thirties with long, raven-black hair and piercing blue eyes, she could simultaneously size you up and cut you down with a glance. In addition to her impressive credentials, the only things Kai knew about her were she had a close connection to someone at the Foundation and she kept her own schedule. She'd always been pleasant to Kai, but they were far from friends. If asked, he'd describe her as cold and calculating.

Emily clearly wanted to keep the project moving. But he couldn't understand how demanding frequent updates and detailed debriefs of his findings accomplished that. In his opinion, it did the opposite—it slowed him down. Plus, he struggled to understand the value she added beyond delivering genetic donor material to the lab. He wondered, and not for the first time, about the highly unusual nature of this arrangement. The only thing that made any sense was that Forrester must anticipate a lucrative revenue stream from the project.

Kai settled behind his desk with his coffee, and he looked up the number of his former colleague, Dr. Frank Garrett. Frank most likely had signed a nondisclosure agreement while he worked on the project, but Kai decided it couldn't hurt to ask some discreet questions.

Frank had been lured away from Forrester by a competitor, but they still met at scientific conferences and association meetings several times a year. Kai fielded job inquiries frequently himself, but had yet to yield to the temptation of external recruitment. Any scientist who'd published highly visible research within the prior twenty-four months was fair game, and Kai's last paper on a breakthrough protocol for a rare blood cancer had attracted some attention. The protocol, originally developed for a strain of liver cancer, had unexpectedly shown excellent results in an experimental trial for Leiomyosarcoma—a disease with only a few thousand documented cases. Kai's protocol had arrested all cases of the disease, resulting in the test patients living cancer free.

It was nearly eight o'clock. Kai picked up the phone and dialed before Frank disappeared into the lab for the day.

"BioLife, Dr. Garrett speaking," Frank answered.

"Hi, Frank. It's Kai Solomon. How's it going?"

"Kai! Good to hear from you. What has you calling so bright and early?"

"Other than the fact that we should meet for drinks soon?"

"That may be sooner than you think. The next Biotech Association Meeting is in two weeks. At least they picked the Fairmont Hotel this time. I swore the last place had hourly rates. Are you going?"

Kai chuckled. "I forgot about that. I'll see you there. It'll be great to catch up. In the meantime, do you have a few minutes to talk shop?"

"Sure thing. What's up?"

Kai hesitated. "Remember the project I couldn't tell you about? The one I'm working on?" He rubbed his chin. "I was asked to take over Project Firefly."

Dead air filled the phone line.

"Frank, are you still there?" Kai asked, suddenly nervous. He heard Frank let out a breath.

"Yeah. I'm here. It's tragic what happened to Tom. How's it going? The project, I mean." He lowered his voice. "Is the Ice Queen still working there?"

"So, you've met Emily. Yup, she still haunts Forrester's halls." Kai sidestepped any discussion about the project. "How closely did you work with Tom while you were here?"

"Not too close. I just pitched in my last few months at Forrester." Frank took the phone off of speaker, and as he picked up the receiver he said in a low voice, "Listen, I'm not giving away any trade secrets here if I tell you that Firefly was one bizarre project."

Kai gripped the phone tighter. "In what way?"

"Well, the Ice Queen for one. Also, it bothered me that we needed to use a series of undisclosed proteins as donor cells for the splice. I like to know what I'm working with to anticipate reasons for mutation, but we didn't have that luxury. Funny, I'm calling something a luxury that's a given on any other project. The project made me uneasy. I can't explain it beyond a feeling in my gut."

Everything Frank said resonated with Kai, justifying his own conclusions.

Kai rested one of his elbows on the desk. "Interesting. We're using some advanced mammalian cell lines patented by the Foundation as a fixed variable within the testing. I figured the secrecy, and the boatload of cash they're paying us, would allow them to commercialize the product under their own brand and maybe throw us a bone on production. Otherwise, I can't see a reason for Forrester to do it."

"I can't say either way, since I was only a minor contributor to the project. Sorry that I can't be of more help."

Kai tried another angle. "Speaking of, you were trained by Noble while you were here, weren't you?"

"Yeah, all of us old guys were taught by the great Noble. It was impossible to escape the old codger."

"Do you still use the Noble Method?"

"Of course. It was pounded into my head, as well as being a truly brilliant method of scientific notation. Why?"

"Tom's lab notes are *missing* a couple of sections based on the notations. The time period is the last three to four weeks before his death." Kai decided to leave out his suspicions that the notes were fabricated.

"Hmm . . . Something happened, but I'm not sure it's related."

Kai's senses ignited. "What do you mean?"

"Rumor had it that Tom had been working very closely with Stanford University on a few projects. According to my sources, I understand his wife's cousin was a respected scientist and prodigy in their Genetics Research program."

"Was? Where is he now?"

"*She* . . . Dr. Sandra Wilson. She was murdered last year about three weeks before Tom died. From what I understand, her car broke down in dicey section of the city, and she was attacked."

Gooseflesh rose on Kai's arms. "What makes you think the incidents could be related?"

"Her death hit him hard. He took a week off after she died. That could explain a partial gap in the time period of the notes."

"How sure are you that they were working together and it wasn't just a coincidence?" Hope welled up in Kai that maybe he'd found a lead.

Frank took an audible breath then lowered his voice again. "Well, a couple of months before Dr. Wilson was murdered, we received a fresh shipment of the cell samples. They were different, but I'm not sure why. Tom had been pretty baffled and, for some reason, he'd decided to perform the full genome sequencing on some of the samples. I was there when the results came back a week or so later. Some of the results agitated him. No more than ten minutes later, he headed to the door with some samples. I asked him what I should tell

Emily when she asked where he'd gone. He looked around nervously and then came over to my lab table. He whispered that he'd found something interesting and was on his way to Stanford to get one of his consultants to take a look at his results. He told me to tell Emily he had a dentist appointment. I couldn't stand the witch, so I'd happily lied for him. Other than that, I didn't think anything more about it at the time. And given the nondisclosure agreement, I didn't expect he would tell me anything further. Now, looking back, these events could all be connected."

"Okay, that makes sense. Thanks, Frank. I appreciate your time."

"No problem. Good luck, Kai. I mean it."

"Thanks," Kai responded absently, tapping a pencil on his desk and already thinking about his next move. He wondered how close of a connection the deaths had to the notes and shuddered.

"See you at the Fairmont in a couple of weeks," Frank added and hung up.

Kai's fingers raced across the keyboard and did a web search on Dr. Sandra Wilson. The first listing was a small story on her murder in the *San Francisco Chronicle*.

> *The esteemed Dr. Sandra Wilson, thirty-five years old, was found murdered on Saturday morning in the Lower Haight district of San Francisco, not far from her home in Haight-Ashbury. Her time of death was around 1:45 a.m. All indications show that she was killed while attempting to flee an attacker.*
>
> *The attack did not appear to involve rape or robbery. However, the police are not releasing information about the weapon used in the attack. The autopsy revealed that she died of massive internal injuries. Colleagues, friends, and family are baffled as to the motive.*
>
> *The funeral will be held this coming Tuesday at 9:00 am at St. Agnes in Haight-Ashbury.*

Kai continued to read the remaining articles, but nothing further about the attack was mentioned. With some additional research, he found more information about her professional life and her work. Apparently a prodigy, she had graduated from Stanford with a PhD at twenty-three years old, and by thirty-one she had already published some impressive papers on genomics in regards to aging and longevity.

Rather than meeting Kristi in the lab, Kai had a better idea. He freed his calendar of meetings until early afternoon and decided to visit Stanford for some external research.

But before he did anything, he needed to send Cara the electronic card he promised or he'd be back in the doghouse.

He chose a funny card with animation and typed in a personal message begging more forgiveness. He hesitated for only a moment before signing it, "Love, Kai."

He hit Send and wondered if he should give Cara a heads-up on what he learned, since it might be connected to Tom's death and the dream.

His fingers hovered over the keyboard as he thought. A moment later, he abandoned the idea. There was no need to freak Cara out until he knew more.

Chapter 13

CARA RODE THE ELEVATOR up to the penthouse. The doors opened into a semi-private hallway, a foyer for two apartments—Penthouse A was hers. If appointed even half as beautifully as the entryway, with its mahogany paneling, original marble floors, and what looked like museum-quality paintings, the place would be a palace.

She shook her head, still trying to absorb her sudden wealth and all its trappings. Taking a deep breath, she walked to the door.

For about the fifth time that morning, Cara reminded herself that she wasn't starring in a movie or going to spontaneously turn into a superhero. Although her position on gun control had changed since she'd woken up.

She twisted the key in the lock, and Cara heard the familiar clatter of doggie toenails on the wood floors inside. She pushed open the door to find Chloe anxiously awaiting her arrival with a wagging tail, just like home . . . well, almost.

Cara leaned down to kiss her dog's head and ruffle her ears. "Hi, Lovey Dovey. Want to show Mommy around our new home?" The words felt surreal rolling off of her tongue.

But rather than walking any deeper into the prewar apartment, Cara stood rooted in the entry foyer assaulted by more marble, chandeliers dripping with crystal, and fine wood paneling. The large, opulent space with its high ceiling was suddenly oppressive.

Breathe, she thought, nervously fingering her diamond necklace.

She took a few tentative steps, and scanned the exquisite architectural detail of the square receiving room, feeling like a trespasser in someone else's home. In the center of the room a circular table supported a large oriental vase and a three-foot floral bouquet like the one she'd seen at the Four Seasons. No sooner had she spotted the flowers than the sweet aroma triggered a tickle in her nose, setting off a chain of sneezes.

Note to self: find a garbage bag and get rid of those flowers, she thought while her eyes watered.

She walked straight ahead into the living room with Chloe trotting next to her. The space held old-world charm, but the leather mid-century modern furniture didn't appeal to her. The décor was nothing like the cozy comfort of her West Village apartment.

Heading to the kitchen next, she walked through the double doorway and let out a low whistle. Her apprehension turned to awe.

Now this is my idea of a kitchen. She despised cooking, but lusted after kitchens the way some women lusted after a hot man. The only thing better would be a hot man cooking in this kitchen.

The kitchen was done in a traditional style with warm, cherry flooring, white maple cabinets, and sleek black granite countertops. All the appliances were high-end and professional, including a six-burner Viking stove, and a built-in Sub-Zero refrigerator that took up a large chunk of one wall. A huge island dominated the center of the room, with modern pendant lighting hanging overhead.

To the side of the island, Cara spotted a pair of plain, white porcelain dog dishes filled with food and water. "Looks like you're taken care of," she said, looking down at her canine sidekick, who stared back with an ear up.

Cara toured the rest of the penthouse. The bedrooms appealed to her taste, feminine with luxurious beds, seating areas, exquisite rugs and window treatments. The bathrooms—all four of them—were modern, and impeccably decorated with marble tiles, steam showers, and soaking tubs. She also found a library with a fireplace resembling something out of *Masterpiece Theatre* at the end of the hall next to the bedrooms, a dining room, and—best of all—a balcony overlooking Central Park.

This is just too . . . too much, Cara thought as she opened the glass doors leading onto the deck. Tall shrubs lined the exterior walls for privacy. There were even trees planted in a large rooftop garden, a dining area, and some lounge chairs for sunbathing. Muted street sounds filtered up from below. Over the treetops, she could see the Conservatory Water inside Central Park, where one could rent model boats to sail, and even farther west, the Angel of the Waters on top of Bethesda Fountain.

"This . . . is all mine . . . " She could hardly believe it.

Her head throbbed from the stress of the morning. What she needed was a good run. Looking across the street with yearning, she desperately wished to do just that—jog until she dropped. But she couldn't leave. Someone she loved could die. She wasn't safe. She needed to stay here until she was contacted.

It took every shred of her remaining control not to scream out loud. Much like a bird in a gilded cage, she was trapped. Only her cage was a multimillion-dollar piece of real estate.

Loneliness hit her, mixing with an overwhelming sense of claustrophobia. She couldn't share the truth with anyone. Not to mention she needed to give serious thought to the answers to all the questions that would come her way and practice them until they sounded natural.

Glancing down, she decided a change of clothes might relax her. She headed toward the bedrooms, and opened doors until she found the master one, assuming she'd find her stuff in there. The room was sumptuous yet feminine, like in a fine resort. It had chocolate textured walls, and a beautiful landscape oil painting hung over a bed covered in crisp white linens. In front of the window was a chaise, a throw casually draped across its back, and a small side table with a reading lamp.

Cara released a breath when she opened the door to a closet the size of her small second bedroom downtown. The walk-in closet was filled with lit racks inside wooden cabinets. Wooden drawers and shoe cubbies covered the entire back wall. Letting the room embrace her, she couldn't imagine her modest wardrobe filling it.

Her cell phone chimed with a new text message. She walked over to the nightstand and fished her phone out of her purse.

> SO WHAT HAPPENED WITH THE LETTER? DID YOU INHERIT SOME MONEY? SENNY, XOXO

"Yes, but at a price that might be too high," she mumbled and plunked herself down on the bed. Chloe jumped up to join her. For someone used to having control over her life, Cara felt powerless. Even the empowerment from deciding to quit her job couldn't compensate for the lies she was about to tell.

"Chloe-girl, what should I say to Aunt Senny?" Cara tensed, realizing that Chloe was the only one with whom she could share the truth. Chloe licked Cara's face before curling up into a ball next to her.

Cara sat numb and statue-still for what felt like an eternity before she picked up her phone.

> NOTHING BIG. BORING FAMILY STUFF. FILL YOU IN ON SAT NITE. LOVE, CARA.

With the exception of the "Love, Cara" part, almost nothing she wrote was true. Her whole body slumped. Would her life be an endless stream of half-truths and lies?

Her phone chimed again.

REALLY? THAT'S WEIRD. SEE YOU SAT! XOXO

Her friend's response brought both a smile and tears. Suddenly exhausted, Cara lay down on the bed and snuggled next to Chloe, taking comfort in her warm little body. Maybe this would all seem better after a nap.

Chapter 14

KAI ARRIVED AT THE Stanford University campus and parked his car close to the School of Medicine, where several of the genetics labs were located. Since Dr. Sandra Wilson was known for antiaging and longevity research, Kai assumed the most logical place to start was at the lab currently affiliated with that research. According to the online directory, a Dr. Philipp Granger had taken over after her death. Even if Dr. Granger wasn't in his office, chances were high that he would have a lab manager or assistant on duty.

Following the signs to the Alway Building, Kai moved with the crush of passing students and faculty along the sidewalk. He'd taken off his lab coat before he left Forrester. Wearing khakis, a polo shirt, and sneakers, he realized he looked more like a student than a scientist in his street clothes. Even his briefcase was back at the lab. The opportunity to do some detective work unrelated to scientific experimentation exhilarated him. Being a detective took the same type of curiosity, and he'd admit to having no shortage of curiosity.

Kai rubbed his hands together, anxious about dropping in on the university unannounced. He wasn't really sure what he was looking for beyond some sort of linkage between Dr. Wilson, Tom, and Project Firefly. On the other hand, nothing ventured, nothing gained.

The elevator doors opened opposite the reception desk for the genetics lab. An attractive girl with brown hair pulled back into a ponytail manned reception—a student, based on her intense absorption in a large textbook and her copious note-taking.

"Excuse me, I wonder if you could help me," Kai said, leaning his elbow casually on the counter.

Startled, the girl's head popped up. "Oh, sorry, I didn't see you. Can I help you?"

He attempted a warm smile, hoping to hide his discomfort. "I'm looking for Dr. Granger. Is he in?"

"No, he's teaching a class, but he should be back at eleven o'clock."

Kai had no desire to wait around for another hour. He leaned in closer. "Is there anyone here right now who worked with Dr. Sandra Wilson?"

Mild surprise passed over the girl's face. "Oh, yeah, um, I think Calvin might be here. He used to be assigned to her. Let me go check." She rested her pencil on her notebook and got up. As she reached the entrance into lab, she turned back. "Who should I say wants to speak with him?"

"Dr. Kai Solomon."

She disappeared behind the door. A few minutes later she reappeared with a tall, gangly young man wearing a white lab coat and glasses.

"Dr. Solomon? Hi, I'm Calvin Wright." He approached, extending his hand. "Wendy mentioned that you were looking for someone who'd worked with Dr. Wilson. Why don't you come with me, and we can talk in my office. But I'm not sure exactly what I can tell you."

"Thanks. This may be a long shot, but you never know," Kai said. He followed Calvin back through the lab and into one of the small offices along the perimeter. Stacks of paper and volumes of scientific books filled the shelves and littered the floor.

"Have a seat." Calvin gestured with a sweep of his hand toward the two guest chairs and sat down behind the desk. On closer inspection, Kai noticed the funky style of Calvin's black glasses and a small tattoo of a Chinese character peeking out from above his collar. "What can I do for you, Dr. Solomon?"

"I'm currently working on a genetics project at Forrester Research Labs that I believe Dr. Wilson was consulting on for my former colleague, Dr. Tom Peyton."

Kai noticed a subtle shudder pass through Calvin, who looked at Kai blankly for a few seconds before replying, "Oh, you work at Forrester. They have a great rep. We haven't had any active projects with them for a couple of years, so I'm not sure I can be of much help."

Kai shifted in his seat and leaned forward. "I'm sorry. I don't mean to barge in here asking uncomfortable questions. I'm just trying to make sense out of some findings Dr. Peyton left behind. After speaking with another colleague today, I discovered a possible connection between Dr. Wilson and my project. I understand this may be a long shot, but have you ever met Dr. Peyton?"

Calvin visibly relaxed.

"I can't say that I have. I worked on a lot of projects for Sandra, but none for Forrester. I'm really sorry that I can't be of more help."

As Calvin spoke, he glanced toward the ceiling and then wrote something on the back of a business card. He stood to shake Kai's hand. Confused, Kai played along. Calvin pressed the card into Kai's hand, which he surreptitiously slid it into his pocket.

Is the room bugged? Kai wondered. It was the only explanation he could think of for Calvin's body language not matching their conversation.

"Thanks anyway, Calvin. Is there anyone else that I can speak to? Did she have any other lab assistants? Maybe Dr. Granger would know?"

Calvin caught his eye and gave a slight nod, signaling he knew Kai was following his lead. "Dr. Solomon, if there was a Forrester project, I would've definitely known about it. We all would've. Our projects are posted, and findings are shared weekly. There was never a project mentioned associated with your lab."

"I guess this is a dead end then. Sorry to have bothered you."

"No problem. Let me take you back to reception."

Kai followed Calvin out in silence.

Calvin turned when he reached reception. "Again, sorry I couldn't be of more help." He shook Kai's hand a final time and then disappeared behind the door into the lab.

Safely inside his car, Kai extracted the business card from his pocket. The inscription on the back read: *Califon Café, tomorrow, six p.m., table on the back wall.*

Calvin knew something. Maybe Kai was right after all.

He shifted into reverse. Suddenly, a strange pulsing resonated inside his head—like the start of a paralyzing migraine. The hairs on the back of his neck stood on end, and he jammed his foot on the brake. While rubbing his temple with one hand, he caught sight of an inky black haze in his rearview mirror and froze. Seconds later, both the pain and the black haze were gone, but the goose-flesh remained. He shuddered.

What the hell was that?

Chapter 15

HOURS INTO AN HGTV marathon with Chloe, Cara had learned how to renovate a good portion of a house, but still hadn't heard anything from anyone. She let out her hundredth deep sigh, and stared down at her canine companion fast asleep next to her.

A loud knock at the door jolted Cara and Chloe out of their seats. She'd expected the doorman to ring her before a guest was sent up. Her feet flew silently over the marble floor to the door, followed by the tap-tap-tap of whippet paws.

She peered through the peephole and did a double take, suddenly sorry she wasn't dressed in anything better than yoga pants and a T-shirt.

Through the fish-eye lens, she studied the young man standing outside. He looked like he had exploded off the pages of *GQ*, or had taken a wrong turn on his way to a fashion shoot. Stunning blue eyes that could melt your socks right off stared patiently at the door from underneath high-arching, dark brows. Expertly tousled black hair topped his heart-shaped face, which was punctuated by high cheekbones and ended in a sexy cleft chin. Her eye traveled over him quickly, taking in any other details she could glean through the peephole. His style was clean-cut yet hip: a white collared shirt open at the neck, a brown leather jacket, and jeans made up his ensemble.

Unconsciously, she slipped the elastic out of her hair and onto her wrist. Giving her hair a shake, she let it cascade down around her shoulders.

No reason to look like a total shlub, she thought, using one of Sienna's Yiddish expressions. She smiled, thinking he was Sienna's type. Glossy. Cara preferred more of a khakis-type guy.

Trusting her gut that she wasn't in danger, she unlocked the door and opened it a crack.

"May I help you?" she managed to ask.

"Cara Collins?" he inquired with an amused twinkle in his eye.

"Yes?" Her pulse sped up.

"Hi, I'm Michael Swift. Your grandmother sent me . . . kind of," he said with a tentative smile. Inexplicably, his words washed over Cara like a warm bath.

And the weirdness continues, she thought, standing frozen as she stared at Michael.

"May I come in?" he asked, snapping Cara out of her momentary lapse.

She opened the door wider. "Sorry, please come in. I've been expecting you." Slightly shaken, she added in a whisper, "Well, actually, I was expecting someone . . . um, older." A sheepish grin formed, and she cringed. "Actually, I didn't mean to say the last part out loud. It's been a crazy couple of days. Can I get you something—water, soda, a glass of wine?" *A dose of reality?*

He reached out to shake her hand and met her gaze. The glow of his eyes, an intense royal blue with flecks of steel gray, drew her in. "I'm glad to meet you. I hope my age isn't an issue," he said, amused. A small dimple appeared on his cheek when he smiled—a bright, showstopping smile that looked vaguely familiar.

She noticed the simultaneous warmth and strength in his handshake, not to mention an electric sensation that caused a blush to spread across her cheeks. Her brows knit together briefly. She was sure they'd never met. Yet, there was something.

Chloe whined, impatient at being ignored, and jumped up to greet Michael with a flying face lick, her tail wagging so vigorously it moved her entire backside.

"Well, who do we have here?" Michael asked as he bent down for a supplemental face wash.

"I'm so sorry. Chloe, off!"

"No, it's fine. I love dogs," Michael said, giving the Whippet Princess a good petting.

"You're too kind. Please let me know if she starts to annoy you. She's a huge flirt, and won't stop until she can add you to her list of admirers."

Michael scratched Chloe behind the ears. "What a beautiful girl," he crooned.

"I'm fully convinced she's a person masquerading in a dog suit."

Michael chuckled, got up, and slipped off his jacket.

"Here, I'll take that," she said. He handed it to her. The buttery leather was soft on her fingertips. Stopping at the coat closet, she put it on a hanger and detected the mild scent of his cologne clinging to it.

They moved toward the living room. Michael rolled up the sleeves of his white shirt as he walked, revealing the Patek Philippe he wore on his wrist. Her eyes widened—the watch cost as much as a car. Had Sienna not been her best friend, she wouldn't have been able to tell the difference between that and a Timex.

Maybe she wasn't the only one with money, but now didn't seem like the time to ask.

His soft leather loafers moved silently across the marble floor of the foyer. Cara stole another glance at her guest. He stood just over six feet tall. Although lean, the line of his shoulders in proportion to the size of his waist hinted at a V-shaped muscular build hidden underneath. If that hadn't been enough, the shape of his biceps through his white shirt and his exposed forearms confirmed it.

"I'll take a glass of water, if you're still offering." He walked over to one of sofas. As soon as he sat down Chloe settled in next to him, nuzzling her head into his lap. Michael didn't seem to mind. He sat with one leg resting on top of the other, one hand petting the dog, and his other arm leaning along the back of the sofa, relaxed and graceful.

"She likes you. It means you're a good soul. She knows." Cara gave him a wry smile and headed off to get her guest a glass of water.

When she returned, she settled on the adjacent sofa, her legs tucked up underneath her. Still wary, she asked, "So my grandmother sent you? Don't take this the wrong way, but weren't you still in diapers when she died?"

He chuckled. "Well, technically, your grandmother didn't actually know who would be sent, only that someone would. I was just chosen as your Messenger a short time ago."

Cara admired his poise and confidence. "Then please tell me you have some answers to help explain the most bizarre thirty-six hours of my life."

Michael's eyes softened. Unfolding his leg, he leaned forward and rested his elbows on his knees. "Some answers, yes."

He was saying the right things, and Cara let down her guard. Yet, she wondered if she should. Could the inheritance be linked to people wanting to kill her? If that were the case, wouldn't she be safer in her own surroundings with no one the wiser? Patience. She had to have patience and let him explain things.

Cara squinted, torn between apprehension and curiosity. "First, tell me what you meant when you said you were my Messenger." Something about the way he'd said it made it seem more permanent than: "Hi, I'm here to tell you a few things and then leave."

"That's just the beginning of a long discussion and probably a long night. There's a lot you need to be prepared for in the coming days. This discussion will only be a small introduction."

Score one for my intuition. Her heart beat more rapidly. "Prepare me for what?"

Michael grew more serious, his eyes seeking hers. She noticed his eyebrows weren't truly black, but rather a deep, rich mahogany. The dark contrast with the royal blue of his eyes gave his stare a power that wouldn't allow her to look away. "Listen, I know your world's been turned upside down, and I apologize for that. I also can't begin to emphasize the magnitude of what you're about to become a part of."

A chill traversed her spine. "Michael, you're scaring me a little. Um, make that a lot."

He smiled. "I'm sorry. That's not my intent. Hey, before we begin, do you like pizza?"

She tilted her head, confused at the shift in conversation. Her traitorous stomach rumbled at the suggestion.

"I'll buy," he said. "I'm not kidding. This is going to be a long night, and I'm starving."

Why not, she thought and shrugged. If this was his attempt to put her at ease, it worked. "Pizza it is. I know less than nothing about takeout in this neighborhood, so if you don't mind chancing it, I'll call down to the doorman for a recommendation."

"I'm willing to chance it if you are," he replied.

"Okay, what do like on your pizza? Personally, I stick to veggies, but we can do half-and-half if you're a heart-attack-on-a-plate type."

"How's mushroom?" he asked, a crooked smile twisting on his lips—as if he knew that's what she'd choose.

She narrowed her eyes. "My favorite. How did you know?"

He smiled wider, exposing his dimple again, and winked. "Just a lucky guess."

Cara went into the kitchen to use the intercom. Not only did the doorman have a bead on where to find good pizza, but she had a line of credit for takeout deliveries. Another happy discovery.

"Pizza should be here in about thirty minutes. I appear to have a house account," she said, walking back to the sofa. Not able to wait any longer for explanations, she swept her hands around the penthouse. "Michael, do you know about any of this?"

He glanced around. "Some of it, but not everything."

Encouraged that he might actually answer her, she asked the one question she wanted most to understand. "Okay, spill. Please tell me why someone could die if I tell anyone about the inheritance."

He studied his hands and hesitated. Was he trying to figure out what to tell her? She studied his face as she waited for his answer. His high cheekbones were his next best feature, after his eyes and his cleft chin. Then again, his face didn't have a bad feature.

He slowly released a breath. "I can't tell you specifically *why* someone could die. But after what I tell you and what you'll learn over the next several days, you should have the answer to your question."

Releasing a sigh of her own, she accepted his answer . . . for now. She tracked back to their earlier discussion. "You never answered my question. What's a Messenger, and how exactly did you find me?" She wanted to know her trust wasn't misplaced.

"Cara, let me ask a favor first. If I promise to answer your questions, will you agree to let me explain things in a way that makes sense and unfolds in a digestible way?" His eyebrows arched and his body tensed.

His looks faded into the background when he spoke. She found the rich timbre of his voice soothing, and there was such sincerity and a genuine sense of honesty in his words, they worked like a protective spell woven together to draw her in and make her feel safe. She admired that he seemed comfortable in his skin; for someone his age, his manner and maturity far exceeded his years. She couldn't explain it, but she was drawn to him like an old friend.

"Sure," she conceded, half-heartedly tossing her hands up and leaning back on the sofa.

The tension in his shoulders eased.

"Thanks. I promise to make this as easy as possible," he said, his lips turning up in a warm smile. "Let me start by asking you a question: In your life, have you ever experienced a time when you met someone and had an instant connection? Like you'd known them forever?"

Cara didn't need even a moment to think of the answer. "Yes," she said, immediately thinking of Kai. "Why?"

"Many people get that feeling, but when *you* do, it means something powerful. You recognize their soul. You're connected to them in a meaningful way."

She looked down at her hands and said quietly, "If you believe in that stuff, I guess."

"Cara, do you believe in that stuff?" The strength of his tone drew her eyes back to him.

She sensed a challenge in his voice and answered with conviction. "Yes. I've always believed in more than I can see. I might not consider myself religious, but I do consider myself spiritual. I believe in God and the power of love, if that's what you're really asking. I believe love survives outside of our physical body, that it's transcendent."

"You've only had an instant connection with two people so far, am I right?" His voice was soft.

A familiar tingling sensation filled her. "How did you know that?" *Can he read my mind?*

He shook his head, indicating he wanted her to pay attention. "Please, just tell me about them."

She sighed and clasped her hands together. "The first is my friend Kai whom I've known since college. The other, Tyler, was later, but we haven't been in touch for many years, and I want to keep it that way." The last thing she wanted to do was discuss Tyler . . . ever.

Michael didn't press her, and gave her a brief, empathic look. "Any strange occurrences involved in either of those two relationships?"

Cara furrowed her brow. Her eyes widened when she made the connection. "This is going to sound crazy, but I think I have a psychic connection to both of them. I have dreams that come true."

"That's not crazy. Think of it like an iceberg—a small part is visible, but your full abilities are lying in wait under the surface of your consciousness. Everyone has the ability to use intuition, but some people, like you, were chosen to have more. Up until now, you've only experienced the normal bleed-through of your abilities. After your training, the veil will be removed, and you'll have full access to why you're having those feelings. You'll even be able tap into your ability to heal others, among other things."

"Heal others?" She stared at him, her mouth dry, thinking back to the home-less woman on the street. "An old woman . . . she stopped me on the street yester-day. I touched her, and I made her younger."

Michael nodded and looked down. "Yes, that was unexpected," he mumbled.

Cara frowned. "*You knew?*"

He let out a deep breath, his face etched with worry. "Yes. We've been follow-ing you since early yesterday to ensure your safety."

She stared at him, stunned, not knowing whether to be relieved or more frightened.

Reaching out, he touched her arm. "You're safe at the moment, Cara. But that's why we took these extra precautions and moved you here directly."

Questions flooded her mind, too many to even know which to ask first, but she fished one out. "Who is 'we'?" Cara pulled her legs up and wrapped her arms around them, wanting to place some sort of barrier between her and what Michael was about to tell her.

"I'm only one of the people who'll enter your life," he said, leaning forward and resting his elbows on his thighs. "If you'll have us."

Cara placed her chin on her drawn-up knees and narrowed her eyes. "What do you mean *if* I'll have you?"

"Cara, no one will force any of this on you. You can say no. It's your decision. These gifts, both your abilities and the money, come with responsibilities and obligations, but ultimately you can reject it all."

"You mean I can say no and give all the money back?"

"Yes. You can also live out your life as it was before I came and before you received your grandmother's letter. But given what's already happened, it might be too late."

"Too late? If I refuse, will someone die?" She asked her question again, determined to eventually get an answer that satisfied her.

Michael dipped his head, hiding his face. "Hasn't someone died already?"

His words made her stomach lurch and raised the hairs on her arms. "What do you mean?"

Michael looked up, his eyes blazing. "You saved one, but sacrificed another. Didn't you?"

The breath left Cara's lungs. The dream. He knew about the dream. Tears sprang to her eyes. "I didn't know! I didn't know that man would be killed in Kai's place." *Next time it could be Kai,* she thought with horror.

Michael moved closer and took both of her hands in his, trying to calm her. His hands were warm and strong as he held her tightly. "For you, both paths come with peril. I'm here to help."

"Do I have to choose now, right this second?" she asked, her vision still blurred and her voice small.

He dropped her hands and sat back. "No, you have some time to decide. You'll receive a formal Calling. That's when you'll make your final decision."

"So who are the other people that I'll be meeting?" She wiped her eyes with her fingers and sagged in her seat. She didn't think she had as much of a choice as Michael said she did, especially if she'd already set herself on a course that put danger into both paths. At least having the financial resources and others to help beat going it alone.

"There are two more that I know of. One will be your mentor who'll be responsible for your training and explaining exactly what it is that you've stepped into. She should be arriving soon. The other will be your Guardian, Chamuel, who's been assigned to protect you."

Another bolt of fear shot through her. "Protect me from what exactly?"

Michael shook his head and sighed. "I know this is going to sound cliché, but there are dark forces interested in thwarting your success."

Her eyebrows drew together. "Success?"

"Yeah. Chamuel and I have been assigned to you. Together the three of us make up what's known as a Trinity, which is formed to help a Soul Seeker fulfill their covenant."

"Okay . . . " Cara said slowly as she kept her arms wrapped tightly around herself. "What does *that* mean?"

Michael took a deep breath and let it out slowly. "Those connections we spoke about earlier, they were to illustrate a point. Cara, before you were born, you tied yourself to another soul through a promise, and together in this life, you're both attached to an event that could tip the balance between good and evil. You are the connection point to the event and the person at the core of the mission, who is known as the Center Stone. You're a Soul Seeker, and I'm your assigned Messenger. My job is to provide the communication bridge between our Trinity and those guiding us."

Cara's skin tingled; this was followed by a wave of dizziness and a sweet sensation on her tongue that was odd yet familiar. "Whoa, that's a lot to take in."

He reached out for her hand. "I know. I'm sorry."

For some reason, the solace of his touch helped her. "No, it's fine. When is this mission coming? Do we know what the event is and the identity of the person I'm tied to?"

"The only thing we know about the event so far is that it *is* coming. Your Center Stone will be revealed when you accept your Calling. In the meantime, we all need to prepare you. The training will help you awaken the skills and abilities I referred to earlier, which will be critical to your success."

Cara nodded, her forehead crinkled. "When will I meet my Guardian?" She was relieved that someone would be there to watch over her, but freaked out that she needed a bodyguard in the first place. God, what a difference a couple of days could make.

He shrugged. "That'll depend on him. And just because you don't see him, doesn't mean he's not there. From what I've been told, the Guardians prefer to stay unseen so their presence is less invasive, and they especially like to stay out of sight until after the Calling is accepted."

"That's okay, I guess." She relaxed a little. "Is this your first Messenger assignment?"

"Yes, but I was only approached a little more than a week ago." He gave her a sheepish grin. "So you could say that I'm new at this too."

Relief filled her—she wasn't the only newbie on the team. She smiled warmly. "What do you do in real life, Michael?"

He brightened instantly. "I own a martial arts studio in Brooklyn."

Well, that explains why he's in such good shape, she thought. His disclosure gave her an added sense of comfort. At least he'd be able to defend himself against danger, and defend her, if need be.

"You?"

"Investment banker." She cocked her head to the side. "But you already knew that, didn't you?" For some reason, she sensed he knew more about her when he walked in the door than he'd ever let on.

He gave her a cryptic smile and a noncommittal shrug while he petted the sleeping dog next to him. He was smooth, she'd give him that.

Searching for a deeper connection, she asked, "So, can I ask? Were you given a choice?"

His gaze was steady and emphatic. "I was, but there was no way I would have said anything but yes."

The strength of his words surprised her, flaring her curiosity. "Who approached you? Were you chosen by a grandparent?"

"No, not exactly. My father approached me," he replied.

Envy flashed through Cara. "I think it would've helped me if my grandmother was alive."

"Cara"—Michael leaned forward in his seat again, and locked her in an unflinching blue-eyed stare—"my father died six months ago."

Chapter 16

As TEMPTED AS CARA WAS to call in sick again and delay her resignation, she knew she had to deal with it at some point. Normally, after missing a day of work, she'd be eager to check her e-mail. But ever since she'd read her grandmother's letter two nights ago, she hadn't been tempted to check in, even once. Astounding how so much had changed so quickly. She'd been too busy making sense of the last couple of days, and her brain didn't have a whole lot of excess capacity to deal with work.

Michael left around one in the morning. She still had tons of questions, but for what Michael could share with her, he'd done a brilliant job. Then again, as a Messenger, delivery of news was part of his job description, wasn't it?

Over pizza, he'd lightened up, and she discovered he was originally from Chicago and that he'd studied martial arts since he was a small child and had a true passion for it. When the evening was over, she was sure of one thing: she liked him. His warmth and maturity impressed her, plus he was smart and could even be funny based on a few of their lighter moments. She'd choose him as a friend any day. Bottom line, he was solid—a pillar, which was just what she needed right now. She couldn't imagine having someone better than him as a partner. Even though Michael seemed almost too perfect, she decided she would have a little faith in him.

Still, not fully accepting her situation, she'd lain in bed this morning thinking about how her life had transformed into a game show parody. Behind door number one lay wealth, secrecy, the ability to help those she loved, and some unknown mission to stop an event that will tip the scales of good and evil. And people close to her could die. Behind door number two was her current life: a job she hated and was about to quit, the inability to help those she loved, and people close to her could die. Behind door number three . . . well, there was no door number three.

With her letter of resignation in her purse, Cara rolled into Cabot Investments in a mental fog. She hadn't quite settled on when she planned to hand it in. The office was already alive and buzzing with activity.

She didn't give it a second thought when she found a sticky note on her computer screen from her boss: *Please meet me in my office when you arrive. Thanks, Rick.*

Bring it on, she thought. After last night's discussion, she still considered herself undecided and hesitant. But whatever she'd stepped into had come at the right time. She was open to a change, and if Michael was any representation—she knew it couldn't be all bad.

Cara hung up her coat and then headed to Rick's office down the hall. When he spotted her through the glass, he motioned for her to come inside. She clicked the door shut behind her.

Only a few years older than her, Rick was a chauvinist who continually bordered on inappropriate, and an active member of Cabot's good old boy network comprised of rich and entitled Ivy League fraternity brothers. If her former boss and mentor, Bob, hadn't died last year, she wouldn't be sitting in front of this slimy horse's ass right now. Rick, by far, was the biggest reason she hated her job.

Rick wore his insincerity like an accessory. "Cara, please sit. You were sick yesterday. How are you feeling today?"

"Doing fine," she replied tersely. "What's on your mind?"

He clasped his hands in front of him and put on his serious face. "Let me cut to the chase. As you know, we've been up against some hard economic times, and we need to make some additional cuts across the junior leadership of the organization. As a result, I'm really sorry to say this, Cara, but we're eliminating your role within the company." He quickly added, "Of course, given your tenure, you're entitled to a severance package and your prorated bonus."

Had this news been delivered on Tuesday, she would have been upset. Then again, she'd always been a big believer in the philosophy that things happen for a reason.

"Um, that's fascinating, Rick. Who else was eliminated?" she asked, not willing to let him off easy. "Were there any *men* eliminated? Given my performance scores, I'm surprised that I was chosen. Care to elaborate?" Unflustered by the news, she stared at him with mock innocence in her green eyes. For fun, she batted her eyelashes twice.

Rick was clearly taken aback, like he expected her to break down and cry or something equally as girly. "Uh, I don't believe that should be part of this discussion," he replied.

Cara knew beneath all the bravado of his shiny exterior, he was a total wuss.

"You know what's really interesting, Rick? Including me, you've single-handedly eliminated all the women at the leadership level within this firm. Aren't we publically traded? Doesn't that open the company up to, I don't know, EEOC issues? I'm not a lawyer, but I'm sure an employment attorney would love to chew on this for a while, especially with the history of the last five women downsized from the company. Smells like class-action suit to me. Just saying . . ." *You misogynist prick.*

She tried to keep the self-satisfied smile off her face and almost managed to do it.

"Cara, will we have an issue here?" A nervous edge was evident in his voice.

She boldly leaned on his desk. "Absolutely not, Rick. However, I will expect the documents on my desk within the next hour to sign. They will include extending my benefits for one year, vesting and payment of all my options on exit, my *full* bonus, and acknowledgment of today as my last day in the office as part of a sixty-day notice period. Are we on the same page?" She smiled sweetly, but it didn't reach her eyes.

As mercenary as this tactic was, she felt justified. She knew Rick understood his own culpability in the firing of her former colleagues. He may be part of the boys' club, but he was a junior member that could easily be shed if his actions meant negative press or any kind of legal action. The firm's reputation couldn't survive the blow, especially given the current economic and political climate.

"W-well, I believe we're close," Rick stammered. "Can you give me until eleven?"

Severance package in hand and her letter of resignation still in her purse, Cara left the building, closing the Cabot Investments chapter of her life with both sadness and relief.

Her driver wasn't due back until later. She'd been instructed to use him for all her transportation, but, frankly, having a driver felt constraining. It gave her that bird-in-a-gilded-cage feeling, just like the thought of returning to the penthouse.

Suddenly free with time on her hands, she decided to take a quick trip back to her West Village apartment. As much as she liked the penthouse, she wanted some of her things to make it more like home. She'd called to have the Watson & Haskin movers pick up her stuff. All she had to do was tag them with the stickers they'd left behind on the table next to her front door.

Rather than call the driver to take her, rebellion welled up inside her and she traveled the way she always had—by subway.

Cara hopped off the number one train at Sheridan Square and Christopher

Street and walked the remaining four blocks up and over to her Perry Street apartment. She loved the intimacy of this part of the city, with its narrow, tree-lined streets—some of them still cobblestone. Buds covered the trees, but they hadn't opened to the point of setting off her allergies. She hoped to find the familiar surroundings comforting; instead she found them unsettling.

Her post-war building stood among the brownstones in front of her. She'd been gone for a little over twenty-four hours, but somehow it felt like more time had passed. She couldn't shake the feeling that her world had shifted, widening the distance between her and the life she knew only two days ago.

As she walked out of the elevator onto her floor, a prickling sensation hit her on the back of her neck and a mild headache formed.

Am I coming down with something? As she slipped her key into the lock, the throbbing in her head grew stronger. She entered the apartment and closed the door behind her. With the exception of the stillness of the air, the living room was exactly as she'd left it yesterday—cozy, inviting, and organized.

Placing her purse and briefcase on the floor, she kicked off her heels and picked up the stickers from the tray where the warehouse manager said they'd be. She laid her jacket down on the table inside the door and dropped her keys in the tray. She stood for a second to think and then decided to start in the kitchen. She wanted to tag her cupboard and a few other kitchen items.

As she worked her way around the kitchen, half her stuff covered in moving stickers, she heard the soft click of the lock on the front door. The simple sound raised an alarm inside her.

She froze, and the pain in her head thumped harder. Adrenaline shot through her, sensing danger. Through the silence, all she could hear was the pounding of her heartbeat echoing in her ears. Gooseflesh rose and covered her entire body. Was she being paranoid and overly sensitive?

Quietly, she crept over to the kitchen doorway and peeked around the corner. The living room was empty, but the door stood open—wide and menacing. Had she latched the door all the way? Gladstone had said that they didn't think she'd be safe here, but he'd also said she could drop by to pick up a few things. And wasn't she supposed to have an unseen Guardian now?

Cara tried to rationalize her fear as she continued to hover in the doorway of the kitchen. Taking some deep breaths, she managed to slow her heart rate down a few beats, but the nagging pain still throbbed in her head, and the pebbles of fear remained on her skin underneath her sweater.

In her stocking feet, she silently eased herself into the living room and looked around. Everything appeared the same, but the energy in the room had changed. It was darker, oppressive. Her instincts screamed for her to run.

Taking quiet, shallow breaths, her heart hammered as she judged the distance between herself and the open door. She took a step, and the door slammed shut, revealing an inky, black haze that grew larger before her eyes.

Terrified, she stood transfixed, the air slowly seeping from her lungs as the taste of tar coated her tongue.

A solid shape slowly emerged from the haze. Her senses screaming, Cara's brain worked overtime to process what her eyes saw standing before her. Much taller than a human, it filled the room up to the ceiling. The beast's black, glowing eyes locked on her and roared inside her head. Its body resembled a satyr: human-looking on top, with hands ending in clawed fingers, and goat-like on the bottom, with legs ending in cloven hooves. Scaly skin, so red it was almost black, covered its body. Horns grew in curved points out of its forehead, and strings of drool dripped from a mouth of razor-sharp teeth.

Her heart almost stopped in terror. She had seen enough religious art in her life to conclude this was either a demon . . . or the Devil himself. She forced herself to take a step back, the front door no longer an option.

Fire escape, she thought on reflex. Her head filled with excruciating pain as she turned and ran blindly back toward the kitchen.

Within a few steps, hot hands wrapped around her neck. Jerking her to a stop, it lifted her off the ground. Her feet frantically kicked empty air beneath her. Its hot breath burned her scalp while the heat of its form seared her back. Her eyes bulged as she choked for air, and her hands tore at the scaly skin surrounding and burning her throat.

No! she cried silently in frustration. She didn't want to die.

After her last intake of breath, everything went black.

Chapter 17

New York City. Perry Street Apartment. Friday, March 21, 1:35 p.m. EDT

THE SOUNDS OF CARA CHOKING and her panicked struggle filled the air. Chamuel held his breath. His palm wrapped around the empty hilt of his weapon, and he silently invoked the blade to life. Brilliant light sprang from the sword's hilt as Chamuel crept up behind the demon and rammed the blade home into its back. Cara dropped from its clutches and hit the floor, unconscious. An ear-splitting shriek escaped the demon before it disintegrated, turning into a column of black ash and falling into a pile next to her.

The blade gone, Chamuel's hand shook as he clipped the hilt back onto his belt next to the rest of his weapons. Stepping over the demon ash, he dropped to his knees next to Cara. He turned her over and stuck two fingers to her jugular to find her weak pulse. He scanned her quickly. The strength of her energy told him she'd recover.

The breath he'd been holding escaped with a whoosh, and his large shoulders slumped in relief.

That was too close.

He glanced around Cara's living room. Other than the signs of a struggle, the apartment was meticulously organized and inviting. Not unlike his own personal space. Looking down at the ash pile, he made a mental note to dispose of it before he left. A bucket, a broom, and a vacuum would do the trick. The demon had conveniently collapsed downward, leaving Cara covered in only a light coating of ash. Chamuel hadn't escaped so easily, taking an extra dose of ash through the blade's exit wound.

Removing his demon ash-covered duster, he turned it inside out and laid it over the back of the nearest chair. His T-shirt and cargo pants were more or less dust-free. He knelt down next to Cara, and opened up his silent telepathic line to Michael.

Before Chamuel could say a word, Michael's voice rushed at him. *"I'm on my way. What the hell just happened?"*

"Did you see it?" Chamuel asked, more interested in if Michael had gotten the vision through the Flow in advance than if he was close by when it had happened. New Trinities usually required an adjustment and fine-tuning period before they fully bonded.

He could hear Michael's agitation. *"Of course I saw it. I ran out of class and jumped in a cab as soon as it hit me. But why wasn't she at work?"*

Chamuel ground his teeth in frustration. She should still have been at the office. Otherwise, he would have been guarding her more closely and this would have never happened.

"I don't know," he said to Michael, his jaw tight.

"I'll be there in about twenty minutes," Michael said. *"By the way, Constantina just arrived."*

Chamuel could hear the weariness seep into Michael's voice. Visions required energy. *"I know. She called me earlier."*

"Take care of Cara, please." Michael's request was more of a plea.

Chamuel frowned. Did Michael actually think he wouldn't? True, they'd met only recently and hadn't yet formed a proper working relationship, but still. *"Of course I will. One thing: I don't want her to see me when she wakes up. I'll be close by, but not visible."*

"No problem. I won't give you away."

Chamuel closed down their telepathic link and looked down at the unconscious yet beautiful woman lying in a heap at his feet. Her stocking-covered feet poked out from the pair of brown slacks she wore with a matching sweater. A diamond solitaire pendant lay at her throat. Her long auburn hair fanned out in a halo around her head. Glancing around, he noticed her high heels lay inside the door next to a table that held her discarded suit jacket and keys.

He brushed his hand down his face. His cheeks burned as his blood pressure rose, livid that he'd misjudged the situation. Had he known she planned on leaving work early or not using her driver, he would have stayed with her all day. Under standard rules of engagement, demons rarely took native form in front of human witnesses. Outside of a safe house, like the penthouse, Cara was safest in places like Cabot.

Luckily, he'd been close by when he'd picked up on her distress, but not close enough to prevent the attack. Again, he had to ask himself: was he up to the task? He couldn't live with a second mistake. He'd been on the job less than twenty-four hours, and he'd almost lost her.

Fortunately for them all, he'd arrived in time, but the nasty bruise circling her neck reminded him he hadn't arrived early enough.

He reached down and gently scooped her up. Waves of hair draped over one of his arms; her legs draped over the other. His weapons dangled from his belt as he carried her limp body over to the sofa. But rather than laying her down, he folded his large frame into a sitting position on the cushions and continued to cradle her. She felt small, fragile, and strangely at home against his chest.

There's barely any weight to her, he thought. She couldn't be more than one hundred twenty pounds, nothing like the solid weight of a Nephil woman.

Despite her unconscious state, he didn't want to let her go. The second he'd touched her, an odd sense of peace rushed over him. Holding her satisfied something deep inside him and quelled his restlessness. Granted, a long time had passed since he'd touched a woman, yet there was something more significant and special about touching her. He couldn't quite place it.

He studied the delicate beauty of her face with wide-eyed fascination, drinking in her creamy pale skin and the long lashes that brushed her cheeks as she slept. Her lips, soft and full, begged to be kissed. His eyes lingered there a moment longer, wondering what her lips would feel and taste like on his.

Leaning down, he breathed in the scent of her hair, its sweet bouquet filling his senses. He drew a deep breath, and his groin stirred. Someone like her could tempt him out of his self-imposed celibacy. He'd denied himself a pathway for his physical desires as part of his atonement. Had he paid enough yet?

As she lay in the crook of his arm, the softness of her hair touching his bare skin made it tingle. A strand of it, the color of autumn leaves, lay over her face. Instinctively, he reached his hand up to brush it away.

But as he was about to make contact, he froze.

Forbidden.

That's what she was to him, forbidden. The rules were clear; she could never be his.

His lips could never touch hers. The realization unexpectedly caused his heart to lurch in his chest. He didn't know what surprised him more: his unexplainable desire for her or that he considered breaking his celibacy. Closing his eyes for a second, he took another deep breath to compose himself.

Forcing himself to stand, he set her down gently but was unable to tear himself away completely. He knelt down next to the sofa until he heard Michael's knock at the door.

After putting his duster back on, he let Michael in. Michael's effort to get there quickly was evident by the *gi* and martial arts shoes he still wore from teaching his class.

"How's she doing?" he asked as he walked past Chamuel and straight to where Cara lay on the sofa, kneeling down beside her.

"Her energy is strong. She's coming back, but I think she needs some help."

"Let's check to see if she has anything containing ammonia. It's the next best thing to old-fashioned smelling salts." Michael got back on his feet. "You take the bathroom, I'll check the kitchen."

Chamuel checked the bathroom cabinet underneath the sink—nothing.

"Found it," Michael yelled from the kitchen.

He met Michael back in the living room. "If you don't want Cara to see you, I'd suggest you cloak now," Michael said, waving the bottle at him.

Begrudgingly, Chamuel agreed. "Fine," he said and disappeared.

Michael turned back to Cara.

"Cara, wake up," he whispered, ammonia fumes wafted out of the open bottle close to her nose. "Cara, can you hear me?"

Her eyes flew open as she coughed and sputtered. Her chest jolted up and off the sofa. Michael moved the bottle away, and she fell back, sucking air into her lungs in greedy breaths. Closing her eyes, she moaned, her hands cradling her head before they moved down to her battered neck. And then her moans transformed into soft cries, and tears streamed from her eyes. She looked at Michael, at first unseeing, then focusing in on his face.

In a hoarse voice, she tried to choke out a few words. "Demon tried . . . kill me. Hurts. Everything hurts."

Chamuel cringed. He could only imagine the pain in her throat and the rest of her body.

There was a look of kindness in Michael's eyes, and he said softly, "I'm sorry. This shouldn't have happened." His words hit Chamuel like a punch in the gut.

Michael put down the bottle and reached for her hand. "We're safe now. Chamuel killed the demon. Just rest for a minute until the driver gets here. He'll take us back to the penthouse. There's someone there who wants to meet you."

Another tear fell from Cara's eye. "I thought I was dead."

Michael squeezed her hand, and his gaze locked on hers. "Don't worry. It'll never happen again. I won't let it."

Chamuel watched with longing the way she clutched Michael's hand tightly and wondered what her hand would feel like in his before he angrily pushed the thought away.

Forbidden, remember?

"Guardian?" she choked.

Chamuel closed his eyes and shook his head. Her words cut right through him, and his heart dropped. *She thinks he failed her.*

"We didn't know you'd be leaving work early. Like I said, this won't happen again."

Chamuel couldn't escape hearing Michael's accusation repeated. He wanted to scream in frustration. *I got it! I fucked up!*

When the driver arrived downstairs, he watched Cara collect her things before she and Michael disappeared through the door.

Staying behind, he cleaned up the demon ash and put off making the one phone call he dreaded. But Constantina's words couldn't sting any more than the verbal lashing he'd already given to himself.

Ten minutes later, Chamuel walked out onto the sidewalk and his head jerked to the side. There it was again, the wisp of Nephilim energy from the day before. He recognized the energy as belonging to the one who helped the Sentinel escape. Had the Nephil assisted the demon in finding Cara?

Chamuel pushed his energy out, searching for the other Nephil, prepared to flush him out. But as quickly as he'd come, the traitor disappeared off the grid.

Then something struck Chamuel as off. If the rogue had been present during the attack, Chamuel would have sensed him, but he hadn't detected him until now.

Maybe he'd asked Isaac the wrong question yesterday. Rather than asking who was scheduled to be in Lower Manhattan at the time, maybe the right question was: who had shown up in Lower Manhattan?

Chapter 18

CARA RUBBED HER NECK, her skin tender to the touch and her throat raw. She'd recovered as well as possible for someone who'd almost been killed by a demon. Her rebellion had answered one question for her: now she knew how someone could die. She might be far from fine, but at least she was safe . . . for now.

During the long ride back to the penthouse, Cara had stayed wrapped in Michael's embrace, her head tucked beneath his chin. His strong arms secured her as she rested her cheek against his warm chest, listening to the steady thump underneath. They didn't talk, but she found Michael's presence calming as she drank in the faint smell of his cologne. His fingers traveled in a soothing path, up and down her back. Though intimate, Cara knew Michael's gesture held no romantic intent. Nonetheless, she appreciated it, and her affection for him grew.

They rode the elevator up to the penthouse after a dizzying ride of twists and turns through the underground garage. One of the measures imparted on Cara earlier that morning by the Chief Security Officer of the building was how she would enter and exit the building both on foot and by car. Unlike the rest of her neighbors, she was given an alternate pathway along the ground level and through the garage, taking her in and out of a different building.

When they entered the apartment, a woman wearing a full-length, blue velvet cloak sat waiting on the sofa.

She rose with Chloe at her side, and smiled in greeting as they approached. She was petite, with silky blonde hair that was straight and long; her eyes had a slight glow and resembled the blue of the ocean. She looked no more than thirty-five, but the way she carried herself hinted she might possibly be older. Her face, flawless and glowing with an aristocratic yet warm demeanor, reminded Cara of Grace Kelly.

Cara blinked. She couldn't quite put her finger on it, but there was something slightly off about the woman's face.

"Cara, it's a pleasure to finally meet you." She took Cara's hands in both of hers. "My name is Constantina, and I'll be your mentor." The woman's eyes were filled with warmth and kindness. The muscles of Cara's arms relaxed as Constantina held her hands. A sense of calm took hold within Cara, moving through her like the gentle lapping of waves rolling back and forth over the sand.

Did this woman just do that? "Pleased to meet you," Cara replied, suddenly feeling refreshed and alive—and confused.

Constantina released Cara's hands and turned to Michael, kissing him once on each cheek. "Michael, so good to see you again, dear one. Chamuel filled me in on what happened."

Cara detected a slight European accent—French, with other influences.

Constantina glanced back at Cara with a look of worry. "I'm sincerely sorry for what happened to you today. You're already on the radar of the Dark Ones, and this means we have much less time than anticipated to train you."

Finally, answers. Cara was surprised by her own steel-willed determination to get on with whatever she needed to know. "Michael briefed me on the basics, but I'm eager to learn more. When can we start?"

Constantina's face lit up with a smile. "Right now." Her eyes shifted to Michael, "Would you mind taking your leave, dear one?"

Still wearing his karate clothes, he gave a small bow of his head, hands crossed in front of him at the waist. "Not at all. Call if you need me." Cara sensed Michael's gesture had less to do with martial arts etiquette and more to do with Constantina's position, highlighting to Cara how much she didn't understand.

Constantina returned the gesture. "Please join us in the morning for our lessons."

"Sure thing," he said. He leaned down and ruffled Chloe's ears as she sat quietly next to Constantina; then he moved to leave. "Have a good evening, ladies."

A small rush of panic set in. "Constantina, please give me a minute?" Cara asked before turning to Michael. "Let me walk you out."

They walked back through the foyer, and Cara stopped Michael with a touch of her hand before they reached the door. She found herself needing his reassurance, both trusting and relying on him more and more.

"Is this okay?" she asked in a small voice. "I wish you were staying."

Leaning down, he put his arm over her shoulder and pulled her closer so their foreheads touched. "It's more than okay. Constantina's amazing, you'll see. You're safe now."

"I felt this weird, calming thing when she held my hands."

"She did an energy push to soothe you. You'll learn how to do it too. Don't worry. It's all good." His voice was warm and confident. She relaxed. If Michael trusted Constantina, she guessed she could too.

She gave him a half-smile. "Thank you for before. It meant a lot to me."

His eyes softened, and he brushed back a strand of her hair. "Hey, I'm just sorry I didn't get there sooner. I know I'm not your Guardian, but I'd still protect you with my life."

A lump formed in her throat at his words, and she wrapped her arms around his warm, muscular body. "Thanks, again."

With a squeeze, he hugged her back. Her cheek brushed against the stiff cotton of his *gi*.

"See you tomorrow," he said. He placed a kiss on the top of her head before closing the door behind him.

Cara returned to the living room and remembered her manners. "Constantina, can I get you anything before we begin?" she asked, her voice still scratchy.

"No, thank you. I hope you don't think me too presumptuous, but I've already put my travel case in the guest room at the end of the hall. Many years have passed since I've been here, but I've always been fond of that room."

Cara suppressed her surprise. She hadn't realized she would have a houseguest, but what the hell? It was no stranger than inheriting the penthouse in the first place, and she had plenty of room. Truth be told, she was glad for the personal attention and the company. She also felt safer.

"You're quite welcome to stay wherever you'd like. I can close Chloe in my room at night, so she doesn't bother you. She's very fond of that guest room."

"Not necessary. She's a dear companion. You're fortunate to have her," she said. "Why don't you change into something more comfortable, and then we'll meet in the library. Will fifteen minutes suffice?"

When Cara arrived in the library, Constantina was already there. Unlike Cara, who wore yoga pants and a T-shirt, Constantina wore loose fitting pants and a tailored tunic made of a flowing material that looked like silk. Its color was the same ocean blue as her eyes. Her silky, blond hair fell free around her shoulders.

Constantina gazed at Cara and smiled warmly. "I've been looking forward to our meeting for quite some time, and I hope to share whatever wisdom and skills you'll need. But first, let me share with you one of the secrets of this room."

She walked over to one of the floor-to-ceiling bookcases, and just like in the movies, moved a hidden lever behind the last book on the sixth shelf from the bottom. The bookcase slowly swung forward, revealing a staircase leading up.

"There's a release on the other side to close it once we're through the door."

Of course there is a hidden door behind the bookcase, Cara thought, caught between surprise and an eye roll.

She followed Constantina through the opening. Constantina touched the release, and they ascended the steps into what looked like a meditation room, yet was far different.

Cara's eyes were drawn upward to the barrel-shaped ceiling made of heavy plaster and painted elaborately with frescos of angels and various scenes, reminding her of those found on the ceiling of the Sistine Chapel in Rome. The pastel blues, greens, and pinks of the ceiling reflected off the white walls, giving a warm glow to the entire room. A high table-like structure to her right, at the far end of room, held lit candles of various colors surrounding an elevated golden orb at the center.

The room was expansive, nearly as large as the penthouse, with a thin, padded mat that spanned most of the floor in lieu of a rug.

"What is this place?" asked Cara quietly, looking around. The space was reminiscent of a church, its beauty held within its simplicity.

"It's one of our meeting places. As a matter of fact, this whole apartment is considered a safe house," said Constantina. She pointed toward the table. "Do you see the golden orb on the altar?"

Cara turned to look where Constantina indicated and nodded.

"Come," she said and took Cara's hand, leading her to it. It reminded Cara of the one in her Catholic church growing up, just higher. Constantina, who stood no more than five feet two inches tall, was shorter than the height of the table. As they drew closer, Cara noticed a box of long matches and a candle snuffer on a small table next to it. A set of stairs was built into the back of the dark wood altar. A white cloth covered the surface, overhanging at the sides; twelve candles of different colors were cradled in a tall, wire stand that circled the orb.

"The orb prevents our energy from being detected, hiding us and making this a safe dwelling. I should also mention that the presence of the altar makes the penthouse hallowed ground, protecting you from demonic forces. The apartment has been in our possession for almost a century. Although you can see many renovations have been done over the years."

That could explain why the space had the feeling of a church and was rocking the angel theme.

"Is that why I inherited this apartment, and the Connecticut farmhouse?" Cara asked. "Are they both safe houses?"

"Yes and no. Yes, they are both safe houses, but that's not why you inherited them. Many factors go into the bequests of the Soul Seekers. Not everyone is as richly gifted as you, dear one. As a matter of fact, very few are gifted this handsomely, and some are not gifted at all. The danger and importance of the mission are key factors, but not the only ones. Trust that over time you will come to discover why. My only advice is to caution you against frivolity in regards to this gift, because you may have need of it in the future. You would do well to remember that money affords privacy, security in the manner of safety, and freedom when needed."

Cara listened carefully and nodded. Given that lens, she grasped the logic but wasn't fully satisfied with the answer. She decided not to push. There were other things she was much more interested in learning. Spending any of the money had been far from her mind.

Constantina dropped her hand and walked to the back of the altar, picking up the matches on her way. She ascended the stairs in the back, and knelt on top, positioning herself to light the remaining candles. "I'd hoped to have all of these lit before I met you in the library."

"What are the candles for?"

"Ah, each of the candles represents one of the twelve Orders of Angels in Heaven."

Interesting. Cara dug into her well of questions. "Constantina, who are we? And why do we need to be hidden? Michael was a little vague on the topic. I'm hoping you can help me understand what I've just stepped into . . . and why people may die."

Constantina descended the altar stairs and came around the front. "As a matter of fact, that will be our very first discussion. You've been patient and rightly inquisitive as to who we are, who you are, and how this all comes together. I intend to make it as easy to understand as possible."

There was an air of calm and serenity about Constantina that Cara appreciated. Constantina picked up her hand again. "Come and sit," she said, and led her to the middle of the room, where they both sank into a seated position on the floor facing each other. "Let us start with a little prayer and then take it from there. Shall we?"

Cara shifted uncomfortably, and Constantina tried to put her at ease. "I will lead, you just think about good things." She smiled and took Cara's hands. They both closed their eyes.

"Our Father, we gather in the name of peace and love, and we ask all the Angels to lend their celestial support in goodness, love, wisdom, power, and light, that they may watch and banish any whose intentions are less than pure. We embrace your gifts with a pure heart. Amen."

"Constantina, I believe in God, but I'm not very religious," Cara blurted out, feeling a little sheepish and embarrassed, but wanting to set the record straight. "I'm also not a big Bible reader. It's hard to explain, but I've always felt suffocated by religion. Like I'm fighting against the control it places on people. I don't believe in scaring people into having faith and obeying rules that don't always make sense." Cara had long since stopped attending the Catholic masses which were so important to her parents.

Constantina gave her a curious but unconcerned look.

Her parents would be mortified at what she'd just revealed, but Cara found it easier to be forthcoming with a virtual stranger. Given the circumstances, she had nothing to lose putting it out there.

"I hope I don't sound like a heathen." Cara added, hoping her honesty didn't offend Constantina.

Constantina smiled and surprised Cara with her reply. "Not at all, and I dare say, you're not altogether wrong. Unfortunately, the purity of the Scriptures has long been tainted by man. Many choices, additions, and deletions have been motivated by politics and control.

"For many centuries, the overlap of church and state has driven the contents that we know as the Word of God. But that really is the least of it. What saddens me the most is that what you know as today's modern Bible will always be incomplete. There are many books and omissions that were not included, many of which you've heard about in other contexts. And there's one very specific book known to a very limited few. It's the book which has resulted in you and I being who and what we are."

Cara stared wide-eyed at Constantina. "This is starting to sound like *The Da Vinci Code*." Cara read voraciously, especially thrillers. *Am I the next Dr. Robert Langdon or Sophie Neveu?* she wondered.

Constantina smiled. "Dear, that's a work of fiction, but there's some truth in such stories."

"So, are you saying the world's been duped for thousands of years?" Cara asked.

"No, Cara, not specifically duped. There's much truth in what you know as the Scriptures, the issue has always been with the interpretation. Please don't get me wrong; religion has an indisputable purpose for humanity by driving faith. Faith is essential for our collective physical and spiritual well-being. But make no mistake, good and evil are very real. Just like faith, the duality of good and evil transcends all religions—so does God, by whatever name He is known by—and love.

"At the end of your days, God has no preference on which path you take to find Him, or which religion you follow. He's satisfied that you find Him. He only wants to welcome you home. Religion, on the other hand, is sometimes just a handy face behind which good and evil do battle. Many crimes have been committed in the name of religion—look at the Crusades. Yet, many wonderful things have also been accomplished through faith in God and love."

Cara's mouth hung open slightly. She couldn't agree more. Constantina captured perfectly what she's always believed. "I've never heard it explained that way before, but that makes sense to me. So, what's the Book that's missing?" Cara was practically croaking; her throat, already sore from the attack, worsened the more she talked.

"Before we begin, let me fix the rasp in your voice and the injury to your neck."

Constantina closed her eyes, clasped her hands together at her chest, and said a few words in a language Cara didn't understand. An angelic glow entered the top of Constantina's head and radiated out of her hands as she separated them and gently placed them on Cara's throat. Warmth penetrated Cara's neck, chasing away the pain.

"Feel better?" she asked.

The difference was unbelievable. "Yes, that was amazing. What did you do?"

"All I did was channel the healing energy that surrounds the earth into your throat, raising your molecular vibration and accelerating your healing. You have the same ability. Learning how to call upon it will be part of your training." She winked at Cara. "It was the same thing I did when we met earlier."

Just like Michael had said.

Cara's pulse quickened. Being able to heal others was something she wanted to learn. "Did Michael tell you about the woman on the street?"

Constantina's face clouded over. "Yes, the Sentinel."

"Is that what I did to her? Heal her?"

Rather than answering her question directly, Constantina asked, "Have you ever used a tire gauge?"

What did the woman on the street have to do with cars? Cara leaned back on her hands. "What's the connection?"

"A tire gauge shows you how much pressure is in the tire. Similarly, a Sentinel draws the Flow through a Soul Seeker to measure their power by the number of years they can remove from her face. And you, my dear, did quite well."

Cara's eyes were round O's. Now she got it.

"Are you ready to begin?" Constantina's warm gaze reflected in her smile.

Cara nodded, having decided to sit back and shut up. Constantina rose to her feet.

"Come," she requested. Cara got to her feet and followed the smaller woman to the far end of the room.

Constantina stopped and glanced at her. "Okay, look up." Cara did as she was told. The ceiling was covered in painted vignettes, mostly angels with wings, but some mortals too. The lights that circled the walls illuminated the ceiling from all angles.

Constantina pointed upward. "See the man writing the book?"

Cara looked at the sea of images above her, and pinpointed the one Constantina wanted her to see. In the picture a man sat scribing a book next to a cave opening with water visible outside in the distance.

"Our scripture is called the Book of Human Angels, translated from the Latin name *Libre Homo Angelorum*. It was written over two thousand years ago by the same priest who penned several of what are now known as the Dead Sea Scrolls, which includes the Books of Enoch."

Constantina pointed again. "The man standing off to the left of the priest is his brother from the first Messenger family. Since the completion of its penning, our scripture has traveled among the Messenger families in order to keep it safe and hidden."

Cara shifted her gaze back down to Constantina. "Is there a reason why the book's been kept hidden?"

"Yes, a very good one," Constantina replied with conviction.

Something puzzled Cara. She tilted her head to the side and frowned. "Wait. Why would the book be written and then hidden? Why write it at all?"

"Our scripture contains more than our story; it contains information that will be needed later . . . by others. This information is one of the reasons the book must remain hidden."

Cara gave her a questioning look. "One of the reasons?"

Cocking her eyebrow at Cara, Constantina asked, "How about I tell you our story, and then, if unanswered, you can ask your question again?"

"All right, but where is it now?"

A look of sadness momentarily passed over Constantina's features. "We have it and protect it with our lives." Then, shaking off whatever thought she'd had, she said, "Let's move over here." Cara trailed behind her to the next location. She was taken aback when Constantina sunk down, laid flat on the mat, and smiled up at her. "I don't know about you, but my neck can take only a few minutes of staring up at the ceiling, and this part of the story may take a while."

The move was so unexpected Cara chuckled and joined her on the floor.

Yes, this was much better, she thought as she lay on her back. Light bathed the ceiling from a set of lights on the surrounding walls, while another set lit the floor. The effect provided a warm glow that filled the room.

Constantina turned her head toward Cara. Roughly eighteen inches away, this was as close as Cara had been to Constantina so far, and she took a moment to notice her soft, smooth skin and the unusual color of her eyes, a shade between green and blue.

"I know you mentioned you're not an avid Bible reader, but have you read about the Great War in Heaven in the Book of Revelations? Can I assume you've heard of Lucifer?"

Cara gave her a wry smile. "I did listen in church once in a while."

"Very good. Look up at the center picture."

The center painting was by far the largest, most violent of all the images. Too many angels to count were depicted in battle against demons in the midst of a bright cloudscape. It was the only image that included the color red.

"See the large angel to the left, the one with the dark hair?"

It took Cara a moment, but she located him. "Yes."

"Lucifer, named after the Morning Star, was a beautiful and beloved angel responsible for leading the Order of Angels known as the Cherubim. One of the reasons why you and I are sitting here today is because of him and the subject of this painting, the Great War in Heaven."

"I vaguely remember the story. Didn't the Great War start because he was jealous of man?"

Constantina smiled. "Yes, that's partially correct. There were two incidents, really. The first occurred when God called his only begotten son, Jesus Christ, home after the Resurrection. He loved Jesus, and mankind, so much that he expected the angels to bow down to Jesus. Lucifer thought himself better than man. He refused to bow to what he considered an inferior being. The other incident involved Lucifer himself—he had higher aspirations, you see. He believed himself superior to God and convinced a faction of the divine host of angels to follow him in an attempt to overthrow God as the Ruler of Heaven. And so started the Great War."

Rolling her head to the side to look at Constantina, Cara said, "So, he pissed everyone off and got kicked out. Does that about sum it up?"

Constantina chuckled. "Yes it does. See the other prominent angel in the painting to the right?"

"Yup," Cara said as she looked at the very beautiful, yet fierce-looking angel wielding a sword of brilliant light.

"That is the Archangel Michael who led the angelic army as they waged war and defeated Lucifer and his minions. In the end, Lucifer and his followers fell from the grace of God and were literally stripped of their wings and cast out of Heaven down to earth . . . where they still reside. At his inception, Lucifer had been one of the most beloved and beautiful of all angels. Today, we refer to him and his fallen angels as the Dark Ones."

"I find it interesting that the Devil started out as an angel. Why wasn't he painted as a demon?" she asked, looking back at Constantina, who wore a sad smile, her brows furrowed.

"To remind us all that he was once loved and that sometimes evil comes in beautiful packages," she said softly. Cara wondered if she'd hit a nerve, but Constantina recovered quickly.

"God loved his angels enough to create them like man, as beings with free will. But with free will comes the ability to sin. In essence, Lucifer was undone by both his sins of pride and envy. What happens next is where we all come in." Constantina lifted her small frame off the mat and moved to stand underneath another large angelic mural.

Cara followed and they both dropped down again on the mat. With all this staring up at the ceiling, she understood why they needed the mat. Another crowd of angels hovered in the painting above; this time no violence was evident. Angels were crowded around, all facing a brilliant light. With the exception of their wings, they all looked different. They all wore different forms of dress with various implements in their hands. Some held swords, some books; others held farming implements or other objects.

"Many angels couldn't understand Lucifer's decisions. A particular faction of angels across the twelve Orders worried about mankind now that Lucifer and his minions were living among them. God couldn't interfere, since he'd given his children the gift of free will to choose their own path and to make their own decisions."

Cara furrowed her brow. "If He can't interfere, what happens when He hears our prayers?" She'd been raised to pray to God for help and guidance, and it didn't sit well with her that her prayers may have been in vain. That was one belief she hadn't abandoned.

With a smile Constantina answered, "Just because He cannot interfere, doesn't mean He doesn't listen or help you. But what you ask for may not be what you really need. His love for all of you is why the Book of Human Angels exists and the reason for our meeting here today."

"Fair point," Cara conceded, relieved.

"After the war, three hundred angels from various choirs approached God and made an unusual request: to form an additional angelic protectorate of mankind by descending from Heaven to live among men. They would provide a hidden resource to protect man and help to maintain the balance of good and evil on earth. They wouldn't directly interfere with the free will of man, but they would provide guidance when needed, working through Trinities to carry out their work. This group of angels is known as the Sanctus Angelorum."

"So, we have angels living among us. Are you an angel?" Cara asked, looking over at her and going for broke.

Constantina smiled at her question. "I'm as human as you are Cara. However, I'm also . . . different."

Cara had already suspected that, but she had trouble pinpointing why. "What do you mean?"

"One of the conditions of the agreement was that the angels could not descend in Angelic form. They had to be born and live as humans. But, there's one difference between the descended angel and an ordinary human soul. These angels were to be born in an 'awakened' state."

"What does that mean, exactly?" Cara rolled her head to the side.

Constantina, still focused on the ceiling, lifted her finger and held it above her. "According to the Kabala, the Night Angel Layela accompanies a soul on its journey down to earth. As the soul enters the unborn fetus, she erases any memories of Heaven and all past lives by placing her finger against the lips. The tip of her finger lies right under the nose—leaving that vertical dent over the center of the upper lip." Constantina touched her finger vertically to her upper lip. Then she turned her head toward Cara and removed her finger. "Layela does not accompany us."

Understanding crashed over Cara. "Oh, my God! I mean, gosh," Cara blurted as her hand flew up to cover her mouth, finally placing what was slightly off about Constantina's beautiful face.

She was missing the vertical indentation above her upper lip.

Chapter 19

"You're one of the three hundred descended angels . . . " Cara stared in wide-eyed amazement, springing up into a sitting position to face Constantina. She couldn't believe she was talking to an angel. Well, a human one anyway.

"Yes, Cara, I am," Constantina replied, sitting up straight and bowing her head in a timeless and noble gesture. "I'm sure you have many questions, but I'll start by telling you that I've lived many lives over many centuries, and I remember them all."

"Are you immortal?"

Constantina shook her head. "No, I'm just like you. My body is human, and my soul is immortal. The only difference between us is my ability to retain my memories of past lives and of Heaven. I also clearly understand why I'm here and what I must do, unlike most humans who must make that discovery on their own."

Cara lowered her head. "I wish I had that knowledge." Then she wouldn't be fumbling around trying to make sense of her life.

"All souls have a divine purpose, which they may or may not ever realize during their lifetime." Constantina reached for her hand. "Cara, look at me."

Cara obeyed.

"You may not have that knowledge now, but you will. You're destined to know."

Then curiosity got the best of her and she had to ask, "Heaven exists . . . and you remember it?" Cara had always hoped that Heaven was real. The belief made her less afraid of death. But then again, she also believed that the only people truly afraid of death were those who had never lived a full life.

"As much as I remember my lives here."

Constantina's words warmed Cara, and she couldn't help but smile. "What's it like? Heaven, I mean."

A dreamy, faraway look came over Constantina. "Ah, that's much harder to describe. In its simplest form, Heaven contains all that is good—love, light, beauty, peace, happiness. It's like nothing you've ever experienced here on earth . . . but you will one day."

Cara took comfort in her answer, feeling the love in her words, so much so that it brought a tear to her eye. She drew in a breath and asked the next logical question. "Does Hell exist?"

Drawing her eyebrows together, Constantina leaned her hands back on the mat. "There are many answers to that question, but yes, there are places shielded from the Light where the Dark Ones exist. Evil, like good, is part of the duality and balance of life and existence. Where there's choice, there's duality. Our job is to keep the balance."

Cara sat mulling over Constantina's words. "So, how do I fit into all of this as a Soul Seeker in a Trinity?"

Constantina smiled and said with her indiscernible accent, "I think that's what you would call a 'good segue.' When we struck our agreement with God, there were conditions to that agreement. For one, we don't carry out our work alone; we're assisted by the Trinities. One of the conditions we must abide is that we cannot interfere directly with other human beings. It would be unfair, you see. We are awakened, meaning we have knowledge and access to information that's forbidden to share, because sharing it could change an individual's destiny without allowing them the ability to choose their own path. That's why Soul Seekers exist; that's why you exist. Your destiny is tied to an event and to a person that will impact the balance of good and evil that we've been tasked with protecting for the last couple of millennia."

"How did my grandmother know about me? Was she a Soul Seeker too?"

"No, she was a Messenger, like Michael. Messengers can sense others like us. Your grandmother, Hannah, sensed it in you as a child. But we've actually known about you longer, since your birth."

"Michael told me a little about Messengers. Can you tell me more? Are they angels too?"

Constantina shook her head. "Messengers, and Messenger families, are human like you. They connect the Soul Seekers to the Sanctus Angelorum. Remember the energy that I channeled to heal your neck earlier? That energy, beyond supplying healing power, also carries messages. We call it the Flow. Messengers have direct communication with us through the Flow, since it's safest for us to keep our distance from the Soul Seekers for their own protection, and ours. The Dark Ones usually have more difficulty spotting Soul Seekers and Messengers. Due to my awakened state, my angelic essence as one of the Sanctus Angelorum is like a beacon for them."

"Wait. If the Messengers are meant to keep us separated, then why are you here?" Cara asked, alarmed that Constantina had put herself in harm's way to be here.

"Ah, not everything is always so simple. Your Trinity is extra special." Constantina released a deep breath and squeezed her hand. "There is more to our story, Cara. When God granted our request, He attached a prophecy that a battle would occur and be led by twelve souls known as the Holy Twelve. You, my dear, are believed to be the First of the Holy Twelve."

It took a minute for Constantina's words to sink in before the air rushed from Cara's lungs. "What?" she breathed. *Battle, what battle?*

"Don't be afraid, dear one. You'll not be alone if the prophecy comes to pass."

Cara pressed her palms to her temples and closed her eyes. "But why me? I'm a *banker*, for Pete's sake. I've never even touched a weapon!" Cara heard Constantina sigh.

"Dear one, life is rarely as obvious or convenient as it is portrayed in books and movies. Real life is messy, Cara. Nothing comes wrapped with a neat bow. The thing you need to understand is that wrapped within your humanity is a spark of the divine. It's that spark that will lead you into battle."

Opening her eyes, Cara tried to control her rising anxiety. "Who are the others, and what's the prophecy?"

Constantina shook her head. "Too much is yet to be determined, and too many free will decisions are yet to be made. It's best if we prepare you for your Calling first. In the interim, I ask that you trust me and not share this knowledge with anyone yet. It would only put you in more danger."

Cara chewed on her lip and reluctantly nodded. Not knowing scared her, but knowing scared her more. For the moment, she could live with not knowing.

"In time, you'll learn more and understand more. But, I'll share with you this—you're the first Seeker that I've ever trained personally," Constantina said, taking Cara's hands and bowing her head. "And, I very much look forward to it."

Cara brows knit with worry. "Won't this be dangerous for you?" Even though they'd just met, Cara felt a connection to Constantina, and her presence drove home the seriousness of their situation.

"Danger is relative. You need not worry about me. I've been around the block a few times, as they say." Constantina gave her a wink, a twinkle in her eye. "As for Messengers, Michael will teach you much in time, but he's still a novice."

"Could have fooled me. He seems to know exactly what he's doing." Michael struck her as one of the most competent people her age she'd ever met and gave the impression he had this Messenger thing down pat.

"Need I say that appearances can be deceiving? He's a strong and wonderful man, but he's still finding his way like you." Constantina settled into a comfortable position, her hands on her knees. "Contrary to what I told you about Seekers who have only spiritual ties to us, Messenger genes run in families, giving them latent psychic abilities buried within their physical brain. They are fully attuned to these abilities during the sacred ceremony when they accept their Calling."

Cara smiled. Maybe Michael was psychic after all, given what he somehow knew about her. "What kind of abilities are we talking about?"

"That depends on the family line, but mainly the ability to speak telepathically to the members of their Trinity and to access the Flow to communicate with the Sanctus Angelorum. All these abilities are tied in one way or another to the manipulation of energy."

"How is it tied to energy?" Cara asked.

"Ah, it's in the laws of physics, my dear. We vibrate at a higher frequency. Think of the Messengers as a radio receiver that is tuned to a specific station. And in turn, each Messenger has their own frequency, like a phone number, so we can communicate with them individually."

Cara tilted her head. The simplicity intrigued her. "Funny, that actually makes sense to me." *What Daniel Bernoulli would have given to have been part of this conversation*, she mused, thinking of the eighteenth century Swiss mathematician and physicist who discovered frequencies through string vibrations.

"That's because you're now looking through a clearer lens," Constantina replied.

"What about me, as a Soul Seeker—what're my abilities?"

Constantina's face lit up. "Why, you're a healer, of course. You have the gift to heal people both physically and spiritually. I'll help you to unlock your gifts as part of your training."

Finally—some clarity. "Thank you." Cara whispered, sincerely feeling more at ease. "What about the Guardians? Who are they?"

"Yes, the Guardianship." Constantina let out a sigh. "Our protectors were a hard-won concession in our agreement. But first, I must tell you the story of the first Watchers and the Nephilim."

Chapter 20

Hell. Friday, March 21.

"IMBECILE," LUCIFER HISSED through his fangs in hellspeak, looming large in full scales and scarlet red skin. Only when his Master went topside did he take on an attractive human guise.

Achanelech knelt down before Lucifer, in his true demonic form, on a bed of hot coals, his flesh bubbling and popping from the heat as pain permeated every nerve ending. His suit of human skin had melted away once he passed through the gates of Hell.

He wanted to cry out but knew better. His carelessness had delivered him straight down for a fireside chat with the Morning Star. Honestly, Achanelech hadn't released his demon to hunt the Soul Seeker. The demon had slipped out without his permission. He suspected his discussion with Emanelech about Cara making a hearty meal was too much for his child to resist—now a bucket of black ash for its poor judgment. Meanwhile, Achanelech was providing supplemental payment using his own demon flesh.

"She's mine and mine alone. Capture her; don't kill her." Lucifer eyed the demon behind Achanelech, and the whip cracked down on his bubbled flesh, ripping a chunk free. Pain shot through him, making him weak. His body stung like he'd stepped on a mountain of scorpions.

"Yes, Master," he replied, his serpentlike voice strained and panting.

"Bending the rules is permissible, but forfeiture is not an option if you plan to continue eating, which I most certainly do."

The whip came down again for good measure, nearly toppling Achanelech where he knelt. Repairing these injuries would take more than changing forms when he returned topside. He would need to eat . . . a lot.

Lucifer gnashed his teeth. "Be gone, and keep your demons fed and under control."

Achanelech pried open his eyes to find he was back in his mansion on the bedroom floor. The low hiss of his burned flesh sizzled in his ears. Engulfed in pain, his skin felt like it had been flayed from his body. If he had working tear ducts, he would have cried.

His consort ran over to him and leaned down.

"Acchie, what's been done to you?" she whispered without touching him. Despite her sometimes cruel and amoral behavior, she always managed to display compassion after his rare visits to Hell. It had been almost a century since the last time, and this was by far the worst visit he had experienced this millennia.

"I've prepared a good meal for you, my darling," she said.

If only he could get up and eat . . . But his skin was fused to the Persian carpet, and to move would risk agony.

"Who are they?" he managed to ask.

"No one who'll be missed," she said in a sing-song voice. "We'll train them and then hold them in reserve until the time is right. But first, let me make you presentable."

An icy coldness swept over him, soothing the burning within and around his body. She gave new meaning to the phrase "When Hell freezes over." Fire and Ice, that's who they were: he the Archdemon of Fire, and her the Archdemoness of Ice. Achanelech and Emanelech, two halves of a whole. That's what she liked to tell him anyway.

I'm a sentimental idiot, he thought, knowing in this moment this was the closest he'd ever come to love.

She reached down and helped him up. His flesh was still charred but no longer painful, and she led him to sit on the chair next to their bed.

"Wait here." She disappeared through the bedroom door to return a few moments later escorting a large human male. His eyes were glazed under Emanelech's spell; he walked trancelike to where Achanelech sat. Hunger rose up inside him, consuming him from the inside out. He did everything in his power not to drool.

"Do you willingly give yoursssself?" Achanelech asked with a breathless hiss, awaiting permission to strike. *Another asinine ground rule in the battle between good and evil*, he thought, thoroughly aggravated.

"Yes." The man said, unseeing to what was to come.

With lightning speed, the man was in Achanelech's embrace. His mouth hovered over the open lips of the man as one of his hands turned to mist and reached inside the human's chest next to his heart. His demonic fingers searched for the ethereal silver cord connecting the soul to the body. Snipping it between two clawed fingers, he sucked out the soul of the man through his open mouth and consumed it. Now trapped within his own body, the human's life force worked to repair the damage to his form and to take the edge off of his hunger. The skin on his hand turned from a crispy black to a reddish pink, and the human turned to dead weight in his arms.

"Darling, please help," Achanelech asked.

"Got him." Emanelech whisked the man out of his arms with little effort. "I'll be back with the next one after I dump this one into recovery." She paused when she reached the door. "I hope you're hungry." She winked and closed the door behind her.

Recovery, he thought with a snort. A nice word for dungeon. Recycling human bodies to serve in his soulless army was the ultimate in "being green," but a good week or two of confinement and "training" was required to get them used to their new state. Better than in the old days, when they would just kill them and leave the carcasses to rot.

Achanelech sat back in his chair and waited for his next course. After dinner, he planned to have a "Come to Lucifer" discussion with his demons. They'd been quiet since his return. They knew they were in trouble, but some of them were as dumb as a box of rocks. He shook his head. No more unsanctioned assassination attempts, or he would turn the lot of them into black ash and call it a day.

He sighed. Once the vaccine was complete . . . that would change everything.

Chapter 21

KAI ENTERED THE RESTAURANT and had a clear view to the kitchen and across the room. He easily spotted Calvin hunkered down behind a menu at one of the tables along the back wall.

Kai hoped for a bite to eat during his meeting to avoid having to forage around in the kitchen later. Melanie and Sara had left earlier, heading down just north of Los Angeles to see Melanie's mother for the weekend. Normally, he would have accompanied them, but he was playing in a golf tournament early the next morning. The timing couldn't have been better. Now he could concentrate on his investigation without having to explain his absence to Melanie.

Kai had received the results of Wednesday's experiment earlier, and they looked promising. Finally, things were moving in the right direction. If he could just get his hands on those lost lab notes, perhaps he'd learn something new, a surefire way to accelerate his success.

The hostess looked up to greet Kai, but he just smiled and signaled that he'd spotted his party. He passed the long, narrow communal table on his way to where Calvin sat, and slid into the chair opposite him.

"Hey Calvin, thanks for meeting me. I have to confess, the secrecy threw me for a loop."

Calvin blushed and gave him a shrug. "Yeah, I'm sorry about that. You weren't the first person to come looking for answers."

"What do you mean?" Kai asked, caught off guard, his radar suddenly up.

"Can I take your order, hon?" The waitress appeared from nowhere.

"Uh, can you give us a few minutes?" Kai hadn't even picked up the menu. "By the way, this is on me," he said to Calvin, trying to put him at ease. The waitress left them alone.

"Thanks, Dr. Solomon. As a cash-strapped grad student, I appreciate your offer. I hear the chef makes a mean short rib," Calvin said, clearly more relaxed.

"Call me Kai."

He nodded. "Will do."

Kai lowered his menu and leaned in. "I have to ask. Are you afraid your office is bugged?"

Calvin answered in a low voice. "I'm not sure, but I've suspected it might have been in the past. With Sandra and Tom dead, I'm not taking any chances."

"Smart," Kai said more to himself than to Calvin. "Do you think it's related to this project?"

"Let's just say this was the only project that was being worked on under the radar, and the two people you're asking me about were killed within three weeks of each other. Call me crazy, but once I tell you what I know, I calculate the probability of a connection at 99.9999 percent."

Kai's heart sped up. "Gotcha."

Calvin discarded his menu and leaned forward. "Dr. Wilson—Sandra—ran an amazing lab, and she was absolutely brilliant. I loved working with her. I told you the truth in the office; we had no projects for Forrester Research on our docket. I wasn't directly involved with Firefly, but I know that she consulted with Dr. Peyton."

The waitress returned. They'd both settled on the signature short ribs. She disappeared with their order, and Kai resumed his questioning.

"Who else has been sniffing around?" Kai asked.

"A couple of days after Sandra died, a woman named Emily paid a visit. Long, dark hair, frosty exterior—do you know her?"

Kai tried not to scowl. "Yes, I do." *Intriguing*, he thought, this meant that Emily also knew a connection existed between Firefly and Stanford.

"Well, she told me she represented something called 'the Foundation' and wanted access to any work resulting from Sandra's research with Dr. Peyton. She believed there was a nondisclosure violation and that all the work was inadvertently owned by them. But, I didn't tell her anything more than I told you yesterday." A mischievous grin spread across Calvin's face. "That made her very angry. She threatened all sorts of legal action and took the matter to the department head. Since the project wasn't official, there wasn't any paperwork to turn over. Anyway, you were the one I was waiting for."

Kai raised a brow. "Why someone like me?"

Calvin scanned the restaurant, leaned in closer to Kai, and lowered his voice to a whisper. "Not someone *like* you, Sandra told me *you* would come. Here's the creepiest part. When Wendy told me you were here to see me yesterday, the moment I heard your name it was like a curtain lifted. What I'm about to tell you popped into my head and sent a shiver up my spine. Not only that, but I experienced this nagging urge to tell you about it. So, believe me when I say, this is a little weirder for me than it is for you."

Gooseflesh covered his arms. Kai remembered the strange look that had passed over Calvin's face when he'd spoken to him in the office. "Okay, man, you're blowing my mind. I wasn't even on the project when she died, so how on earth did she suspect that I'd come snooping around after all this time?" Then a radical thought entered his mind. If she'd been trained in hypnotherapy, she could have done it. "Do you think she buried the story in your subconscious?"

"Yeah, I'm almost positive on that one." He chuckled. "The other question, about why she suspected you'd come . . . I don't have a clue." Calvin folded his arms, his brown eyes locked on Kai from behind his funky black glasses. "Everything started when Dr. Peyton came barreling into the lab late one morning last January. That was the first time I'd ever met him. He introduced himself and asked to see Sandra, but she was finishing up a class. So, I left him in her office and then went about my business. She came back when I was restocking supplies in the room next to her office. I don't think Dr. Peyton meant to speak so loud, or knew the walls were paper thin."

The waitress reappeared with their drinks, breaking in on their exchange. Calvin paused, tracking her with his eyes until she left.

He turned his attention back to Kai and continued. "Dr. Peyton had found something unexpected in one of the samples from the Foundation. His research had been restricted to gene samples, and he thought he had finally isolated some of the single nucleotide polymorphisms, or SNPs, that were driving some genetic changes affecting the traits associated with longevity. He was tracking success in some test and control mice. He also suspected that multiple labs were involved, beyond Forrester—basically, that the Foundation was piecing out the work on Firefly.

"But the samples he received that day were clearly not meant for Forrester. They contained samples of the full cell nucleus. Peyton had wanted to get his hands on those samples for some time, but he had been denied access. So, from what I overheard, he put three of the samples through full genome sequencing. They contained the same markers as the samples he'd been working with, so he knew they'd come from the same source of genetic material that he'd been testing. But something about the genome didn't make sense."

"What did he find?" Kai asked.

"Let me first ask you a question. The donor cells. Where were you told they came from?"

Kai's eyes narrowed a bit. "What are you asking, Calvin?"

"It's a simple question—animal, mineral, insect?"

"They're *supposed to be* samples from human cancer donors. Are you telling me they're something else?"

"I can only tell you what they're *not* . . . After Dr. Peyton compared the results to the HapMap, he realized that whatever they are, they're not human. As he put it, they were 'beyond human.'"

The hairs on Kai's arms stood up for a twenty-one-gun salute. The genome didn't appear on the HapMap's catalog of common genetic variants. How was this even possible?

The waitress arrived with their order, but Kai's appetite had disappeared.

Calvin's appetite clearly wasn't affected. He launched an attack on his short ribs. "These are really good. There's more to tell, so dig in," he said with his mouth partially full.

Kai's head spun. The implications of what Calvin told him opened up a world of possibilities. He couldn't begin to fathom the impact of the situation or what it all meant. But it did shed some light on why he kept running into dead ends with the current research. He needed to find those hidden pages from Tom's work now, more than ever.

"So, what happened after that?" Kai asked, hoping to speed things up.

Calvin rested his fork on the side of his plate. "Sandra took me into her confidence right away and asked me to help conceal the connection between the lab and Forrester. Then Dr. Peyton showed up more frequently to work with Sandra, but only on my shift."

"Do you think Tom ended up with all the research?"

"I think so. The night she was killed, her lab and office were ransacked. But the university asked the police to keep that part out of the papers."

"Ransacked, huh? What are the chances they found something worth killing over?"

Calvin shot him a wicked smile. "They were too late."

"How do you know?" Kai asked, knitting his brow.

"I saved the best part for last. The night before she died, when she came to do her hocus-pocus on my head, she made me promise that I would tell this story only once . . . and only to you. She also instructed me to give you the final piece."

An icy finger danced along his spine. "What final piece?"

Calvin reached into his pocket and pulled out a business card. In black letters, Kai spotted the address for Watson & Haskins in downtown San Francisco.

"The code word is *Ishmael*."

Chapter 22

New York City. Meeting Room. Friday, March 21, 7:00 p.m. EDT

AFTER A QUICK BREAK and a bite to eat downstairs, Cara ascended the stairs back into the glowing warmth of the meeting room. The angelic faces on the ceiling stared down at her in greeting.

Constantina's face brightened when they reached the center of the mat. "Cara, now that you know who and what I am, rather than me telling you about the Watchers and the Nephilim, why don't I show you?"

Cara eyes widened. "Show me? How?"

"Through a shared vision. All the moments of human history on earth are stored in the Flow, similar to a vast library of three-dimensional movie recordings. I believe learning works best through experience."

Cara stared at Constantina, incredulous. "*Seriously*? Let me guess, physics?"

"Of course, dear."

"Wait—does that mean you can see *anything*?" Cara frowned, thinking about the "Big Brother" implications.

Constantina patted her hand. "Worry not. There are certain rules around access. The Flow isn't meant to spy on humanity, but rather to archive its history. The Irin, our archivists, guard against any misuse. Only the High Council can request access, and it must be for a specific purpose like education."

Cara's shoulders relaxed. After all these years, she finally felt that the torture of her high school science classes had paid off. Her eyes lit up. "Does the Flow carry the future, as well as the past?"

Constantina shook her head. "Just the past. Only the Trinity Stones hold snippets of the future, but sharing that knowledge directly is expressly forbidden." She reached out to Cara. "Come take my hands. Are you ready?" A glow developed around Constantina that hadn't been there a minute ago.

"Ready as I'll ever be," Cara said and swallowed, placing her hands in

Constantina's. A warm, flowing energy coursed into one of her hands, circled around inside her, and exited through her other hand. Her nerve endings tingled with energy.

"Close your eyes."

Cara obeyed, and a soft breeze enveloped her, adding to the energy coursing through her. She heard the candles flicker on the altar in the distance. Soft tendrils of air swirled clockwise, sweeping her up and transporting her along a current, her body as light as a feather. She couldn't tell if she actually moved or if it was an out-of-body experience. She found the sensation both strange and comforting.

"You may open your eyes," said Constantina, and the breeze died down.

Cara found herself standing next to Constantina on a mountain, one among many surrounding them in the barren, rocky terrain. Dry air filled Cara's lungs with her first breath while her vision captured the dusty, ochre landscape contrasted by the pale blue of the sky above. Light shifted over the range, casting shadows above the mountaintops and into the valleys below. She felt small, lost among the vastness as wind whistled by yet left them untouched. She pivoted in a full circle, her arms outstretched as she took in the mountain desert beauty. The scene reminded Cara of an IMAX movie, only more real.

"Where are we?"

"Mount Hebron, the mountain used by the Watchers."

A man approached from the distance using a staff as he hiked up the mountain. His clothes confirmed for Cara that this image had occurred long ago. The man wore leather sandals and a homespun garment that was draped around him and held in place by a rope belt.

"He can't see or hear us, can he?"

"No, dear one. Yet, we'll be close enough to witness the upcoming exchange. You'll also be able to understand their words, despite the fact that in this life you don't speak Aramaic."

Cara looked over at Constantina, who appeared solid and fully human standing next to her. "How's that possible?"

"This vision is filtering through me, and as a result, you'll share my ability to understand the languages that I speak."

Okay, now that's seriously impressive. Cara nodded.

The man stopped and waited about fifteen feet away from where they watched. Within minutes, movement from above caused Cara to look up.

Thwap! Thwap! Thwap! She heard the powerful sound of wings beating the air as an angel descended before gently touching down on the ground in front of the man. The angel easily stood several feet taller than the man, his snow-white wings alone tripling his size. Cara stared, awestruck, by its luminescent beauty. She'd never expected to see an angel up close and personal.

"Enoch, why did you call me forth?" The angel asked the man. Constantina had been right—Cara understood every word. *Weird, but very cool.*

"My worry grows, Semyaza. You are the leader of the Watchers, so I'm taking my concerns to you. The Watchers have violated both of their covenants with God. Knowledge of the stars, weapons, and sorcery are being freely shared, and now there are many young girls heavy with child from your brethren. In my dreams, God has expressed his displeasure."

The angel's face darkened. "Why would God speak to you, rather than to me?"

"That I cannot answer, but the Nephilim you are spawning are an affront. They're selfish and evil, causing great harm to humanity. There will be consequences if you do not take control of this situation," Enoch said.

"You are but a human. How dare you insert yourself into our affairs," Semyaza scolded.

Enoch face crumpled in sadness. "I fear for you, Semyaza, and for the Watchers, as much as I fear for man. Mark my words, your entrance back into Heaven is no longer guaranteed."

"We shall see. Our meeting is concluded." With a few powerful thrusts, the angel launched himself into the air leaving behind an ochre cloud.

"The sin of pride will be your undoing," Enoch said under his breath while he wiped the dust from his eyes.

"Close your eyes, Cara." As soon as she did, the breeze swept her up and engulfed her, transporting them to another location.

When Cara blinked her eyes open, she stood in a beautiful desert valley. Sunlight streamed over the mountains from behind, creating shadows at her feet. There she saw a large boat nestled against the side of the rocks. The boat's construction consisted entirely of wood, but its most striking feature was its size, nearly three times the size of an ocean liner. What Cara found more astounding than the size of the boat, was the cargo. Pairs of animals lined up at the base, as far back as Cara's eyes could see.

Holy crap, she thought, gaping at Noah's Ark.

Constantina chimed in. "Let me take you back a little further, now that you know where the conversation will lead. Close your eyes so you don't get dizzy."

The breeze engulfed her again, and when it settled, Cara opened her eyes to the same valley. Darkness consumed the landscape, the Ark nowhere in sight. A brilliant, winged figure stood speaking in front of a campfire to a man of much smaller stature.

"Noah, great-grandson of Enoch," the angel said. "I carry an urgent message from the Lord our God. You must hide thyself! On His command, the whole world will be destroyed by deluge. You must save male and female pairs of all manner of beast."

"If that is what must be done, I shall do it. Why is the Lord so angry?"

"Man has strayed far from the fold. Our Father looks to cleanse the earth not only of man, but of the Nephilim abominations. The angel Semyaza and the rest of the Watchers have already received their punishment. They are locked away in darkness to await their fate during final Judgment."

Noah bowed his head. "Uriel, I will not fail. His will be done."

"Close your eyes," Constantina whispered, as the breeze kicked back up.

This time, when she opened her eyes, Cara recognized the warmth of the meeting room. Her hair settled back onto her shoulders, the breeze gone. She swayed for a moment and then sank down with Constantina onto the mat so that they were facing each other.

Cara tried to wrap her head around what she'd just witnessed. Leaning over her crossed legs, she blurted, "That was amazing, like we were there. When did that all happen?"

"Before the Great War. But depending on which religion you follow, the time-line and circumstances may be represented differently according to scriptures and texts. My representation to you is that of our reality and timeline. So, what did you learn from our brief journey?"

Cara took a deep breath and collected her thoughts, knowing she would need to remember it all. "Angels were sent to earth and broke the rules God set. Specifically, sharing knowledge and impregnating human women whose off-spring were called Nephilim. In anger, God locked up the angels and washed away the Nephilim in the Flood. Am I close?"

Constantina nodded as she sat with poise and perfect posture. *Like a yogi*, Cara thought.

"Very. Two hundred angels called the Watchers were sent to earth to help man, but were given certain boundaries. Angels, by their nature, have access to powerful knowledge that can usurp free will and the destiny of man. Therefore, we must be very careful what we reveal. Unfortunately, these angels, by their own free will, chose to disobey God. As a result they fell and became a form of fallen angel. But, unlike Lucifer and his minions, they were all captured and imprisoned before the Flood."

"It doesn't seem like the Nephilim were very pleasant," Cara said.

"True. These half-breed angels were corrupt. So, now you can imagine what

God thought of our request to create Nephilim as part of our plan," Constantina said with raised eyebrows.

Cara grinned. "The suggestion didn't go over well, did it?"

She gave her a wry smile. "Not at first, no it didn't. But we spent much time thinking through our final proposal. Remember Uriel, the angel who delivered the message to Noah?"

Cara nodded.

Turning her body to the left, Constantina squinted at the ceiling and then pointed. "See that warrior angel, right there?"

Cara's eyes followed the direction of her finger. She located the vignette she was supposed to find. "Is that him? The one with the sword next to the painting of the golden chariot?"

"Yes, very good. He is a Watcher, as well as the leader of the ninth Order of Angels, the incorruptible Powers. We, the Sanctus Angelorum, are the next generation of Watchers here on earth, and the Archangel Uriel is our angelic sponsor. The Guardians are Nephilim, *our* Nephilim."

Cara's eyes widened. "Nephilim? But, how—"

Constantina put a finger to Cara's lips and a small hand on her shoulder. "Shh, I will tell you. We knew we would need protection given our human vulnerability and the knowledge of what we were up against. We believed that with some adjustments, we could create the right kind of Nephilim, rather than the abominations of the past."

"What kind of adjustments?" It sounded like they'd need a lot of them from what little Cara knew.

"We proposed that only women of the Sanctus Angelorum could bear and raise these children fathered by Uriel's Order of Angels. We needed these births sanctioned by Heaven. We further agreed to control their number. They would carry both human and angelic characteristics, but they wouldn't be given the ability to procreate on their own."

Cara was fascinated, bursting with questions. "Wow. How are they created? Do the angels of the Powers take human form?"

"We offer a visitation prayer in the angelic language. Once granted, the result is an immaculate conception of a Nephil child, which is born in the same fashion as a human child."

Cara's eyes popped open wider. "Whoa! Really? An immaculate conception—as in the Virgin Mary brand of immaculate conception?" *This is even better than the Da Vinci Code!*

Constantina smiled, amused. "There are some answers that I cannot give you, but I will say it's similar to the Biblical interpretation with slightly different paternity. Each woman bears several Nephilim children during her human life-time. Presently, we have over three thousand Nephilim in our ranks."

Cara did some quick math. "How did you get so many with only a couple of children per lifetime?"

"Ah, one of the angelic characteristics—the Nephilim lifetime spans five hundred years. Their physiology slows their aging, so they age differently than a normal human after the age of twenty-one."

Cara continued to stare in a state of wide-eyed wonder. "Really? I'm sorry, I must sound like a broken record," she said, and then fired out questions. "What other characteristics can you share with me? Do Nephilim look like human babies when they're born? Do they have wings?"

Constantina held up her hand and let out peal of melodic feminine laughter. "Slow down, we have plenty of time. And, yes, they look like every other baby when they're born, because they're human . . . with a few added qualities. For instance, they're all fair of face, meaning they have angelic beauty. I cannot lie—there have been none that I've seen that are less than beautiful unless scarred in battle."

"So, you're saying they're all good-looking?" Cara asked, wondering about Chamuel.

Constantina nodded. "Yes, dear, they're all physically appealing. They also tend to be physically larger, both taller and more muscular than humans. Beyond physical characteristics, they have the ability to command energy and manipu-late the laws of physics as it relates to the physical world, while you and I use it for healing. Simply put, they possess a form of magic and can do special things. For instance, they can cloak themselves."

"What does *that* mean?" Cara asked.

"They can hide behind a veil of invisibility."

Well that explained a lot to Cara. When Michael had said Chamuel was unseen, she'd thought that he lurked around corners and watched her from a dis-tance. She found the realization that he could be much closer unsettling. "What else can they do?"

Constantina smiled. "I cannot give away all their secrets, but I will answer your other question. They do have wings, but they're not always visible."

"Do they hide them by cloaking them?" Cara said, venturing a guess.

"No, they're hidden inside themselves. One of the reasons Nephilim tend to be larger in scale is to compensate for their wingspan."

Cara sat dumbfounded, believing, without a doubt, that a hidden world oper-ated around her, including men who were half-angels. *Cool.*

Constantina continued her storytelling. "We chose the Nephilim to be our Guardians, since our foes aren't always human, as you've already seen."

A chill traveled through Cara. Yes, she knew exactly what Constantina meant. Humans were no match for demons.

"The Nephilim are the sole members of the Guardianship. They possess the battle resolve of their fathers, the angelic Order of the Powers, making them the perfect warriors to protect us. When Nephilim children reach sixteen, they graduate from the Angelorum Sanctuary and enter the Guardianship to begin their warrior training, which lasts until they're twenty-one years old. Then, they're officially Called and Marked."

Cara squinted. "What does it mean to be Called and Marked?" Having spent the last couple of days desperately trying to make sense of her life, Cara happily soaked up every detail Constantina gave.

"Cara, I think you missed your human calling as an attorney," Constantina teased and then popped up off the mat and reached for Cara's hand. Constantina pulled Cara up with an iron grip. Cara's eyes widened with surprise at the strength of the petite woman in front of her who'd just lifted her off the mat with one arm.

"You're very strong," Cara said, agape.

Constantina shrugged. "Perhaps, but I'm still flesh and blood like you." Without any further elaboration, she led Cara over to yet another vignette on the ceiling. "Let's save the topic of the Calling for later, since it's much more complex and something also very pertinent to your role as well. How about we talk about what it means to be Marked instead?"

Constantina pointed up to a grouping of twelve angels, eleven males and one lone female, each bearing an elaborate red tattoo on their chest.

"Are those Nephilim?" Cara asked. They looked like angels to her.

"Yes. Also, the number holds significance. Only one in twelve Nephilim is born female."

For some reason Cara had assumed all the Guardians were male. She gave herself a kick for setting feminism back a few decades.

"When the Guardian takes their oath to serve the Guardianship, they're Marked with red tattoos on the pectoral muscle closest to the heart. The Mark is comprised of the sigil representing their Angelic name over the crest of the Guardianship. A similar process is followed for Messengers, except their crest represents their father's family lineage instead."

Cara narrowed her eyes. "Will I be getting a tattoo?" *God, I hope not.* Cara didn't mind tattoos on others but didn't relish one of her own.

"Actually, the Soul Seekers are never Marked on the outside. Even though you accept a Calling, it's only the Guardians and the Messengers who are truly ever in our direct service. If you ask politely, I'm sure Michael would be happy to show you his." Constantina smiled.

Relieved, Cara let out the breath she hadn't realized she'd been holding. "Can I ask a few more questions about the Guardians?"

Constantina nodded. "Of course."

"What are the Nephilim like as people? Do they act like us? Have the same feelings, emotions?"

"They're a very loyal and passionate group with their own subculture. They're raised to be that way, having the best of both of their parents. The differences between us and the Nephilim are not only physiological but also psychological. Mainly, this is due to their longevity. As a result, they tend to stick to their own kind."

Maybe that's one reason why Chamuel hadn't revealed himself yet, Cara thought.

"You mentioned the Guardians can live up to five hundred years. How old is my Guardian, Chamuel?"

"Let me see." Constantina paused to think. "He's almost one hundred and fifty."

Cara didn't know why that surprised her, but it did. "So, how old would he look if I saw him on the street?"

Again, Constantina paused to think. "I believe that he would appear to be only a few biological years older than you."

"So he'd look about my age?"

"Yes, dear, I believe so," Constantina said, covering a yawn. "We should probably take a break for the evening. I'm weary from my travels."

Cara looked at her watch and noticed it was almost midnight. She'd forgotten that Constantina had a long journey prior to her arrival to the penthouse.

"Thank you for all your help," Cara replied, grateful for the detailed explanations. And even more grateful that she wasn't as lost.

Constantina reached out to touch Cara's arm. "There's one more thing regarding your Guardian Chamuel that I must mention to you before we end this evening."

"What's that?" Cara asked, taken aback by the sudden reference to Chamuel.

"You're forbidden from becoming romantically entangled with him while the Trinity exists. We believe romantic attachment compromises the safety of a Trinity. The penalty is great for the Guardian who crosses that boundary."

Cara eyebrows flew up. "I thought you said they couldn't procreate?" It surprised her that Constantina would think she'd even consider the possibility. Then again, she'd been asking questions about him.

Constantina's melodic laughter escaped before she could cover her mouth with her hand. Clearing her throat, she said, "I'm sorry I wasn't clear. They may not be able to father children, but they're fully equipped to, um—conduct a physical relationship."

A beet-red blush spread across Cara's cheeks. "My bad. Has this ever happened before, a Soul Seeker getting involved with her Guardian?" Now, *this* was a good reason for her Guardian to keep his distance. Perhaps it would be better if they never met. *Hot or not, he's off-limits.*

"I'm afraid it's happened enough over the centuries for the necessity of the rule."

Cara arched a brow, her face cooler now. "Good to know. You mentioned 'while the Trinity exists' . . . at some point does it cease to exist?"

"Remember, the Guardian will most likely outlive both the Messenger and the Seeker, and ultimately be part of multiple Trinities. Some missions are lifelong and others are finite, causing a Trinity to end either in death or the successful conclusion of a mission."

"Right . . . that makes sense," Cara said, now truly grasping the impact of the Guardian's role within the Trinity. "So, are all Guardians off-limits to me or just mine?" *Better to be clear*, she thought.

"Just yours." Constantina tried to stifle another yawn with the back of her hand. "Let us continue in the morning when Michael arrives, shall we?"

"Yes, and thanks again. This is a lot to absorb. I appreciate your patience." Cara was grateful for the day she'd just spent with Constantina. Relief filled her now that she had answers to many of her questions.

Constantina touched her shoulder. "You're making it easy, my dear," she said before leading them in a closing prayer.

Cara hadn't realized the depth of her exhaustion until she stood on legs filled with pins and needles. She waited for Constantina to snuff out the candles, then she dragged her weary body down the stairs after her.

Upon opening the door, they were greeted by a very hungry whippet.

Chapter 23

WITH A FORK MIDWAY to her mouth, Cara's head turned at the sound of the doorbell. She shot a look at Constantina and got up from the kitchen island to answer the front door. Chloe bounded out of the kitchen ahead of her, tail wagging.

Cara looked through the peephole, and smiled. Michael.

She pulled open the door. "Hi, come in."

Dipping his head down, he gave her a quick peck on the cheek in greeting as Chloe tried to jump up in between them.

"Down, Princess, no one is trying to steal your man," Cara told Chloe before turning back to Michael. "Would you like something to eat?"

Cara had made her signature breakfast consisting of coffee, scrambled eggs, and toast, which exhausted her morning repertoire of menu options. Cereal and frozen waffles were her guest's only other choices.

He gave her a wry smile. "I downed a protein smoothie before I left." Then he leaned in and winked. "I've been up since six and already put in a full workout."

The night they'd met she'd been impressed when he'd spoken to her about his workout schedule. She'd confessed to being woefully inadequate by comparison with a mild routine of three-mile runs a couple of times per week.

She gave him a small shove. "Show off."

He just chuckled and reached down to greet his four-legged fan club.

Cara's nose caught the warm notes of amber and rosewood in his now-familiar cologne, and she noted the smoothness of his clean-shaven face. How is it that he managed to look stylish, even in exercise gear, without ever appearing to put in a conscious effort? His almost-black hair was stylishly mussed, while she had a serious case of bed head concealed within her ponytail.

"How did yesterday go?" he asked, following her.

She smiled. "Really well. You were right. Constantina is amazing. She's down here."

They moved through the double doors into the kitchen.

"Michael, dear one, welcome." Constantina rose, bestowing him with a double-cheek kiss before sitting back down to her coffee. "When we're finished eating, I'd like to retire to the meeting room upstairs to introduce Cara to the basics of her training. I believe it will benefit you both."

Cara looked forward to resuming her training. Yesterday's session had been so intense, spurring a shift within her as she eased into the acceptance of her new normal. She wanted to discover the gifts and abilities buried within her, especially if they could help the people she loved and ultimately tip the balance toward good in the world. There weren't any rules preventing her from being both a banker and a healer, were there? Assuming she could get another banking job . . .

Cara cleared the dishes into the dishwasher, and they headed to the library. Filing up the secret stairs to the meeting room, they left Chloe asleep on the library couch below.

Constantina lit the candles on the altar before they convened in the center of the floor and sat. Eyes closed, she led the opening prayer to the Angels to protect and guide them in their training. When done, she gazed at them and nodded. With a clap of her small hands, she began.

"I'd like to share a series of energy-related exercises. We'll start with something simple and a bit fun—how to use energy to tell if someone is telling you the truth."

A small thrill went through Cara. That did sound fun, not to mention extremely useful.

"When you want to sense the truth," said Constantina, "use your sense of taste—literally. You breathe in the energy surrounding a person, which extends on average between two to three feet from their physical body." She traced the air around them with her hands as she spoke.

"Michael, I want you to tell Cara something true." Constantina then turned to her. "Cara, after he tells you his truth, breathe in his energy. Like this . . . " She ran her fingertips gently over Cara's forehead and down over her cheeks. "Focus on absorbing it through your skin right here. Then wait and notice the flavor on your tongue. Okay, Michael . . . " Constantina prompted.

"I grew up in Chicago," he said.

Cara did what Constantina told her. She let his words wash over her face, noting any taste on her tongue. There wasn't a particular flavor that she noticed, just sweetness. She nodded when she finished her assessment.

"Now, tell her something false."

"I have a brother and a sister."

Cara repeated the process, and this time her tongue tasted bitter.

"Did you taste a difference?" Constantina asked.

Cara nodded vigorously, her eyes wide. Then a thought struck her. "Constantina, do demons have a taste? Right before the demon attacked me, I tasted . . . tar." She wrinkled her nose in disgust.

A startled look passed over Constantina's face. "Yes. That's exactly how evil tastes to me."

Cara looked over at Michael, who shrugged and answered the unasked question. "I haven't experienced that yet."

"Count your blessings, dear one. Let's try this again. Make up one true and one false statement and then let Cara guess the difference."

Michael gave Cara a blank stare. "I'm a fantastic singer." He paused to watch Cara. She nodded for him to move on, and he said, "I graduated from Yale University with a BA in English."

Michael and Constantina waited.

"Michael, I'm so sorry you can't carry a tune, but I'm impressed by your educational background."

He gave her a crooked smile. "By the way, I only have a younger sister, no other boys in my family."

"Very good." Constantina beamed like a proud parent. "Okay, now switch. Cara, it's your turn. Tell Michael something true about yourself."

"I own a car."

Michael motioned when he was done.

"Something false: I've successfully run the New York City Marathon," she said, and he nodded.

"Now guess the next two, Michael." Constantina tipped her head at Cara.

"I love mid-century modern furniture." Cara waited for his response. When he nodded, she said, "I make a fabulous smoothie."

Michael responded, "I guess you will be swapping out the furniture downstairs in the living room one of these days, and I'd happily try one of your smoothies."

The corner of Cara's mouth quirked. "Anytime."

"So, what did you taste?" Constantina asked Cara first.

"I clearly tasted sweetness for truth, and bitterness for falsehood," she said.

Michael nodded. "My experience was similar."

"Very good. The tastes will get stronger with practice to the point you'll find richness and nuance in the flavors beyond truth and lies, but also across many emotions."

Cara, invigorated by the lesson, could barely contain her amazement. Who would have thought you could actually taste the truth? It seemed so intuitive and simple.

"Let's take a break and then we'll move on to channeling energy. Like what Cara did when she encountered the Sentinel," Constantina said.

Cara's footsteps echoed across the wood floor in the kitchen as she raced toward the counter to scoop up her vibrating cell phone. A text from Sienna lit up the screen.

"Shit," Cara blurted.

Michael and Constantina turned their heads to look at her from the island where they ate lunch.

"What is it, dear?" Constantina asked.

"I'm supposed to meet my best friend Sienna tonight for a belated birthday celebration." In all the excitement, Cara had forgotten about her plans. She watched a look pass between Constantina and Michael before his eyes closed and his face fell into a look of peaceful contemplation.

He opened his eyes twenty seconds later. "No warnings in the Flow regarding Cara. I'll check during the evening, but she should be fine."

Turning to Cara, Constantina said, "Go out and enjoy yourself. We'll contact you if anything changes." Glancing at the clock, she motioned to the door. "Let's get back to work to finish our lesson in time for Cara to prepare for her evening."

Michael volunteered to take Chloe for a quick walk before they continued, while Cara accompanied Constantina back up to the welcoming faces of the angels gazing down from the ceiling of the meeting room.

Cara's mind shifted to her plans for the evening and was suddenly aware of the potential for her two worlds to collide. "Constantina, what do I say to people, like Sienna, about all this? Mr. Gladstone suggested that I tell them I'm house-sitting."

Constantina blinked. With a look of innocence in her ocean-blue eyes, she said, "That's a very good suggestion. It's the truth. You're caring for it. She need not know about the change in ownership. As an alternative, you'd be an asset to the Watson & Haskins investment team, given your background. They're a company owned entirely by us."

Cara's eyes lit up. She loved what she did for a living. She'd just hated her boss. "Thank you. I'd like to continue to work. I'll consider it." Her spirits lightened.

Michael came up the stairs two at a time. "Okay, our four-legged friend is taken care of and resting comfortably on the library sofa under a blanket."

Returning to the center of the meeting room, they dropped back down onto the mat and faced one another. Constantina suggested a few cleansing breaths to start.

"Next, we'll cover energy healing. Cara, you've seen me do this before, but I'll explain it this time as I demonstrate. Remember the prayer I opened with earlier?"

Cara nodded.

"That was a prayer of protection, which is the first step. It can be either spoken silently or out loud. It's best to use the angelic language since it can be condensed into fewer words, but any language will do since it's the intent that matters." Constantina spoke a few sounds that must have been angelic words. Either way, Cara had never heard anything like it before.

"The second step is connecting to the Flow. Imagine reaching up with the top of your head and then breathing down the energy, welcoming it inside you."

Constantina closed her eyes and her chest heaved slightly. A pillar of bright light traveled down through the ceiling, connecting to the top of Constantina's head as she sat.

Cara eyes widened as she watched the threads of energy pulsing down through the glow and into Constantina.

She opened her eyes, but the light remained. "The third step is coalescence. In simple terms, the energy is swirling around my heart. Through my intent, I must add love," Constantina said and then looked at Michael.

"Can you remove the blade I requested, dear one?"

Blade, what blade? Cara wondered with alarm.

Michael moved to sit closer to Constantina and then removed a small dagger from inside the pocket of his hoodie. He unsheathed the dagger before handing it to her.

"What are you doing?" Cara asked, her heart kicking in her chest.

Michael leaned over and reached for her knee, the pressure of his strong, tapered fingers were reassuring. "It's okay," he said softly. "I've done this before." Yet somehow that wasn't quite enough for Cara.

He moved closer to Constantina and pushed up his sleeve, holding up the exposed underside of his rippled forearm.

The pillar of light still funneling down from overhead, Constantina took the blade and passed it over Michael's arm. Cara saw him wince as his bright-red blood flowed from the gash. Her heart hammered and she leaned back, subconsciously trying to distance herself.

Constantina leaned forward and placed her hands on Michael's shoulders. Suddenly, they disappeared from view, engulfed in bright light. Cara suspected the same phenomenon had occurred with the Sentinel, except she hadn't done it on purpose.

A moment later the light disappeared and they were both visible again.

Michael turned to her to show her his arm, now perfect, the gash gone. "See, I told you."

Cara's jaw hung open. "I'll be able to do that?"

"Yes. Now it's your turn."

A tingle of anxiety passed through her. "My turn? Now? I don't want to hurt anyone," she said, scooting crab-like even further back on the mat. What if she couldn't do it?

Michael grabbed her shoulders gently, pulling her forward while locking his gaze on her from under his mahogany eyebrows. "Hey, don't worry. I've gotten my ass kicked much worse than this in the dojo. That was nothing. Just trust us."

He planted a quick kiss with warm lips on her forehead to soothe her before he settled back down next to her. Even though they were only friends, she liked his openly affectionate manner, as if he knew that's what she needed. His touch held a protectiveness that offered her security and elicited her trust in him.

"Don't be afraid, dear one. Get comfortably seated," Constantina said.

Tentatively, Cara took a deep breath and followed her direction.

"Now, ask for protection from our Creator and his angels, banning any forces with ill intent. Envision yourself surrounded by their protective light."

Okay, she could do that. Cara mentally said her silent prayer.

"Are you ready to call down the Flow?"

Cara nodded. *As ready as I'll ever be.*

"Picture reaching up through the top of your head and then breathe out."

Cara closed her eyes and pictured a trap door, like on a jack-in-the-box, opening on the top of her head. An imaginary hand catapulted straight up into the stratosphere as she let out her breath.

"Now, breathe in and pull down the Flow."

Cara wrapped her imaginary hand around the Flow, pulling it down with force then tucking the hand back inside her head. Her body rocked and her eyes flew open when the blazing light slammed through her crown. The light traveled into her chest, where it settled, awaiting her next instruction. Its path connected her head to her chest, filling her with a tingling vibration. Had she really done that?

She stared wide-eyed at Constantina and Michael. They were smiling at her.

"Well done," said Constantina. "Now imagine the energy swirling around your heart, and fill it with your love."

Without needing much thought, Cara spun the energy inside her chest, and she visualized her feelings for those she loved. Exhilaration filled her senses until her nerve endings crackled.

In a lightning-quick move, Constantina slashed her own forearm. "Now heal me," she commanded.

Instinct propelled Cara forward, her hands latching onto Constantina's small shoulders. The energy swirling inside her blazed out through her hands, engulfing them in a ball of light. Traveling in a circuit from her, into Constantina, and then back, the energy warmed her from within. As she held on to Constantina, the energy traveled back into her and grew stronger until it became the same as the energy leaving her. The sensation overwhelmed Cara with happiness.

"You can drop your hands now. When the energy coming in feels the same as the energy leaving, that's the signal the healing process is complete."

Cara removed her hands from Constantina's shoulders and the light disappeared, but Cara remained invigorated. That had been so much different than her experience with the Sentinel on the street. From the outside, it looked the same, but what she'd experienced inside had been so much different. Constantina sat before her unharmed and beaming. "Now say a silent prayer of thanks."

Thank you! Cara launched herself forward and threw her arms around Constantina's petite shoulders, the smell of lavender wafting up from her hair as she hugged her. "That was the most amazing thing I've ever felt. Thank you."

"It's always been inside you, dear one. I only showed you how to unlock it on your own." She squeezed her back, and Cara released her. Constantina rubbed her hands together. "Later, I'll show you how to temper the energy to use it for smaller remedies and how to conceal the light."

Cara cast a glance at Michael. "Wait. Doesn't Michael get a turn?"

Constantina smiled at Michael. "His gifts are many, but not the same as yours, and vice versa. Healing isn't one of his gifts."

Cara looked back at him and suddenly wondered what other gifts Michael had outside the standard-issue Messenger abilities Constantina had mentioned the day before.

Michael peered at her sheepishly with his fingers interlaced in front of him, and shrugged.

"Enough chatter, dear ones. Next, I want to attune your empathetic abilities to read and taste emotions." Constantina clapped her hands together. "Let's get started."

Bring it on, Cara thought. She was ready.

Chapter 24

CARA STEPPED OUT of the taxi in front of Raphael's in SoHo feeling like she'd gotten a get-out-of-jail-free card. The last couple of days had been both exhilarating and exhausting. As each hour passed, she eased more into the new life that had been offered to her, but she also welcomed a reprieve from the impending responsibilities. Helping good triumph of over evil could wait for a night.

She was glad that Constantina and Michael agreed it was safe enough for her to keep her plans with Sienna to celebrate her birthday, which felt like a lifetime ago. The hardest part of the evening for Cara would be *not* talking about any of this with Sienna. They'd shared everything ever since they were teenagers.

At least she solved the problem of how to explain the letter to Sienna. With a stroke of brilliance, she'd come up with an acceptable half-truth for Sienna while browsing through the bookshelves in the library. Cara was shocked when she'd picked one first edition after another of all the major titles of the eighteenth and nineteenth centuries. Her fingers caressed the soft leather covers, unable to believe her find. Charles Dickens, the Brontë sisters, and Jane Austen were only a few of her favorite authors she'd found. She decided she'd tell Sienna her grandmother had left her a rare book collection—which was true in a sense—without telling her about her change in location. She could make the apartment caretaker role work to eliminate questions about her new residence while she explained her pursuit for a new job. But that lie could wait for another week or so.

For tonight, she would just live normally, painting the town with her best friend and enjoying her new Christian Louboutin shoes, which had survived her sprint through Lower Manhattan no worse for wear.

Cara approached the hostess, a young woman in her early twenties who looked like any number of struggling models or actresses working in the NYC restaurant business. She looked up and smiled as Cara approached.

"May I help you?"

"Hi, yes, seven o'clock reservation for Sienna Sargent?"

The hostess perked up at the mention of Sienna's name. "Ah, yes. She hasn't arrived yet. Would you like me to seat you or would you like to wait at the bar?"

"Thanks, I'll wait at the bar." Cara handed her red swing coat to the hostess in exchange for a coat-check ticket.

It was still on the early side, and the restaurant was only partially full. Knowing Sienna, they would be there for several hours, then bar-hop to meet friends the rest of the evening. Counter to the late-night Manhattan dinner culture, Cara and Sienna both enjoyed eating dinner early.

Plenty of bar stools sat empty, with only a party of four having drinks, and a gay couple chatting quietly over what looked like a couple of glasses of champagne. By eight thirty, the place would be jammed.

Built at the turn of the century, the restaurant's bathrooms were located at the very top of a narrow, spiral staircase in the center of the restaurant next to the bar. Obviously, an addition made at some point in the very long history of the building, and one that would never be considered up to code today. The first floor still retained its original tin ceiling and late-Victorian charm.

Cara eyed the staircase. *Better to take this on sober than after a few glasses of wine*, she thought. She carefully climbed up the narrow stairs in her new heels.

The bathroom was small and tight, but the mirror was well lit. She checked her reflection. She had taken some extra time to give her hair a full-bodied wave, making it fall down below her shoulders.

Constantina's energy treatment had helped, allowing Cara's makeup to cover the residual bruising on her neck from the attack and the dark circles from the long and mentally draining last two days. Giving herself a once-over, Cara concluded she looked just fine, with the smoky eyeliner, mascara for her long lashes, and her favorite red lipstick—all showing her china-doll skin to perfection. She smiled at the reflection of her new black dress—another splurge, like the shoes. It hugged the shape of her small waist and hips perfectly, giving tasteful emphasis to her nicely endowed chest. Sienna would be pleasantly surprised.

She stood back and breathed a sigh of relief. Why was she continually surprised when she found no physical evidence of the changes happening inside her? Outwardly, no one would ever know her world had turned upside down.

Cara gripped the pole tightly on her perilous journey back down the spiral staircase. Rounding the last turn, her breath escaped in a large whoosh when she spotted the man heading for a seat at the bar. Not only did the sight of him catch her attention, but the warm wave of energy that followed sent a prickling sensation from the top of her head all the way down to the bottom of her spine.

His dark-blond hair fell in waves around his chiseled face, touching down just below his shoulders. Well over six feet tall, he towered over everyone else in the bar. He wore a black V-neck sweater tucked into jeans that hugged the contours of his muscled body. It wasn't until he looked up and his vivid, crystal-blue eyes locked on hers that the shock of recognition washed over her . . .

Right before her foot missed the last step, and she took a header off of the stairs.

In a blur, strong arms caught her before she hit the ground. A jolt of electricity made her heart skip a beat as her fingers grazed the warmth of a massive bicep under black cashmere. She was close enough to catch his clean, citrus scent mixed with something deliciously male. He pulled her up onto her feet.

"I have you," he whispered in her ear, his warm breath caressing her cheek as he steadied her. He smiled warmly, and the color of his eyes was even more startling up close. "Are you okay?" His voice was soft and intimate, a tone she would've used only with her closest friends.

A flush hit Cara's cheeks as she stared dumbfounded at the Greek god from the subway; she tried to coax her mouth to form words. Struck by the beauty and kindness in his eyes, for a split second she believed she could happily drown in them.

"New shoes," she mumbled mindlessly. "Thank you . . . " Trying to get her bearings, she did the only safe thing she could think of—she turned and walked briskly toward the front of the restaurant.

Great. I see the most beautiful man on the planet and make a total ass out of myself. It figures.

Sienna walked into the restaurant or, more accurately, made her entrance, while Cara muttered to herself.

"Hi sweetie! Happy birthday!" Sienna ran to Cara in way-too-high heels. She carried a huge Prada handbag and wore some runway creation that wasn't suitable for normal humans. It looked like an orange, asymmetrical box in the shape of dress. Cara knew the outfit would look ridiculous on her, but Sienna managed to make it wearable and incredibly chic. She threw her arms around Cara and bestowed a kiss on each cheek, European style.

"Hello," Cara squeezed out and then stood back to do a surreptitious assessment.

Sienna's long, jet-black hair was pulled back in a chignon using chopsticks to hold it in place—at least that's what Cara thought they were. With her hair back, Sienna's sky-blue eyes and thick black eyelashes were on full display—her eyes looked *huge*. Despite her unconventional apparel selection for the evening, Sienna looked stunning. She'd always been the center of attention when they were growing up. Some things never changed.

"You look great! I love that dress, Carissima." Sienna glanced down at Cara's chest. "I'm glad you listened to me. It does a nice job of packaging your wares."

Cara rolled her eyes and smiled. This was high praise coming from Sienna.

Sienna turned to the hostess. "Gabrielle, *darling*, it's so lovely to see you again! Did you get me my favorite table?"

"Of course. Anything for you. The chef prepared something special for you this evening. He'll be out later to greet you personally." She led them back toward their table.

Gabrielle and Sienna were lost in chatter in front of her while Cara trailed behind.

Passing through the bar, Cara spotted the blue-eyed Greek god seated on a barstool. The handsome outline of his face and the luminescence of his skin magnetized her, propelling the beat of her heart. The curve of his back called to her, begging her fingers to run down his spine.

Whoa! She gave herself a mental kick and did her best to sneak past him unseen.

Just when she thought she'd made it, he turned and leaned back. Catching her eye, he smiled and said quietly, "Have a nice dinner."

Trapped in his gaze, her feet kept walking. She turned her head just in time to avoid running into a man who was getting up from his chair.

Great. Another suave move for the home team, she thought, and instantly blushed. Thankfully, this time he couldn't see her face. She slipped into the booth facing the bar, opposite Sienna.

"What's wrong? You look distracted," Sienna asked.

"Nothing. I'm just the klutz of the century. Before you arrived, I tripped on the last stair of the spiral staircase coming down from the bathroom."

Sienna's face registered alarm, and she reached for Cara's arm. "Are you hurt?"

Cara sighed. "I'm fine. A tall, gorgeous, blond man caught me."

"Really? Where is he?" Sienna asked, ready to turn around and gawk.

"He's at the bar." Cara glanced to where he'd been sitting—but his seat was empty. "That's strange. He was there a minute ago."

Sienna leaned across the table. "I think you should give him your number if he comes back. No offense, honey, but you could use a date."

Cara rolled her eyes. "Thanks."

The waitress arrived a moment later, but rather than take their drink order, she presented them with one of the more expensive bottles of red wine on the menu. Placing it on the table, she looked at Cara and smiled. "A gentleman at the bar sent this bottle with his compliments. He understands you're celebrating a birthday." She set the two glasses down on the table and proceeded to uncork the bottle. Cara and Sienna looked at each other, stunned.

"Is he still here?" Cara inquired, now realizing her disappointment when she'd thought he'd disappeared. Butterflies tickled her stomach, and relief washed over her. As embarrassed as she was, she didn't want him to leave. At least until she knew his name.

"He was here a minute ago," the waitress said, and they all turned around to look at the empty seat at the bar. "Let me check with the bartender." She left them to their wine.

"Carissima, I like him already—classy move. He must have thought you were hot to drop some serious coin on this wine. You better not let him out the front door without a number. Oh crap . . . He wasn't wearing a wedding ring, was he?"

Cara wrinkled her brow, annoyed. "I didn't notice during my death-defying midair acrobatics. It if makes any difference, I didn't pick up a married vibe. But men like him don't normally look at me."

Sienna slapped her hand on the table. "Yes, they do. You're just too oblivious to see it. You've probably passed up thousands of opportunities to meet someone gorgeous. You just don't pay attention. My new name for you is Clueless Cara. You need to stop looking at the ground when you walk and look at people."

"I wasn't looking at the ground, which is why I almost face-planted."

"And look at who you met. Case in point," was Sienna's smug reply. Then she leaned across the table closer to Cara, wearing a self-satisfied grin. "Maybe that wish I made for you on your birthday will come true, and you can finally dump that married loser Kai."

Cara narrowed her eyes. "He's my friend, not my lover, and you don't dump your friends."

"Some friend," she shot back. "He didn't even call you on your birthday."

Cara gave Sienna a sheepish look. "He called the next morning and sent a card." She hated when Sienna bashed Kai and she had to jump to his defense. Then she took the chance to deflect Sienna. "Speaking of doomed romances—how's Oliver?"

"Not fair. You know he's only my Hamptons connection with a few fringe benefits. However, there's this hot model I met in Paris, who, astoundingly enough, is straight and lives in New York."

"Well, now that sounds promising," Cara snorted with another roll of her eyes.

Sienna gave her a hurt look. "Hey, you know I'm not shopping for anything serious right now. I'm not ready. Mark crushed my heart. I need to have fun for a while."

Sienna and Mark had dated for four years. Last summer, when all signs pointed to a proposal, he had left her for another woman he'd met in the Hamptons. He'd been the stereotypical handsome, rich, arrogant Wall Street banker. But, to his credit, he'd always been generous and treated Sienna well enough. Sienna seemed very happy with him, but he'd let her down in the end. Secretly, Cara was happy when their relationship ended, suspecting he'd been cheating on Sienna for some time. Cara wanted more for her friend—someone who could make her happy and treasure her for who she was.

The waitress returned. "I'm sorry. He left. But he asked me to give this to you." She handed Cara a small, neatly folded piece of paper.

She accepted it and thanked the waitress.

Sienna stared at her with impatience. "Well, what're you waiting for? Your next birthday?"

Cara slowly unfolded the paper, revealing a note written in neat, looping script, and read it to Sienna. "'It would be my pleasure if you would meet me here on Tuesday evening at eight o'clock for dinner.'" There was no signature.

"Excuse me one second," Cara got up from the table and went to the bar. Now she really needed to know his name. She called the bartender over. "Do you remember the tall man with the long, blond hair who was sitting here earlier?"

"Sure. He's a regular. Comes in for dinner a couple times a month and eats at the bar," the bartender replied.

"Do you know his name?"

The bartender paused a moment to think then frowned. "I don't think he's ever told me. For what it's worth, he seems like a nice guy. Very low-key and friendly. Generous tipper."

"Is he always alone?" she asked, stepping into more dangerous territory.

He shrugged, cleaning a glass with his bar towel. "He's been alone whenever I've seen him."

Cara thanked him and returned to her table.

She slipped back into the booth across from Sienna. "The bartender doesn't know his name."

"So, you're going to meet him, right?"

"Well, I have a couple of days to think about it . . . "

"You'd better go. Otherwise, I'll show up and meet him," Sienna said, dead serious. "Listen, not to get all princess-y on you, but this is what fairy tales are made of. Don't overthink it; just do it."

"Okay, Mother Goose, let's order," Cara replied, thinking she'd had her fair share of fairy-tale moments lately, and not all of them good.

Sienna looked at Cara over the menu. "Okay, and then I want to hear what happened with that letter."

Cara sighed. *Let the games begin.*

Chapter 25

CHAMUEL CLOAKED AND EXITED Raphael's detected, but unseen, by the Guardians sent to relieve him. If it hadn't been for Isaac, he'd still be in there instead of taking his dinner to go. Normally, he would've stopped to greet the Tri-State guys, but the last thing he needed was to be seen out of uniform.

He had been surprised when Constantina had called earlier to tell him Cara planned to meet a friend for a belated birthday celebration at one of his neighborhood restaurants. That's when he'd gotten his crazy idea: to dress in street clothes and watch her from inside the restaurant. He had just ordered when Isaac texted to say they needed speak ASAP, and that Zeke and Noah were waiting outside the restaurant, ready to take over his surveillance for the evening.

It was at that point that he had done the unthinkable and sent her the note.

When he'd spotted her descending the spiral staircase, she'd unexpectedly taken his breath away—again. Sheer instinct had taken over next when she'd slipped and fell forward. Before he could even think, she was in his arms. The electricity that had passed between them when he'd touched her and she'd gazed into his eyes was stronger than when he'd cradled her unconscious body after the attack. When their eyes had locked, everything else receded.

Their souls touched.

Could it be soul recognition? he wondered, thinking of a phenomenon he'd learned of in his training as an adolescent Nephilim.

A rush of heat raced through his veins, awakening the full force of his desire and unleashing something he'd long since suppressed. Cara was even more enticing wide-awake than unconscious, and the thought terrified him. He'd only suspected it before, but he was sure of it now: she threatened to break through the shell he'd spent years building around himself. For the last couple of decades—damn it, who was he kidding, the last century—he'd been impervious to the lure of a beautiful woman and living a monk-like existence ever since . . . that fateful night.

Breaking his celibacy was one thing, but that paled in comparison to what would happen to him if the High Council found out. Cara was expressly forbidden to him. The law left no room for misinterpretation. A Trinity Guardian was forbidden to engage in romantic conduct with any member of the same Trinity.

Period. End of story. His punishment would be severe for crossing the line, least of which included one hundred years of mandatory imprisonment.

He released a deep sigh. Why did he choose to recklessly barrel down this path and send her that note? The wine, well . . . okay, that could be easily construed as a gesture without strings.

But, dinner?

His eyes widened. What if soul recognition was the impetus behind his lunacy?

Is that the inexplicable force driving me forward? Is she my soul mate? He couldn't think of anything that could fuel the strength of his desire so powerfully that it transcended even his fear of punishment. Or maybe he just deserved more punishment for his recklessness.

His head hurt with all the questions spinning around inside it. Besides having much to lose personally, meeting her again under false pretenses would be unforgivable. His job as her Guardian was to protect her, and so far he'd done that sight unseen. But inevitably, they'd be in a situation where she would see him. Despite that, he hungered for her to have the opportunity to know him first as a man.

He shook his head. This could all end with disastrous consequences.

But then he smiled like an idiot. The chance to feel her lips against his may be worth a century of imprisonment.

Absorbed in his thoughts as he walked home with his dinner, he nearly passed the doorstep of his Greene Street loft.

He checked his watch. Isaac had given him thirty minutes to get home before he called. He had ten minutes left.

Chamuel had bought his fifth-floor loft in the early seventies when New York City real estate was dirt cheap. He owned the loft under his current human identity, Simon Young, as was standard practice for the Guardians. Given the Nephilim longevity, choosing multiple, alternate human identities over their lifetimes came in handy for financial and estate dealings outside of the Angelorum. And there was no denying that Simon Young looked a lot better on a driver's license than Chamuel, Guardian of the Angelorum.

The generously sized loft contained an art studio where he spent time painting.

He'd always been a lover of the arts, and given his lifespan, he'd had many years to hone his talent. Many of his paintings, which he had framed himself, hung on the walls throughout his apartment. He'd appointed the rest of the apartment tastefully with a mix of antiques and modern pieces for a comfortable, chic, and eclectic vibe. But his true joy was his kitchen.

Chamuel had spent a small fortune designing and installing a chef's kitchen, and, despite his desire for dining out at the bar at places like Raphael's every couple of weeks, he loved to cook—he found it therapeutic. Most recently, he'd studied in Paris during the nineties while on hiatus from the Guardianship, and over the last century he had mastered the art of cooking in many styles. Up until a week ago, when he'd moved back full-time to his loft, he'd only cooked here occasionally. For years he'd made dinner on Saturday nights at the Connecticut Tri-State house, trying out new ideas and serving multiple courses with wine pairings to his appreciative brethren.

Chamuel sat down at the kitchen island to eat his meal.

It's only dinner, he thought, as he took a bite of his hanger steak. *What am I doing?* He shook his head. *I'm not thinking with my brain. I must be insane.*

Despite his misgivings, he couldn't contain his excitement for his potential dinner date. Then the thought struck him that she might not show up on Tuesday, eliciting a stab of disappointment. He was a stranger, after all. Mentally he kicked himself.

Get a grip, man.

His cell phone rang, a welcome interruption from the mental gymnastics he inflicted on himself. He glanced at the caller ID and answered.

"Isaac, what's so important?"

"We have another problem. There's been an attack on our Seeker in Boston, and her Guardian has been taken."

As if a rogue Nephil and Cara getting spotted by a Sentinel and attacked by demon hadn't been enough on their collective plate over the last two days. Isaac had sent the report to Chamuel last night, and no one within the Guardianship had been anywhere near Cara or the Sentinel. Also, the only energy detected near Cara over the last two days had been his. Energy footprints don't lie and can't be replicated. The report left Chamuel absolutely perplexed.

"Xavier has been taken?" Chamuel was concerned about the attack and another missing Guardian.

"Yes," Isaac replied, "can you get up to Boston? Given the sensitivity of this situation, I don't want to alarm the rest of the team. With the exception of Zeke and Noah, many of them just left to go to the Angelorum Sanctuary for the spring induction ceremony at the Guardian Academy. I've already spoken to Constantina, and she's cleared it."

When Isaac called him yesterday and confirmed that Constantina was the Council member sent to mentor Cara, Chamuel hadn't been surprised. Given his history with Constantina, he realized that he'd been hand-selected for this assignment. He'd suspected as much when he'd spoken to Isaac after the Sentinel incident.

"I'll drive up this evening and see the Boston Seeker first thing in the morning. Any more news on the rogue Nephil?"

"None. All the House leaders are double checking. But you know as well as I do, our technology is flawless, and none of us can hide or manipulate the data. I'm quickly starting to think we have a Nephil who exists outside of the Angelorum Guardianship. Regardless, a footprint should have appeared besides yours. Constantina and I are meeting tomorrow to discuss a plan of action."

"Hmm," Chamuel mumbled, thinking how much he missed his privileges as a Guardian House leader.

"Chamuel, be careful tomorrow. I'm not sure if the rogue Nephil incident and the abductions are related, but we have a pattern that's been emerging over the last couple of years and increasing in frequency. This is the third Guardian disappearance this year, which is highly concerning. The Angelorum assigned a task force to look into it further. If you weren't part of a Trinity . . . "

"Maybe we could get someone else assigned to Cara," he offered, knowing the probability was a big fat zero.

"Cham, you know that's not possible. There's no arguing with Constantina."

"Don't I know it," Chamuel muttered. "Anyway, I'll give you a call once I get a handle on the situation. Give me twenty-four hours."

"Fair enough. I'll text you the additional details. Thanks, brother."

The call disturbed Chamuel. He couldn't escape his feelings of restlessness over the Boston incident and his reckless decisions regarding Cara. But he now had some time tonight and knew how to cure what ailed him.

After finishing his dinner, he headed up to the roof, his own private retreat. He'd cultivated small fruit trees, perennials, herbs, and vegetables in and among statuary and fountains all held within an elaborate system of built-in containers that bordered the full-sized deck. In the center was a pergola-covered dining area with a bar, grill, table, and enough seating to host a sizable party. Too bad it hadn't seen one in a while. Not to mention he'd never enjoyed this space with anyone special.

Maybe that would change soon . . . He was momentarily hopeful before he cast the thought away. Tending to his garden gave him such joy, but tonight he needed something more. He needed some freedom, something to release him and free his mind.

He removed his black sweater and laid it on the nearest lounge chair, revealing the hard pectoral muscles of his chest and a single, red tattoo over his heart—his Mark as a Guardian. Rippled abs disappeared into the top of his jeans, which he slipped off and laid on top of his sweater. He stood on the roof in only his boxers. His Nephilim DNA protected him from the effects of heat or cold in either extreme, eliminating the need for any body hair. The brisk night air brushed softly over his bare skin. He could fly fully clothed in his modified wardrobe, but near nakedness heightened his pleasure.

He looked around, trying to decide which direction to go for a quick flight, and finally settled on heading south toward the ocean and the moon. With a quick cloaking prayer to hide him from human sight, his wings rapidly emerged from between his shoulder blades, growing and unfurling with snow-white feathers. His full wingspan extended over triple his height.

A light breeze rolled across his face and caressed his feathers. Flexing his shoulders, he stretched and shook his wings to ready them for flight. Anticipation brought a smile to his face and a stronger beat to his heart. With a crouch, a leap, and two flaps of his powerful wings, Chamuel soared up into the night sky, enjoying the pure freedom of flight.

Chapter 26

New York City. Fifth Avenue Penthouse. Sunday, March 23, 2:00 p.m. EDT

THIS MUST BE WHAT *it's like to be on the verge of death*, thought Cara, her head pounding. She tried to coax herself into consciousness after her alcohol-fueled night. After she and Sienna left Raphael's, they'd met some friends of Sienna's at a club in the Meatpacking District. Cara couldn't remember what time she'd gotten in or even how she made it home, only that she should have passed on the last tequila shot.

Her nose twitched, tantalized by the aroma of coffee. She unglued her right eye with the back of her hand. Staring out through a tiny slit, a figure slowly came into focus.

Michael, wearing a crooked smile, waved a mug in front of her.

"Is that what I think it is, or am I still dreaming?" she mumbled, her face still buried in the pillow.

"Wake up, sleepyhead. It's way past lunchtime," he replied softly, putting the coffee on the nightstand.

Her right eye opened wider. "Really? What time is it?" She felt like she'd just gone to bed.

"Two o'clock."

She groaned and tried to gather her wits. "Crap . . . Did you happen to bring any aspirin with that coffee?"

He picked up the bottle hiding behind the coffee mug on the nightstand, and shook it. Her oversensitive ears magnified the sound of the pills slamming up against the interior plastic walls of the bottle.

"*Ahh*, that's loud," she wailed.

"Two?"

"Yes, please." Then the thought struck her. "Isn't it Sunday? What're you doing here?"

"Constantina hoped to have another session. But it looked like you might sleep the day away, so she asked me to drop her off at church." He plucked two pills out of his palm and placed them next to her coffee.

"Constantina went to church?" Technically, Constantina was an angel, but it still struck Cara as odd.

"It's an Angelorum affiliate. And don't waste time feeling bad; she would've cancelled anyway. Isaac, the head of the Tri-State Guardians, called her unexpectedly and asked her to meet him there." Michael looked at his watch then poked at her. "Rise and shine. Get dressed and meet me in the kitchen in ten minutes."

Cara eyed him warily from her horizontal vantage point. "Why?"

"We're going for a run in Central Park," he smiled wickedly, closing the door behind him.

With her hair up in a ponytail and her running clothes on, Cara slunk into the kitchen, her legs moving like they were disconnected from her body. Taking a seat on one of the counter stools, she propped herself up on her elbows. Michael unceremoniously plunked down a glass filled with green fluid in front of her.

"What the hell is this? It's *green*." Cara stared at it in horror.

"Wheatgrass. Drink up." Michael said sternly before cracking a smile. "I promise you'll be good as new afterward. What did you drink last night, anyway?"

"It would be easier to tell you what I didn't drink. Mixing alcohol never works for me," she grumbled, pressing her hands against the sides of her throbbing head.

"Well, a good run will help you work out the toxins."

Cara narrowed her eyes. "Really? You're not doing this just to torture me?" Resting her head on her hands, she glowered at Michael, who looked like he just stepped out of a Nike catalog dressed in a white T-shirt and navy running clothes. The sleeves of his jacket were pushed up, striking the right note of casual style. His impeccable grooming made her seem lacking. She wanted to find his flaws: a bad hair day, a hang nail, something.

He placed his hand on his chest and gave her a wounded look. "Would I do that to you?"

"In a word: yes." She detected his intentions were good, but suspected he wasn't above giving out a little punishment when necessary.

He winked at her. "You're right. Come on, it's a beautiful day. I'd like to think that I didn't waste my time trekking into Manhattan for nothing."

"Grr." She conceded, hoping her head wouldn't pop off from the exertion.

Michael glanced down at Chloe, who sat at his feet with her head cocked and ear extended upward. "Want to go for a walk, girl?" She jumped up, tail wagging furiously at the word *walk*.

Cara smirked. "That's like asking a child if it wants candy."

Michael grabbed the lead off a hook in the kitchen, and the dog bolted ahead of them to the front door. Cara followed, snatching her sunglasses on the way out to cover her photosensitive eyes.

They headed outside using the underground passageway and found their way across the street into Central Park. The day was sunny and in the low sixties—perfect for a nice run when sober and hangover-free. Birds chirped happily above them, celebrating spring. They were probably cute robins or chickadees, but in her debilitated state they sounded more like pterodactyls.

"Will we be safe?" Cara asked as they strolled toward the running path. "Just you and I?"

"We should be. Chamuel is away for the day on Guardian business, but the Tri-State Guardians sent someone else to watch over us."

Cara raised a brow. "Chamuel gets time off?"

Michael shrugged. "Something came up that needed his attention. We'll be fine."

Not that she wanted to dwell on it, but she had to ask. "Michael, what was that demon thing that attacked me in my apartment?"

His shoulders tensed, and he replied in a low voice. "A Hunter for the Dark Ones."

"It looked like it crawled straight out of Hell."

Michael gave her a piercing look. "It did."

"Why am I not surprised?" She snorted, prepared to let it slide. Fallen angels, demons, Hell—it was all so surreal, but no crazier than angels, healing energy from the heavens, and handsome Messengers.

Michael, scowling, grabbed her arm and pulled her to a stop before they reached the jogging path. His fingers dug into her upper arm. "Cara, don't shrug this off. The Dark Ones usually send the soulless human Hunters in daytime, not demons. They must consider you very dangerous to have taken that chance."

A chill shot through her. "You're afraid for me." It wasn't a question, but a statement. His concern rolled over her and clung to her skin.

He let go of her arm and avoided her gaze. "Yes, very."

"What are soulless humans?" Neither he nor Constantina had mentioned them before.

"They're a type of Hunter, and just what their name implies. They're humans without a soul, damned to darkness when they die."

Cara frowned. "How can you tell them apart from normal humans?"

He turned to her. "They're surrounded by a black haze. A byproduct of the energy they steal. It's like the black haze of the demons before they manifest."

The hairs rose on her arms as she remembered the black demon haze from her apartment, still fresh and raw in her memory.

They started walking, but hadn't taken more than a few steps when he stopped her again. "There's one more difference between the soulless and the demon Hunters."

"What's that?"

He dipped his head, hiding his face. When he looked up, anxiety filled his eyes. "I can kill a soulless Hunter, but only a Guardian can kill a demon."

She understood now. Michel had told her he would protect her with his life, but he was as defenseless as she against a demon, and that scared him as much as it did her. She pressed her lips together and nodded. Wrapping her fingers in his, she squeezed his hand.

They passed the Alice in Wonderland installation and the Conservatory Water, where model boats graced the pond, before they reached the jogging path. With the nice weather came a crowd, and the park was filled with runners, bikers, parents pushing strollers, and even a few policemen on horseback.

Cara was thankful when Michael let her set the pace, adjusting his stride so they could run side by side. Chloe eagerly ran next to him while he held her lead. Their conversation had been sobering, allowing her to momentarily forget about the pain in her head.

She stole a glance at Michael as they ran, capturing a snapshot of his now-familiar profile with its cleft chin and high cheekbones. Within such a short time she'd come to depend on him. She didn't find it alarming to wake up and find him standing over her bed waving a cup of coffee. Instead, she found it comforting. Her heart stirred with affection for him, and she realized she wanted to know more about him. Plus, she needed a distraction from her throbbing cranium.

She picked a question off her burning questions list. "What was it like visiting the Angelorum Sanctuary?"

Michael glanced quickly in her direction, and his face lit up. "It was amazing. Like nothing I've ever seen. Picture a small city the size of the West Village. It's complete with cathedrals, residential buildings, a luxury hotel and conference center, a medical center, a training facility—you name it, they have it—all shoved underground. Just don't ask me where it is."

She rolled her eyes. "Let me guess—secret location?"

The pounding of her running shoes synchronized with the pounding of her head.

He glanced over at her and smirked. "Exactly. Windowless transportation is arranged for guests. Based on the time it takes to get there, my guess is it's somewhere within a fifty-mile radius of Paris."

The level of security didn't surprise her, but made it seem more real. "Did you get to see the whole place?"

"Not by a long shot. I was restricted mainly to the Guardian training facility and the residences. Oh, and my induction ceremony took place in one of the cathedrals."

"So what did you do there?"

Michael shrugged. "Messenger training. Some of it was classroom, like the history of the Angelorum and Angelology, and the rest was field training. Since I've trained extensively in weapons and martial arts, it wasn't a major part of my curriculum like some of the other Messengers in my class."

Cara had never seen Michael in action, but reckoned he could more than hold his own. "Do you have a favorite weapon?"

"My signature is the throwing star. They're easy to carry and within my comfort zone. Not that I've ever killed someone before . . ." His voice trailed off. Cara sensed his discomfort and remembered that, like her, he'd been plucked from his life, where killing wasn't part of his job description. He added, "I had a batch of them blessed before I left the facility, just in case."

"Fascinating." Cara swallowed, wondering what the probability was of Michael having to kill someone in the future. "What other types of training?"

"The rest mostly centered on unlocking my abilities."

"Like what?"

His shoulders stiffened as he ran next to her. Not at all the reaction she'd expected.

"How about we talk about those another time?" His words echoed in her head rather than her ears. She froze mid-step. He stopped a couple of yards away when he realized he'd lost her and eyed her quizzically. "Constantina mentioned that I could speak to you telepathically, right?"

Cara nodded, attempting to wipe the deer-in-headlights look off her face. She had mentioned it, but experiencing it firsthand was entirely different.

With a look of amusement, he came back with Chloe and grabbed her hand. "Come on. Don't look so shell-shocked." He pulled her forward, and they were off and running again.

"Can I talk to you that way?"

"Yeah," he answered telepathically, *"It's based on intent. Just think a sentence to me."*

She shot him a look, not fully believing him. *"Do you have a girlfriend?"*

A pink blush spread across his cheeks, and his lips parted in surprise. He turned his head to look at her. *"Now who's torturing whom? Why do you ask?"*

She hadn't expected to hit a nerve. He wasn't just embarrassed, a wave of bitter-lemon fear rolled off him. Playing it off, she lowered her sunglasses and switched back to verbal communication. "Just curious. With all the time we've been spending together lately, I wondered if I was stealing you away from someone."

Even though Michael was undeniably hot, she never thought about him as more than a close friend. She had someone else in mind for him . . . Sienna's image kept passing through her mind whenever she looked at him. Realizing maybe she'd asked the wrong question, she flushed.

"Um, you don't have to answer if you don't want to, but should I have asked if you had a boyfriend instead?"

It took her a second before she realized he'd ground to a halt behind her. She stopped and looked over her shoulder as other runners dashed by.

He stood glaring at her with Chloe straining against the leash at his side, his jaw tight and his arms locked across his chest, not caring that he created a traffic jam. "Why would you ask me that?"

If she thought she'd struck a nerve last time, this time she'd hit it with a sledgehammer.

Oops.

She cringed and gave him a shrug. "Sorry . . . No reason, really, other than the anti-girlfriend vibe I picked up. Either preference is fine with me." So what if he's gay? All it meant was that she couldn't play cupid between him and Sienna. She hadn't expected the rush of emotions from him that she felt coming at her.

He raked his fingers through his perfectly tousled hair and a muscle jumped in his cheek. "I'm not gay. Not even close," he said, his eyes flashed from royal to steel blue.

"I didn't mean to upset you. There's nothing wrong with it if you were," she replied evenly, trying to diffuse the situation. It's not like she would've asked if he hadn't clenched in fear when she asked if he had a girlfriend. And there wasn't anything openly gay about him either, quite the opposite, but you never knew these days.

He shook his head and deflated. "I know. I'm sorry. It's just that . . . " His voice trailed off again. "There's baggage on my side, that's all." They resumed a slow jog in silence. A few moments later, he said, "Honestly, between work and being the Messenger to a hungover Soul Seeker, my plate is full. I can't imagine having a girlfriend right now."

Cara accepted his answer, but she received a powerful taste of cinnamon, in what Michael had said, indicating something very personal was hidden behind the truth. He held his baggage with an iron grip, whatever it was.

She hit a comfortable stride running next to Michael and Chloe. The sun warmed the top of her head as she ran. She let the mood settle for few minutes.

"So, tell me more about the Sanctuary."

"There isn't a whole lot more to tell, other than it's been a mind-blowing couple of weeks."

Boy, did she know that feeling.

"And you received your Mark at the end?" she asked, thinking of the red tattoo Constantina had told her about.

He relaxed more and touched his chest over his heart. "Yeah, at the ceremony. Me, and about twenty other Messengers from around the world were inducted together. What surprised me the most was how it affected me." Michael's eyes softened, and he caressed the watch on his wrist. "Accepting my Calling made me feel closer to my father and helped fill the void left behind when he died. Also, that's where I met Constantina."

Cara glanced at the Patek Phillipe watch on Michael's muscled forearm and it clicked. "Was that your father's watch?"

He stayed silent for a moment then glanced over at her. There was no mistaking the grief surrounding him. "Yeah."

So, his inheritance had been gained the old-fashioned way. "You mentioned your dad passed away six months ago. He must've been fairly young."

The sound of their running shoes thumped rhythmically against the pavement as they ran.

Nodding, he said quietly, "Fifty-three. Heart attack. It was a complete shock." He added, "We were very close. It's been tough."

Michael's pain, still fresh and raw, made her heart ache. She kicked herself for not being more sensitive. "I'm sorry, Michael. I'm sure he was very proud of you." She reached out to touch his arm as they ran, offering him a physical gesture like he'd done so often for her.

He reached up and brushed her hand with his fingers. "Thanks."

"Did it freak you out when he visited you . . . you know . . . afterward?" Loved one or not, Cara didn't know how she'd react to having a ghost deliver a message.

He shrugged. "My family line has some unique gifts. So, I wasn't surprised, if that's what you're asking."

"What kind of gifts?" Her senses tingled with intrigue.

Michael tensed again next to her. He gave her an earnest look. "Can we save that answer for another time?" Like his reaction to the girlfriend question, she couldn't escape the sense that Michael had some secrets. She decided not to push.

"Sure," she said. "I hope I get to see the Sanctuary for myself someday."

"Seekers aren't usually brought there since the Angelorum tries to keep its distance. Maybe since you're a special case . . . you never know," he said. "Before

I forget, Constantina asked me to train you in Tai Chi this week. I won't have enough time to make you a martial arts expert, but I'll take you as far as I can in the time we have."

"Sounds perfect. I'd love to see your dojo." Michael may have some secrets, but she had a few of her own. "Um . . . do you think my kickboxing experience could be useful?" In addition to their shared sisterhood of anxiety, she and Sienna had taken kickboxing lessons together throughout high school to "kick anxiety's ass"—up until the summer before Cara left for college and refused to leave the house. Cara continued taking lessons for safety after college when she moved to Manhattan.

His head snapped around, and his eyebrows shot up. "You kickbox?"

She answered with a smug smile.

Chloe jerked Michael to a sudden stop and pulled him onto the grass. Nose to the ground, she sniffed for a spot to do her business. Cara followed, welcoming the break to catch her breath. The pain in her head had eased, or maybe she'd just gone numb. Either way, she felt marginally better. She kicked the grass with the toe of her running shoe. "Um . . . something else happened last night."

"Oh?" Michael frowned. The sniff-fest exhausted, Chloe pulled Michael back toward the running path, and they were off again.

Cara gave Michael a conspiratorial look before dropping her bombshell. "I met someone." She sped up, overtaking him.

"Wait!" she heard him call from behind as he and Chloe gave chase. She managed to stay ahead of them for all of a minute and a half before they caught up. It was worth seeing Michael partially out of breath. "For someone with a hangover, that was a nice sprint. What happened last night?"

They slowed their pace, and Cara recounted her experience with the handsome stranger.

"When he caught me, it blew me away. In the note, he asked me to come back to meet him there on Tuesday night for a date. I haven't decided if I should go. On the other hand, it's the best offer I've had in years. Maybe the date will renew my faith in men."

That drew Michael's eyebrows together. "Hey, we may only be friends, but I hope I've represented my gender well," he teased. Without a doubt he had.

She moved her sunglasses up to rest on the top of her head and smiled. "You're definitely a credit to your gender." But credit to his gender or not, friendship was their one and only option. Per the rules of the Trinity, like the Guardians, Messengers were also cautioned against romantic contact within a Trinity. She'd clarified that with Constantina after their discussion about the Guardians.

"Apology accepted. So what does this gift to women look like?"

"Tall, blond, and handsome. You'd approve of his fashion sense," she said with a wink.

He grinned. "I'm flattered that you trust my fashion sense. With your truth training, you should be able to figure out if the guy is a jerk or not."

"I guess. I still have a day or so to decide."

"What's his name?"

"That's the strangest part—he didn't sign the note. I asked the bartender, but he didn't know his name either, only that he came in often and seemed nice."

"It's not every day you meet someone who gives you that kind of reaction. It's been a while for me," he said.

"You never know, Michael, you may find someone when you least expect it."

He just gave a shrug. "Not looking, remember?"

We'll see about that, she thought with a smile.

Chapter 27

San Francisco. Forrester Research. Monday, March 24, 7:00 a.m. PDT

KAI STARED DOWN, daydreaming into his coffee cup. His curiosity had been in overdrive since Friday night and, as far as he was concerned, Monday morning hadn't come fast enough. Fortunately, he'd managed to distract himself with the golf tournament over the weekend, playing respectably and coming in fifth overall. Melanie and Sara had gotten back late from visiting Melanie's mother the night before, so essentially Kai had had the entire weekend to dissect his discussion with Calvin.

Kai tried researching the word *Ishmael*, but all he'd found were Biblical and *Moby Dick* references. He was sure this was the missing link. What else could it be? The visit to the law offices of Watson & Haskins filled him with equal parts excitement and trepidation. Tom may have made a breakthrough discovery, but Kai couldn't avoid thinking that whatever he'd discovered was related to his death. Sandra obviously believed the knowledge was dangerous enough to protect Calvin by burying the information in his subconscious. If so, what did that mean for his safety and the safety of his family? He needed to be more cautious.

At least ten times over the weekend he'd picked up the phone to call Cara to get her input. Each time, he ended up putting the phone back down. The last thing he needed was for her to freak out on him. What if this turned out to be dangerous? He needed to minimize the number of people he put in danger, not add to it. Nothing he'd learned so far was related to anyone named Le Feu anyway. Kai decided to wait until their scheduled call on Wednesday. Maybe he'd know more by then.

Sara wandered slowly through the kitchen doorway in her pajamas, rubbing the sleep from her eyes with balled-up little fists. She spotted Kai seated at the counter and, without a word, propelled herself toward him. Noticing her in time, he prepared himself for impact, using her momentum to scoop her up onto his lap.

"Well, hello, sleepyhead. How was Grandma's house?" He kissed the top of her head as she snuggled close.

"Good," she said in a muffled voice, speaking directly into his shirt.

"Did you miss me?" he asked quietly. She nodded *yes* against his chest. "Where's Mommy?"

"Shower."

"Do you need help getting ready for school?" They referred to preschool as *school* in an effort to get Sara used to the idea before she started kindergarten next year.

She shook her head *no* as Melanie walked into the kitchen, still in her bath robe, her hair up in a towel.

Melanie kissed Sara on the head and kissed Kai warmly on his lips. "Good morning," she purred. "Hey, would you mind pouring me a cup of coffee while I get the milk?" She continued on to the refrigerator. Behind the warm greeting, she sounded like she desperately needed a cup.

"Tired?" he asked, carrying Sara to the coffee machine. He opened the cabinet above it and reached his free hand up to extract a mug.

"Sorry we got home so late. I wanted to leave earlier, but Sara was having such fun with Maggie, the little girl next door." She fetched her daughter and her coffee.

He was glad they were back. The house seemed empty over the weekend without them. "I missed you both."

She smiled. Leaning up against the counter, she cradled Sara close. "We missed you too. Fifth place in the tournament was a nice finish compared to last year. Are you happy with it?"

"Happy enough, I guess." He had been too distracted to really savor his result, but the memory brought a smile to his lips. "Sorry I was asleep when you got home. I was exhausted." Hesitating momentarily, he continued, "I may be on to something at work."

"Really?" Melanie asked, surprised. "Like what?"

"I'm not sure. But I may have found a clue to turn these experiments around."

A moment later, she grimaced and put down her coffee. She wobbled as she lowered Sara to the ground, trying not to drop her. Steadying herself against the counter, her free hand shot up to rub her temple.

Kai stood with a frown. "Honey, are you all right? Is it another headache?" He rounded the island and pulled Melanie into his arms. Sara reached out and clung to his leg.

"They've been worse lately, especially this past week."

Kai's frown deepened. "Hon, aren't you taking the meds I picked up for you?"

"Yeah, but they make me groggy. I'm concerned that I won't be able to take them while I'm in China. I leave tomorrow."

Shit. He'd forgotten about her buying trip. Well, not really forgotten—he actually thought it was next week. Melanie made quarterly trips to China as part of her job as a retail buyer for a clothing manufacturer.

"Maybe you should postpone the trip," he offered. "I think it's time to get that MRI we've been talking about." Melanie had put off setting the appointment for more than a month.

She pulled away, and lifted Sara back into her arms. "Sweetie, I can't postpone the trip. Can you get my meds changed? I'll schedule an MRI when I get back."

Kai had a few physician friends with whom he traded services as professional courtesy. He frowned and placed his hands on his hips. "For the record, I'm not comfortable with this. We need to get these headaches diagnosed. They could be any number of things. Will you at least promise to set the appointment before you leave?"

"I promise," she said quietly. "Good luck today. Let me know how it turns out." She looked at Sara. "Someone needs to get ready for school." She turned back to Kai. "I need to get moving."

Kai gathered them both into his arms and hugged them. Resting his cheek on Melanie's hair, he said softly, "Hey, I love you. I'm just worried about you."

"I know. I love you too," she whispered.

He leaned down and kissed her tenderly on the lips. "Go get Sara ready, and I'll give you a call later to see how you're doing. I'll get a new prescription on my way home."

She smiled. "Thanks."

Kai watched as she padded out of the kitchen with Sara. He looked at the time. If he planned on fighting the traffic into downtown San Francisco, he'd better make a move. He finished his coffee and left with the business card for Watson & Haskins tucked safely in his wallet. He'd call in sick on the way . . .

Watson & Haskins was located in the Financial District in an old art deco building on Montgomery, across from Sutter. Kai smiled when he saw the building. There was something magical and charming about the little building—with its King Tut–themed relief carvings on either side of the arched entrance—tucked between two taller, more modern buildings.

Kai rode the elevator up. Watson & Haskins appeared to occupy the entire fifth floor. The décor reflected its historic thirties flavor with original marble floors and architectural details.

An elegantly dressed receptionist sat at a large wooden desk. A huge set of double doors behind her led into the offices. "May I help you?" she asked.

"Yes." He showed her the business card and added, "The password is *Ishmael*." He hoped he didn't sound as ridiculous as he felt.

"I understand," she said in a neutral tone. "Please have a seat."

Taking the card, she disappeared through the double doors. Kai headed over to one of the plush, leather chairs to wait patiently for her return.

He didn't have to wait long. Within five minutes, she settled back down behind the reception desk. "Mr. Gladstone will see you shortly."

While Kai waited, he noticed the classical music playing in the background. The surroundings calmed his nerves to the point where he didn't mind lingering. A couple more minutes passed before the phone buzzed softly.

After a few muted words into the handset, she stood up. "Mr. Gladstone will see you now. Please come this way."

Kai passed through the double doors to meet the waiting Mr. Gladstone, a tall, stocky man in his midsixties with white hair and a good-natured twinkle in his blue eyes.

"Dr. Solomon, we've been waiting for you. I'm so very pleased to finally meet you." He took Kai's hand inside both of his and shook it vigorously. A twinge hit Kai in his gut. Gladstone expected him too?

"Follow me, please." Turning on his heel, he led Kai to his office through a mazelike hallway filled with beautiful paintings and more wood paneling. It was decorated in the style of a clubby, personal library, with built-in bookshelves on the surrounding walls; a partner's desk dominated the room, with a pair of guest chairs in front to conduct business. For more relaxed conversations, two leather club chairs and a small table sat in front of a fireplace. The placed looked best suited for a smoking jacket and a Meerschaum pipe.

"Please sit." Gladstone motioned toward one of the chairs. Gladstone's attire, an expensive gray flannel suit and bowtie, made Kai appear woefully under-dressed by comparison in his khakis and Merrell shoes.

Kai took a seat. "Thank you for seeing me without an appointment."

"Think nothing of it. I don't believe this will take very long," he replied. Reaching into his desk, he pulled out an ornate leather folder with a strange, round metal seal. He pushed down on the gold seal, and it opened with a snap. Looking inside, he pulled out a small object. "I'm afraid this is all there is . . . " He slid a key across the desk to Kai.

Kai deflated like a leaky balloon. "That's it?"

"Yes, I'm afraid so."

"Do you have any idea what the key opens?"

"No, but I hoped that you would."

Gladstone's kind demeanor reminded Kai of a thinner, beardless Santa Claus. Kai sensed the man's sincerity. "Do you know what *Ishmael* means and why Dr. Wilson chose that password?" He figured there was no harm in asking.

With a twinkle in his eye, Gladstone responded, "Why, it's a name, of course."

Kai couldn't fully appreciate Gladstone's attempt at humor, but he didn't want to be rude and hid his impatience. "Do you know whose name?"

"That is something you must discover on your own. What I can tell you is that 'Ishmael is the key, and the key is Ishmael.'"

Kai picked up the key and examined the engraved number: 550056-94306. Caught somewhere between disappointment and defeat, he mumbled. "This could mean anything."

"But that's where you're wrong, Dr. Solomon. It could mean only one thing, and that's the thing you must find."

"Is there anything else you can tell me?" Kai asked in a final effort to extract meaningful information.

"There's nothing more to tell," Gladstone said, rising from behind the desk. He pointed to the key. "You have everything in your hand as we speak." He walked to the door, signaling the meeting was over.

Kai pondered the meaning associated with this piece of the puzzle in the shape of a key. Although he believed he was one step closer to the notes, he didn't know how big of a step he'd taken.

As he left the building, he was assaulted by the same migraine-like sensation he'd had leaving Stanford. His hand flew to his temple, and the hair bristled on the back of his neck. He thought briefly of his discussion with Melanie earlier. Could they both be ill?

The pain intensified, blurring his vision. He stopped in the middle of the sidewalk, unable to continue, a tar-like taste passing over his tongue. Kai's heart hammered, not knowing if he could make it back to the car, much less drive. Suddenly, the sensation was gone.

Shit, that was weird.

Maybe Melanie should schedule an MRI for both of them.

Chapter 28

New York City. Fifth Avenue Penthouse. Tuesday, March 25, 2:30 p.m. EDT

CARA HAD LOOKED at the looping script on the note about one hundred times over the past few days. After talking to Michael on Sunday, she knew she'd keep the date. In truth, she hadn't really considered not going. She couldn't push the image of the Greek god's startling blue eyes—or the thought of the electricity that had passed between them—out of her mind.

During her afternoon training session of protective energy shielding, Cara told Constantina she intended to keep the date.

"Fine. I'll alert Chamuel."

Cara groaned, unable to stop herself.

Constantina gave her a sympathetic smile. "I respect that you have a life, but danger is close, and you can't be too cautious." The set of her petite shoulders told Cara this topic wasn't up for discussion.

She sulked, less than thrilled to think someone would be watching her on a *date*. "Will I actually get to meet him at some point? It's kind of creepy that he's watching me and I have no idea what he looks like." Ever since she found out he could watch her under a veil of invisibility, she wondered how close he'd come to her. Did he peek in her windows at night?

Constantina nodded. "When the time is right, he will reveal himself. Think of your Guardian like you would a Guardian Angel—someone who is there to help when needed, not to spy on you."

"At least with Michael I know him, and he's not watching me," she said and then her lips turned up into a smile. "He's turning out to be a good friend."

"I can see that. He's a good man, very kind and caring. We're lucky to have Michael in our lives. He's actually quite a unique young man," Constantina said. Cara wondered, in addition to the skills he refused to disclose, if his baggage contributed to his uniqueness.

Constantina tilted her head and gave a nod for emphasis. "And I assure you that Chamuel is also very special. I've known him for many years, and there's no one I trust more to be your Guardian."

Ugh, privacy is the issue, not trust, Cara thought with her arms folded. She embraced her new life more and more every day, but ironically, one of the more difficult changes had been the lack of boundaries regarding her personal space and alone time.

Constantina gave Cara a thoughtful look. "Your Calling is expected soon. I believe Michael told you that you had a choice. None of this will be forced upon you. You can reject what's been offered. What we've been doing up until now is preparing your mind and body for your mission, since there'll be little time between your Calling and when your mission begins. Your soul has been pre-pared since before your birth, but, as a conscious being, you retain your free will. Therefore, you must formally accept your Calling."

Cara understood, but her curiosity stirred. "What happens if I reject the Calling?"

Constantina's mouth set in a worried line, and sadness touched her blue eyes. "If you reject the Calling, your life would be set back to the way it was. You'd move back into your residence and pick up your life where you left off. All the newly acquired assets would revert back to the trust, and your memories of me and all that I've told you would be taken away. But, because of your Sentinel encounter, we can no longer remove you from the sight of the Dark Ones. They'll always believe you're a threat, leaving you and your loved ones at an even greater risk."

Cara considered what Constantina told her. It didn't seem like much of a choice. Losing both Constantina and Michael was too painful for her to ponder, and putting herself and her loved ones in danger was absolutely out of the question.

She took a deep breath.

Let's do it.

At six thirty, Constantina stopped the lesson and smiled. "Okay, enough. Shall we get you ready for your date?"

Cara grinned and nodded enthusiastically.

"Can I arrange your hair for you?" Constantina asked, and Cara could hear the girlish excitement in Constantina's voice. Her choice of words reminded Cara that Constantina was, in many ways, from another time and place.

"I would be honored," Cara replied, genuinely touched. It warmed her heart. Constantina glowed at her response and clapped her hands together in delight.

Less than an hour later, Cara stood before Constantina in a simple black dress that clung to the right curves yet left something to the imagination. Cara chose a pair of black Dior heels and a black alpaca shawl to wrap around her shoulders. Her diamond pendant hung at her throat. Constantina had brushed Cara's hair and curled it, giving it body and fullness so it fell in waves and pooled around her shoulders. When she'd applied Cara's makeup, it brought back memories for Cara of the many sessions she used to have with Sienna in high school. Constantina beamed when she'd finished and handed the mirror to Cara. Her hand flew to her mouth, overcome with emotion. She looked beautiful in a way she'd never been able to accomplish on her own.

Embracing Constantina, she whispered in her ear, "Thank you."

"Well, don't stand here all night with me," Constantina said, pushing her away. "The driver should be waiting downstairs. If you plan to meet your gentleman by eight, you'd better go." Holding Cara at arm's length, she gave her shoulders one final squeeze.

At one minute of eight, Cara stepped out of the car and onto the sidewalk. Her stomach filled with the flutter of a butterfly symphony. The night, beautiful and crisp, was filled with promise.

Before Cara could open the restaurant door, an arm extended from behind her followed by a deep, rich voice. "Allow me." She looked over her shoulder, and there he stood, wearing dark tailored slacks and a wool jacket over a white-collared shirt, open at the neck.

Her breath caught, aware of his nearness. His dark-blond hair was neatly pulled back from his face, exposing his chiseled bone structure—the same as when she'd seen him on the subway.

Wow. He was even more stunning than she'd remembered.

She smiled up at him. Even though she wore heels, he stood over a head taller than her. In turn, he gazed down and smiled, blinding her with his vivid, crystal-blue eyes. Their smiles were enough to form a connection. She led the way, speechless, into the restaurant as his warm energy followed.

Gabrielle was off for the night; another model-actress type staffed the hostess station. As soon as she saw Cara's date, she lit up. "So good to see you again. I have a nice table for you in the back. Follow me." Grabbing two menus, she led them deep into the restaurant.

Gently placing his fingertips on the small of her back, he guided Cara to the table. His physical contact surprised Cara, making her skin tingle under his touch. With anyone else, she would have interpreted the gesture as forward, but instead she attributed it to the rarified manners of a man with good breeding.

Given their first encounter, maybe he was afraid she might trip on the way to the table? She was definitely steadier on her feet tonight, making another blow to her dignity unlikely. His movements were elegant and graceful for a man of his stature, making Cara feel petite and delicate beside him.

The hostess stopped at one of the more private tables covered in a white table cloth. "Here you are."

Cara moved to take the seat on the far side of the table, when the gentle pressure of his hand redirected her to the other chair. He stood behind it, holding it out for her. She lowered herself to be seated and caught the clean, citrusy scent of him behind her. He took his seat, the hostess handed them menus, and departed.

Still smiling, he leaned forward and broke his silence. "Thank you for accepting my invitation. I hope you don't mind, but I don't like having my back to the door." The rich, deep, and melodic tone of his voice almost stopped her heart, but she wondered about his level of vigilance.

Breathe, she reminded herself. She parted her lips to speak and realized she still didn't know his name. She couldn't resist teasing him on his omission. She batted her eyelashes. "Um . . . Would it be too forward of me to ask your name?"

His eyes held only the smallest flash of surprise, and she suppressed a smile. In her opinion, the fact that he couldn't hide the faint blush blooming across his chiseled cheeks made it all worthwhile.

"My apologies. Yes, I guess introductions are in order." His hand extended across the table. "Simon Young."

Electricity danced across her fingers as her hand disappeared inside his. Her father taught her that you could learn a lot about a man from his handshake, and she liked what his told her. Warm, firm, and full of confidence. Large and nicely shaped, his hand was too soft to belong to a manual laborer. She wondered about his profession.

"Cara Collins." Leaning in, she said, "Thank you for the bottle of wine, and for preventing my unceremonious fall. I'm sorry I ran away." Thinking of the mortifying incident, she was unable to hide her own blush. She unwound the alpaca shawl from around her, revealing her bare shoulders and the thin-strapped dress underneath.

His eyes gently caressed her every move. "It's been a long time since I've had the unexpected pleasure such as catching a beautiful woman in my arms."

"Somehow, I have trouble believing that." Cara found his manner simultaneously formal and unpretentious, a refreshing combination, in her opinion. She arched a brow and did a quick read on his energy. What he gave off was strong, positive, and just plain luscious, ruling him out as someone intent on harming her. When he smiled, it reached his eyes, making her want to melt at his feet.

"I'm flattered, but believe it. My career is a bit consuming. As a matter of fact, this is the first date I have had in . . . Actually, I shouldn't answer that; I might embarrass myself," he said, shyly averting his eyes.

His admission warmed her. She liked his self-deprecating manner, a rare and attractive quality. But she found it shocking that someone like him had gone without a date for a while. Yet, it did set her at ease. Her dance card wasn't exactly full either, but he didn't need to know that.

"What do you do?" *Please don't say professional athlete*, she thought.

He hesitated for a moment before responding. She sensed nervousness behind his smooth and confident demeanor. "I'm in the private security business. There aren't a lot of women in my line of work, and the hours can be . . . undesirable."

For the first time since he'd spoken, she detected a slight accent. She breathed an internal sigh of relief that his profession didn't involve chasing balls down a field, and it explained his desire to protect his back.

"Where are you from—originally, I mean?"

Another look of mild surprise crossed his face. "I grew up in Europe as a child, in France. Why do you ask?"

"I heard a slight inflection in your voice," she said. "It's nice." She was a sucker for a sexy accent.

He blinked, and a soft coloring formed above his cheekbones at her compliment. He cleared his throat and laid his napkin across his lap. "Thank you. I didn't realize I had an accent."

"Most people with accents say that," she teased him in an attempt to help him relax.

His eyes twinkled again with interest. "What about you, Cara? Where did you grow up?"

"Summit, New Jersey, but I've lived in Manhattan since I graduated college. My family still lives there. What about you? Do you have family here or are they in Europe?"

She could see that she'd caught him off guard again. Was it her or did he seem to be tiptoeing through her questions with the same care he'd use to walk through a minefield? This was the easy stuff. How was he going to react if she asked him anything more complex?

"I have some brothers, but my parents are both *gone*," he replied with tenseness in his square jaw. His answers bathed her tongue in sweetness. At least he was telling the truth.

"I'm sorry. It's not often someone our age has lost both of their parents."

A startled look passed through his eyes.

Cara cringed. "Um, was that the wrong thing to say?" She hoped she could get through the evening without repeatedly sticking her high-heeled foot in her mouth. At this rate, they'd never make it to dessert.

His face softened, and he leaned in closer, his arms folded. "You didn't say anything wrong. They've been gone a long time, that's all."

Ah, that rich, sexy accent again. Some of the tension disappeared from his shoulders, and the gap between them started to close as they talked. Not wanting to ruin the moment, she moved to safer conversational ground.

"So, the bartender says you come here often. He had some nice things to say about you."

"You asked the bartender about me?" He raised his eyebrows, and his lips twisted back into a smile.

"Well, I'd hoped he knew your name. By the way, he didn't," she teased, inching forward.

"I've never thought about it. I'll be sure to properly introduce myself next time," he replied. "This is one of the places I come to unwind and have dinner when I don't feel like cooking. I live only a few blocks away."

"You cook?" Cara's eyes lit up. "I love to eat, but I'll confess that I don't love to cook."

"Yes. I studied at the Culinary Institute in Paris. A while back, I took a break from my career and decided to do something else for a while."

"Very impressive," replied Cara, and she meant it. He didn't just cook, he *cooked*. To her there was nothing sexier than a man who knew his way around a kitchen. She found the juxtaposition of a man who looked like a linebacker standing in a kitchen, wearing an apron and holding a whisk, intriguing.

He gave her another shy smile. "If our date ends well, will you permit me to cook for you sometime?" His eyes held a look of hope and honest desire. She was so used to men who offered things they had no intention of delivering that she found his honesty uplifting.

He's almost too good to be true, she thought.

"I'd be honored." Cara already sensed this date would lead to another, unless he sprouted another head sometime during the evening. "I recently took a break from my career too."

"Really? What career?"

"Investment banking," she said. "Like your career, it doesn't leave much time for forming quality relationships. I'm thankful that I have time to do something else now."

"So what are you doing, if I might ask?"

She paused for only a moment before she met his gaze and answered. "I'm still trying to figure that out."

Glancing over quickly at the waitress, he asked, "Are you hungry? I've been holding off the server, since I didn't want her to interrupt. Would you have a glass of wine if I ordered a bottle?"

"Yes and yes." Cara couldn't remove the smile from her face as she basked in the pleasure of his company. In this setting, he was nothing like the intimidating man in black she'd spotted on the subway. Instead, she found him charming and engaging.

He signaled the waitress. Without opening the menu, he asked Cara, "Do you trust me?"

She nodded. Regarding food, absolutely, but the rest remained to be seen.

Turning to the waitress, he said, "Tell the chef we're a *go*, and a bottle of this." He opened the wine menu briefly and pointed to his selection. The waitress collected their menus and left.

"He'll prepare us a five-course meal. I promise it'll be fantastic."

"Well, this is your neighborhood," Cara replied, "and after what you've told me, I think I feel safe putting myself in your culinary hands."

Simon leaned forward and the collar of his shirt opened wider, revealing the smooth, hairless skin below the hollow of his throat. "Let's hope the chef isn't in the mood for tripe tonight."

Cara paled.

"Just kidding," he said, grinning. "When I called him earlier, I requested no organ meats."

She narrowed her eyes. "That was kind of mean." She liked his sense of humor and the fact that he'd relaxed enough to tease her back.

Amusement in his eyes, he chuckled. "You seem like the kind of person who can hold her own against a little teasing." Then his eyes softened, and his face grew serious. He hesitated before leaning in even closer. He extended his hand across the table and swallowed hard. She sensed the energy from him shift and tingle. Her breathing quickened and she placed her hand in his, drawn into his gaze. His fingers wrapped around hers, surrounding them with soft warmth.

"You look very beautiful tonight. I want you to know that it didn't go unnoticed, or unappreciated," he said softly.

Cara blushed. "Thank you. You're too kind." Her hand felt good inside his. Energy snapped over her skin and ignited her desire to get closer to him.

His face was only inches from hers. "Kind or not, I'm being honest."

Simon's words made her heart beat faster. Trying not to stare, she surreptitiously drank him in. The skin of his face was smooth and flawless, projecting an underlying radiance. His features were strong enough to be masculine but not overly so with full, kissable lips. Beyond his packaging, what she glimpsed inside him interested her most of all—a good soul.

The sommelier arrived with a bottle of white wine and a corkscrew. Sadly, Simon relinquished her hand and sat back in his chair. There was a pause while a sample of wine was poured for him to taste. Simon studied the color, swirled the wine, observed the legs as they meandered down the side of the glass, took a sniff, and finally took a taste to roll on his tongue. He nodded, accepting the wine and allowing it to be poured.

"This is a very good French white, which should pair with whatever the chef serves as our first course." Noticing the look on Cara's face, he continued, "Before you're too impressed, the chef made the recommendation when we spoke earlier. A toast?" He raised his glass, and she lifted hers. "To getting to know you and to unexpected encounters," he said, gently tapping his glass to hers.

"So, tell me something about you," she said.

He tensed. Was that panic she sensed? Were they reentering the question minefield?

"I'm afraid I'm not very good at talking about myself," he said, trying to cover his discomfort.

That's a switch. Usually men can't stop talking about themselves, she thought. She took a deep breath. Icebreaker exercises worked in most situations, why not on a date? "Okay, let's do this: what's the most beautiful place you've ever visited?"

His tension appeared to ratchet down a notch. He folded his hands in front of him and thought for a moment. "The Grand Canyon."

"Why?" she asked.

Squinting into the distance, he collected his thoughts and said, "Because it's so beautiful. It's like seeing a part of Heaven when I look at it."

She liked his answer. The stiffness eased from his shoulders, and he loosened up more.

"What about you, Cara? What's the most beautiful place you've ever visited and why?"

Her expression softened. "I love the South of France, but Monaco was the most beautiful place I'd ever seen. The views left me breathless. I've never been to the Grand Canyon, so I don't know how it compares." She'd spent a semester abroad in Nice during her junior year of college, but hadn't traveled much since because of her job.

He nodded. "A lovely choice. They're both beautiful in their own way and for different reasons. Someday, you must see the Grand Canyon. It'll take your breath away."

"Have you traveled much?"

"Enough," he answered, "but, there's no place like home. Like you, that's New York City for me."

Sensing his evasion, she let it slide this time. She clasped her hands together and tried another question.

"What's your favorite book?" An avid reader her whole life, she loved to get a sense of a person by what they read. Her tastes varied from the classics all the way to trashy thrillers, but her favorites held universal appeal.

"Ah, great question. I love many of the classics, but I believe that one of my favorites is a twentieth-century novel, *Siddhartha* by Herman Hesse."

Pleasantly surprised by his choice, Cara smiled and took a sip of wine. "I love that book. What makes it your favorite?"

Simon's eyes held a faraway look as he spoke. "Although a person's life may not be perfect, there's still hope that he can learn to live and ultimately achieve Nirvana."

His words sounded personal to her. *Is there something holding him back from finding meaning in his life?* she wondered.

He looked back at her. "And what's yours, Cara?"

"It's a children's fable, actually." She looked at him shyly. "*Le Petit Prince* by Antoine de Saint-Exupéry. I was required to read it in French class during my last year of high school."

"I know it." Simon's face lit up.

"Then you know the story." She was so pleased that he knew her selection.

His delight was unmistakable. "Please, tell me why you found it so impactful." Looking at her with anticipation, he folded his hands in front of him and leaned halfway across the table.

She cleared her throat softly. "I've always loved what the fox taught the Little Prince—that to love someone is a great responsibility and opens you up to loss. To love, you need to trust your heart."

With a thoughtful look, Simon quoted, in French, the gift bestowed from the fox to the Little Prince: "*It is only with the heart that one can see rightly; the essential is invisible to the eyes.*"

Her heart quickened as he spoke. He actually knew her favorite line.

"It struck me that in the end, the Little Prince was willing to do anything to get back to the Rose he loved, even if that meant he had to die." Her eyes watered a little thinking about it.

Simon took her hands from across the table. "You have a strong heart."

Cara surprised herself by opening up so quickly. Something about Simon made her want to bare her soul. With a lump in her throat, she wondered if

Simon was the kind of person who would do anything to be with the one he loved.

The first course arrived. Two bowls of chilled spring pea soup with pancetta and a small swirl of crème fraîche were placed in front of them. The waitress also took the opportunity to refill their wine glasses before departing.

"Bon appétit," said Simon, lifting his spoon.

The soup was absolutely amazing, and so was the wine. Cara couldn't believe what a great time she was having. So far, Simon had exceeded her expectations. Granted, her expectations had been pretty low. But Simon was the first man who had made her forget about Kai, even momentarily, in a very long time. As a matter of fact, up until now, she hadn't realized what had actually been the problem.

As she sat with Simon, she had another realization. Regardless of how much things had changed, she wanted a relationship to be part of her new life. She wanted a chance to be with someone like Simon, if not Simon himself. Deep inside, she hungered to move on and to take another chance.

The rest of dinner passed quickly. The chef stopped by once to check on them, and by the time dessert had arrived, it was almost eleven.

"I can't believe it's so late. The night just flew by." Cara was amazed, not able to remember the last time she'd enjoyed herself this much.

"I believe that's the sign of a good date." Simon's eyes blazed with hope. "What are my chances of a second?"

Tilting her head to the side, she smiled, and the corners of her eyes crinkled, unable to hide her pleasure. "My crystal ball says they're pretty good."

"Do you like art?" he asked.

Her eyes widened. "I love art."

She sensed his nervousness like she had earlier, and watched him unconsciously wring his hands. "I have some flexibility in my schedule this week. Um . . . Would you like to go the Met with me tomorrow?"

Her stomach did a backflip. Even if she had to fight a horde of demons with her bare hands, she'd be there. She did a rapid mental review and calculated her schedule for the next day. Maybe if she agreed to have Chamuel shadow her . . . She'd check with Constantina when she woke up.

Her plan in place, she said, "I'd love to. I have a commitment in the morning, but let me see what I can do about rearranging my schedule for the afternoon. Does that work?"

"It works fine."

"I'll text you in the morning once I've worked out my schedule." She dug her cell phone out of her purse and handed it to him. "Program your number in, and then I'll call you with mine."

He accepted her phone in his large hand. When he handed it back, she hit Send and his phone rang in his jacket pocket.

"We're all set," she said, hanging up.

He gave her an appreciative look. "Clever girl."

Simon called the waitress over to take care of the bill. Cara's heart sunk. She wasn't ready for the evening to end and hoped Simon felt the same way.

As if reading her mind, he asked, "Would you like to take a walk? Some fresh air would be nice after such a long meal."

Cara glanced down at her high heels. "I believe I can manage a couple of blocks."

He came around to her side of the table and pulled out her chair. She wrapped her shawl back around her shoulders, and he escorted her out of the restaurant into the brisk night air.

"It's a bit colder. Are you sure you'll be warm enough? Let me give you this." He moved to slip of out his jacket.

Cara touched his arm and shook her head. "No, I'm fine. Which way?" She pulled her shawl tighter around her shoulders, determined to tough it out.

He pointed east and extended his elbow so that she could hook her arm through his. "May I?"

"Absolutely." She slipped her arm through and they set off. Cara loved his impeccable manners. There was a practiced ease and comfort there. Not once did he appear to force or fake it. Usually, she spent half the night wondering if her date would offer to pay for his half of the dinner bill, much less hold her seat out for her or appreciate that she'd accepted the date.

"There's a lounge around the corner. Would you like to go for a quick night cap?" he suggested. "Then I promise to get you home safely."

"Thank you. I'd be happy to take you up on your offer, kind sir. One condition—my treat for the night caps."

He stopped her on the sidewalk. "Cara, please don't think I'm old-fashioned, but I was raised to believe that a man of worth always takes responsibility for the first date. My mother wouldn't have approved of anything less."

Cara narrowed her eyes. "Cheap shot, using your mother like that . . . "

He smiled. "I know, but it's true."

She surrendered. "Okay—this time. But if you always insist on paying, I might start to think you have something against independent women."

His lips parted in surprise, and he looked taken aback . . . for about the millionth time that night. "I love independent women, but there's nothing wrong with showing respect and honoring your relationships."

"I give up for tonight, but I plan to bring it up again."

Just before they rounded the corner, Simon froze, coming to a dead halt on the sidewalk.

The taste of lemons tickled her tongue as his fear collided into her.

Chapter 29

New York City. Prince Street. Wednesday, March 26, 12:31 a.m. EDT

FEAR BARRELED DOWN his spine like a runaway freight train the moment he sensed the energy. Another Nephilim, close by. But this time it wasn't the rogue, it was Zeke. Taken by surprise, Chamuel ground to a halt on the sidewalk with Cara on his arm. If Zeke spotted him out of uniform with Cara, it wouldn't take an advanced degree in rocket science to guess what was going on. Not to mention what would happen if Cara found out she was a hair's breadth away from violating Angelorum law.

Chamuel had skated on the edge of recklessness from the moment he'd arrived on the date, and the temptation to kiss her grew every millisecond longer he spent with her. Asking her to come with him to the lounge could easily turn into a mistake. He kicked himself for not ending the date at the restaurant.

She clutched his biceps firmly, looking at him with wide eyes. "Is everything okay?"

He reached into his breast pocket. "Sorry. For a moment I thought I'd left my wallet behind," he said, making himself believe it so she wouldn't taste his bluff.

She relaxed next to him. Then he did the only thing he could think of: he said a silent cloaking prayer and they both disappeared from sight. This way, Zeke would only be able to sense him and would assume he was on duty. If all went according to plan and he navigated well, Cara would never be the wiser. From her vantage point, nothing would change. She'd never know they'd disappeared or couldn't be heard by anyone else.

When they arrived at the lounge, Chamuel uncloaked and breathed a sigh of relief. A warm rush of air hit them as he opened the door and guided Cara inside.

A jazz musician played on a small stage in the front of the crowd. Red and purple velvet drapes lined the walls, and clusters of small seating areas created an intimate atmosphere. Already densely packed with a post-dinner crowd, he managed to find them a seat on an open banquette with two round tables tucked in the back of the room.

The waitress arrived a moment after they sat down, ready to take their order. He looked down at Cara next to him. "What would you like?"

"What're you having?" she asked. The sparkle in her green eyes warmed him.

"A glass of port. Can I tempt you to join me?"

"I believe you can," she answered. His traitorous face flushed when her eyes settled on his lips.

Turning away, he ordered two glasses of twenty-year-old tawny port and then concentrated elsewhere to avoid coming undone. Gazing around the room at the other couples, a fierce yearning to have a normal, romantic relationship with Cara gripped him hard. Even the small taste of her company and attention this evening had shifted something inside him. But it wasn't just that, it was because the attention came from her—no one else would do. After tonight, the thought of continuing on in his state of lonely self-depravation gutted him. His resolve was weakening.

He fought back a frown and forced his eyes to settle on the musician, listening to the bluesy notes of the saxophone. Within minutes, the waitress returned with their drinks and the check.

"This should warm you for the ride home," he said, handing her one of the glasses.

Cara shifted into him, and a jolt of electricity sizzled over his skin. He resisted throwing his drink back in one swallow. Maybe then he wouldn't be so hyper-aware of her thigh brushing up against his. The scent of her perfume was closer now than it had been in the restaurant, and he found himself wanting to press his nose to her neck and inhale deeply.

Rational thought temporarily deserted him, and desire rushed through his veins like water through a fire hose. It took all his control to breathe evenly, and he considered sitting on his hands to prevent them from doing something stupid.

As they sat listening to the music, he tried to beat his desire back into submission, but his resistance eventually waned and he slipped his arm around her. She felt so satisfying in his arms, so small and delicate. He couldn't stop himself from drawing her closer.

She leaned into him and rested her head on his shoulder. Her gesture triggered his need to both protect her and to share a lover's touch. His fingers crept up to touch her hair and he drew in a sharp breath. He had to turn his head away and close his eyes so he could luxuriate in the silken strands he caressed.

By the time the musician finished his set, their drinks were empty.

Ready to end their evening before he crossed the line, he dipped his head to whisper in her ear and found himself staring down into her green eyes gazing up at him with invitation. His sense of smell sharpened and the wildflower scent of her longing pierced through the aroma of her perfume, wafting up to greet him. Images of the day he'd held her after the attack slammed into him, and he froze.

Her full red lips cried out to him.

Am I the only one who can hear them?

The ache to kiss her grew until it nearly cracked him open. His heart pounded, and his breath left him as he fought to retreat—when all he wanted to do was gather her up into his arms and never let her go.

Her eyes fastened to his, unmoving. He could tell she sensed his inner turmoil as easily as she could read words on a page. Then she moved her eyes down to his lips, and touched them lightly with her finger.

He felt his eyes dilate; surely the blue rim was almost gone, overpowered by the black center. It took all his willpower not to jump out of his skin. His razor-sharp hearing could hear her breath quickening through her parted lips. There was nothing he wanted more in that moment than to break his celibacy. His hand caressed the delicate ivory column of her neck, and an undeniable need rose up, ready to consume him.

God, if I do this, there's no going back, he thought. His lips moved in silent protest. No reprieve or forgiveness. What he was doing was wrong on every level.

How could I have been so naive to think I could escape my attraction?

He took one more look at her ripe, red lips. Coupled with the feel of her full breasts pressed up against him, it was more than he could handle. Like a pane of glass battered by hurricane-force winds, his resolve strained under the mounting pressure until it shattered into a million tiny pieces and the world receded around them . . . and she was all there was.

He cupped the petal-soft skin of her cheek.

She closed her eyes, and her small hand covered his before she took it from her cheek and touched her lips to the tips of his fingers.

Oh, Heavenly Father . . . His blood flowed faster, and his breathing grew ragged. Had he been fully human, he would've broken out into a sweat. He closed his eyes, and for a moment savored her feather-like touch. Swallowing, he reopened his eyes. Hardly able to believe the longing he saw reflected in her eyes, he was honored to be chosen by her.

Surrendering, he bent down and touched the velvet of her lips with his. Soft and full, the sensation was so much better than he'd imagined. A warm wash of energy engulfed him and the tension melted from his body. Slowly, he sank his fingers deep into her auburn waves and lost himself in the taste of her lips. The sweetness of the port greeted him first. His tongue gently parted her lips, and he deepened the kiss until their tongues met in a divine dance of exploration. His senses exploded, and visions of making love to her slammed into his consciousness.

One transgression at a time, he chided himself.

He kissed her until they were both breathless then slowly disengaged his lips from hers.

Before he could pull away completely, her hands clasped the sides of his face. With a half-lidded gaze, she captured his bottom lip in a gentle kiss before moving to the corner of his mouth. From there, her lips traveled, leaving a trail of sensuous kisses over his jaw and down the sensitive skin of his neck. His nerve endings snapped, and an ungentlemanly moan escaped through his lips.

A release of long-forgotten hormones surged through him, and he prayed he wouldn't have to stand anytime soon. Between the weakness in his knees and disproportionate amount of blood in his groin, he couldn't get up even if he wanted to.

His foggy brain thought to stop her before he lost total self-control. With every last shred of restraint he could muster, he tipped her head up and pulled away.

"Thank you for the most wonderful evening," he said in a deep, thick voice and tucked her head underneath his chin, hugging her petite body against his. He memorized how every inch of her felt pressed against him, knowing these memories would be the only thing sustaining him if and when he got caught.

He almost laughed, because all he wanted was to do it again.

"We need to get you home," he said finally. Forcing himself to his feet, he shifted his jacket closed before helping her up and gently propelling her toward the door.

The night air slapped him back to his senses. Thank God they'd been in a public place. He wished he could say he was shocked at his actions, but he'd be lying.

"Simon?" Cara stopped short in front of him and turned into his arms.

"Yes?"

Rising on tiptoe, she leaned into him and gave him a dazzling smile. "Thank you for a really great night."

He'd surely be punished for this, so why not make the most of it?

He pulled her into his arms and lowered his lips to hers for one last kiss. Breathing in the wild bluebell fragrance of her desire, he impressed the memory of it on his senses.

"Until tomorrow?"

"Yes, until then," she said with a warm smile.

With a two-finger salute, a yellow cab stopped for him at the curb. Opening the door, he ushered her inside.

"Here's the lady's fare," he said, pushing a wad of cash through the slot in the Plexiglas partition.

Chamuel watched the taxi drive away, Cara's kiss still tingling on his lips. The feel of her in his arms tonight had awakened something powerful inside him, and the strength of it rocked him.

Nice job, he thought facetiously. He'd succeeded in crossing the line into forbidden territory within one night. He'd gravely miscalculated, thinking he could resist kissing her for at least two dates.

Self-deluded idiot. Now it would take imprisonment to keep him away from her.

Releasing a long breath, he passed his hand down over his face. Thank God Constantina only knew him by his given name and had no idea what name he'd chosen for his latest human identity. If Cara mentioned Simon Young to her, she'd never make the connection.

The night had been one of the best nights of his life and also one of the most difficult. Knowing she'd already completed truth training, he'd spent some time preparing for the date. But even though he'd carefully constructed answers to questions he suspected she would ask, she'd still caught him out a few times. Not only that, since they were in the same Trinity, he had to block any accidental telepathic thought projections.

He smiled. He'd forgotten how it felt when a woman looked at him with desire and interest, like she'd done this evening. It felt good, really good.

I'm so screwed, he thought, envisioning the lonely cell with his name on it. Adding to his agenda of self-destruction, he planned to see her again tomorrow. His smile widened. He couldn't wait.

Wiping the idiotic grin from his face, he put his thoughts aside and got moving. He still had to ensure that she arrived home safely. With a quick cloaking prayer coupled with a prayer for swiftness, he followed the taxi on foot through the city until it dropped her off. He watched her walk into the building that led to the underground pathway back to the penthouse. Sensing no danger, he relaxed. From there, the orb in the meeting room above the library would hide her presence.

Sending a quick text to Constantina, he let her know there were no incidents to report on his watch and that Cara should be arriving upstairs momentarily. He couldn't resist adding that he approved of the gentleman who'd taken Cara to dinner.

He smirked when he thought back to the one moment of the evening when

Cara had made the assumption that they were approximately the same age. *Give or take about one hundred and twenty years.*

Chamuel thought about heading across the street to the park, launching himself into the sky unseen and flying home. Instead, he decided to walk with his memories of the evening to keep him company. He'd worry about her forbidden status another day.

Was her kiss worth one hundred years of imprisonment?

Abso-fucking-lutely.

Chapter 30

San Francisco. Forrester Research. Wednesday, March 26, 8:00 a.m. PDT

KAI HURRIED INTO HIS OFFICE. He was late after dropping Sara off at preschool. He hung his messenger bag on the back of his door while trying not to spill the cup of coffee in his other hand. Taking care of Sara while Melanie traveled gave him a renewed respect for all she did. He just wished she'd take the headaches more seriously. At least she'd scheduled the MRI before she left for China and took the new prescription with her. Hopefully, her headaches wouldn't ruin her trip.

He'd driven himself half-crazy on his way into work, racking his brain about the key. Since leaving Watson & Haskins on Monday, he couldn't stop thinking about it. Maybe he'd ask Cara after all.

Picking up the phone, he dialed her cell. Wednesday morning at eight a.m. Pacific Time had been their standing call time for the last five years.

"Hey! The Hoyas kicked butt last night," Cara said, giving a nod to their alma mater for their win against Florida in the NCAA's March Madness tournament.

"I caught the highlights—it was fantastic! The win put me ahead in our basketball pool," he said, perking up for a moment. He'd dreamed of playing hoops for Georgetown, but soccer turned out to be better suited for his time and talent.

"Oh, and thanks for the eCard. So, what up? Anything related to the dream to tell me?" she asked.

He thought for a second, and decided he wasn't ready to mention anything. "Nothing yet. So, how's the boss from Hell?"

"Um . . . I was laid off a couple of days after my birthday."

Kai bristled. "Why didn't you call me or send me a text or something?" It wasn't like Cara to keep something significant like this from him for almost a week.

"Why? There's nothing you could do about it, and I'm not that upset anyway. Besides, I found another job." she said nonchalantly.

His eyebrows flew up. "Already? That was fast."

She chuckled. "Kai, you just sounded like my dad."

"Yeah, well, he's a smart guy." He hated when she said that, almost as much as when she accused him of sounding like a big brother. "Don't keep me hanging. What's this other job?"

"Are you okay? You sound tense."

He let out an exasperated breath. God, this woman sometimes knew him better than his own wife did. Should he tell her? He trusted her more than anyone, but she was prone to overreaction. Next thing he knew, she'd be on a plane flying out to babysit him—and it wouldn't be the first time. He'd love to see her, but if this broke bad, he'd have his hands full just keeping Melanie and Sara safe. If anything happened to any of them, he'd lose it.

"Kai, are you still there?"

"Yeah, sorry. Melanie left for China this morning on business, so I'm Mom and Dad this week. I'm a disorganized wreck already." He hated keeping this from her, but he couldn't tell her. He just couldn't.

"Just stick to the shopping list Melanie leaves you, and the microwave. You'll be fine."

"Anything new with Sienna?"

Cara groaned. "We went out on Saturday night, and Sunday I was a hungover mess."

Kai chuckled, and they spoke for a few more minutes. As he signed off, she stopped him.

"Wait! One more thing . . . Be careful. I haven't been able to shake the feeling about that dream."

A twinge of guilt cut through him. His instincts told him he should tell her, but his mouth refused to cooperate. His jaw opened, but the words failed to arrive. He blew out a silent breath.

"I will," he said, and signed off with the promise that he'd be in touch if anything involving the mysterious Le Feu cropped up. Uneasiness settled in his gut after he hung up.

Preparing to enter the lab for the day, he noticed the pile of mail left by his secretary on his desk. On top of the stack was a brochure for a laboratory supply company. Picking it up to throw it in the trash, Kai spotted the postal address and froze.

Kai's hands shook as he went to retrieve his wallet from his messenger bag. Sitting back down at his desk, he removed the key from the leather pocket behind his driver's license and looked at the last five digits on the key—94306. The zip code on the brochure was 94301, and the company was located in Palo Alto, California.

Kai's heart thumped. Not wanting to leave a trail on his work PC, he took out his smartphone and looked up the post office locations in Palo Alto. There were two; one located on Hamilton Avenue in postal district 94301, and a second on Cambridge close to El Camino Real in 94306. He did one last search . . . for the post office box addresses in the zip code 94306. They all came up six digits.

Kai punched the air. *Bingo!*

The Palo Alto post office was spitting distance from the Stanford Campus. He could kick himself for not thinking of it sooner.

Triple W, Emily, was at work today, which would call for some evasive action on his part. He checked his electronic calendar against Emily's to figure out the best time to slip out and still be back in San Jose by six o'clock to pick up Sara from preschool.

He grabbed the phone and dialed his intern. "Hey, Kristi. It's Kai. Can you do me a favor?"

"You betcha," Kristi said. "Were the samples I ran viable?"

Kai cringed. He hadn't checked them yet. "Uh, give me an hour and I'll let you know. In the meantime, can you set up the next set?"

"I surely can. What's your favor?"

"I have to run over to Building Seven at around ten forty-five for the rest of the day. If anyone asks, just let them know. I'll be in Lab Four until then."

"Not a problem. I'll stop in when I'm done setting up the next splice."

Satisfied with his plan, Kai slipped the key back into his wallet and slid it in his back pocket. He felt better keeping the key on him now. In the meantime, he had to force himself to work when all he wanted to do was to discover the meaning of "Ishmael."

"Our little scientist is on the move again." Emanelech's voice purred through the speaker phone on Achanelech's desk. He'd been attending to his businesses all morning and his leg ached with stiffness from sitting for hours. The downside of living topside was that one needed to make a healthy living to blend in and to hide one's activities. After all the years he'd spent on earth, you'd think he could retire and live off of his interest. If the Master stopped tithing him to death, maybe one day he could do just that. Ironic, but the Angelorum did the opposite. They *bestowed* wealth on their most valuable Soul Seekers, which was both good and bad, he supposed. Sudden wealth made those Soul Seekers more conspicuous—easier to hunt down and kill.

Achanelech's lips twisted into a frown. "It took him long enough. Hopefully, he'll lead us to the prize this time."

"Dr. Solomon's not the only game in the casino, you know."

He rolled his eyes at her use of the modern cliché and hissed at her. "Sssss . . . Em, we're not playing roulette here. The Forrester research is the most promising, but we're running out of time. Like it or not, our decision to solve two problems at once will be construed by the Angelorum as us throwing down the gauntlet. Expect the Master to flay us both if we fail."

"We won't fail." Her icy voice froze the air on his side of the phone. "We'll get our vaccine *and* capture her for Lucifer." Then she added with glee, "The plan's actually brilliant, if I do say so myself. Then again, I did think of it."

"I admire your confidence, *ma chérie*. I wish I shared it," he said dryly. "Just be prepared to act fast."

She sniffed. "Aren't I always? My bigger problem is keeping your demon fed so that it doesn't swallow our prize. Having the scientist as a snack won't get us any closer to a vaccine and will surely get us disemboweled."

He'd chosen the best behaved of his demon children to accompany her. Gritting his teeth, he said, "If that happens, I will flay you myself."

An icicle popped through the phone and struck him on the head. "Promises, promises. I'd like to see you try. Later, Gator." She hung up on him.

Bitch, he thought and turned the ice to a boiling puddle on his desk. He seethed, rubbing his forehead where he'd been struck. Some days he envied humans their ignorance. Today was one of them.

Kai arrived at the post office on Cambridge, not far from the Stanford campus, a solid fifteen minutes before lunch. The lot was peppered with a few cars when Kai pulled in.

Taking a deep breath, he grabbed his bag and went inside. He tried to shake off the uneasy sense that he was being watched.

He entered the post office and looked around. With the exception of a couple of people at the counter making purchases, the place was quiet. Heading straight to the section with the post offices boxes, he studied the first number and did a quick calculation. Within a minute, he found a box with a number that matched the key: 550056.

Kai eyes nervously darted around. Another patron walked in to pick up mail. A bead of sweat formed on his upper lip. Slipping the key into the lock, he did something uncharacteristic for an Agnostic—he said a little prayer. The key turned effortlessly, and the small door opened. Kai blew out the long breath he hadn't realized he'd been holding.

When he looked inside the square cubby, he found ten envelopes of varying sizes. He pulled them out. Flipping through the mail, his mouth went dry when he noticed they were all addressed to him.

His hands shook as he removed the envelopes and relocked the box. Scanning the room, he quickly deposited the mail into his messenger bag and slipped the key back inside his wallet.

Suddenly, Kai thought of something. He went over to the closed window designated for assistance with packages and post office boxes and rang the bell.

Moments later, a postal worker opened the top of the Dutch door.

"May I help you?" he asked.

Kai said politely, "I don't remember when the contract for my mailbox runs out. Can you check for me?" Kai supplied him with the number.

"Sure," the worker said, "I'll be right back." Disappearing behind the door, he reappeared five minutes later shaking his head. "Well, you don't have to worry. It's paid up until 2023."

Stunned, Kai thanked the postman and headed back to his car. Obviously, Tom was prepared in case it took Kai a lot longer to make his discovery.

He slipped into the driver's seat. He needed a place to review all this material, someplace public yet private. A quick search on his cell phone revealed a Starbucks less than half a mile away. Since it was midday, he would blend in with the college crowd. Cara always said he looked more like a college student than a scientist. It was time to test her theory.

Despite the temperature in the sun-warmed car, goose bumps rose on Kai's skin. His pulse jumped in his neck. He heard the blood rush through his ears, and his head began to throb.

Another migraine? He hoped it was just stress. He wrinkled his nose when he caught the faint smell of tar. Scanning the lot one more time, he expected to spot a road repair crew nearby. But there was nothing out of the ordinary. As he drove off, he was unable to escape a pervasive sense of dread.

Kai ordered a decaf coffee and retreated to the back of the café, finding a private table that suited his needs among the packed crowd. Cautiously, he removed the stack of envelopes from his bag and ordered them by date based on the postmark. He opened the oldest one first—it contained a letter from Dr. Tom Peyton.

Dear Kai,

If you're reading this letter, it's because I'm no longer alive. As scientists, our intellectual curiosity is unparalleled, and at times we're fortunate enough to discover something both earth-shattering and life altering. I've made one of those discoveries, which I will pass on to you. By now, you've realized that the last part of the research I conducted is missing from Forrester and was replaced with notes that I fabricated. Since we were both taught by Noble, I placed a bet that the notations would provide enough of a clue for you. I'm not sure how complete my research will be before you read this letter. However, you must keep it safe and hidden.

Project Firefly isn't what it appears to be . . . it never was. With Dr. Sandra Wilson's help, I was able to piece together the true intent of the project. As I write this, Sandra has been dead for less than twenty-four hours, but she made some provisions for me before she died to ensure that eventually you would find these documents. As you read, I beg you in advance to put aside your preconceived notions of what is scientifically probable and possible, and be willing to suspend your disbelief—it will get you closer to the truth. Kai, it's imperative you complete the work, but not at Forrester. The Foundation is a front for a ruthless and nefarious group of people who will do anything to get their hands on this discovery, including killing you and your family. It's why both Sandra and I are now dead, regardless of how our deaths were staged to look. Sandra convinced me that you're the only one who can help. Something about your destiny, if you believe in that sort of thing. I'm so sorry that you're now involved in this . . .

Sandra has assured me that there will be an opportunity to get this into the right hands, and it will come by means of someone you know, trust, and love. When you're sure you're safe, you must find Ishmael and the others. The DNA fueling the project hasn't been coming from where you think. What you've been working with in the lab is DNA belonging to Ishmael and others like him. At this point, here is where I'll ask you to suspend your disbelief—Ishmael is not 100% human.

Stay safe and watch your back.

Sincerely,

Tom

Holy shit! Kai stared at the stationary in his trembling hands. He managed to get the letter back into the envelope as a chill passed through him. Carefully, he looked around. Everything looked normal. Resting his head in his hands, he pressed the heels of his hands into his eye sockets and took several deep breaths to calm his pounding heart. A few moments later, he picked up his cell from the table and started to punch in Cara's number. Mid-dial he threw it back down. He couldn't drag her into this . . . Not yet.

What the hell does this all mean?

Pulling out the next envelope, he swept his hand over his face and opened it. Unfolding the pages, he stared at the first section of real lab notes belonging to the Noble annotations. The contents started at a brand-new point, not part of his current research.

Kai swallowed and then his scientific curiosity kicked into overdrive, absorbing him instantly into the research, which seemed closer to science fiction than to scientific fact. Although nervous, his excitement quickly outpaced his fear. His eyes couldn't travel over the pages fast enough, wanting to soak in every detail.

The genome sequenced by Tom and Sandra held 99.99 percent human genes with a few distinct differences. The senescence displayed in the cells was almost nonexistent, indicating the longevity of the owner was closer to half a millennia. In addition, they held the ability to rapidly replace cells, greatly accelerating the healing process beyond normal human abilities. Finally, there was one gene that had been edited out, and there was a note explaining that under no circumstances should it be reintroduced into the genetically engineered product. The final notes centered on creating a DNA-based vaccine to introduce the material into a host subject. Kai was experienced in vaccine creation as part of his cancer research.

Kai flipped through the pages again. The research notes appeared to be complete. Tom must have had just enough time to finish the work once he knew what he was looking for. But Tom never again mentioned the reason for the genetic abnormalities found in Ishmael or why he believed Ishmael wasn't human.

This is like an episode of the X-Files *for Flip's sake!*

As Kai reread the notes, many things clicked into place and he understood why he'd made so little progress within the last year. The more he read, the more he suspected it wasn't safe to keep any of this material on his person or easily accessible.

I need a plan, he thought, nervously tapping his fingers on the table. If he ever hoped to reproduce the results without the luxury of consulting these notes, he needed to remember the right gene markers and a few other critical pieces of information. Putting his photographic memory to work, he memorized the critical passages and took some cryptic notes in Noble notation on the notepad he had with him.

He glanced at his watch and panicked—it was almost five o'clock. He'd need to hustle in order to arrive back in San Jose in time to pick up Sara. Gathering up the documents, he hurriedly stuffed them into his bag and headed back to the post office to get there before it closed.

When he arrived, rather than returning to his post box, he made a beeline for the man behind the counter. Tom's letter mentioned getting the notes into the hands of someone Kai knew and trusted. He bought a large padded envelope then dashed out a quick note: "Keep this safe. Kai."

Slipping the key and all the documents inside the envelope, he addressed it to one of the only people he trusted with his life. He printed Cara's West Village address on the envelope with no return address and handed it back to the postal worker.

"Six dollars ninety-five cents," the man said after he'd affixed the metered stamp.

Kai handed him seven dollars and left without waiting for his change.

Chapter 31

New York City. Fifth Avenue. Wednesday, March 26, 1:55 p.m. EDT

CARA LEFT THE BUILDING out of the now-familiar underground maze. Getting to the Met was easy. It was located only a couple of blocks away on Fifth Avenue at Eighty-Second Street—barely a five-minute walk from her building. She had texted Simon earlier, and they'd arranged to meet at the bottom of the steps in front of the main entrance of the museum at two o'clock, but she hoped to get there a few minutes early.

Her morning had been frantic. She'd talked to Kai. He'd seemed a little distracted, which worked in her favor, allowing her to avoid leaking any information about her new life, especially her date. She noticed a shift within herself since the night before regarding Kai. This call had been the first time she'd spoken to him without the pull of longing which usually accompanied it. That was the good news. The bad news was she still couldn't escape the nagging feeling regarding the dream of Le Feu.

She and Constantina had met earlier to do another session before spending some time training with Michael. They'd spent time on the solo form of Tai Chi and how to use it as a form of self-defense to move with the force being exerted as opposed to meeting force with force. Michael had also spent some time introducing her to his case of weapons and reviewing knife holds in advance of incorporating weapons into her training.

Cara had taken some extra time selecting her outfit for her date—a nice pair of jeans and a black cashmere scoop-neck sweater—which she adorned with a long silver necklace. She also decided on black boots with a sexy medium heel that were high enough to be flattering, but not too high to be uncomfortable while walking around the museum for a couple of hours.

Cara thought briefly about Chamuel, who was probably hot on her trail as she blazed a path to the Met. She'd been taken off guard by something Constantina had said right before she'd left the penthouse.

"Chamuel has confirmed he'll be near. He liked your young man," she'd said.

Cara had stopped and turned back. "Really? He said that?"

"Yes. He texted me when you entered the building last night, not only to tell me you were safely back, but also to say he approved of your Simon."

Cara's eyebrows had risen in surprise.

Trusting that Chamuel was close enough to protect her, she allowed her thoughts to drift to Simon as she walked. She loved the museum and couldn't imagine a more perfect date.

She approached the magnificent Beaux-Arts structure with its four giant pairs of columns framing three sets of doors, each covered by an arch containing a triptych of windows. The stairs leading up to the entrance from all three directions were filled with people either sitting or standing, preparing to go inside, or just relaxing and enjoying the sun with no plans to go any farther. Passing by a street vendor, she caught the scent of spicy roasted nuts.

She spotted Simon sitting midway up the steps waiting for her to arrive. His hair was secured in a ponytail, and he was dressed casually in a black leather jacket and black jeans. A white button-front shirt, open at the neck, and Italian leather loafers added a dressy touch. He turned his head and looked her way; a smile spread across his face when he saw her. She returned his smile.

He rose and walked down to the street to meet her. When she was within arm's length, he pulled her in against him, lowering his full lips onto hers. Her head tilted back and her hand naturally gravitated up to caress his smooth cheek before she slid her fingers back to stroke the softness of his dark golden hair. The feel of his large hand splayed on her back and his gentle kiss sent a delicate shiver through her while a flash of warmth shot to her core. Unable to resist, she snuggled into the solid muscles of his chest, hungering to know what they would feel like under her fingertips.

Her heart raced as his tongue gently parted her lips, deepening the kiss. Her face flushed, and her knees went weak. She held back a moan, right before his lips deserted her. Holding her in his arms, he pressed his forehead to hers, the blue pools of his eyes captivating her.

"I had a great time last night," he said softly with the barest hint of an accent.

"Ditto," she said, trying to get the heat and tightness at the center of her thighs under control.

Does he realize how breathless he makes me? She wondered. Not to mention hot. After their date last night, she couldn't stop thinking about their first kiss. He awakened sensations in her that she'd given up hopes of ever feeling again. If he tried to make love to her right now on the steps, she might not stop him.

Slowly, he released her out of their embrace.

"So, how about we go enjoy some art?" he asked.

Cara took a few more breaths to recover and opened her purse. "Brilliant idea. By the way, I'm a member, so we don't need to pay admission," she said, pulling out her membership card. When she looked up, he held up his own, wearing a shy grin.

"Me too."

She gaped. He was a President's Circle donor, one of the highest levels of patronage, costing twenty thousand dollars annually. She was a Contributing donor, since it had privileges associated with the Costume Institute. At twelve hundred dollars annually, she considered it expensive but worth it.

"You're a true patron of the arts," she said. *And round two goes to Simon*, she thought.

He winked at her, and put the card back in his pocket before reaching for her hand. "You could say that. Let's go."

They entered the main hall, where Simon showed his membership card and received two little, round, blue metal tags. They affixed the buttons to their clothing, and Cara stopped to check her coat before they entered the gate.

Pausing at the bottom of the large central staircase, Simon turned to her. "Where would you like to start?"

Cara thought for a second. "Well, I guess my favorite places are the American Wing, European Paintings, and the Sculpture Garden, but I'm open to anything. My first love is American landscape painters of the Hudson River School, but I also love the Impressionists, especially Renoir. What about you?"

He smiled. "I guess my bias runs toward European Paintings, but I love all your favorite wings. Did you know that when John Kensett died in 1872, thirty-eight of his paintings were donated to the museum?" Simon said, referencing one of the most prominent Hudson River painters of the time.

Cara tilted her head, impressed by his knowledge. "I knew a lot of his paintings were here, but no, I hadn't realized there had been such a large bequest."

"Why don't we start on the first floor in the American Wing? Then we can move on to the European Paintings." he suggested.

She smiled. "Excellent idea."

They set out for the Charles Engelhard Court, a large, open structure anchored on the north side by the multistory, neoclassical façade of the Branch Bank of the United States, originally located on Wall Street.

Cara enjoyed having her hand inside Simon's as they meandered through the court, looking at the Tiffany glass along the way.

"You mentioned you paint. What's your favorite subject?" she asked.

Simon paused to think. "I find landscapes inspiring," he said. Then he glanced at her with a mischievous glint in his eye. "I've also been known to paint some full-bodied portraits in my time."

"Nudes, you mean?"

He looked at her innocently. "Of course. What other way is there to paint them?"

She chuckled, but she couldn't decide if he was teasing her or if he was dead serious until he didn't seem to get the joke. Then he smiled.

"It would give me great pleasure to have you as my model someday."

A blush warmed her cheeks. "I'm flattered that you'd consider me." She could hold her own with a piece of charcoal and wouldn't mind him returning the favor.

"Do you collect?" she asked, changing the topic as they climbed the stairs to the second level of the American Wing.

"Mostly everything I own, I've painted myself. You?"

"I have a few painting and sketches, but I'd hardly call it a collection," she replied. "Would you mind if we moved to the European Paintings galleries? With all this discussion about paintings, I'm anxious to see some."

Simon smiled, his eyes crinkling at the sides. "I'd love to."

The first gallery they entered had several Rubens and pieces from his contemporaries. They paused in front of one of the largest paintings in the gallery. Simon pulled her back so that her body rested against the warm ripples under his shirt, his arms encircling her waist and his chin rested gently atop her head while they admired the work. As much as Cara enjoyed the art, she enjoyed being in Simon's embrace more. Her body melted under his touch, and she badly wished that they were someplace private so they could get even closer. She craved the touch of his skin directly on hers.

"I'd like to see your paintings some time," she whispered.

"That could be arranged." His breath warmed her hair as he spoke, and then he kissed the top of her head.

Their moment was interrupted by the vibration of Simon's cell phone in his jacket pocket. She felt his body tense.

"Excuse me one second," he said, stepping away to reach into his pocket for his phone. He looked at the number. "I have to take this call. It's work. Can you wait here a moment?"

She nodded.

"I'll be right back."

A couple of minutes later, Cara turned to see Simon reenter the Gallery as a chime sounded from inside her purse. It was a text from Constantina: CALLED BACK TO THE SANCTUARY ON UNEXPECTED BUSINESS. I'VE ASKED MICHAEL TO STAY WITH YOU IN THE PENTHOUSE. CHAMUEL WILL STAY CLOSE. ENJOY YOUR

DATE. NO NEED TO RUSH HOME. I'LL CONTACT YOU AS SOON AS I CAN. LOVE, CONSTANTINA.

Warm hands clasped her shoulders from behind. "Did you get a message?" he whispered in her ear.

"Yes. Good news. My appointment was cancelled for tonight," she whispered back.

"Well, that *is* excellent news. Can I tempt you with a dinner invitation?"

She smiled. "I think I can be persuaded."

"Would it sweeten the deal if I said that I'd be the one doing the cooking?"

"Perhaps . . . as long as you don't throw in a cheesy line about showing me your etchings. Otherwise, I'll think that you're just trying to get me alone." She turned into his arms.

"No chance of that." He pulled her back into his hard warmth. "I don't own any etchings. But I'd love to show you my paintings."

"I'd love to see them."

His lips turned up in a sexy smile. "I can't lie. I want to get you alone. But I promise to be a gentleman. Your virtue is safe with me . . . this time."

They spent another hour and a half exploring the European Paintings galleries. Simon's extensive knowledge impressed her as he pointed out the significance of the sociopolitical climate during the time periods the paintings were made, as well as technical observations on brush strokes and styles. He knew a broad range of artists, time periods, and styles.

Her connection to him grew with each passing minute. Two days ago, she didn't even know him, and now she couldn't imagine spending time without him. She hoped she wasn't headed for disappointment. Pushing those feelings down, she decided to enjoy the moment. One thing was for sure: there wasn't any place she'd rather be or anyone else she'd rather be with.

Simon looked at his watch. "It's almost five o'clock. Are you ready to head downtown? I want to get to the market while we still have a good selection for dinner."

"Sounds good. Lead the way, kind sir." She linked her arm back through his, and they headed for the exit.

Chapter 32

THE CABBIE DROPPED Cara and Simon off at the Gourmet Garage, a specialty food store on Broome Street in SoHo. Cara normally despised food shopping but even taking out the garbage would be fun with Simon. He carried a small basket, filling it with some artisanal cheeses and a fresh baguette to start. Along the way, he added some fresh tuna, salad greens, and a few other items needed to prepare the meal. Cara happily trailed alongside him, watching him in motion as he talked to various people whom he seemed to know. His familiarity with the store extended to every kind of food, vegetable, and spice.

Color me impressed, she thought with delight.

When they were finished gathering their groceries, they walked the one block to Simon's Greene Street loft as darkness fell. Cara loved this section of the city. SoHo held the largest array of historic cast-iron architecture in the world, and Greene Street was a great example. Its nineteenth-century buildings and cobblestone streets had served industrial purposes in the 1880s and '90s. Cara guessed a loft in one of these buildings would sell for anywhere from two to five million dollars depending on the size of the apartment. She smiled to herself, thinking this was the perfect place for someone like Simon who was an avid painter.

He led the way into one of the row houses. The foyer was decorated in what Cara would term modern industrial; the lines were clean and sparse with framed black-and-white photographs and a heavy dose of metal furniture.

"Interesting choice of décor," she said.

Simon gave the foyer a quick glance. "The co-op committee wanted to give a nod to the building's industrial roots," he said. "The décor isn't really my taste, but it doesn't offend me either."

They took what was the original elevator, common in the old converted loft spaces, to the fifth floor. The elevator required a key and an access code.

"You have the whole floor?" Cara asked, stepping out directly into his apartment and an open plan hallway. There was a six-foot partition wall to the right, a narrow hallway down to the left, and a large opening into a magnificent gourmet kitchen straight ahead. The ceilings were easily fourteen feet high, painted black to hide the ductwork and to draw the eye downward.

Simon set the bags on the floor and hung their coats on hooks next to the elevator.

"It's not as big as it looks at first blush," he said. He retrieved the bags before heading into the kitchen. "Each resident has their own floor. I'll take you to see the best part later." He flashed a smile and started to unload the food onto the center island.

Somehow she trusted he wasn't referring to the bedroom. She glanced around. "I remember you promising earlier to show me your artwork."

"And I always keep my promises," he said. That didn't surprise her. "My studio is on the other side of the living room around the corner."

He emptied both bags. "Would you mind being my sous-chef this evening?"

Giving him a wary look, she asked, "Does it involve sharp objects?"

Simon's shoulders tensed and his dark-blond eyebrows drew together in a frown. "Are you afraid of knives?"

She wondered why that worried him and laughed it off. "When I say I'm a disaster in the kitchen, I'm not kidding."

He looked relieved. "Don't worry. I'll teach you how to handle a knife properly."

Okay, she could feign ignorance for an evening since Michael had already taken her through the full gamut of knives at his dojo. Knives weren't the problem. She could burn water.

After he washed the fish, he set it on a plate and turned to her. "Let me go change into something better suited to cook in, and then I'll give you a tour before we start dinner." He disappeared down the hallway to the left of the kitchen.

Cara looked around the spotless kitchen. The counters were free of clutter other than an espresso maker, a knife block, and a basket of fresh fruit. A truly magnificent space, it showcased a heavy-duty stainless steel industrial stove with a hood and exhaust that disappeared up into the black painted ceiling. Simon had chosen sleek, modern European cabinets and a dark granite countertop. It rivaled her kitchen back at the penthouse.

As Cara looked around, taking everything in, she noticed four exceptional paintings on the partition wall separating the hall from the kitchen. Three of them were food-themed still lifes—fruit, vegetables, and fresh seafood—executed in the style of Severin Roesen, an American mid-nineteenth-century painter. The fourth painting, although framed in the same nineteenth-century style, didn't seem to belong with the rest. The portrait contained a young woman's face, the look in the sitter's eyes capturing her love for the painter.

Puzzled, Cara hopped down from the counter stool. With a twinge of guilt for snooping, she lifted the picture off the hook to examine it. Her art history training had taught her to examine the back of a canvas when judging the age of an unrestored painting. From what Cara could determine, the painting appeared to be a late nineteenth century work. Carefully, she placed the painting back on the wall.

Simon returned wearing a black V-neck cotton shirt that hugged his torso tucked into old faded blue jeans. She'd never seen him without long sleeves and was surprised at both the broadness of his shoulders and the density of muscles on his arms. He was leaner than a bodybuilder but as well defined.

It should illegal to look so delicious in old jeans, she thought.

"I was admiring your paintings. Are these all yours?" she asked, and then added, "Well, except for the portrait."

Simon furrowed his brows as he looked at her. "They're all mine. Why would you exclude the portrait?"

She flushed and clasped her hands. "I'm sorry for snooping. I took a look at the back and the canvas looks like it's from the late nineteenth century."

An uneasy look traversed Simon's face, and after a brief pause, he spoke. "I love old canvases and have painted on many you'd now consider old. I like the way they hold the pigment. Did you know that a lot of artists paint over existing paintings at some point in their careers?"

Cara could taste the truth in his words despite his rigid posture.

"Did you know the woman or was she just a model?"

A multitude of emotions washed over Simon's face, ending in a pained expression and a sad smile. "Her name was Calliope. I guess you could say she was my first love."

Cara's heart caught in her chest. "Where is she now?" For some reason, she didn't think she'd need to deal with past girlfriends this soon.

He stared off, his eyes unfocused. "She died a while back."

Okay, not the answer she'd expected. Despite being hit with a pang of regret for asking, she sensed something cryptic in his answer. "I'm sorry. I didn't mean to pry."

Shaking his head, he sighed deeply. "You didn't. Sometimes I think I should talk about her and about what happened. But there's never been anyone . . ." He turned away from her. Leaning his hands on the counter, he hung his head. She heard him mutter softly to himself.

Sliding off the stool, she walked around the island until she stood looking up the rippled mountain of his back. Her hands reached out and made contact with the soft cotton of his shirt. He drew in a sharp breath as her fingers glided over the black fabric, her hands exploring the chiseled terrain. His tension slid away under her touch, and he leaned back against her. Reaching around him from behind, she traced the hard ridges of his pectorals before traveling down over the bumpy muscles of his midsection until her arms encircled his lean waist. She rested her ear against the hollow of his spine. Breathing in the clean scent of the cotton, she caught a pleasant muskiness permeating his citrus cologne. The moment she sensed it, her body flushed with heat and she had a déjà vu moment—she had comforted him before. In a flash, the memory faded.

"If you want, you can share it with me," she offered gently. She meant it. The sadness inside him spoke to her, and her first instinct was to heal him in any way she could.

He curled his fingers around one of her hands. "Cara, I—" he started, then captured both of her hands in his, moving them from his waist to his mouth, and kissing them with soft lips. He twisted around to face her and closed his eyes, tucking her into his chest.

She unwittingly held her breath while he just stood there, holding her. Fierce protectiveness welled up inside her, and she realized that she wanted him to confide in her. She'd be his pillar of strength if that's what he needed. Sensing his discomfort, she nestled her hands in the small of his back and looked up, catching his gaze. "Sometimes it's better to touch someone when you have a hard story to tell."

His lips quirked in a small smile tinged with sadness. "I like that thought." He hugged her tightly, his large arms forming two pillars of warmth along her sides. Her ear rested back on the soft cotton next to his beating heart. She felt the warmth of his cheek on her hair.

He cleared his throat. "My family and Calliope's knew each other well. We grew up together, practically since birth. But we didn't discover our feelings for each other until we were adolescents. Actually, I think a more accurate statement would be that I didn't realize how much she loved me until I became an adolescent. Boys are generally more naive when it comes to love than girls. You girls tend to have that advantage over us. Our families were in the same business so it only made sense that we would choose the same careers, so to speak. We were educated and trained to fight together."

Cara interjected. "You were both in private security?"

"Yes. I mentioned there weren't many women in my line of work, and it's true. Calliope was one of the few whom I've ever worked with. Somehow, I don't know if she would've ever chosen this career if it hadn't been for me. The job can be dangerous, and I think her family would have preferred for her to have chosen a teaching career."

"That sounds a little old-fashioned. Sounds like she wanted to play with the big boys," replied Cara.

"She did. At least she said she did. We'd been a couple for several years, but our relationship had become strained. I loved her, but felt guilty for being restless and wanting more out of life. I hungered to see the world, while she wanted to remain in Europe close to her family. Anyway, my team had a particularly dangerous assignment, guarding a highly visible target being pursued by some pretty rough people. We gathered intelligence indicating the situation could escalate, so I called in reinforcements. Calliope wasn't supposed to be there that night. Under normal circumstances, we were prohibited from working together on assignments for safety reasons. As it turned out, her team was the only one close enough to respond.

"All hell broke loose, and we were ambushed. We worked in pairs, and my primary role was to protect the target while my partner protected me. Almost immediately, my partner was wounded, preventing him from signaling me when an attacker came at my back. Calliope spotted the danger and left her formation to protect me while her partner fought to hold off the enemy. In the seconds she left her back exposed and killed my attacker, she was killed by another as I watched, helpless to save her . . . " he paused, and Cara heard him swallow.

"It's okay," Cara whispered, stroking his back with her hand as she stayed pressed against him.

After more throat-clearing, he continued. "We went in with eight that night and came home with six. The rest of us barely made it out of there with our own lives. After I told her family, I made my decision to take a break for a while. I left right after her funeral and came to the United States."

Her heart hurt for his loss. Her long-standing heartache over Kai seemed so small and insignificant in comparison. She moved her head out from underneath his chin and looked up at him. He'd turned away. She could swear he wiped a tear away with the back of his hand, not wanting her to see it. Reaching up, she gently turned his head back to face her.

"Look at me," she said. His gaze was bright.

She locked her eyes on his, her hands clutching the sides of his face tenderly. "Her death wasn't your fault, Simon," she said, going straight to the root of his pain. "It wasn't your fault." A look of surprise shone in his eyes along with something else—a blazing desire.

His mouth came down on hers, and his need washed over her in a warm fiery wave, igniting her nerve endings with an energy and passion that rocked her. Any reserve she had dissolved. She kissed him back with everything she had, tasting and probing as a moan escaped her throat. His large hands wound into her hair, and he pressed her into the hard muscled landscape of his chest. Without warning, he scooped her up into his strong arms and carried her down the hall into his bedroom. The room was masculine and stylish. He headed for the king-sized bed. The only light in the room was given off by the Impressionist-style painting hanging above his headboard.

He set her down at the edge of the bed, and bent down to nibble the side of her neck. His touch made her tingle all the way down to her toes. A sudden whiff of his pleasant, musky scent assaulted her senses, triggering a shudder deep in her core. All she wanted in that moment was to touch, tease, and taste every inch of him. Overtaken by blind desire, Cara brushed the palm of her hand down the front of his jeans, and her lips parted in surprise. His hands wrapped around her shoulders as he threw back his head and groaned. Lifting his shirt from his waistband, she slipped her hands underneath the worn cotton and brushed her fingertips over his abs, surprised at the smooth, silky texture of his skin. She had a deep impulse to run her tongue over the hard ridges of his stomach, but his hands reached under to gently capture her wrists. Lifting them to his mouth, he kissed her palms. Then he scooped her back up, and lowered her lightly onto the bed. He lay down, leaning on his elbows over her with blue fire burning in his eyes.

"I want to make love to you so desperately, I can barely stop myself. But I don't want our first time to be overshadowed by my past. You deserve the right experience and to know it's only about you and not my baggage. Do you understand?" His brow furrowed, his rich voice pleading.

She looked up at him from the bed and nodded, at a loss for words, wondering what to do with the all the hormones coursing through her body. But the passion behind his disclosure moved her. She'd only been with two men, in the Biblical sense, before him, and would have added him as the third without question. Her body wilted in disappointment at the sudden stop, but her respect for him deepened.

"I just want to lie with you for a couple of minutes. Is that okay?" he asked softly, still balanced over her.

She smiled, putting both her arms up to him, inviting him down to rest on top of her. He came toward her, and in one swift movement shifted her on top of him. "If I lie on top of you, I might crush you," he teased.

It was crazy, but in that moment, she knew she was falling in love with him. Without a word, she leaned down, her hair creating a curtain around them, and pressed her lips tenderly to his. He reacted with a soft moan, his fingers digging gently into the curve of her hips. Then she did something she'd wanted to do since the night before. She reached around to the base of his neck and pulled out the leather tie that held his hair back, releasing the dark golden waves onto the pillow.

"I want to see you with your hair down," she said softly.

He gazed up at her. "I thought you already had."

Emotionally, she guessed she had.

Wrapping his arms around her, he snuggled her on top of him, unable to hide the evidence of his desire pressing up against her. He sealed his mouth over hers, kissing her at first gently, and then with a hungry passion. His fingers trailed down the length of her back then his arms wrapped her in steel bands of warm flesh. Cara melted into his strength, savoring their kiss. She was exactly where she wanted to be. She wanted this—she wanted him—it felt right and good.

Pulling his lips from hers, he looked at her. "We better start cooking before the fish goes bad. It's still on the counter."

"Okay," she conceded, trying not to look too disappointed as she rolled off him and into a sitting position next to him.

He sat up and wrapped his muscled thighs around her from behind, whispering into her hair. "Thank you." Then he hoisted them both up.

Cara's eyes widened at his strength and she laughed. "You make me feel like this delicate little flower next to you."

"Aren't you?" he asked as they headed back toward the kitchen to cook their meal.

Chapter 33

New York City. Greene Street Loft. Wednesday, March 26, 8:00 p.m. EDT

CHAMUEL COMBED HIS FINGERS through his hair and cringed as he followed Cara out of his bedroom. The jagged edges of his emotions, laid bare and exposed for Cara to see, had ripped a raw hole in his chest. He never thought he would have shared Calliope's story with her this soon. On one hand, he could kick himself for not removing the painting; on the other, this had been an impromptu dinner invite, and the painting had been there so long he failed to consciously give it a second thought.

But he hadn't told Cara the whole story. He couldn't, not without exposing his true identity, and he wasn't ready to make that leap. He needed to relish this evening with her, ensuring it was filled with only happy memories, since they might be the only thing that kept him company in his prison cell.

He'd mentioned eight went in and only six came out, but he didn't explain the other casualty. Calliope's death had been tragic, but his shame came from the other he'd lost: Mina, the Soul Seeker in his Trinity. She'd been the target. The Dark Ones used Calliope as a distraction to pull his attention away from her. Their ploy worked, and he'd failed them both. That's when he had earned his badge of shame, why he'd avoided the Trinity rotation, and why he'd denied himself the pleasure of female companionship . . . until he'd met Cara. Intellectually, he knew every step he took with Cara put him dangerously close to repeating history, but his soul hungered for her in a way he couldn't deny or contain.

Within a few brief moments, Cara had managed to release part of the burden he'd been carrying for well beyond a century. Her empathy moved him. Maybe being with Cara could help him heal the rest of the way. Maybe, as with Siddhartha, his imperfect life could lead him to Nirvana. Maybe history didn't have to repeat itself.

His masculine pride was still bruised for shedding a tear in front of her, a true rarity. But he trusted her, and in that moment, he knew with conviction that he was falling in love with her. She tested his self-control when she'd touched him through his jeans and then ran the silken tips of her fingers over his naked skin. The male in him hadn't wanted to stop her, but the gentleman in him knew he had to.

It was true when he said he didn't want to use her as a balm to soothe his guilt over Calliope's death. That had never really entered his mind. It was bad enough that he already violated the law. He couldn't take it any farther with a clear conscience while this falsehood existed between them. Had that not been the case, damn the fish, he would have spent the entire night pleasuring her in every way he could think of—and there were many. God knows, he'd been at the top of his class when it came to Sensual Pleasures training.

By the time they reached the kitchen, the mood had lightened considerably. He tucked his hair behind his ears. Normally, he didn't like to cook with his hair down, but Cara seemed to like it that way. And he wanted to please her.

Chamuel turned on the CD player to a contemporary mix so they had some lively music to cook to as they prepared the meal.

Cooking gave him time to gather his thoughts as she watched, smiling from the center island. He gave her manageable tasks, and, true to his word, he taught her how to use his Henkel knives. Her only job requiring a knife was cutting up the romaine lettuce heads for their salad, which she could have just ripped with her hands.

He'd been alarmed earlier when she seemed hesitant to use a knife, since part of her training with Michael would be weapons training. Given what she was up against, she would need to be able to defend herself even with him guarding her. Once she knew the truth, assuming they could keep their relationship secret, he hoped to take over some of her training personally.

As the meal cooked, he went to retrieve a bottle of wine out of one of the two tall wine towers. "I know fish requires a white, but would you mind a red?" he asked, standing in front of the open refrigerator.

"Sounds good to me. I don't stand on ceremony."

Chamuel selected a bottle and took two red-wine glasses from the bar in the kitchen, pouring them each a glass.

Raising her glass, Cara looked at him with a sparkle in her green eyes. "To new beginnings?"

"I'll drink to that." He smiled and tapped his glass with hers. He only hoped this beginning wouldn't be short-lived and followed by an unhappy ending.

Remembering he owed her a tour, he picked up the small timer for the fish and his glass of wine. "Take your wine, and grab your coat. I want to show you something." He wanted her to see his pride and joy.

He led her past his bedroom through a door at the end of the hallway to the stairs. They climbed to the top and he threw open the exterior door, flicking on the lights to the roof deck as he passed.

Cara gasped. "This is yours?"

His heart swelled with happiness at her delight. "Yes, it's mine. This was one of the perks of buying the top-floor apartment."

Cara's eyes held a look of awe while she took in the view of the deck and the city beyond. "Simon, this is absolutely gorgeous. If it wasn't so chilly, we could have eaten up here tonight."

He wrapped his arms around her from behind and pulled her into him, carefully balancing his wine. She felt so good next him to like this, he couldn't resist burying his face into the hair by her neck and breathing in her scent laced with the wildflower notes of her desire. "We will, when the weather gets warmer," he said, dreaming of their future as she stood in his arms. He pictured hosting parties together and enjoying the warmth of summer, sunning on the deck.

The timer for the fish rang. She turned to him. "Can we come back later?"

"Your wish is my command. In the meantime, we should rescue the fish."

They ate dinner by candlelight in the dining room. Not wanting her to go, Chamuel convinced Cara to stay and watch a movie.

Settling on the large sectional, he lay sideways with Cara snuggled in front of him, her head leaning back against his chest and his arms at home around her. They chose a new action thriller on pay-per-view.

Before he pushed play, he took her hand and whispered in her ear. "Cara, the call I received in the museum earlier? It turns out I'm needed at work this week after all. I'd like to see you again, but I don't know what my schedule will be like. Can we be spontaneous?" He kissed her palm as he waited for her answer.

"We'll make it work," she replied. "If you can get away Friday night, I have plans with my friend Sienna, and she's dying to meet you. I would love for you to join us." She twisted her head and stared up at him with expectation. The last thing he wanted to do was disappoint her.

"I'll do my best."

Before the introductory credits finished rolling, she was asleep on his chest.

Chamuel had never been this happy or this concerned. He knew two things: he craved Cara with every fiber of his body and soul, and this was the first time he'd felt like this in his one-hundred-forty-seven-year life. If he could freeze time, with her body melded to his like it was now, he'd gladly stay this way for eternity.

Punishment be damned.

He hungered to do what every Nephilim does when he or she is in love. He wanted to surround them both within the comfort and safety of his snow-white wings. But right now he prayed for one thing—that she'd forgive him for his deception. Making love to her would be impossible without her forgiveness.

Chapter 34

San Jose. Country Day School. Wednesday, March 26,
6:20 p.m. PDT / 9:20 p.m. EDT

SARA'S PRESCHOOL TEACHER stood outside the one-story ranch-style building with both Sara and another child, her arm resting gently around them as they waited, backpacks slung over their small shoulders.

"Daddy," Sara shouted, dropping her backpack and launching her body into his arms as he approached. Kai leaned down to scoop her up.

"Miss Jessica, I'm really sorry I'm late," Kai said, addressing the young teacher with kind eyes. Kai felt better knowing Sara wasn't the only one waiting for a parent. Not that it allayed his guilt.

Jessica smiled warmly. "No problem, Dr. Solomon. Sara was keeping Tucker and me company until his parents could get here." Hearing his name, the small boy snuggled up closer behind Miss Jessica. Her face lit up and she added, "Big news. Sara did very well on her alphabet test today."

Sara beamed at her teacher. "Miss Jessica put two gold stars on my paper, not just one," she said, excited with her accomplishment.

"Wow, that's great," he said to Sara, reaching down to retrieve her backpack before turning back to her teacher. "Thanks, again, Miss Jessica. We'll see you tomorrow morning."

The little boy peeked around Miss Jessica, and Kai gave him a wave. "Bye, Tucker."

Kai buckled Sara into her booster seat in the back of the A6, and they set off for home. He only half listened to Sara jabber about her day filled with lost lunchboxes, projects involving crepe paper animals, and chocolate chip cookies brought to class to celebrate a student's birthday. His mind was consumed with what he'd learned from Tom's notes and a plethora of questions. Where did he go from here? Did he go back to Forrester and continue with his current work like nothing had happened? Did he look for an independent lab and try to replicate the work? Did he ask for a transfer? For the first time, he almost regretted making the discovery. With the knowledge came a responsibility he wasn't sure he could fulfill. Why him? Why was it so important that he be the one to make this discovery? He got a brain cramp just thinking about it.

He pulled into the driveway and pain slammed straight into him. An angry throbbing started behind his eyes, causing pinpricks of white to cloud his vision. His hand flew up to rub his temple, while steadying himself on the steering wheel with his other. Thank God he had some extra meds for Melanie in the house.

Taking a deep breath, he tried to manage the pain. He eased his way out of the car and around to the other side to get Sara. Opening the door, he found her staring up at him with wild eyes.

"Daddy, I'm afraid."

Her words struck him in his crippled state. "What are you afraid of, sweetie?"

"Monster."

A shiver passed over Kai.

"What monster?"

"The one in the house." She whimpered, her corn-silk blonde hair falling down around her face.

Her words slapped him in the face, and the pain in his head intensified. He glanced over at his split-level house, and everything looked in order. The security system would have notified him had anyone entered his residence. He desperately needed something to quell the pain in his head, and now wasn't the time to indulge in monsters-under-the-bed discussions.

"Come on, honey. Daddy will protect you," he said, unbuckling her and lifting her out of the car.

"No! Luke!" she squirmed out of his arms, and ran headlong down the narrow pathway along the side of the house, which led through the gate into the backyard.

"Sara!" Kai staggered after her, but the painful throbbing prevented him from moving any faster. *Luke? Who the hell is Luke?* Then he remembered her telling him about Luke the night she'd crawled into his bed.

After the gate banged closed behind Sara, Kai heard the sound of shattering glass a moment before Sara's scream pierced the air. His heart jumped to his throat and his legs moved as fast as they could. He crashed through the gate and into a scene that stunned him to a halt. Sara was crouched between a tree and the side fence ten feet away.

In the center of his yard, between the back patio and the swing set, a large man in black clothing and a large creature circled each other, ready to fight. The creature, a ten-foot-tall horned demon with talons and cloven feet, was surrounded in a black shadow. Its skin was a combination of scales and feathers, so red it was almost black. The face had glowing red eyes and needle-sharp teeth. The man stood before the demon with a sword of blinding light thrust out in front of him. Neither of them took notice of Kai or Sara.

The air wavered around them as the demon swatted at the man with a hand of talon-tipped fingers. Molten waves of heat rolled toward Kai. The painful throbbing receded slightly as Kai stood rooted in place, gaping in stunned disbelief.

The man and the demon continued their circular dance, the demon taking random swats, and the man ducking out of its way. In a blink of an eye, the man transformed into a white blur of light, and in a blinding flash, rammed into the demon. The demon let out a roar, and then there was silence.

Kai's headache disappeared. He stood with his jaw hanging open, staring at the empty backyard and the pile of black ash where the demon had stood. The man with the sword disappeared without a trace.

"Daddy!"

Kai turned his head as a fist slammed into his face, knocking him to the ground. Kai scrambled to get up, but a hard kick landed in his side, doubling him over and knocking the wind out of him. He fell to the ground, groaning in pain.

Sara screamed. He looked through a swelling eye to see a man he didn't recognize grab her from behind, her feet kicking the air. Panic seized him, and he forced himself to move before being pulled roughly to his feet. Hands encircled his throat from behind with an iron grip, constricting his airway. Kai struggled against him while Sara screamed in the other man's arms.

"Where are the notes?" asked a cold and controlled voice an inch from his ear.

"I don't have them," Kai choked out through gritted teeth.

"That's unfortunate."

"Daddy, they have our angel!" Sara cried.

Kai turned his head to see what she was talking about. The man who'd fought the demon earlier was pinned inside the arms of a much larger man who stood over seven feet tall and didn't look altogether human. His eyes widened when he saw a woman with raven-black hair standing next them. It all clicked into place.

"Emily." Her name slipped from his lips right before a sweet, cloying smell covered his mouth, sucking him into darkness.

Chapter 35

KAI EDGED INTO CONSCIOUSNESS, his head a pulsing mass on his shoulders. The ground was hard and cold beneath him. His senses awakened to the combined smell of dampness and rotting garbage. Slowly opening his eyes, he surveyed his surroundings in the semi-darkness and concluded he was in some kind of underground prison cell.

A couple of oil lamps cast dim shadows along the rough walls, illuminating just enough for Kai to make out a few more dark cells across the way. No movement or sound within, they all appeared to be empty. He was alone.

He took a deep breath and let it out slowly to calm himself.

Shivering on the ground with his hands tied securely behind his back, he fought back a wave of nausea. He gave himself another minute then did an inventory of his extremities, testing them one by one in an effort to diagnose any potential injuries. Other than the cold and stiffness from his concrete bed and his bound hands, he determined he was in reasonable shape. Digging deeper into his memory, he tried to recall what had happened.

Closing his eyes to focus, he remembered picking Sara up from preschool a little late but without incident. Then the scene from the backyard came crashing back. Kai's eyes popped open and his heart raced; his concern for Sara escalated to panic.

What have they done with my little girl?

Instinctually, he wanted to scream for help, but instantly recognized the futility of it. He used the chill of the concrete next to his cheek to ground him and get his breathing back under control. His second strongest gift after his near-photographic memory was his ability to manage a crisis. Sara's safety unwound him, but losing his cool wouldn't do her any good.

Summoning all his willpower, he shifted into crisis-management mode. A deadly calm settled over him as he engaged his most valuable asset: his analytical mind.

Kai struggled to push himself up into a sitting position, the restraints cutting into his wrists when he moved. The throbbing in his head intensified with the change in elevation, followed by an urge to vomit. After giving himself a minute for the pain and nausea to subside, he assessed his situation.

Creating a mental checklist, he took a deep breath and collected his thoughts. He was still alive, which meant he had a chance. Check. It was fair to assume his abduction was related to Tom's work. Check. The Foundation was involved. Check. He would be needed in some way to create the vaccine. Check. They both had leverage—he had what they wanted inside his head, and they had his daughter. Double check.

His thoughts shifted back to getting help, and his anxiety flared.

Just think, he told himself sternly.

Even if Miss Jessica at Sara's school grew concerned, with Melanie away on business in China until the weekend, it could be a while before anyone started to look for them.

Shit.

Multiple pairs of footfalls approached from the distance. Adrenaline tore through Kai at the sound of his approaching captors. He drew himself up onto his feet.

Slowly, they came into view. A sharply dressed man of average height holding a cane led a small entourage. The man's jet-black hair brushed the top of his suit jacket. His eyes were dark coals, and a V-shaped scar was etched in his cheek.

Kai narrowed his eyes the moment he recognized the oh-so-familiar face of the woman standing at the man's side. They were flanked by two oversized men who hung in the shadows.

Kai's eyes bore into Emily.

I knew I hated that bitch for a reason, he thought. Turning his attention to the man, Kai projected a picture of utter calm. "Who are you?"

If his smirk was any indication, the man was somewhat amused by Kai's question. He spoke in a smooth and slightly accented voice. "You're the Messenger—you tell me?"

Kai tried to hide a genuine look of confusion on his face. "I'm sorry, what?"

"Ah, I see . . ." the man said, squinting. "You don't know. Very smart, that Sandra was."

Mystified, Kai kept his face blank. *What the hell is he talking about?*

The black-haired man paced using his cane, his gait showing a slight limp as he walked. The large red jewel on top of the cane caught Kai's eye.

"Dr. Solomon, we've been waiting for some time for you to lead us to Dr. Peyton's work. We had started to lose hope." The man's voice took on a slithery quality that sent a shiver across Kai's skin. Stopping in front of Kai, he gave him a piercing look. "We were disappointed to find you were no longer in possession of what we're seeking. Let's hope you can remember what you read."

"Where's my daughter?"

"Oh, she's quite safe . . . for now."

"I want to see her," Kai demanded.

A malevolent grin spread across the man's face. "Dr. Solomon, you're hardly in the position to make such demands." He waved his hand at Kai as if trying to shoo away a pesky insect. "You'll see her in due time. In the meantime, why don't I tell you what you'll be doing while you're our guest?"

Kai gritted his teeth and projected a composure he didn't feel. Better to shut up and listen.

"First, please allow me to introduce myself. I am Le Feu, and of course you already know my consort, Emily."

Like the pieces of a puzzle locking into place, everything clicked at once for Kai, and his knees went weak. He could hear the roar of his pulse thundering through his ears.

Cara's dream.

Le Feu regarded him shrewdly and smiled. "Ah, I see you've heard of me. My reputation precedes me."

Kai said nothing but continued to stare.

Le Feu clasped his hands together and pointed them toward Kai. "Well! Let's get started. We have so little time to do so much. You have many questions, I know. What I'll tell you is that you're a guest of the Foundation." He swept his hand out in front of him. "My apologies for the harsh accommodations. You'll soon be moved to more comfortable quarters in the lab upstairs, but make no mistake—they'll be no less secure. Our lab is fully equipped. I believe you'll be quite impressed."

Le Feu pointed to the two enormous men, who stepped out of the shadows from behind him. "Chaos and Destruction will guard you at all times," he said.

Kai recognized their faces. One of them had been in his backyard the night before, holding the man wearing black whom Sara had called Luke. The identical twins stood over seven feet tall with faces that held an unnaturally white pallor. They'd never be mistaken for human in a crowd.

An icy energy radiated from them, chilling the air and raising gooseflesh on Kai's arms under his jacket. They provided a sharp contrast to the malevolent heat radiating from Le Feu.

Kai simultaneously sweated and shuddered from the effect.

"Let me get to the point. You have five days to create the vaccine that we need."

"Five days? Are you *nuts*?" Even with the notes and a clear road map, Kai anticipated the vaccine would take at least a couple of weeks to develop correctly.

Le Feu's eyebrow flew up. "I may be many things, Dr. Solomon, but crazy isn't one of them. I'll remind you, there's a lot at stake." There was no mistaking the toxic tone of his voice.

Kai returned to a healthy state of fear. "Why only five days?"

"Because that's when you become the bait we need to reel in the fish we've cast our net out to catch. We've been waiting for so very long," he said, a snakelike hiss becoming evident in his diction. Kai could have sworn he saw a fork in the man's tongue.

"Who would that be?" Kai asked, genuinely curious.

Le Feu stared at Kai, sizing him up as he leaned on his cane. "You really don't know, do you?"

Kai answered honestly. "No, I don't."

"This is going to be so much fun." Le Feu cackled. "Why, your precious Cara, of course."

The air left Kai's lungs. "What does Cara have to do with any of this?" He struggled to mask his fear.

Le Feu winked at him. "You'll see. I wouldn't want to spoil the surprisse." He hissed the last word. "In the meantime, Chaos will take you to the lab. You'll get to have a brief visit with your daughter through a video monitor, and then tick-tock, you'll need to get to work."

"What if five days isn't enough?" Kai had to know.

Le Feu pushed a finger of burning energy in his direction. Kai jumped back when it connected with his chest. "I'm in need of a couple human sacrifices, Dr. Solomon. Your wife and daughter would do nicely. I'm sure you understand the need for us to provide a strong incentive for your success."

Kai fought against his restraints to get to Le Feu. "Who the fuck are you?" he yelled.

Coal-black eyes blazed at Kai. "*Who* I am is unimportant. It's *what* I am that should concern you."

Am I the only fucking human in the room? Kai wondered with alarm.

"If I give you what you need within five days, then what?" Kai asked, reaching for his options.

"Then you all get to leave, unharmed."

Kai was immediately suspicious. "How can I be sure?"

Le Feu looked him straight in the eye. "You can't."

"What about Cara?"

Le Feu shook his head. "Oh, I'm afraid she's not mine to release. And I suspect her death will be slow and painful."

"You bastard!" Kai screamed, launching himself at Le Feu. The restraints dug deeper into his wrists. Within seconds, Chaos had Kai in a vicelike grip, chilling him to the bone.

Le Feu turned to leave, giving Kai a blank stare. "I dare say that's impossible, given my lack of parentage," he said dryly. Emily, who hadn't said a word since she entered the cell, swept her gaze over Kai and brushed him with a look of satisfaction before turning to leave.

"And you . . . you cold, evil bitch. I hope you rot in Hell!" He spit after her.

"With pleasure," she said and continued to walk at Le Feu's side.

After they disappeared around the corner, Chaos roughly turned Kai around and removed his bindings. Relieved, Kai rubbed his battered wrists, trying to get the circulation back into his hands.

"Come with us," Chaos breathed in a hollow, inhuman voice. The sound caused the hairs on the back of Kai's neck to stand on end.

Kai's mind reeled as he followed Chaos. Destruction trailed behind them. Tom's words echoed in his head: *Ishmael is not one hundred percent human.* In less than twenty-four hours, Kai had seen a lot that fit into the not-one-hundred-percent-human category. He no longer needed to suspend his disbelief. He believed every word.

Chapter 36

NO ONE SAW CHAMUEL as he sat alone, cloaked, on a park bench across the street from Cara's penthouse, where she was safely ensconced. Both he and Michael had been put on high alert by Constantina. As a result, they were both sticking close to Cara, making it next to impossible for him to get another chance to see her alone as Simon.

Chamuel had been working since Cara left his apartment, starting with trailing her back to the penthouse. He'd stayed close to monitor the area, catching a few hours of sleep in Penthouse B next to Cara's—part of the Angelorum's real estate portfolio. Theoretically, he could have gone back to his loft at some point, since Cara was protected by the orb, but he hated the thought of the loneliness his place held without her there. He wanted to be as close to her as possible, He was unable to imagine himself without her.

During his long hours of surveillance, he'd come to a decision. Before they went any further, he needed to reveal his identity. The thought left a hard knot of fear in his gut. He believed that they could deal with the consequences together, if her feelings were the same as his. He'd surely be ejected from the Guardianship and probably forced to undergo the transformation to remove his wings as part of the punishment. Maybe he could petition the High Council to mitigate the prison sentence. He had one favor he knew he could call in. Regardless, he was prepared to make the sacrifice required to be with her. But would she accept him when she found out who he was? That was the question.

His phone vibrated in his pocket, pulling him away from his contemplation.

"Michael?"

"Hi, Chamuel. I sense you close by. Thanks for the tight surveillance. Constantina called earlier. The monitors have noticed a significant drop in dark energy in the New York City area. She thinks it's only temporary, and that we should still be cautious. She's also convinced Cara's Calling will happen soon."

"Constantina must've called me right before she called you. I also spoke to Isaac. He noticed the same pattern along the eastern seaboard. The Guardianship shares Constantina's opinion. They're trying to locate where the dark forces have migrated to, which could give us a clue to what lies ahead. In the interim, we shouldn't let our guard down, but you can have some freedom to move around if you'd like."

He heard Michael breathe a sigh of relief. "I'm glad you said that. Just a heads-up, I thought maybe I'd take Cara out after our morning session. We're going a little stir-crazy locked up in the penthouse. We even have the dog walker taking Chloe out four times a day. Anyway, I have my monthly class for adults with disabilities tonight. Just wanted you to know."

"What time?"

"Class starts at eight thirty, and we usually finish around ten. I think Cara and her friend Sienna plan to go out for drinks downtown. She invited me, but I can't go since I have class."

"No problem. I'll stay close," he replied.

"Thanks." Michael hung up.

Chamuel's heart leapt. This was his chance to see Cara again without accidental exposure. He'd call Cara later and let her know that he could meet her and Sienna this evening.

As he sat on the park bench weaving a strategy, he looked down and noticed a dog sniffing his leg.

"Chloe, what are you sniffing? There's nothing there," said the young woman walking the dog.

Realizing the dog with the girl was Cara's, Chamuel looked down into the big brown eyes staring up at him. Reaching down, he petted the whippet's narrow little head. Chloe licked his hand and he smiled in amusement as she tried to jump up and kiss him on the nose.

"Chloe, what are you doing, silly girl?" the girl asked. "There's nothing there." The dog walker pulled on her lead, trying to get her to continue her walk.

Chamuel whispered to Chloe in the angelic language. The dog listened intently with her ear cocked, and gave him a last lick before continuing on her way. Chamuel watched her go off to do her business, thinking that surprises were sometimes found in the most interesting packages.

Chapter 37

CARA HAD BEEN WALKING on air since she'd left Simon's apartment after their date. Her spirit was light and alive with hope. It wasn't until the next morning that she'd realized, with jarring clarity, she hadn't thought about Kai even once during her date.

Simon had texted her several times, just to wish her a good day or to say that he missed her and couldn't wait to see her again. Since Constantina was away, that left only her lessons with Michael.

Under Constantina's suggestion, she and Michael used the upstairs meeting room in lieu of the Brooklyn dojo for her training. Between Cara's kickboxing experience and her new proficiency in basic Tai Chi moves, Michael felt comfortable introducing basic weaponry. They put in a full day on Thursday, ordering takeout and collapsing Thursday evening. Friday morning, they continued and put in another full session.

They were just sitting down for lunch in the kitchen, when Cara's cell burst into "Teenage Dream" by Katy Perry, the ringtone Cara had assigned to Simon. Her stomach lurched with excitement as she snatched up the phone.

"Hi," she said, grinning wide.

"Hi, back," he said, his voice a deep, sexy purr. "If your offer still stands, I can get away for a couple of hours to join you and your friend Sienna for a drink this evening."

She brightened even more. "That would be great. She's been dying to meet you. She wants to know who stole her friend and left me in her place."

He chuckled. "I'm impressed that I've had such a transformational effect."

She was already planning how she could get some extra time with him after she left Sienna. "We're meeting at nine o'clock at the Standard Grill, down in the Meatpacking District."

"I know of it," he said. "How about I meet you at nine thirty? That will give you some time alone with your friend first."

"Perfect. I'm looking forward to seeing you." *All of you, preferably naked*, she thought wickedly.

"The feeling is mutual. Until later?"

"Yes, until then. Bye." She hung up, elated, and had trouble erasing the sappy look of happiness from her face. She glanced at Michael. "I wish you could come tonight. I want you to meet Sienna and Simon."

"I know. I'm looking forward to meeting them," he replied. "Let's play it by ear. Maybe I'll be able to join you afterward."

"Great! I think you'll love Sienna."

He stepped back, holding up his hands. "Not looking for a girlfriend, remember?"

"I'm not trying to fix you up. Honest. Girl Scout's honor. I just think you might have things in common, as friends . . . as my friends." But Cara couldn't stop picturing Michael and Sienna together. Even though Michael seemed adamantly opposed to getting involved in a romantic relationship right now . . . you never know. She was so happy that she wanted everyone to share in the same happiness, especially the people she loved.

"Thanks." He smiled. "I have no closet space for a girlfriend anyway." He gave her a devilish glance.

"Now the secret comes out; the fear of releasing closet space," Cara teased. "You can get help for that you know."

He laughed and cocked his head. "Are you saying I need a shrink?"

She looked at him, straight-faced. "No, a storage unit."

They stared at each other a moment and burst out laughing.

The more time she spent with Michael, the more he surprised her. She kept thinking back to their conversation in the park and about the secrets he kept so tightly guarded.

Unprompted, Michael hopped off the barstool. "Since we've been killing it the last two days, why don't we go out and do something fun this afternoon?"

Cara looked at him sideways. "Really? Can we do that?"

"Yup. I cleared it with Chamuel."

They spent the afternoon shopping, of all things. After they returned to the penthouse, Michael took his bags and left for Brooklyn with the promise that he'd try to meet them later. He'd let her know, but either way, he would meet her back at the penthouse.

Cara arrived at the Standard Grill, on time and before Sienna, as always. Cara loved the buzz of Meatpacking District, especially on Friday nights when it filled up with the post-work crowd. Between the Grill, the beer garden next door, and the Boom Boom Room at the top of the adjoining hip-and-chic Standard Hotel, a whole evening's worth of entertainment possibilities existed within a tiny cobblestone city block. If it had been daytime, the park on the Highline above them would have been added to the list. Cara hoped the familiar setting, and seeing Simon and Sienna, would allow her to pretend she still led a normal life.

She navigated her way to the bar and decided to make wise choices regarding her alcohol consumption for the evening by sticking to red wine. She had no desire to experience another hangover like the one she'd had the previous Sunday.

The restaurant was crowded and the bar mostly full, but Cara managed to score a barstool anyway. She ordered a cabernet sauvignon and waited for Sienna.

Sienna entered the bar at nine fifteen and beelined her way to Cara.

"Sweetie, how are you?" she said, giving her a quick peck on the cheek. "I can't wait to meet your guy! When is he going to be here?" She sat down on the stool Cara managed to procure from the couple who had just left.

"He should be here at about nine thirty. Oh, and Michael might stop by later, but it's still up in the air. By the way, you'll never guess what we did this afternoon."

Sienna raised her eyebrows. "Does Simon need to be worried?"

Cara rolled her eyes. "Of course not! Michael and I did a little shopping at Barney's this afternoon. His idea."

Cara mentally patted herself on the back for another stroke of brilliance she'd had. How do you explain to your longtime, nosy best friend that you're spending time with your new martial arts instructor outside of training? You subtly hint that you're working an angle to fix him up with her. Cara expected Michael to be less than happy with her cover for him, but she had to work with what she had.

"*Really?* He shops without the threat of Chinese water torture? That *is* interesting. What did you buy? More important, what did *he* buy?" Sienna asked.

Cara swept her hand down in front of herself. "I bought this lovely ensemble, which he selected for me. And if he comes, you can ask him yourself."

Sienna gave Cara a quick, appraising look and nodded her approval. "I'm impressed. You sure he isn't gay?"

Cara gave Sienna a look of mild exasperation. "He's not gay, that I can promise you. But I'm not sure he's on the market either. I think you'll like him as a friend, if nothing else."

Cara's phone rang in her purse, and when she picked it up, she saw Constantina's name on the display. "I need to take this," Cara mumbled as she got up and left Sienna. She answered the phone on her way outside where she could be alone.

"Constantina?" she asked.

"Cara, dear one, how are you faring?"

"I'm fine. Will you be coming back soon?"

"I expect so. Could you manage a trip to the farmhouse in Connecticut for a few days?"

Cara knew Constantina wasn't really asking, but rather politely making a request that couldn't be refused. She gave the only acceptable reply. "Of course."

"Take Michael with you, and if she is willing, your friend Sienna," she said.

Cara raised her eyebrows. "Really? Sienna?" Why on earth would Constantina want her to bring Sienna? That was like inviting the press to a closed meeting in the Oval Office.

"We've been watching the Trinity Stones very carefully. It might not make sense right now, but at some point it will, that I promise. Trust me."

"I trust you implicitly," Cara said, and she meant it.

"Good. Leave as soon as you can tomorrow morning. Journey forth in peace and love, Cara."

"And you, Constantina." Cara hung up.

Her face folded in disappointment. After tonight, she was guaranteed not to see Simon again for a few more days. She sighed. This probably wouldn't be the last time duty would call, tearing her away from personal plans. She went back inside to join Sienna and slid back onto the stool next to her.

"I got a call from the owners of the house in Connecticut and they want me to go up there for a few days and check the place out. Would you be able to get away? I know it's short notice, but I thought I'd ask Michael too. The place is supposed to be magnificent, and there's a spa close by." Earlier in the week, Cara had told Sienna about her new house-sitting gig.

"Spa? Did you say spa? I'm in. I can definitely escape until Tuesday or Wednesday at the latest."

"Would you be able to leave early tomorrow morning?" Cara asked with a wince, knowing Sienna wasn't a morning person.

"As long as you're providing the Starbucks, and no coherent conversation is required until at least ten o'clock," she replied.

Cara threw her arms around Sienna. "Thanks. I love you."

"I think I'm jealous," a male voice said from behind them.

Cara's heart skipped a beat when she heard his voice, and she spun around. "Simon!"

He put his arm around her shoulders and leaned in to give her a kiss hello.

Cara's skin tingled as his lips met hers. She kissed him back enough to show him she missed him but not enough to get arrested for lewd behavior—which is how she really wanted to kiss him.

When their lips parted, Simon turned to Sienna and took her hand. "Sienna, I presume? I'm Simon Young. It's good to meet you."

Sienna just stared, awestruck, as he shook her hand.

"It's rare that I get to see Sienna speechless," said Cara.

Sienna recovered and shot Cara a look before cocking her head to the side. "Our little Cara here has been living a nun-like existence before she met you. Let me be the first to thank you for rescuing her from herself."

Cara's jaw fell. She was semi-horrified. "Thanks, Senny. Let me take a second to bask in the mortification."

Simon smiled, amused. "She's not the only one. Living a monastic lifestyle, that is." He turned to Cara with a look of adoration in his eyes that made her melt on the spot.

"I can't imagine why," said Sienna under her breath. "Well, you're just as gorgeous as she described."

"She said I was gorgeous?" He looked back at Cara, and his expression softened.

"Yes, she did," answered Cara on her own behalf.

Simon ordered them a round of drinks. Before they'd finished, he looked at Cara with regret. "I'm sorry, but I can't stay. I was called back in, and it looks like I'll be away for a couple of days."

Cara gave him a sympathetic smile. "That's okay. My side job is house-sitting, and the owners just asked me to go to Connecticut for a few days to check in on the place." She pouted. "I'd hoped we could spend some time together, but it looks like our next date will have to wait until I get back and your work schedule frees up." She reached out to take his hand, which he surrendered to her willingly.

He drew her into his arms and rested his head on top of hers. "I'll miss you," he said. He looked down into her eyes before his lips met hers in a reassuring kiss. "Either way, we would have missed the opportunity for a few days."

Simon turned to Sienna. "Sienna, it was lovely meeting you. I hope to see you again soon." He leaned over and gave her a peck on the cheek, as one would bestow on a friend in greeting or departure. "May I borrow Cara for a minute?"

"Sure, just make sure to send her back sometime tonight. It was great meeting you, too, Simon."

Cara and Simon stepped outside to say their good-byes.

As soon as they were on the sidewalk, he enveloped her in an embrace. His lips were electric velvet on hers and their kiss deepened until she melted into him.

The energy of his longing pulled at her, drawing her tight against the warm, firm contours of his body. If she could have gotten any closer to him, she would have. She turned liquid in his arms, wishing their night didn't have to end here.

"I have to go." His eyes burned vivid blue, gazing down at her with disappointment. More than anything she wanted those eyes to consume her and fulfill her desire.

She tried to keep her misery from showing by offering a small smile. "I know. See you soon?"

"Sooner than you think." He winked and released her. She hugged herself to replace the void left behind from his warmth and watched his large figure walk across the street and disappear into the night.

Chapter 38

CHAMUEL SWORE under his breath as he left Cara, thinking how his plans had turned to dust before his eyes. He'd almost made it to the bar when he'd first received a text from Cara to let him know Michael may be joining them. Disappointment slammed into him. The last thing he needed was to be caught by his own Trinity Messenger. That was Plan Combustion Element Number One. Then his phone had rung in his pocket.

He looked to see the caller—Constantina—and suspected he'd just found Plan Combustion Element Number Two.

"Chamuel, dear one," she'd said. "I tried Michael, but he didn't answer his phone. I'm sending Cara to Connecticut for a few days. Be prepared to follow her. I'll send Michael with her and her friend Sienna."

He wondered why, but knew better than to ask. It was an order, and in their long, shared history, she never offered details about orders. Either she wouldn't or couldn't.

"Any luck locating the shift in Dark One activity?"

"We're close," she replied, "but don't be surprised if we find out at the same time."

"Fair enough. I'll be close," he said, frustrated he wouldn't be close enough.

"Journey forth in peace and love."

"And, you."

His disappointment outweighed his relief in postponing the gut-wrenching discussion he'd planned to have with Cara. He figured that if he told her about himself now, it would be far easier on her than if she found out accidentally. Not to mention, it would also be better for him in the long run.

At least he'd enjoyed one drink with her before they were torn apart for the next few days. Well, not exactly torn apart. He'd be with her, but as her unseen

Guardian and not as the man in love with her. Chamuel knew his time was running out to tell Cara, and his resentment at being separated from her surprised him. Being with her had opened a Pandora's box of emotions he hadn't expected, knocking him slightly off balance.

He was a block away, still cursing his luck, when the faint wisp of Nephilim energy tickled his aura.

The rogue. A low growl rose from his throat, and his hands clenched into fists. This time, he wouldn't let him get away. There was only one sure way to draw him out, but first, he had to get somewhere more private.

He thought for a second and grinned. Pier 54 on the Hudson River, five minutes away, would do nicely. At this time of night it would be deserted and covered in shadows, with the sounds of the West Side Highway to cover any noise—if there happened to be any. Chamuel relaxed and changed direction, strolling along, acting as if nothing was wrong.

The rogue's energy curled around him, following from a safe distance. Chamuel crossed the West Side Highway toward the towering, semicircular archway. Made entirely of iron girders from the facade of a former pier shed for ocean liners that once occupied the space, the archway loomed ahead like a skeletal ghost, providing entrance onto the desolate, parking lot–like pier. Ducking into the shadows, Chamuel felt the energy behind him.

He needed to make his move quickly. In a blink of an eye, Chamuel threw down his suit jacket, and cloaked, unfurling his wings in a smooth burst through the modified shirt he wore. He leapt up and sliced through the air as fast as his wings would allow, directly at the other Nephil.

Chamuel tackled his stalker, connecting solidly with the other man's body through the veil of invisibility. Chamuel retracted his wings before they both slammed down onto the asphalt at the edge of the pier, rolling together to absorb the impact. The back of a blond head, snow-white plumage, and a white tunic came into view as their veils of invisibility connected.

"Who are you?" Chamuel snarled, gripping the rogue securely from behind. In answer, the man retracted his wings swiftly with a whoosh, the coarse edge feathers slicing across Chamuel's shoulders right before he landed a reverse head butt into Chamuel's face. Stars sparkled across his field of vision as he lost his grip. Blood trickled from his nose and mixed with the blood already on the sticky ribbons of his torn shirt. Still reeling, the attacker elbowed him in the ribs. Their connection broken, the rogue disappeared from view.

Using the Nephil's energy to guide him, Chamuel struck straight out into the air, and his fist connected with the man's side. A loud grunt from the Nephil traveled between the intersecting veils. He flashed into view for only a second, but not long enough for Chamuel to see his face. Funny how the laws of physics applied: sight, sound, and physical contact could be made when two cloaks collided, yet invisibility and silence remained for everyone outside of the veils. There wouldn't be any reports of men with wings having a throw-down unless their energy waned to the point where one or both of them had to stop cloaking.

Just when Chamuel thought he'd recovered, a fist connected with his jaw, slamming him backward into the ground. His head spun as he tried to lift himself up and get his bearings, but his body failed to cooperate, and he collapsed back onto the asphalt and winced. When he touched the back of his head, blood dampened his fingertips.

The wisp of energy disappeared into the night. The rogue had escaped once again.

Shit.

Chamuel rested on the pavement, rubbing his aching jaw. Other than getting his ass kicked, he'd confirmed one thing. If the rogue had wanted to kill him, he'd passed on the chance.

The questions remained: who was this guy, and what *did* he want?

Chapter 39

Connecticut. Greenwich Farmhouse. Sunday, March 30, 6:30 a.m. EDT

SILENCE. Such a beautiful thing. Cara relaxed and enjoyed the quiet while sitting on one of the shabby-chic couches in the living room with Chloe curled up next to her. She thought about what to do next. It was still too early for either Michael or Sienna to be up. Thank God. She hadn't fully recovered from last night and their nonstop bickering.

Michael and Sienna had been like oil and water since the moment they'd met. Michael never made it Friday night, but the fireworks had started immediately when Cara picked up Sienna at her apartment yesterday morning. She'd thought they would hit it off. Rather, they took an instant dislike to each other. It had started with Sienna slamming Michael's "gay" button by making a snide comment about his shirt and the type of men who wore them. Michael zapped back a snarky reply questioning how she would even know what brand of shirt he wore. She basically called him a moron, and spouted off her fashion credentials. From there, it quickly devolved into a verbal ping-pong match that left Cara wishing for earplugs. It made for a *very* long trip to the farmhouse.

Relief flooded her the moment they turned onto their private road, which split in three directions, leading to three private residences. The farmhouse was the one on the left.

Cara had been pleasantly surprised when they drove up. Only "farmhouse" seemed like such a quaint description for something that was more of a cross between a mansion and an estate.

As they drew closer, the woods opened into a clearing that exposed a large house covered with gray cedar shingles, white trim, and a wraparound front porch. Impeccable landscaping surrounded the house. A grassy area with a flagpole, and a perennial garden that had yet to bloom for the season, was contained within the center of a circular driveway. Cara thought the house looked better suited for the Hamptons than tucked away in suburban Greenwich, Connecticut.

Watson & Haskins had taken the liberty of freshening it up for her arrival. No doubt the Chanel-clad Claudette was behind the update. Unlike the modern décor of the New York apartment, the house was decorated in a cottage style appealing to Cara's taste.

Cara petted the sleeping dog next to her, savoring her alone time. She equated the whirlwind of activity over the last couple of weeks to watching her life through the Plexiglas door of a dryer on a spin cycle. In the scheme of things, this getaway was a welcome break, especially since they'd received word that the Dark Ones' energy had dropped off substantially along the eastern seaboard, making it safer to move around. The question was: why had they fled? She sensed this was only the calm before the storm, but even a few days of peace and quiet would be worth it before all hell broke loose.

One thing was for sure: she already missed Simon. Their timing was a little crazy, but was there ever a good time to start a relationship?

Relationship. She smiled. She liked the sound of the word. Finding him was the last thing she'd expected, and now she couldn't imagine giving him up.

Too bad Constantina hadn't sent me to Connecticut alone. She could've asked Simon to join her. Cara was still baffled as to why Constantina wanted her to take Sienna, Michael, and Chloe with her. She could understand Michael and Chloe—but Sienna? This could be a little dangerous, especially given Sienna's inability to keep a secret. Cara decided to trust that Constantina knew what she was doing.

Thanks to Constantina, Cara grew more comfortable with her new life as each day passed. She still had questions, but not nearly as many. It felt like an eternity since she'd read her Grandmother Hannah's letter. As surprising as it was to her, Cara didn't miss her old life. Not even a little bit. She was amazed at how easy it had been to let it go.

She looked at her watch and did some quick calculations. Two hours, easy, before Sienna crawled out of her room looking for coffee. With Michael, maybe another hour and a half before he emerged after primping to perfection. He may be an early riser during the week, but he'd confessed to sleeping in on Sundays if he could. Their little jog around the park last weekend had been retribution for dragging him out of bed and making him wait around for her. If she left now, they'd never know she'd been gone. And she wouldn't have to worry about them killing each other before she returned.

Cara sighed. A long walk in the fresh morning air would do her good. It was only a mile and a half to downtown, and she'd be safe enough with Chamuel watching over her. Then a thought struck her, and she chuckled as she wondered if he actually walked or just flew behind her . . .

She popped off the couch with Chloe in tow and slipped on a light sweater. She grabbed her cell phone and stuffed her pockets with essentials. Chloe raced ahead to the door; her tail was in hyper-wag.

Chloe approached the walk with gusto, dragging Cara along behind her. Before Cara knew it, they'd turned the corner onto the main street and headed for the dog-friendly café Cara had spotted yesterday.

As they drew closer, Cara noticed the umbrellas closed the night before were now open, indicating outside seating was available. Several of the tables were already occupied. She was mildly surprised that she wasn't the only soul intent on catching some early-morning sun over a cup of coffee.

They'd almost reached the gate when Chloe pulled sharply on the lead, freeing herself from Cara's hand. Cara bolted after her, arriving just as Chloe hurled herself right onto the lap of a young guy with a baseball cap pulled low on his head sitting at one of the tables. Chloe jumped up and kissed him on the lips.

"Oh my God, I am so sorry! Chloe, get down!" Cara grabbed Chloe's lead, trying to pull her away. Straining against the leash, Chloe whined, her tail whipping from side-to-side as she frantically tried to get back to him.

After taking a few seconds to recover, he laughed and leaned back in his chair. "No problem. I haven't been kissed like that in a while, but I usually prefer my women on two legs rather than four."

Cara caught a glimpse of his blond hair tucked under his cap, suspecting it was pulled back and some of the length hidden underneath. She chuckled, and her face brightened. "Thanks for being so great. This wanton hussy is Chloe. She's never done that to me before. She usually saves that greeting for her most ardent admirers." Cara dropped to one knee next to her dog, and glanced between them. "Do you guys have something to tell me?"

She was relieved the guy didn't seem upset, and happy she wouldn't get ejected for Chloe's bad behavior. He seemed easy-going, with a warm, dimpled smile and a sense of humor. Not to mention the pair of killer blue eyes that peeked out from under the cap.

She looked up and caught him checking her out. Her cheeks warmed in a blush.

"Hi, I'm Brett." He stuck his hand across the table.

She stood and shook his hand. "Hi, back. Cara."

He sat up straighter in his chair and motioned for her to sit. "Would you ladies like to join me for breakfast?"

What the heck? She'd enjoy the company.

Cara tilted her head and smiled. "Sure." She pulled out the chair opposite him while Chloe disappeared under the white plastic table.

Brett reached down to pet Chloe.

Cara narrowed her eyes. "You know, she's acting as if she's met you before . . ." Truth be told, Cara sensed something familiar about him too, but was sure they'd never met. A quick energy read showed a strong, positive vibrancy.

"I think I'd remember such a beautiful girl," he teased, placing his hand over his heart. "Dogs seem to like me."

"They're wonderful judges of character," she said. "So, any friend of Chloe's is a friend of mine."

The waitress walked over. "Can I get you something?" she asked. Cara ordered a low-fat latte and an egg-white omelet with toast. The waitress leaned down to pet Chloe. "I'll bring some water and a couple of dog biscuits."

"Then you'll have a friend for life," Cara said.

Glancing around, Cara said to Brett, "I'm shocked to see so many people this early on a Sunday morning. I figured Chloe and I would be the only ones out."

Brett gave her a mock wounded look. "Would you like me to go?" He feigned getting up to leave.

Cara face flushed, and she grinned. "No, I didn't mean it that way. I'm just used to Manhattan, where no respectable New Yorker is seen before ten o'clock on a Sunday for breakfast. I think that's why brunch was invented."

He threw her a disarming smile. Something about him put her immediately at ease. In addition to great energy, he seemed genuine and nice. He lit up the more they talked, and she took the opportunity to take a closer look.

She guessed he was close to her age, possibly a little younger. Despite being seated, he looked tall, a little over six feet. He had a slight hint of a tan, setting off his heavily lashed blue eyes and full lips. Masculine enough, his face had a fine bone structure with high cheekbones, a nicely shaped nose, and a sculptured jaw line. The dimple on his cheek when he smiled gave him a boyish charm, which contrasted to the hip style of his black leather jacket, studded belt, and jeans. Her eyes flashed to his hands. He wore a simple silver ring engraved with his name on one of his long, tapered fingers; it appeared to be his only jewelry.

She nearly caught herself panting. No two ways about it, he was hot. If she wasn't already taken . . .

"Earth to Cara . . ." Brett leaned toward her over his folded arms.

Jolted out of her reverie, she blushed crimson. "I'm sorry—what did you say?"

"You were checking me out, weren't you?" An amused smile stretched across his face, and his dimple etched in his cheek.

She flushed a deeper red.

"Caught ya! Don't worry. I did the same thing to you when you were talking some sense into Chloe," he teased.

"You did?" She'd noticed, but his admission surprised her.

He laughed. "Absolutely!" Then Cara caught a change in Brett's expression, followed by a wince. "Listen, I hope I didn't embarrass you just now. I don't always have the best filters."

Without a second thought, her hand gravitated to the back of his and patted it. "Don't worry. I usually have the same problem with filters. Thanks. I'm flattered."

He leaned forward and smiled shyly. "Me too, actually . . . flattered, I mean." He flushed a rosy hue under his tan. For some reason, he reminded her of Kai.

Her pulse jumped, and she swallowed delicately, wanting to shake herself. There was no denying the seed of attraction between them. He had a magnetic pull she couldn't explain. She thought of Simon, and her pulse came back under control.

Clearing his throat, he moved to safer territory. "I've been working alone for the past couple of days, and I'm a little stir-crazy. I hope I'm not being inappropriate." He searched her eyes for a reaction and then added, "Honestly, I'm glad we met. It's the first time I've enjoyed someone's company in a while."

Cara found his candor refreshing, and his company equally as enjoyable.

"Thanks. I'm glad we met you too." She gave him a warm smile and thought back to his initial confession about checking her out. She'd be lying if she said it hadn't given her a little thrill.

The waitress returned with Cara's latte and omelet and Chloe's water and treats. She refreshed Brett's coffee before moving on.

"So, what are you working on so intensely?" Cara asked, taking in a forkful of her eggs and glancing at the notebook he'd been writing in when they'd arrived.

Brett fingered the wire spiral binding the pages and hesitated. "I'm a songwriter. I'm working on some new material. That's why I'm alone. I do my best work when I isolate myself."

Cara was intrigued. She had never met a songwriter—or any entertainers, for that matter.

"That's very interesting. I really admire anyone who can write. I've always struggled with it personally. I guess that's why I became an investment banker." She paused, a pensive look on her face. "Or should I say, why I *used to be* an investment banker?" She shrugged and went back to her eggs.

"Really?" Brett raised an eyebrow. "Now that's impressive. Not everyone is smart enough to be an investment banker. What's the deal with *used to be*?" He took another sip of his coffee.

Cara gave him a whimsical shrug. "Well, let's just say I've undergone a career change lately."

"Well, don't keep it to yourself. What are you doing now?" he coaxed.

"I'm still trying to figure that out." She gave him a sheepish look.

Resting his elbows on the table, he laced his fingers together and leaned forward. "You ever get to San Francisco?"

Cara tilted her head quizzically, and thought of Kai. "Interesting you should ask. I have a close friend who lives there. It's been a couple of years, but I hope to visit one of these days soon. Why?"

"I'm here on a bit of a sabbatical. I actually live there," he replied with a hint of . . . something. She tasted something new . . . something vanilla, followed by an unexpected stab of disappointment.

"Oh, when do you go back?" Cara tried to keep her shoulders from slumping. *Why do I feel like I'm losing a friend?*

He picked up his coffee cup and took a sip. "I'm here for a long weekend while my aunt is in Europe, but I have an open invitation. I get here often enough. What about you?"

"Me too. I actually live in Manhattan. I'm only here until Tuesday this time, but I expect to be here pretty often. So, I guess neither of us really lives here."

The waitress came with the check. Both Brett and Cara grabbed for it at the same time. His hand felt warm on hers as they both covered the check. The touch of his skin sent an unexpected spark through her.

"Let me," Brett said seriously.

"On one condition," she said.

He arched an eyebrow. "Which is?"

"You promise to call me next time you're in town so that I can return the favor." She took the pen from the bill. Ripping off a corner of the check, she wrote her number down and gave it him. Maybe she'd be here alone in the future. For a moment she wondered if giving him her phone number was disloyal to Simon, but her instinct told her it was the right thing to do.

"It's a deal," he said and gave her another dimpled smile. "Hey, I'll do you one better. I'll program you into my phone." Then, his face lit up with a look of hope as his fingers tapped in her number. "What if I wanted to take you up on your offer tomorrow before I leave?"

She wished she could say yes. "You could if you don't mind a crowd. I'm here with two friends. I snuck out on my own this morning while they were sleeping."

He shrugged, but couldn't hide the disappointment in his voice. "Okay, next time, then. I really enjoyed meeting you, Cara. Chloe too."

Cara followed his eyes down below the table where Chloe was curled up, sleeping on top of his motorcycle boots.

Cara frowned. "Has she been on top of you the whole time? I'm so sorry."

"For what? She's very toasty on the feet, even through my boots," he said with a grin.

Chloe awoke with a start and jumped off of him, bestowing one last kiss on his face and then returning to Cara's side. Brett left cash for the waitress, and they stood to leave.

His blue eyes captured her gaze, and he inched closer until he was in her personal space. Her face flushed, and her heart suddenly sped up. He dipped in and paused at her lips, before brushing her cheek with a kiss. Her breath caught in her throat.

"Look forward to seeing you next time," he said.

"You too, Brett," she said, momentarily frozen, her hand sweating on Chloe's leash. *Did he almost kiss me?* She couldn't decide whether she was more surprised or disappointed.

They gave each other one last smile and left the café, each heading off in opposite directions.

Chapter 40

CHAMUEL WATCHED Cara and Chloe at the café with that blond boy, and his heart filled with jealousy. He'd cloaked himself and moved close enough to listen in on their conversation. Yes, he was spying on her. The chemistry between Cara and the guy was unmistakable, piercing Chamuel straight in the heart. He almost jumped out of his skin when she handed him her number and the guy kissed her good-bye on the cheek.

The time he'd spent with Cara over the last week had been magical. He couldn't bear someone else getting in the way. He'd walked into his own trap by following an irrational desire to get to know her. Who was he really trying to fool? He knew he loved her the moment he'd caught her in his arms. It was why he crossed the line to begin with . . .

As they left the café, walking in opposite directions, Chamuel felt a wisp of familiar Nephilim energy approach him. He recognized Noah, one of the Tri-State Guardians. Noah reached out and laid his hand on Chamuel's shoulder to connect their veils of invisibility so they could talk.

"What's up, brother?" Chamuel asked.

"I see your charge met mine," Noah replied.

"Huh? That blond kid with the baseball cap?" This was unexpected. Jealousy still rumbled in Chamuel's gut.

"Yeah, but only for the weekend. He's West Coast. Constantina called in a favor. Brett King, big rock star, ducked out from his tour for a little incognito R&R."

That woman sure gets around, Chamuel thought at the mention of Constantina's name. Then again, she had a gift for orchestration. He frowned, his eyes darkening. "Since when do we provide security for entertainers?" He tried to keep the petulance out of his voice.

"He hasn't been approached or Called yet, so he must have importance to the

Angelorum if he's been assigned security this early. He's on a plane first thing Monday morning back to rejoin the tour."

They watched Brett get into a red Mercedes coupe and drive off in the same direction as Cara, beeping as he passed her on the street.

"I'd better go. By the way, we miss your Saturday night specials at the House. See you soon." Noah dropped his hand, unhooking their cloaks of invisibility, and flew off.

Could this be the reason Constantina hauled them all to Connecticut? Was Cara supposed to meet Blondie?

Chamuel had a bad feeling about this. Clues were beginning to add up. Constantina managing Cara's training personally was enough of a red flag. Now, having Cara make contact with other future Trinity members? This had the smell of something big and unprecedented attached.

He also had an impending sense that his time to come clean with Cara had almost run out.

Chapter 41

Connecticut. Greenwich Farmhouse. Sunday, March 30, 9:00 a.m. EDT

CARA WALKED UP the drive with Chloe to see Michael and Sienna standing with their arms crossed, facing off on the porch. At first she thought maybe they'd been waiting for her to return, but as she drew closer, she realized that wasn't it at all.

Sienna's slim figure was togged out in skinny jeans, high boots, and a purple fur vest over a form-fitting gray shirt. Michael, as always, was perfectly coiffed and dressed in his *GQ* uniform of tailored jeans with a black belt, a fitted T-shirt layered under an Armani long-sleeve shirt, and Gucci loafers sans the socks. They made a striking pair; too bad they hated each other.

"Hey, guys," Cara said as she approached.

Sienna turned to face Cara, arms still crossed in front of her. "He's pissed off because I figured out his little secret."

"Secret? What secret?" Cara looked at Michael; his face blazed red. Embarrassment or anger—she couldn't tell which it was until his energy hit her square in the face with a mixture of both.

Sienna picked up her iPad and shook it at Michael, smirking. "Meet Mr. Times-Square-Billboard-Calvin-Klein-Underwear-Ad circa 2009. I'd wondered why he looked so familiar when I met him."

Cara's head jerked over to look at Michael. Okay . . . that was out of left field. Sure, Michael was hot and handsome enough to model . . . but why keep it a secret?

"*Him.*" Sienna scoffed. "Do you believe it?"

Michael gave Sienna a dirty look. "What do you mean, 'him'? Why is that so surprising to you?"

Sienna glanced briefly at his crotch, looked back into his eyes, and *humfphed.*

Michael's mouth turned into a thin, angry line, and his eyes turned a stormy blue. "You wish," he bit out. Cara watched as he struggled to stay in control. The sour grape taste of his anger was palpable on her tongue.

Sienna looked at Cara with a raised eyebrow. "You sure he plays for the home team?"

Cara stood dumbfounded by the exchange. "Are you serious? Senny, back off. So, Michael's done some 'billboard' time? Good for him." An image of Michael's midsection swathed in designer cotton and large enough to cover a city block flashed through her mind. That could make any woman break out in a cold sweat.

He narrowed his eyes at Sienna and tightened his arms over his chest. "Why would you think that? Not all male models are gay, you know," he snapped.

Sienna shrugged and added some fuel to the fire. "No need to be so snotty about it. You sure argue like a gay man. I should know." With that she started fidgeting with her iPad.

"Sienna, what are you doing?" Cara asked slowly.

Sienna looked up, glanced at Michael, and smirked. "I want to get a better look at the ad and see what was so special."

"Wouldn't you like to know," he growled.

Sienna faced him, coiled and ready to strike. "Some things are better on paper with a lot of airbrushing!"

Uncrossing his arms, his hands clenched at his sides. "I promise you, no airbrushing was required," he said through gritted teeth. A vein jumped in his flushed neck, and Cara's mouth puckered with a second heavy dose of sour grape.

Finally reaching her limit, Cara lobbed in a verbal grenade to interrupt their sparring. "You sure you two aren't in love? You squabble like a married couple."

As annoying and uncharacteristic as it had been, the passion and intensity of their fighting tickled her imagination. Maybe, underneath it all, they were heading straight into each other's arms. *Or maybe not.*

Dead silence. Michael and Sienna froze in place, regarding each other with hostility before turning back to Cara. Michael spoke first.

"I could never be with someone so vapid."

Sienna stamped her foot and chimed in, "Well, Vocabulary Boy, I could never be with someone so conceited. You wouldn't know what to do with me if you had me anyway!"

"Before or after I put you over my knee!"

Sienna put down her iPad and planted her hands on her hips. "Oh, is that the way you like it, *pretty boy*?"

Michael's whole body stiffened, and his face drained of color. Overcome by an unnatural calm, he strode up to Sienna, his face hovering inches from hers.

"Don't. Ever. Call. Me. That. Again," he ground out quietly through his taut jaw. Sienna shrunk away from him.

He stepped around Sienna, and silently headed for the door. Cara caught the flaming hue covering his face as he passed, his anger transforming into something else . . . the unmistakable, cloying taste of shame.

Cara's mouth fell slack. If she thought she'd hit a nerve in the park last Sunday, Sienna had stumbled into something much deeper.

Chloe tugged at her lead, wanting to follow him. Cara unclipped her, and she trotted inside.

Sienna shook the stunned look off her face while her shoulders mildly trembled. "Al-righty, then . . ." She dropped down onto one of the cushioned wicker chairs.

"Hey, you okay?" Cara asked, sitting down in the chair next to her.

She pouted and clutched her iPad, "Yeah, I'm fine . . . I guess."

"What is with you two? Where is all this hostility coming from anyway?"

Sienna shrugged and looked away. Cara's heart leapt a little; Sienna's body language spoke volumes. Cara said in a low conspiratorial voice, "Admit it. You're attracted to him, aren't you?"

"Don't go there, Cara," Sienna said, tossing her tablet onto the table and crossing her arms over her chest. "He's not even remotely interested in me, anyway," she added softly, looking down at her lap.

Cara had known Sienna long enough to understand her insecurities. It was just as Cara suspected. Sienna was pissed Michael hadn't returned her interest.

"What if he was? Attracted to you? What then?"

Sienna jerked her head up. "He's not," she snapped. "Not to mention he's got a serious stick up his ass. So, let's just drop it, okay?"

Cara threw up her hands. "Fine. But Senny, I know you better than anyone. You wouldn't be this upset if you really didn't care what he thought of you."

"Whatever." Sienna blushed. Unable to meet Cara's eyes, she got up and walked inside.

Cara sighed and followed her.

Michael approached Cara when she reached the living room while Sienna settled on the couch and picked up a magazine. There was an earnest look in his royal-blue eyes.

"I'm sorry for my behavior out there," he said. Then he shook his head and whispered, "I know she's your best friend, but she makes me crazy. Why did Constantina want us to bring her?"

Cara just gave him a weak smile. "I'm sorry. I promise she's really a good person." She winked at him. "Calvin Klein model, huh?"

Under his usual smooth and good-natured demeanor, she sensed his underlying discomfort and his effort to hide it. He gave her a wry look. "That was awhile back. I'm not in the business anymore. Promise you won't hold it against me?"

She grabbed his forearm and pulled him closer. "Are you okay?" she whispered, searching his eyes. The muscles in his arm clenched under her fingers, and he looked away. A wisp of shame followed.

"I'm fine." He covered her hand then returned her gaze. "Really." She ignored the bitter taste of his lie, and let him have it.

He gently twisted away, and gave her a warm smile. *"Thanks,"* he said telepathically.

Cara nodded. She'd been right in her assessment of him. There were things he'd rather keep hidden . . . dark things.

"Well, if you're expecting me to apologize, don't hold your breath." Sienna chimed in from across the room, speaking to no one in particular.

Cara rolled her eyes. "Come on, Senny. Don't be that way. Can't we all just get along?"

"Well, I'd be in a better mood if that *GQ*-escapee over there hadn't distracted me before I had breakfast."

Cara immediately understood and turned to Michael. "She's hypoglycemic. She needs to eat when she gets up or she turns into the beast you just witnessed." Michael's eyes softened.

"How about I make you some eggs?" Cara asked Sienna on her way to the kitchen. Michael followed behind her.

"Egg whites with toast would be great," Sienna yelled from the living room.

Cara gathered the eggs and picked up the frying pan.

Michael took it from her. "Allow me." He placed it on the stove. "If I don't cook with this thing, I might end up hitting her with it," he mumbled, facing the stove with his back to Cara.

She smirked. "She really gets under your skin, doesn't she?" She walked over and leaned on the counter next to him.

His high cheekbones reddened, and he pushed his hair back with his hand. "More than you know," he said without looking at her. Then he turned to her and said, "Why did you tell her I might be interested in meeting her?"

Now it was Cara's turn to redden, then she got annoyed. "Can you think of a better explanation for me traveling with a guy I just met when, as of few days ago, I have a boyfriend? I'm not sure how you manage the lying-to-family-and-friends thing, but I'm doing the best I can."

He reached his over and squeezed her arm. "I know. Fair point. Sorry. I'm happy to pretend if it makes things easier for you."

She arched a brow. "Too late for that, don't you think?"

"I'll do better, I promise."

Her heart warmed. He was a good friend. "I'm going back to hang out with Sienna. Will you be okay?"

He nodded. "I know my way around a kitchen."

"Senny, Michael is cooking you breakfast," Cara said as she returned.

Sienna looked up from her magazine, horrified. "What if he poisons me? Shouldn't you be watching him?"

"Well, I couldn't exactly say it would be undeserved," teased Cara. "He's a nice guy. Can you at least try to be civil, for me?"

Not surprisingly, Cara could tell Sienna felt bad and was hiding it behind a brave face, just like when they were teenagers. Behind it all, Sienna was a big marshmallow. Another reason why Cara couldn't believe how awful Sienna was being to Michael—even if he wasn't interested in dating her.

Cara walked over to the large window overlooking the grounds and wondered where Chamuel watched them from before her thoughts turned to her amazing week with Simon.

Out of the corner of her eye, Cara saw Michael arrive from the kitchen. He approached Sienna with her breakfast, eggs artfully arranged on the plate in one hand, and a glass of fresh-squeezed orange juice in the other. Without a word, he set them down in front of her and headed over to Cara. Trying to hide a smirk, she wondered how tempted he was to actually throw the breakfast at Sienna. Poor Sienna. How Cara loved her, but oh, how she sometimes wanted to smack some sense into her. On the other hand, it wasn't lost on Cara that Michael had added a sprig of parsley to garnish the plate.

Michael came over to her and pulled her close. He whispered, "Cara, it's time."

His tone said it all. Icy electric fingers danced along her spine. This was their prearranged signal meaning he'd just been contacted by the Angelorum and told that her Calling was imminent. This would release her final powers and reveal the soul at the center of her Trinity Stone.

She looked at him. "What? *Now*?"

"I just got the message."

Within seconds, both her and Michael's cell phones rang and all hell broke loose. Michael headed off out of earshot to take his call while Cara took her call standing next to the window.

At first, all Cara heard was a woman screaming and crying on the line. She held the phone away from her ear for a second to look at the number on the display. Panic seized her immediately.

"Melanie, is that you? What is it? Did something happen to Kai?" Cara paced back and forth with nervous energy.

"Cara, oh my God!" Melanie screamed into the phone, choking on her tears. "They're gone! Taken . . . "

"What do you mean *taken*? Who took them?" Cara kept her voice steady and calm.

Melanie's unintelligible ranting continued to filter through the phone.

Ready to snap, Cara took a cleansing breath and gripped her phone hard. "I can help, Melanie. Just tell me what happened. But you have to calm down. I promise I'll help."

Melanie dialed down her hysteria half a notch and told her story through a bout of hiccupping. "I got home from China, and got a call . . . said they had them . . . didn't want money . . . said Kai needed to give them what they wanted or they'd kill him and Sara." Her frenzied wailing resumed at a renewed fever pitch.

Cara fought to control herself. "Who has them?"

"I don't know who has them!"

"What does Kai need to give them?"

"Lab notes. They said he has missing lab notes. He sent the notes to someone. Did he send them to you?"

Cara had no idea what Melanie was talking about. She hadn't gotten any mail from Kai before she'd left New York. Then again, she'd moved, and it took a few days for her receive her forwarded mail from the West Village apartment. "No, I never got a package from Kai. Where are you? Are you at home?"

"Yes," Melanie cried as if doubled over in pain on the other end.

Cara spoke softly but firmly. "I can be in San Francisco tonight. Hold tight, I'm coming." She hung up.

As soon as the phone disconnected, Cara crumbled. Her hand shook so violently, she dropped the phone. Michael ran over and grabbed her arm just as her knees buckled underneath her. Sienna, panicking, dashed over to join them and grabbed her other arm. Both of them kept Cara from hitting the ground with a thud.

It all happened in slow motion. A maelstrom of panic hit her. If anything happened to Kai, she'd be destroyed. Fear reached down and touched the center of her being with hostile accuracy. Without warning, an unseen force of energy came slamming down from above, blowing Sienna and Michael off her as it shot outward through her body. She stood wrapped in a blinding white light, which forced both Michael and Sienna to cover their eyes.

A cyclone of energy propelled her spirit upwards away from the depths of the pit trying to suck her down and drown her. Soft, harmonious voices caressed and surrounded her, lifting her higher with every note. Increasing in velocity as it came down through the crown of her head, the energy traveled through her heart and radiated out of every pore taking the darkness with it. Her arms rose heavenward.

Wrapped in the angelic music playing inside her head, a voice spoke, standing out over the melodic song. The voice addressed her silently but clearly. "You have been chosen. Do you accept your place as a servant in this Trinity?"

Silently and emphatically, Cara answered, "Yes, I accept my place."

Upon her response, the disembodied voice continued. "Blessed be your journey. Hold holy your Center Stone."

Then the spirit unleashed another pillar of light. Two threads of energy struck her from above, rattling her teeth as they entered her crown with the precision of an ice pick. Her body shook violently, at odds with itself, as the two separate chords vibrated like dissonant tuning forks down the length of her, nearly knocking her off of her feet. As the vibration slowed, one chord entwined around the other and spun, picking up speed until they reached tornado force and merged in harmony. As Cara thought her body was about to disintegrate from the pressure, the kinetic frenzy peaked, exploding outward and covering the inside of her skin in a gentle molecular rain. Kai's image filled her mind, and her body was temporarily not her own. She instinctively knew the buzzing inside her skin was Kai's frequency—how Kai felt at the cellular level. Her essence was connected to his through the Flow.

The music reached a melodic crescendo, and slowly, the light faded, returning Cara to full consciousness. When the voices and the buzzing were gone, she stood in the room facing her two stunned friends.

Michael and Sienna gaped at her in silence. Only Michael understood what he'd just witnessed. Cara had just made her final transformation and accepted her Calling. No one spoke. The air crackled with residual energy.

With the change, Cara's senses sharpened and her ability to detect energy transformed. She could distinctly feel Michael, almost as an extension of herself. Sienna's energy was different, less intense and steadier in its rhythm. Even Chloe gave off her own frequency.

Sienna clamped her mouth shut, opened it, and then shut it again. Pointing at Cara wide-eyed, words tumbled out of her mouth in a jumble. "What-the-fuck-was-that-glowing-thing?"

Cara traded a look with Michael. *"Um . . . a little help here?"*

He pressed his lips together in a thin line and put his palms up in surrender.

Oh, for Pete's sake, she thought. Cara walked over to Sienna and pulled her into her arms. With a push of calming energy, Sienna stopped trembling and sighed peacefully.

Cara dropped her arms and stepped away.

"What did you do? I feel relaxed . . . amazing even."

"Remember when we got those Reiki treatments last year?" Cara asked.

Sienna nodded and gave her a skeptical look.

"It's like that, just on steroids." Cara wiped her hand down the side of her face and took a deep breath. "Sen, I need you to do something for me."

"What? Anything . . . "

"You can't tell anyone what you saw. It could get people killed . . . it could get me killed. . . or you."

Sienna paled and said in a small voice. "What?"

Cara took Sienna's hands in hers and squeezed. "I'm not telling you this to scare you, but I need to know you won't say anything about this or anything else you might learn about me going forward. You'll have to trust me."

"Okay, I won't say anything. I promise," she said with a wan smile.

Cara turned to Michael. "Kai is my Center Stone."

Michael nodded his head. "That was Constantina who called. The Dark Ones have Kai. We're sure of it. She's arranged a plane for us in thirty minutes at the Westchester County airport."

"Oh, crap. What're we going to do with Sienna?" she asked him.

Sarcastic Michael reappeared. "As much as I'd like to say, 'leave her here,' Constantina told me to take her with us."

"Oh, fuck off, Michael!" Sienna responded in foul-mouthed form. "I'll go pack. And for the record, I'm happy to be here for my best friend during this time of crisis." She strode off, apparently recovered, as Chloe followed.

Michael's eyes followed her. "I can't believe she kisses her mother with that mouth." He looked down at his phone. "Chamuel just sent a text. He'll meet us at the plane."

Cara thoughts drifted to Kai. How could she not have known this would happen?

"Cara?" Michael's voice snapped her back.

Anxiety tingled inside her, and her eyes brimmed. "If anything happens to Kai and Sara before we get there, I'll never be able to live with myself."

Michael wrapped her in a warm, reassuring embrace. "It'll be okay." He kissed the top of her head. "We'll spend some time preparing on the plane. Isaac and Chamuel have already called ahead to connect us with the Guardianship in Northern California."

She relaxed in his arms then pulled away, drying her tears. "Why is Constantina allowing us to take Sienna? From everything she's told me, this is forbidden. I don't get it."

"It seems crazy to me too, but let's just roll with it."

"Sometimes, I would give anything to get inside that woman's head for a couple of minutes," Cara said.

"Be careful what you wish for . . . "

"Did you say Chamuel will be coming with us? You mean I finally get to meet my elusive Guardian?" *Bonus time*, she thought, looking forward to a formal introduction.

Michael shrugged. "Yup. According to Constantina, it's not unusual for a Guardian to stay hidden until the Seeker accepts their Calling and the Center Stone is revealed."

"Guardians, Seekers, Center Stones—what're you talking about?"

They turned around to see Sienna with her suitcase in one hand and Chloe's leash in the other.

Michael and Cara passed each other a look.

Sienna looked from one to the other. "Never mind," she said, exasperated, and continued on her way to the front door.

"We'd better get our stuff. Meet you outside in a couple of minutes?" Michael said to Cara.

With the car packed, Cara locked up as Sienna finished her walk with Chloe. Michael dug the slip of paper with the details and his phone out of his pocket. Sienna walked by and snatched the paper out of Michael's hand on her way to open the car door.

"The least I can do is navigate," she said with an outstretched hand. "Give me your phone. I'll text Chamuel or whatever his name is."

Michael eyed her suspiciously, but rather than fight with her, he handed her his phone.

They rode to the airport in relative silence, the closest thing to peace they'd had all day.

Chapter 42

New York. Westchester County Airport. Sunday, March 30,
12:00 p.m. EDT

It took them less than twenty minutes to arrive at Westchester County Airport and park in the area reserved for the Executive Jet private charter flights. Since their flight was chartered, they had the luxury of bypassing security and heading straight for the hangar where the Gulfstream G650 was parked. Chamuel had texted Michael on the way over to say he would be accompanied by two of the Tri-State Guardians, Isaac and Ezekiel.

Cara milled around with the others on the tarmac close to the plane, waiting for the pilot to give them permission to board. Sienna kept Chloe with her on the lead, giving Cara the freedom to focus on Kai. The air was filled with nervous energy. Even Sienna and Michael managed to stay out of each other's way.

Although Cara was no longer overwhelmed by the intensity of the morning, she still tried to wrap her head around the acceptance of her Calling. Constantina had prepared her as best as she could, but there were some things too difficult to put into words. You had to experience them yourself in order to truly understand, and the Calling definitely fit into that category. She didn't have any idea what her friends had seen while it happened, but the display must have been pretty spectacular, since both of them stood gaping at her, speechless, when it was over.

"Incoming . . . " Sienna's voice broke the silence, jolting Cara out of her contemplation.

The three men walked toward them from across the tarmac. She glanced over to see the Guardians approach in the distance carrying duffel bags. All three of the men were about six and a half feet tall and built like well-muscled WWF wrestlers. Adding to the impact, the black dusters they wore over their black clothing flapped around their legs as they walked. There was a military element in their formation. They were still too far away for Cara to see their faces clearly. Sienna continued to watch as they approached while Cara went back to pacing, anxiously awaiting the all-clear to board the plane.

Michael turned to Cara, catching her mid-pace. "How are you holding up?"

"I'm okay, but this is a lot to absorb in one day. I'm a little overwhelmed."

"I understand," he said and gave her shoulder a quick squeeze.

"Thanks." She smiled and resumed her pacing. Images of Kai tumbled through her consciousness in a nonstop loop. Then she heard Sienna speak slowly.

"Oh. My. God. Those are some fine-looking men."

Cara turned to see Sienna's narrowed eyes glued to the approaching men, and as they drew closer, she said, "Cara, what's *Simon* doing here?"

With that, Cara's head snapped back around to the approaching Guardians to see what Sienna was talking about. Simon led the formation, his blond hair pulled back, followed a dark-haired Guardian and one with a spiky blond brush cut. Their faces were masculine but beautiful, with chiseled good looks. Now closer, she could clearly see the black cargo pants and tight black tees under their dusters. Sienna was right. They were an impressive sight—three oversized men walking with purpose.

On reflex, happiness shot through Cara; but it abruptly turned to confusion as she stood watching his approach. *What's he doing here?* she wondered.

As he came closer, she noticed he didn't exactly appear overjoyed to see her. Simon, flanked by the two Tri-State Guardians, rapidly closed the distance to where she stood with her party. Slowly, comprehension dawned until it shattered inside her . . . and her blood went from a slow simmer to a rolling boil.

Michael was the first to speak. "Chamuel, welcome. Let me introduce—"

"Private *fucking* security!" Cara erupted as her legs propelled her forward. She met the Guardians before Michael could finish his sentence, stopping inches away from Simon. "*REALLY?*" she spat the words at him.

A whole range of emotions struck her at once. How could he have misled her like this? He was her *Guardian*. The only man on the *planet* she wasn't allowed to love. She'd just wasted nine *years* loving a man she couldn't have, and now this?

"I'm so sorry," Simon whispered. His face was stone but his eyes pleaded with her to understand.

"I thought you were away!" Her face twisted in anguish as she tried to apply logic to what he'd told her and prevent her heart from splintering into shards. The bliss from this last week ripped away from her.

Michael stood in shocked silence next to her. She turned on her heel and stormed off up the stairs onto the plane.

Sienna's footsteps followed behind her.

Cara dropped onto the leather bench seating. Chloe jumped up next to her, and Sienna sat down on her other side. The Gulfstream carried thirteen passengers comfortably, not to mention opulently, with enough room to spread out. Right now, she needed all that space to separate her from Simon.

"Carissima, what just happened out there?" Sienna asked softly, wrapping her arm around Cara's shoulders.

Cara wished she knew how to answer that question. The man standing outside wasn't actually a man at all; he was Nephilim. And he was her Guardian. He was forbidden.

"Simon is . . ." She sighed. What could she say? There wasn't much she could tell her. Tears trickled down her face as she looked at Sienna. "He's not who he said he was. He lied to me." If anything, she knew Sienna would understand deceit after her own experience.

Sienna stroked her hair. "I'm sorry, sweetie. Maybe you guys can work this out."

Cara bristled, upset that Sienna couldn't see the egregiousness of the situation. "Are you taking his side?"

Sienna touched her forehead to Cara's hair. "No. Carissima, I watched that man look at you with love in his eyes on Friday night. And when you yelled at him out there, he struggled not to look devastated. Hear him out if you have the chance, that's all I'm saying."

Cara hugged her friend back. "I'm sorry you had to get wrapped up in this mess."

"Hey, that's what friends are for . . . being there to help you with your messes." She patted her back. "Let's just concentrate on Kai right now. We can deal with Simon later. I can tell from the look in his eyes, he's not going anywhere."

Cara looked up at Sienna and sniffled, her nose stuffed from crying. "I cared about Simon, and now I could lose Kai too." Correction. She more than cared for Simon—she was in love with him—but felt too foolish to say it out loud.

Sienna reached down into her bag and pulled out a tissue, handing it to her. "Here, sweetie. I'll help in any way I can."

"Thanks, Senny. I'm glad you're here." Cara gave her a big squeeze.

Cara sighed. The depth of Simon's deception had strong implications on their continued relationship—if it continued. He had more than lied to her; he'd betrayed her trust. She was beyond angry or sad. She was numb. Simon had been off-limits to her without her knowledge. She equated the situation to finding out that he was married, gay—or a priest! They all had the same implications as far as she was concerned, and she knew once the numbness wore off, her shattered heart would prevail and more tears would be shed.

Chapter 43

New York. Westchester County Airport. Sunday, March 30,
12:15 p.m. EDT

CHAMUEL STOOD, with his heart in his throat, staring at the open door of the plane where Cara had disappeared.

"So, you've *met* Cara," Michael stated with his arms crossed in front of him. His judgmental tone wasn't lost on Chamuel.

Chamuel, none too pleased with himself, glanced at Michael. "*Obviously.*"

As soon as the word passed through his lips, Chamuel regretted it. This wasn't Michael's fault. Chamuel had taken an oath to protect and work harmoniously in tandem with his Trinity, but his actions were now the cause of discord.

"I'm sorry, Michael. You don't deserve my anger."

Michael gave Chamuel a hard look, but he kept his voice calm and measured. "Let's speak on the plane. I need to fill you in before we land in San Francisco."

Chamuel nodded absently and glanced back at the open plane door.

Michael raked his hand through his hair and glared at him. "We'll deal with the fallout of your situation with Cara later. Let's focus on the task at hand."

Chamuel knew Michael was aware of the rules, and the last thing he needed to add to his list of transgressions for the day was more discord between he and Michael.

Without another word, Chamuel and the Guardians proceeded to the plane. Isaac and Zeke's concerned energy dogged him from behind. He knew they were eager to question him. He was dreading the flight. This was not at all the way he wanted Cara to find out his true identity. Not to mention that he'd just landed himself in his own pot of boiling water. Best friend or not, he was sure if Isaac got him alone, he'd kick his ass for this.

Chamuel sat cemented to his seat. Given his traveling companions, going over to speak with Cara was out of the question. The last thing he needed was to put his brothers in the position of having information they would be obligated to use against him at the Tribunal.

He'd naively hoped that Cara would stay silent until they were alone. The intensity of her anger had taken him by surprise. He'd miscalculated . . . badly. As a result, she'd inadvertently exposed him. Strung between anger at his own stupidity and hurt that Cara hadn't even given him a chance, he wanted to be anywhere but here.

His love for Cara ignited feelings he desperately wanted to hold on to, even though he knew he had no right to them in the first place. He wondered if Constantina had known this would happen when she assigned him. Of all people, how could she set him up this way?

No use blaming Constantina. She didn't hold a sword to my neck, he thought. As much as he wanted to blame someone, he could only blame himself. He hadn't given Cara a choice; he'd made the choice for both of them—again his fault.

She deserves better than me, he finally conceded. With that, his shoulders slumped, and he decided to push his feelings aside and fulfill his oath, as hard as that would be.

Isaac tapped him on the shoulder. "Chamuel?"

"Not now," he growled under his breath. He was in no mood to speak to him or anyone else.

Isaac's fingers dug into the back of his neck, and he lowered his head to Chamuel's ear. "We can either do this the hard way or the easy way. Your choice. Come with me. Now."

Chamuel got up and followed Isaac forward, ducking behind the curtain into the stateroom behind the cockpit.

Isaac blew out a breath. Passing his hand over his buzz cut, he fixed Chamuel with an icy-blue glare. "What were you thinking?"

Chamuel ground his teeth; there was no way he'd stay for a lecture. He turned to leave. Isaac grabbed his arm and yanked him backward into a choke hold. Isaac's breath warmed his ear. "You'll stay here until I give you permission to leave."

"I'm in charge of this mission," Chamuel said through clenched teeth. Eyeing the tight space, he ruled out having a throw-down with Isaac. Even so, having sparred with Isaac since puberty, he knew his chances were only a hair greater than fifty-fifty.

"Technically, but you're compromised. You put me in this situation, so you owe me the respect of hearing me out. Got it?" Isaac's grip loosened, and his voice softened. "Can I let you go now?"

Chamuel closed his eyes and sighed in frustration. "Yeah."

Isaac dropped his arm and stepped back to lean against the table. He ran both of his hands back through his prickly blond hair. "Cham, we've know each other since before we had wings, and I love you like a true brother. But how did this happen? I've watched you suffer endlessly since Calliope and Mina died." Isaac's voice filled with anguish. "I'm going to have to turn you in. Do you have any idea how that makes me *feel*?"

Chamuel swept his hand over his face. "Listen, can we agree to deal with this after the mission's over? I'm not going to fall apart. I've got this one." Well, he wouldn't fall apart in public at least. But he also wouldn't let his issues with Cara interfere with his job—that he knew with certainty.

Isaac pressed his lips together into a hard line. "We don't have much of a choice. I'll take care of Zeke. And that's another thing. That kid worships you . . . " Isaac shook his head. Suddenly, his head flew up and his eyes turned frigid. "She didn't seduce you, did she?"

Chamuel's spine stiffened, and he gave Isaac a harsh look. "This isn't her fault. And no . . . she didn't seduce me."

Isaac raised an eyebrow. "Well, I know it's been a while. Why didn't you just listen to me—"

Chamuel held up his palm. "Stop, just stop, *I*," he said. "This is about more than breaking my celibacy. If that's all it was, nothing would've ever happened."

Isaac held his hands to his head then pointed to where Cara sat on the other side of the curtain. "But of all the asinine choices. Why did you have to choose the only person on earth forbidden to you? Not only that, she screwed you out there. You're really bent on self-destruction, aren't you?"

Anger and hurt erupted inside Chamuel and he grabbed Isaac by the collar. "She didn't know, and I didn't tell her. This is my fault, *I*. Mine. Not hers."

Isaac wrenched himself free and wilted in front of him. "Shit . . . You're in love with her."

The curtain parted, and Michael poked his head in. "Can I talk to you both?"

Chamuel signaled with his hand for Michael to enter.

"Chamuel? Or would you prefer me to call you Simon?" Michael asked, the curtain closing behind him.

He ignored the barb. "Off duty, I'm Simon. Here, I'm acting in my official capacity as the Guardian of our Trinity, so you should address me as Chamuel." His voice held the same weariness that had settled into his bones.

Silently, through their telepathic link, Michael asked, *"Would you mind if we all moved to chairs toward the back of the plane? I've asked the girls to move up so that we can have some additional privacy."*

The mention of Cara sent a shooting pain through Chamuel's chest. Worse was the thought of walking past her and not being able to take her into his arms. He looked at Michael and gave a reluctant nod.

"Zeke's already there waiting for us," Michael said.

Chamuel followed Isaac and Michael back through the cabin. Lucky for him, Cara was stretched out in one of the reclining seats with her eyes closed, listening to her iPod.

They settled into the two sets of seats that faced inward with a table in between. Once comfortably seated, Michael started the briefing.

"The Center Stone of this Trinity is Dr. Kai Solomon. He and Cara have known each other since college. They have a strong, long-standing emotional bond. This mission is pivotal. Not only do we need to rescue Dr. Solomon from the Dark Ones, but we also need to ensure his discovery remains out of their hands. The Council believes Kai has been given access to knowledge that could enable the Dark Ones to develop an army that could compete equally with the Guardianship." Michael paused and looked pointedly at each of them, waiting for a reaction.

Chamuel frowned. "How would they do such a thing?"

"We believe they're trying to create a vaccine that transforms a human being into a Nephil with the same strength and powers as all of you. We think they're looking to meet us head-on for the final battle."

Alarm spread inside Chamuel. "You mean the prophecy?" he asked, stunned. All the signs were there. He'd suspected something big, just not this big.

"Yes," said Michael.

"But how do we know this?" Isaac asked gruffly.

"Dr. Sandra Wilson and Dr. Tom Peyton were part of a special Trinity that preceded Cara and Kai. An insertion orchestrated by the Angelorum to create an insurance policy for Cara and Kai's success. Sandra and Tom made the initial discovery of the DNA's true origin," Michael explained.

Chamuel looked at Michael with a furrowed brow. "Why was the insertion necessary?"

"The Dark Ones had advance knowledge of Cara's mission."

"I figured that when I saw Achanelech dogging Cara in the subway," Chamuel said. "The Sentinel was his. How'd they find out?" The Angelorum had a long and colorful history with the Demon King of Fire. Achanelech, tongue-in-cheek, chose the name Le Feu as his moniker, which meant "fire" in French.

Michael shook his head. "We don't know."

"That's concerning. What made the Trinity special?" Isaac asked.

Michael took a deep breath. "Sandra was a Three Hundred Class Nephil, and she wasn't the Guardian. She was both the Messenger and the Seeker, and Tom was her Center Stone."

The Angelorum classified Nephilim by the century of their age. Chamuel, at one hundred forty-seven, was part of the One Hundred Class, which made Sandra between three and four hundred years old.

"*How could that be possible? She was Nephilim?*" Chamuel asked. There had never been a Nephil who had been either a Messenger or a Seeker in the history of the Angelorum, much less a combination of both.

"There's more," Michael said.

Chamuel and his brothers stared, waiting for the punch line.

"She was one of Constantina's children," Michael finished.

"*What?*" "*No way!*" "*Are you fucking kidding me?*" Chamuel, Isaac, and Zeke all spoke at once under the veil of silence. None of them had known Sandra when she was alive.

Michael looked intensely at the others. "Sandra, whose Nephilim name was Hope, chose to work in the private sector as a scientist. She was placed in the outside world about fifteen years ago to build her credentials and to blend into human society. That's why none of you knew of her."

Chamuel stared off into space. What Michael told them had serious implications . . . Had the Angelorum violated their own noninterference rule?

"Sandra accepted her fate and made a great sacrifice. At the request of the Angelorum, she went through the transformation."

Michael's words hit Chamuel right in the gut, followed by a sudden wave of nausea. A Nephil's worst nightmare, the transformation was something he could be facing for his romance with Cara. Held as the ultimate punishment against the Guardianship, the procedure consists of the removal of a Nephil's wings, their source of strength, rendering them powerless and weak.

"They needed to ensure she avoided detection as Nephilim. Hope knew this was a potential suicide mission when she'd accepted it. A certain sequence of events needed to take place in order to put Cara exactly where she needed to be to fulfill her destiny. Sandra also had another gift . . . She could see the future, making her the perfect choice. Her challenge was to orchestrate everything without interfering with free will. We still don't have all the answers." Michael sat back for a breather.

Chamuel looked at Michael with laser precision. "But why Cara and why now?"

Michael leaned forward and clasped his hands together. "Think about it. This is the first time in history that science has made it possible. The latest genetic sequencing equipment revolutionized genetic engineering, making research inexpensive and discoveries quick to replicate, but it's only been available for a couple of years. If you stop to think, this is the first point in time this *could* have happened.

"The Dark Ones tried to recover Tom and Sandra's work after they were killed, but Sandra ensured they couldn't. She set it up so that the discovery would be passed to Dr. Solomon, and only to Dr. Solomon. We know it's taken just over a year for him to discover the package Sandra arranged before she died. We think he's been watched since back then."

"What was in the package?" Chamuel asked.

"A key to a post office box containing all of Tom and Sandra's lab notes on how to make the vaccine." Michael centered his gaze on Chamuel when he shared the next part. "We think this could be a trap . . . to capture Cara. The Council discovered the energy shifted to the San Francisco Bay Area after dropping off the grid on the East Coast. They're convinced the Dark Ones knew Cara would come after Kai, so they didn't need to hunt her back home. Basically, we're walking right into their hands."

Chamuel's brow deepened with worry. "If they have the discovery, why do they want Cara?"

"The same reason Sandra sacrificed herself and why Constantina is training Cara personally . . . " Michael took a deep breath. "Cara is the First of the Holy Twelve."

Of course. Chamuel closed his eyes.

"Son of a bitch," Isaac mumbled next to him, while Zeke let out a low whistle.

"You may want to consider some extra backup for the rescue given this development," Michael said.

"The prophecy has started," stated Isaac.

"Actually," Michael corrected him, "the prophecy started when Cara was born, twenty-seven years ago, and the preparation has been underway since the anomaly first appeared in the Trinity Pool."

Chamuel silently reeled from Michael's revelations. Cara was tied to the prophecy, and he was tied to Hope. He needed to have a word with Constantina the next time he saw her.

His shoulders stiffened as comprehension seeped further into his consciousness. Constantina had chosen him as part of this Trinity, not only to fill the role with a warm body she trusted, but also because she needed one of the Guardianship's best strategists. This Trinity and this mission would extend well beyond the rescue of Dr. Kai Solomon—if they managed to live that long. They would be part of the ultimate fight.

The realization took his breath away and placed a much larger burden squarely on his shoulders. Could he take them all the way and not get them killed?

Wanting an intimate relationship with Cara seemed selfish now in the face of what their future held. Still, the thought of turning away from her tore his heart to shreds.

Michael abruptly pulled him back from his thoughts. "There's more," he said. "To complicate matters, Sandra's Guardian, Ishmael, disappeared right before she died. He's believed to have been taken by the Dark Ones."

Chamuel exchanged a glance with Isaac.

"There's something bigger going on here," Isaac said. "There have been other incidents." Isaac proceeded to tell Michael about the recent occurrence with the Boston Seeker and the Guardian who was snatched.

Then Isaac shot Chamuel a look. "We also have reason to believe there may be a breach in the Guardianship. Chamuel reported Cara's incident with the Sentinel. Apparently, the Sentinel escaped with the help of a Nephil who's shown up a couple more times in Chamuel's presence. What's baffling is that we can't tag anyone registered with the Guardianship to the places and times where Chamuel detected him. Is it possible the Dark Ones already succeeded in making their own Nephilim?"

Michael shook his head. "Not likely."

"What does Cara know about any of this?" Chamuel asked.

"She only knows Dr. Solomon is working on a highly confidential project. Nothing more." Michael swept his gaze across their faces before landing on Chamuel. "Let me know if you disagree, but I think we should refrain from giving her too many details."

Chamuel couldn't tell if Michael spoke to him as Cara's Guardian or as the man who loved her. He guessed it didn't matter, since the answer would still be the same. He nodded. "Agreed. It will only cause her more anxiety over his disappearance."

"Do we know when Kai and his daughter were taken?" Isaac asked.

"Based on his wife's response, she believes within the last twenty-four hours, but we really don't have any additional details. Our San Francisco branch of Watson & Haskins sent word that Kai picked up Sandra's package last Monday. However, his wife claims she was in China until last night, so he and his daughter could have been missing for as long as a week. Not surprising, there's been nothing in the news about their disappearance."

"We'll need to be prepared for anything." Zeke, their dark-haired, baby-faced partner, rubbed his hands over his tattooed biceps.

"Agreed," said Chamuel.

"We'll arrive in San Jose by late afternoon, so we should make it to Dr. Solomon's house a little after five o'clock," Michael said. "We'll learn more once we speak with his wife directly . . . But, your observations are good ones and, to your point, we should proceed with extreme caution."

He stood, indicating the meeting was over. "See you on the ground."

Chapter 44

California. Undisclosed Location. Sunday, March 30,
3:00 p.m. PDT / 12:00 p.m. EDT

FIGHTING BACK A YAWN, Kai prepared another sample. He'd worked continuously since being taken to the lab, snatching a few hours of sleep every eighteen to twenty hours. Unable to tell whether it was night or day from inside his underground prison, he used the timer on one of the lab machines to track his five-day countdown. He'd need every available minute to finish the vaccine, and time was running out.

Le Feu hadn't exaggerated. The lab was fully equipped with everything, including a state-of-the-art genetic sequencing machine. His knowledge gaps now filled, Kai's work took on a new pace and direction. Having memorized the key points in Tom's notes, he knew which gene pairs were important and which chromosomes to study. From what he could gather, the vaccine transformed human DNA into the donor DNA, highlighting two specific characteristics: longevity and rapid healing abilities.

His experience making vaccines notwithstanding, using DNA in vaccines was new for Kai. DNA vaccines were already being tested on humans for HIV, malaria, and a few other diseases. Despite the fact there were no bacterium or virus involved, Kai used the same technology to introduce the vaccine into the body and have it replicate. If his calculations were correct, replication would start instantaneously after the injection, reaching a saturation level in the body within an hour.

He yawned, no longer able to suppress it. He had to push through his exhaustion. Sara's safety depended on his success. He'd spoken with her earlier over the video monitoring system, expending his daily allotment of five precious minutes per day. Seeing her on the screen killed him inside. Fortunately, though tired and confused, she appeared otherwise unharmed. During their conversation earlier, she'd told him she wasn't as scared and that she'd been given good food.

A lump formed in his throat as she spoke, terrified of what would happen to her if he failed. He was so proud of her. When he told her how brave she was to be there alone without him or Mommy, she'd averted her eyes, as if she'd wanted to say something but decided against it. Instead, she said, "I love you, Daddy. We'll fight the monsters together." Something about her reaction caused a ripple of anxiety to run through him, and then the video monitor went dark.

Kai was hunched over a lab table in deep concentration when he heard the voice. *"Dr. Solomon, can you hear me?"*

Kai's head flew up, startled. He spun around looking for the person who'd spoken, but found he was alone. "Where are you?" he asked aloud.

The voice responded inside Kai's head. *"Please don't speak. I can hear you through your thoughts. Speak, but not aloud. Think what it is you want to say."*

Kai frowned. *I'm I losing it?*

"No, Dr. Solomon, you're mentally fit." The voice responded matter-of-factly.

Kai squelched a nervous laugh at the literal interpretation and decided to roll with it. This wasn't any more insane than anything else that had happened this week.

"Who are you?" he asked silently.

"I'm Ishmael. We've been waiting for you."

Kai snapped to attention. *"Ishmael is the key, and the key is Ishmael."*

"I see you've received Sandra's message. Good. We have little time. The only reason we can communicate right now is because Chaos and Destruction have left the premises. Their presence interferes with our telepathic communications. Within the next twenty-four hours, a rescue attempt will be made for you and Sara. When they come, tell them I'm here, below you, in a deeper dungeon with the others . . . We're with your daughter Sara."

Ishmael now had Kai's full attention. *"Is she safe? Sara, I mean?"*

"Yes. My brother Luke is with her. He apologizes for his failure to protect you both from the Dark Ones, and for having to kill the demon in front of one so young. They captured him when you were both kidnapped."

Kai flashed back to scene in his backyard and to the man with the shining sword. The one who'd turned into a white blur. The man who wasn't one hundred percent human.

"What are *you?"* Kai asked anxiously.

"I am of angelic nature, Dr. Solomon," Ishmael said. *"Please let them know there are ten of us in all. We've all been injured, and some of us are weaker than others. But you have my word that we'll do whatever we can to protect your daughter."*

Kai, overwhelmed with emotion, whispered, "Thank you."

"*One last thing, Dr. Solomon. You must not let Le Feu get the vaccine. He will kill us all, including you and your family.*"

"*But, he said he'd let us go if I succeeded.*" Kai knew the response he would receive as soon as he thought the words.

"*You know too much for him to let you live, Dr. Solomon. Mark my words, his intent is to kill us all. Now, I must go. The twins are returning. Journey forth in peace and love, Dr. Solomon.*"

The voice was gone.

Kai had anticipated Le Feu's betrayal and already had a plan . . . now all he had to do was escape. He'd created two versions of the vaccine. The one he'd injected into three of Le Feu's flunkies last night would degrade in less than a week. He would hide a syringe of the real vaccine in his sock, and smuggle it out during the rescue.

The door of the lab opened, jarring him from his thoughts. He glanced up and his heart dropped as a tide of emotions swept over him when he recognized the blonde woman standing before him.

Chapter 45

San Jose Airport. Sunday, March 30, 5:10 p.m. PDT

WARM SUN CARESSED Cara's face as they disembarked in San Jose, though the temperature was not much different from what she'd left behind on the East Coast. Three black Escalades waited on the side of the tarmac. Having arrived on a private flight, she and the others were free to leave without entering the terminal.

Cara hung back as the driver of the lead car exited. Her eyes had avoided looking in Simon's direction for most of the flight. Even a mere glimpse of him made her heart lurch in pain. Now, seeing him in action, she had difficulty thinking of him as the Simon she'd spent the last week dating. The Simon whose lips and touch she craved. The Simon whom she was in love with . . .

He walked ahead with Isaac to greet a tall, dark-haired man dressed similarly to him, while Michael and the other Guardians collected the luggage and loaded it into the waiting vehicles.

Simon extended his hand in greeting, placing it on the other man's huge shoulder and using the formal greeting of the Guardianship. "Greetings, Raphael. It's been a long time, my friend. Thanks for your help."

"Chamuel, it's more of a pleasure than a duty to assist you," he responded warmly before turning to Isaac to exchange pleasantries.

Simon handed him a piece of paper. "Here's the address. We'll ride with you. We've learned more since our departure, so I have more to brief you on."

Silently brushing past them, Cara headed for the next car with Chloe and Sienna, relieved to finally escape her Guardian.

Forty minutes later, the Escalades pulled up in a line next to the curb outside Kai's home. Simon, Isaac, Raphael, and Michael exited the first car and approached hers.

A knock sounded on the back passenger window. Cara's cheeks flushed when the black-tinted glass rolled down to reveal Simon. Her feelings came rushing back when she caught a spark ignite in his eyes that he quickly tried to cover. Both her resolve and her anger lost some ground when she heard his rich, melodic voice.

"Cara, bring Chloe with us, please," he said gently. In that moment, she realized she couldn't think of him as Chamuel; to her, he would always be Simon.

Confused, she looked down at the dog curled up next to her on the seat. Why did he want Chloe?

She sighed. At this point, he was in charge, and if nothing else, she trusted him to do his job. Without a word, Cara clipped Chloe's leash onto her collar, and exited the door facing the street. She brought the dog around to the sidewalk.

Isaac hung back while Cara, Michael, and Chloe led the way to the house, flanked by Raphael and Simon. The front door was open behind the screen. Cara rang the bell, and called inside.

"Melanie, it's Cara. We're here."

"Come in," said a familiar voice.

Cara started across the threshold, and Chloe's hackles rose. She bared her teeth, and a deep growl rumbled up from her throat. Tensing her legs, Chloe barked viciously and reared up, ready to attack Melanie as she entered the room.

Too startled to move, Cara tugged back on the lead. She gasped in surprise when the dog's eyes shot out bright blue lasers at Melanie. Shoring up on Chloe's lead with both hands, Cara struggled to hold her back. A flash of white flew past Cara's peripheral vision. The next thing she knew, Simon had his hand wrapped around Melanie's throat and spoke to her in a language Cara didn't understand.

"What are you doing?" Cara screamed at Simon. She was rooted in place, trying to control her near rabid dog. In a panic, she turned to Michael and demanded, "What's he saying to her?"

"He's speaking to her in the angelic language. Give me Chloe," Michael said before wrenching Chloe's lead from her. "Raphael, take Chloe outside to Sienna and come back."

Raphael nodded and dragged the vicious animal from the house.

"Melanie's not what she seems," said Michael and grabbed Cara's shoulders. He was right. When Melanie spoke, her voice was deep and demonic. She choked out a response to Simon's question, trying to wretch his hand free of her throat.

Cara stared, stunned. She understood. "Melanie's one of the Dark Ones?"

"Not exactly," he said, keeping close watch on Simon and Melanie.

Raphael strode back in. With his free hand Simon slid out a dagger from his weapons belt and stabbed Melanie in the chest. She crumpled to the ground, motionless.

"What have you done?" Cara screamed, breaking away from Michael to get to Melanie.

Simon turned to face Cara and spoke calmly. "Relax. I didn't kill her. She's just unconscious. I cast out the demon that possessed her. From what I understand, it's been riding shotgun for almost a year."

"Will she be okay?"

"Yes, she should be." Simon turned to address Raphael and started toward the door. "Can you have your team take care of Melanie? Bring her to the clinic?"

"We'll have the third car transport her," he said.

Simon momentarily stopped and glanced at Cara. "Now we won't be warning our enemies of our arrival."

Struck by a thought, Cara reached out and grabbed his forearm as he turned to go. "Wait. You wanted me to bring Chloe with us because she can see demons?"

A faint smile touched his lips. "Yes. Chloe is a Sentinel . . . for our side." Then his expression turned hard, like the day she'd seen him in the subway, and he walked out the front door.

Chapter 46

San Francisco. Sunday, March 30, 6:30 p.m. PDT

CARA STARED OUT the window of the Escalade as they wove through downtown San Francisco with her whippet Sentinel asleep in an exhausted ball between her and Michael. She tried to wrap her mind around what she'd witnessed back at Kai's house—demons, blue lasers shooting from her pet's eyes, the flash of wings behind Simon. At least the excitement dulled her emotional pain.

Sienna leaned over the back of Cara's seat from the third row. "Carissima," she asked in a low voice, "who are all these men? Do they work for Simon?"

Cara saw Sienna's eyes trained on the tall man with the black braided hair sitting behind the wheel. Cara heard a stifled snort from the driver, and thought about kicking the back of his seat. Too bad she was sitting on the passenger side. The Guardian's face was the color of café mocha and his emerald-green eyes caught her gaze in the rearview mirror. He wore an amused look that said: "I can't wait to hear this."

She narrowed her eyes at his reflection and then glanced at Sienna. "No, sweetie. They all work for the same private security organization as Simon, but for different people." The half-truth felt almost natural passing through her lips.

"If they didn't all have long hair, I'd think they were a military Special Forces team or something. Either way, I'm enjoying the view," Sienna purred.

Michael rolled his eyes and broke his silence. "Are men all you ever think about?" he snapped.

Sienna glared at him. "I could ask *you* the same question."

Anger flared instantly in Michael's eyes. "You're such a bitch."

Cara dove between them as Sienna lunged at Michael with her nails out. "Stop it! Both of you!" Cara pushed Sienna back into the third row. This time the Guardian in the front seat didn't attempt to hide his amusement—he burst out laughing.

"Play nice, children, or I'm going to stop the car and make you all walk," he said with a West Indian lilt. "Pretty One, you shouldn't let him get to you. But, to be fair, you shouldn't question the gentleman's manhood."

Michael gazed out the window and smirked with vindication.

"And you, sir," he said to Michael, "shouldn't fault the woman for going after what she wants. You might profit from her example."

"Ha!" Sienna barked at Michael. The side of his face flushed and Cara felt sorry for him, aware of his extreme sensitivity over being publically embarrassed.

"Thanks for the support, uh . . . " Cara didn't know his name.

"Jade. The name is Jade, Miss Cara," he said in his warm lilt. She caught herself staring at his unusual and beautiful mixed-race coloring, appreciating what Sienna meant about the view. Thinking back to what Constantina had told her about the Guardians and their angelic characteristics, she wasn't surprised that he was breathtaking.

"It's nice to meet you, Jade. Sorry for the commotion," Cara said and glanced at Michael, who sat with his arms crossed tightly in front of him, wearing a tense frown, and then at Sienna, who sat in a full pout behind her. Their energy roiled around them in an angry cloud.

Cara sighed. They acted like a pair of two-year-olds when they were together, but there was no denying their energy carried a certain electricity.

"No problem. Let me know if there's anything else you need, princess," he said.

Cara hoped "princess" was only an endearment and not some title she wasn't aware of.

The SUV turned the corner into a neighborhood in the Marina District.

"Nice place," Cara said to Michael as their Escalade pulled up in front of a blue three-story home. "It looks like someone's house." One glance at him told her that he hadn't fully recovered from his dust up with Sienna.

"It is. Constantina didn't want to draw attention to our arrival, so she arranged a private safe house for us," Michael said with forced nonchalance, his arms still bolted across his body.

Unlike the traditional row houses populating the street, the ultramodern design had a two-story, glass picture window comprised of smaller square windows spreading along the front and right side of the house. A roof deck, surrounded by more glass panels, crowned the top of the house, while the ground floor facade boasted a stainless-steel double garage door next to the front entrance.

The Escalades pulled in one by one and parked in the private lot on the side of house—a true luxury in San Francisco.

"Thanks, Jade." Cara said, catching the Guardian's eye as they exited the SUV. He winked and gave her a bright, white smile.

Cara sandwiched herself and Chloe between Michael and Sienna as they followed Simon and some of the others in through the front door and up the stairs to the first floor.

Cara looked around with appreciation at the large space with its two-level open floor plan. A large kitchen dominated the right wall just opposite the spacious living room area on the left. Open railing like on the deck of a ship edged the second-floor loft space, and stairs behind the kitchen led up upstairs. The entire area was white, with splashes of color added from oversized artwork and upholstered accents sprinkled on the ultramodern furniture.

Was that really a guitar mounted to the wall in the dining room?

"Cara."

She turned at the sound of her name.

"You, Sienna, and Michael can take the upstairs bedrooms," Simon said evenly. "My team will use the lower levels. Why don't you take your bags up?" Then he turned his back in dismissal and huddled with Isaac. She overheard them discussing setting up the command post in the living room.

Sienna led the way up while Cara maintained her position separating Michael and Sienna in case one of them got the overwhelming urge to toss the other over the upstairs railing.

"Cara, Michael, be back down here in twenty minutes," Simon called from below.

Twenty minutes later, she and Michael descended from the upstairs loft and approached the living room. The room was filled to capacity with Guardians dressed in standard-issue black and seated on every available inch of the L-shaped sofa. Isaac, Zeke, Raphael, and Jade sat among six more Guardians Cara didn't recognize—ten of the largest and most beautiful men human eyes could behold, and Simon made eleven. Their cultural diversity actually took Cara by surprise. Jade wasn't the only man of color. There was also an Asian and two Hispanic Guardians in the group. Simon cut a commanding figure as the only man standing among them.

Thank God Sienna's upstairs on the roof deck, Cara thought. Far enough away not to cause a disruption trying to get a closer look at all that rippled muscle.

All eyes fixed on Simon. He looked up as they approached, capturing Cara's gaze for a split second with unreadable eyes before he signaled with his hand for them to join him.

"Brothers, I'd like to introduce you to the members of my Trinity." Simon swept his hand in her direction. "This is Cara Collins, our Soul Seeker." And then toward Michael. "And our Messenger, Michael Swift."

Not knowing what else to do, Cara just nodded as she was introduced while Michael offered a "nice to meet you."

Simon gestured behind him. "Please, sit and join us for the briefing."

Cara lowered herself onto the empty settee facing the crowded sofa. Her pulse raced and heat spread through her. Angry or not, her traitorous body betrayed her. Why was it that being this close to him made her tingle with such awareness?

"Team, please introduce yourselves. Give your name and house affiliation," Simon instructed and sat down next to her on the settee.

Raphael, the dark-haired Guardian leader, stood and gave a small bow. "Welcome to our fair city, Collins Trinity. I'm Raphael, Son of Peliel. I lead the San Francisco City House and this is my team." He spoke with a cordial smile, gesturing toward the seated men further down on the sofa.

Cara had never heard a formal Guardian introduction or their Trinity name spoken aloud before. Constantina had explained the Guardians take on the name of their angelic mother and that the Trinity name was derived based on the Soul Seeker's surname.

Raphael took his place on the sofa while Jade rose up alongside of him.

Jade bent at the waist with a mischievous glint in his emerald eyes. "Princess and Sir," he said, addressing them, "I'm Jade, Son of Arella with San Francisco City House. Glad to be of service in both battle and in dispensing wisdom."

"Whether you want it or not," came the gruff comment from the rusty-haired Guardian on the other side of Isaac.

Jade winked and sat down. "Gabe hates that I'm always right."

Gabe answered with a loud snort.

"Brothers . . . " Raphael said in a warning tone.

Zeke, with his baby face and rakish smile, stood up next and gave them a wave. Cara hadn't paid much attention to the dark-ponytailed Guardian with the warm brown eyes on the trip out, but she found herself smiling back at him, liking his playful energy. Unlike many of the other Guardians whose skin was tattoo-free, intricate tribal designs curled up and around both of his muscled arms, disappearing under his T-shirt sleeves. "Hey. Sorry we didn't get to meet earlier. Glad to be here to help with the rescue and to kick some demon ass." He tipped two fingers at Isaac. "I'm with the East Coast Tri-State House. Oh, yeah. Ezekiel, Son of Itqal."

Alongside him, Isaac gave him an icy glare and shook his head. "Remind me to send you back through diplomacy training," he said dryly before standing and turning his attention back to Cara and Michael.

"He's just a stick in the mud."

Cara jumped at the sound of Zeke's voice in her head. She looked at him to see the corner of Zeke's mouth tipped up in a smile.

"Zeke, get off my Trinity's frequency," Simon growled next to her.

Cara's spine stiffened. She'd never heard Simon speak to her telepathically before. It only served to remind her of his deception.

Zeke shrugged and widened his eyes, projecting a look of innocence from behind Isaac.

"Isaac, Son of Heiglot and leader of Tri-State House. Your Trinity has our commitment to do whatever it takes to rescue Dr. Solomon," he said, and squeezed back on the sofa between Zeke and Gabe.

Gabe lumbered up, bigger and burlier than the rest of the Guardians, but no less muscled. He pawed at his rust-colored ponytail, a few shades redder than Cara's own hair, tightening it behind his head. His eyes, the same color green as hers, caught her gaze and warmed. "Cara, please accept my apology for my rude behavior earlier." He cast a brief glare in Jade's direction then returned his attention to her. "I'm Gabriel, Son of Iahmel, and I'm also a member of the San Francisco City House. I'm here to get down to business and find our prisoners." Jerking his head toward Jade, he cracked his large knuckles and said, "Any of these guys get out of hand, you let me know. I'll take care of 'em for you."

"I've got that one covered," came Simon's chilly response.

Gabe's eyebrow twitched and the corner of his mouth tugged up in a small smile. He put his hands up in surrender and sat down.

By the time all the introductions were done several minutes later, she'd met: Sun, Son of Urpaniel; Jophiel, Son of Harudha; Christian, Son of Jariel; Camael, Son of Liwet; and Isiah, Son of Mehiel.

Simon leaned forward. His thigh accidentally brushed Cara, and she edged away.

"Raphael, please share your update. Then I'll lay out our plan for everyone," Simon said.

Raphael picked up his digital tablet from the coffee table and cleared his throat. "We've done a refresh on all of Achanelech's properties and known associates. He's gotten smart over the years and created some new holding companies, but I've short-listed some possible locations. I've also pulled building plans, architectural drawings, and permits—not that they'd tell the whole story. But at least it's a start."

"Who's Achanelech?" Cara whispered in Michael's ear.

"The one who has Kai and his daughter." A shiver rippled down Cara's back. Michael added, "We think he's interested in Kai's latest genetics project at Forrester."

Uh-huh. That was the first morsel of information she'd heard that made any sense to her at all about Kai's disappearance. Then it clicked into place. The notebooks Melanie had mentioned on the phone . . .

Simon got up from the settee. "Thanks, Rafe. Do you have our final numbers for this mission?"

"Two teams of five are on their way in and plan to meet us at the site once it's found. The other local teams are otherwise engaged in assignments and can't get away. Before we spoke in the car, I'd hoped that would be enough."

Letting out a breath, Simon crossed his arm over his chest and propped his chin on his fist, shaking his head in contemplation. "Barely. I'd be happier if we had some backup."

Raphael scrubbed his face with his hand and shifted up to his feet. "I know. After you all came inside, I put in a call to Angel Benitez and his retiree team in LA, but I haven't gotten a response yet."

Murmurs and looks of discomfort spread through the West Coast Guardians on the sofa.

"You called the Exile?" Gabriel popped up and glared at Raphael. "Why would you drag Benedictine and his Four Hundred Class into active Guardian business?"

"Sit. Down. Gabe. Now," Raphael said through his clenched teeth, goring him with a look until Gabe lowered himself onto the settee.

"But—"

"Don't question my authority again." The living room pulsed with Raphael's menacing energy until Gabriel closed his mouth and shut up. He sat in a stormy sulk with a red face and a deep frown.

"Let me be clear," Simon snapped at the team. "I don't have time for Guardianship politics. I wouldn't care if he and his Nephilim are green, have two heads, and bark at the moon once a month. We need all the help we can get." He scowled and paced while he thought. "When will we know if they're coming?"

"Don't know. They travel a lot. It might take days for Angel to return my call, if he does at all."

Cara sensed Raphael's concern and wondered who Angel was and what had gotten him exiled. Constantina hadn't mentioned that was even a possibility.

Simon shook his head and said, "Then we can't count on them. Right now that makes us twenty-one strong. Michael is a trained fighter making twenty-two." He glanced at Raphael, who had recovered his calm demeanor. "How many listening devices do we have?"

"Six. One for each rescue team of four, and an extra for our explosives team of two," he said.

Zeke, Gabriel, and Sun exchanged quizzical looks with each other on the sofa, reflecting Cara's own confusion.

Michael leaned over to Cara and whispered, "The Guardians innately use telepathic communication during missions, just like we do in our Trinity. Not devices. This is like asking them to use scuba gear on dry land."

"Good," Simon replied and then addressed the puzzled Guardians. "We've been investigating incidents over the last several years of Guardian disappearances during Seeker attacks. The common theme in all the interviews has been the unexpected interference of telepathic communication on our frequencies. Ishmael was taken by the Dark Ones under similar circumstances. Our hypothesis is that these incidents are related. Furthermore, since our communication is based on our ability to bend the laws of physics, the only interference possible must be supernatural in nature. With that in mind, our use of modern technology shouldn't be anticipated by our enemies, allowing us to communicate as we normally would telepathically. Raphael secured state-of-the-art listening devices used by United States Special Forces teams."

Cara watched as the expressions in the room changed from confusion to interest.

Raphael reached inside his pocket and pulled out a small two-part device, handing it to Simon.

Simon set it on the coffee table. He scanned the room and then reached up and removed his hair tie. His hair cascaded down to cover his neck and the tops of his shoulders. He placed the earpiece part of the device under his hair into his ear.

A rush of warmth hit Cara and she wanted to kick herself for acting like a bone-headed schoolgirl. She hated the fact that her heart and her head were having a serious disconnect, and that seeing his hair loose around his face did something extra to weaken her knees.

Simon gave Isaac a wry smile. "With the exception of *I* over there, who felt compelled to leave the reservation and chop off his hair, wearing our hair down will conceal the devices from view." He leaned in and picked up the other small piece on the table. "The receiver is small enough to hide in our belts and won't interfere with wing expansion and takeoff. It's also on a closed frequency that can't be accessed by anyone outside the six teams. The communications booster will be controlled from outside the perimeter in one of our vehicles."

A lot of head nodding and discussion ensued, all of it positive.

"First things first. We need to find out where they're holding Dr. Solomon," said Simon. "You all have your search assignments from earlier. See Isaac for the flight roster. Thank you, Brothers. You're dismissed."

The Guardians hoisted themselves up off the sofa one by one, and broke into individual conversations. Simon turned to her and Michael and lowered his voice. "Stay a minute so I can fill you in."

The doorbell rang.

Simon turned to Zeke with a smirk. "Can you get the food? I can hear your stomach growling from here."

Zeke gleefully rubbed his hands together. "Don't need to ask me twice." His heavy boots echoed across the wood floor as he headed toward the stairs. He yelled back, "Too bad we weren't meeting under better circumstances. We could've strong-armed you into cooking for us, Chamuel."

Simon flushed. "I daresay there'll be no wine pairings for us this evening. Another time, Zeke."

Zeke's voice came up from the door a few moments later. "I need help down here."

Jade and one of the other Guardians milling about in the living room went to his aid.

Simon turned back to Cara and Michael. "We'll search by air in one-hour bursts so that we can grab sleep and reserve our energy for the rescue. The first patrol will leave right after they eat, since we all need to fuel up before we fly. I suggest getting some food with the rest of us to keep up your strength. I'm hoping we find the location before dawn so we can move in while it's still dark. So, get as much sleep as you can. You may be woken up sometime before dawn."

Cara stared at him as he spoke. A shiver rolled through her as the rescue became a reality in her mind. Simon fingers grazed the top of her shoulder. His touch, as always, sent an annoying jolt of excitement over her skin.

"Cara, once we find Kai, you'll be paired with me and Michael. Zeke will round out our team of four. But it'll be you who leads us to Kai's precise location. We'll need to all be on our game if we plan to make it out of there in one piece. Michael and I will rely on you to manage your fear. Trust in your training and your healing powers to keep yourself calm." Simon's eyes connected with hers.

"Good advice." She looked away and swallowed, avoiding any more direct eye contact. She appreciated that Simon didn't try to falsely placate her. Rather, he laid out her responsibilities as part of their Trinity. He was right; there wasn't any room for error or weak behavior. Her mind flashed back to her recent panic attack, and she prayed that it wouldn't be an issue. She needed to hold her own. People were placing their faith in her, and she couldn't let them down. Reaching down into her well of strength, she visualized pushing away her fear and replacing it with calm resolve.

Simon must have noted the shift inside her. "Good girl," he said quietly and turned to Michael. "Michael, stay with Isaac. He'll show you what to do in the command center and fill you in more completely on our rescue plan. I'll see you both later."

Cara glanced after Simon as he strode off toward the kitchen, sensing he was eager to put some distance between them after the meeting. Fine with her. Being close to him only complicated an already complicated situation.

Zeke and Jade unpacked the bags of food as the Guardians filed into the kitchen. Between the peninsula island with six barstools and the huge banquette along the kitchen wall with seating for twelve normal-sized people, there was more than enough room for everyone to comfortably enjoy the feast.

The smell of the warm food drifted over. Ignoring the rumble in her stomach, Cara used the distraction to slip away and join Sienna on the roof deck. She cracked the exterior door open and walked out into the now cooling remains of the day.

Sienna sat on one of the plush lounge chairs facing San Francisco Bay, which could be seen over the rooftops, brooding and mindlessly flipping through a fashion magazine.

With a deep sigh, Cara sank onto the chaise lounge next to Sienna's and rested her head against its bright-blue cushion. Unwilling and unable to deal with any more problems, she decided to ignore Sienna's down-in-the-mouth demeanor. Her plate was full. She was eaten up with worry over Kai. On top of that, her anger over Simon's betrayal was coupled with an intense craving for his touch. She fought the urge to scream as loud as she could.

"It's so beautiful up here," she said, taking in the view of the rust-red Golden Gate Bridge. It seemed strange to be in one of her favorite cities under these circumstances. Ordinarily, she would have spent some time in Golden Gate Park and had dinner at The Slanted Door in the Embarcadero Ferry Terminal. But that wouldn't be happening this time.

Her thoughts flashed to Simon's roof deck. A pang of disappointment hit her as she thought how unlikely it would be for them to ever enjoy it together.

She rolled her head on the cushion toward Sienna. "By the way, the food's here, and we have more company. Counting Michael, there are twelve hungry men downstairs eating as we speak. We should probably get down there to stake out a meal."

"Forget Michael," she said with a sour pucker of her lips. Then her expression brightened. "More men?"

Cara tsk-tsked. "Come on, Senny. Be nice to Michael. And the other ones are here to work, not flirt—I know that wouldn't normally stop you, but they're absorbed in rescue plans." She couldn't mention the fact that they normally stuck to their own kind, but if Sienna wanted to knock herself out trying—who was she to get in the way. It sure beat watching her niggle at Michael.

"We'll see," she said in a sing-song voice and led the way downstairs.

They descended the stairs into the kitchen. The Guardians sat eating, wedged in around the banquette or on stools at the bar.

Sienna pulled Cara aside and whispered in her ear. "O-M-G! This is like Hottie Heaven."

Carrie smiled and whispered back, "Just remember to behave."

"I'll do my best."

Michael spotted them. "Cara, Sienna—chicken, beef, fish, or vegetarian?"

"Fish," Cara replied and Michael handed her a container.

"Beefcake. Sorry, beef," said Sienna, staring openly at all the men.

Michael rolled his eyes and snorted, shoving a container marked *beef* at her.

Narrowing her eyes at him, Sienna ripped it from his grasp and walked over to the island. She sidled up to Jade and turned on her signature Sienna smile. "Is this seat taken?"

He shook his head and grinned. "Be my guest, Pretty One."

"Let the games begin," Cara said to Michael out of earshot from Sienna.

Michael shot Sienna a malicious look. "She's really a piece of work." His voice betrayed his annoyance. He reached for a container of his own. "I put out some food and water for Chloe. No interest. She's working the room for table food."

"I'm not surprised, the little hussy." Cara smiled, spotting her dog under the table.

"Not any little hussy. Our Sentinel. An official part of the team," he said.

Cara slapped her hand on the counter. "That was a surprise! I nearly fell over when Simon told us. To think, all this time I thought she was just a charming little dog who liked men."

She caught Simon gazing at her from the banquette, and her face tingled. Then she gave Michael a pleading look. "Hey, want to come up and eat in front of the sunset with me?" She couldn't bear being this close to Simon right now.

He gave her a knowing smile. "I can go up for a few minutes, but then I need to get back to meet with Isaac."

Halfway up the stairs she heard Simon's voice from behind. "Cara, take advantage of the jet lag and get a couple hours of sleep, so you're ready when we need you."

When she glanced back at him, his body language gave nothing away. "I will. Thanks. And good luck," she said, feeling grateful. Without them, she wouldn't have any way of rescuing Kai. She was indebted to Simon and his team, regardless of the mix of desire and pain that touched her soul from his presence.

Chapter 47

CARA LOOKED AT HIM pointedly under the deck lights, and blurted, "I think Sienna's attracted to you."

Sitting astride one of the chaise lounges, Michael stopped mid-chew. His mouth went dry, and he had the overwhelming desire to spit his rice back onto the plate. He took a swig of water from the bottle to help him swallow it. "Why would you say that? She's thrown herself at every guy we've met since we picked her up on Saturday morning. Besides, she thinks I'm gay."

He couldn't keep the aggravation from his voice. She rubbed him every which way but right, clawing at the fabric of his control every chance she had. She didn't seem the least bit interested in him. Not to mention, she had an uncanny knack for pressing all his personal hot buttons.

"No, she doesn't." Cara put down her food. "I know her better than I know myself sometimes. For all of her crazy faults, the fact that you're the only one in the room she's not throwing herself at tells me everything I need to know. Listen, I know you're not looking, but the fact that she drives you nuts should be telling you something too."

"Yeah, it's telling me to stay as far away from her as possible," he said in a low growl, digging his heels in.

"Really?" Cara eyes bore into him. "Why did you cook her breakfast after you found out she was having a glycemic attack?"

Her words hit him in the chest, and he looked away. Just because they didn't like each other didn't mean he couldn't feel sorry for her or want to do something nice, did it?

"She may not have said 'thank you,' but I know she appreciated it."

She did thank me, he thought. Maybe not out loud, but in her head she did. He couldn't tell Cara that without revealing he had telepathic abilities beyond the Trinity. Not a topic for discussion or disclosure as far as he was concerned. He was still angry with himself for giving in to his curiosity and dipping into Sienna's mind back in Connecticut, breaking his own rule. He'd only gone in for a millisecond when he'd set down her eggs, expecting something awful. Instead, he'd heard her words of gratitude. He forgave her just a little. Too bad it didn't last long.

Cara reached out and touched his hand. "I know it's none of my business, but I care about both of you, and it kills me to see you at each other's throats."

A strange thrill shot through him, and he narrowed his eyes at Cara. "You really think she's attracted to me under all that venom?"

Cara gave him a crooked smile. "I'd take the odds."

He looked at his dad's watch. "Hey, I need to get back downstairs and see Isaac." He swung his leg over the lounge and moved to get up.

Cara's fingers clutched his forearm. "Michael. Maybe I shouldn't tell you this, but I'm going to put this out there, just between us." She hesitated. "Don't let Sienna's rough exterior fool you. Her childhood wasn't easy, and we both shared severe anxiety attacks in high school. That's why we're such good friends. A lot of what you've seen are her defense mechanisms. She's a good person, I promise."

He swallowed. What Cara said about Sienna's childhood resonated with him. They stood up, ready to go.

Pointing to her container, he asked, "Want me to take that for you?"

She picked it up and handed it to him. Her eyes searched his.

"Thanks, Cara. I appreciate you telling me." He only hoped he remembered what Cara said the next time Sienna pushed his buttons.

He went downstairs and headed to the kitchen to drop off the containers. Low-pitched banter filled the living room where the Guardians had all reconvened. He caught Chamuel's eye.

"*Roof deck is clear when you're ready,*" he said telepathically.

Chamuel nodded from across the room.

Michael walked into the kitchen past Sienna, who sat moping at the island, mindlessly poking at her food with her fork. His back to her, he smirked. She'd obviously struck out with Jade.

"Why so glum?" he asked, making an attempt at polite and casual conversation as he took care of his dinner garbage. While he was at it, he grabbed the couple of empty food containers off the counter and put them into a black garbage bag.

"Do you find me pretty?" she asked him.

Michael froze, caught off guard. He tempered his snark. "You sure you want my opinion? Last I heard, you thought I didn't play for the home team."

"I'm unattractive and useless to you, aren't I?" True concern echoed in her voice.

Unable to veil his sarcasm, he said, "Yeah, right—you're a hag. *You can't be serious.*" Pretty wasn't her problem, bitchy was. He turned to face her.

Her shoulders collapsed around her and fat tears spilled down from her eyes into the uneaten food. She dipped her head, using her long, jet-black hair to hide her face.

Did I make her cry? Guilt and panic washed over Michael followed by a stab of empathy. He had to fix this. Since the black day he hid in the woods and had to cry alone when he was eight years old, tears cut him in an inexplicable way, kick-starting his instincts to soothe them away in others. It didn't matter that he'd just spent the most uncomfortable few days of his adult life because of her or that an hour ago they would've gladly thrown sharp objects at one another. Cara's words surfaced, and the only thing that registered in his brain was that Sienna needed him—now. And he wouldn't let her cry because of him.

Michael swallowed hard and dropped the bag. In three steps he stood on the other side of the bar next to Sienna. Before he could stop himself, he pulled her from the barstool and draped his arm protectively over her slumped shoulder. His eyes darted around, looking for someplace private. Spotting a door behind the living room, he led her into what turned out to be a small recording studio. He closed them inside.

For the first time, Michael actually wondered who owned the house. He hadn't thought much about the guitar in the dining room, but seeing the studio and the line of platinum CDs hanging on the wall, he concluded that the owner was in the music industry.

Her sobs grew louder as he led her toward the couch and sat down next to her. He held her while she cried. Her vulnerability touched him deeply and unexpectedly. When her tears slowed, he tipped her chin up so that he could see her face.

"Shh . . . Why would you say something like that?" he asked gently. "I've never said you're unattractive or useless, have I?"

She averted her eyes and dabbed at them with the napkin she'd been clutching from dinner. "You must think it, though," she said, sniffling.

He brushed a piece of her silken jet-black hair behind her ear. "I don't. You're a beautiful woman with a sharp mind. That can't be it. Why are you really crying? It can't be because of what I said to you in the kitchen. What's the matter?" He wanted—no, he *needed*—to know what made her feel bad enough to cry. Granted, she'd been a total pain in the ass, but something about seeing her this way caused a shift inside him; it sneaked past his defenses and resounded with the broken pieces of himself he kept securely hidden.

She wrung the napkin in her hands. "I feel so lost and useless. There's nothing I can do to help Cara, unlike you. I'm usually the one who takes care of her. Now, I'm just a burden." She looked up at him. Spiky wet eyelashes surrounded her sky-blue eyes. "Michael, I'm sorry for the way I've treated you. Cara's right, you're a good person. It's me that's horrible."

Her apology touched him, and a pang of regret echoed inside his chest. Maybe he wasn't the only one who needed to take charge. He pulled her closer and tucked her head against his shoulder, pressing his face into her silky black hair and inhaling a hint of jasmine. "It's okay. You're helping Cara by just being with her. You're her best friend, and she loves you."

As he held Sienna, he realized with a pulse of exhilaration how good her petite frame felt in his arms; it awakened something primal and raw within him. He took special care in holding her, almost afraid she might break. She'd driven him crazy these last few days, but maybe Cara was right and he'd misjudged Sienna. He hadn't exaggerated when he said she was beautiful and smart. If he'd been completely open with her, he would've added sexy. Here like this, there wasn't a man in his right mind who wouldn't fall all over her.

His arms still around her, he leaned back and looked into her downturned eyes. "You better now?"

She nodded, her hair billowing down around her face with the movement.

Tilting her chin up again, Michael's eyes drifted to Sienna's rosy lips, only inches from his. Without thinking twice, he leaned in and kissed her. At first, his lips melted softly onto hers, and then, overtaken by an uncontrollable passion that had been building since they'd met, he increased the pressure and his tongue parted her lips, hungrily deepening the kiss. Desire flared inside him like a flash fire, coursing through his veins with white-hot heat.

"Michael . . . " She moaned, responding eagerly without hesitation. She curled her hand around his neck and drew him closer. Her kiss became more demanding as her free hand traveled down the hollow of his spine, turning his body to tinder under her touch.

Powerless to stop, he met her head-on. His fingers ran through the length of her silky hair before he gathered her tightly into his chest, his groin reacting with a hard, throbbing excitement. If this didn't stop, they'd both be naked on the floor in less than a minute.

The mere thought triggered his internal alarms, ripping him from the moment. He couldn't lose control like this. His stomach flooded with adrenaline and filled him with the sudden urge to flee. On reflex, he jerked back from Sienna and clutched her shoulders, pushing her away to create distance between them.

His gaze glued to hers, he thought as fast as he could for a graceful exit. "I'm sorry. I shouldn't have taken advantage of you like that."

Sienna stared at him with a look of confusion, her eyes not fully dry and her lips pleasantly swollen from their kiss. "What do you mean?"

"I don't want you to think that I'd take advantage of you when you're vulnerable," he said.

"I don't think that," she said in a small voice, shaking her head.

"We should go."

"Okay." Sadness returned to her voice, stabbing him in the heart.

His hands still on her shoulders, he kept his eyes locked on hers. "Don't misunderstand me. I wanted to kiss you, but I need to get back outside." As he said the words, the truth rocked him. He *did* want to kiss her; the problem was he wanted to kiss her until he was buried so deep inside her he couldn't remember his own name. And that wasn't something he could ever allow to happen.

"We'll talk later," he said, the lie tasting bitter on his tongue. Quickly, he led her by the hand up to Cara, leaving them together upstairs.

His encounter with Sienna rattled his self-control and awakened feelings underneath his polished exterior that terrified him. His hands shook so badly, he reached for the railing on the stairs on his way down.

Coward, he chided himself. *She'd never want you anyway if she knew . . . No one would.*

He stopped on the stairs and squeezed his eyes shut, trying to suppress the last thirty minutes—wishing he could erase the memory entirely. The fact that she sidestepped his defenses, even for a few minutes, unnerved him more than he wanted to admit. Sienna would never be a good candidate for his "friends with benefits" approach to dating. Instinctively, he knew she'd want more than he could give. No. The truth was she deserved more than he could give.

"Michael, are you all right?" Michael's eyes snapped open when he received the telepathic message. Chamuel stood at the bottom of the stairs, wearing a look of concern.

He swallowed and nodded, not trusting his voice even to return a silent reply.

Chamuel motioned him down. "Come join us in the command center before I leave with the next patrol."

Chapter 48

San Francisco. Safe House. Sunday, March 30, 8:40 p.m. PDT

CONCERN SPARKED in Chamuel the moment he saw Michael standing with his eyes closed, seemingly frozen in the middle of the staircase. Earlier, he'd witnessed the exchange between Michael and Sienna in the kitchen, watching as Michael led Sienna through the living room into the recording studio.

Had his own emotions not been shredding his insides all day, Chamuel might not have noticed the look of pain on Michael's face. He suspected it had something to do with Sienna, which baffled him considering their apparent dislike for each other . . . or maybe not anymore.

Michael met him at the bottom of the stairs. "I'm fine," he said, his voice barely a whisper. Chamuel noticed the mild tremor in Michael's hands.

He swept a hand over his face and then encircled Michael's upper arm with his fingers. *"Come with me."*

"I said I'm fine," Michael gritted, twisting his arm away.

Chamuel threw his palms up and stepped away.

Michael clutched his head with his hands. "I'm sorry. I . . . Let's go to the kitchen."

Chamuel followed Michael into the kitchen. The black garbage bag still lay crumpled on the floor where Michael had dropped it earlier.

Planting his hands on his hips, Chamuel shook his head. "Listen. You don't have to talk. But I need to know that I can depend on you. Our Trinity has taken some blows today, pretty much all of them my fault. Regardless, I can't jeopardize our safety and the safety of the teams if we can't pull our shit together."

Michael cross his arms and looked away. "I'll be fine, really. I didn't mean to snap at you," he said in a weary voice.

"No problem," Chamuel replied and turned to leave.

"Do you love her?" Michael asked silently from behind him.

Chamuel stopped and spun on his heel to face Michael; his blue eyes blazed and his jaw was taut. *"Yes."* Then Chamuel turned and strode out of the kitchen. "Meet us in the living room," he said aloud.

He reached the sofa, huffing with frustration. Isaac looked up.

"You okay?" he asked, cocking a blond eyebrow.

Chamuel paced, taking deep breaths. "Yeah. Fine."

"Cham—"

He held up his hand. "Don't, okay. Just don't."

Isaac fixed him with a hard stare. "Trade places with me. I'll take the next patrol with Zeke." Chamuel and Zeke had drawn the short straw, having to split three vectors between the two of them due to the odd number of Guardians.

A low growl rose from Chamuel's throat in response. He didn't need Isaac to coddle him.

"Yo. You ready?" Zeke entered the living room, and Chamuel unintentionally rounded on him.

Zeke took a giant step back. "Whoa, Cham. Take it easy, man. What's going on?"

Chamuel blew out a breath. He wanted so desperately to punch someone. Michael's question blew the lid off the calm he'd been fighting to keep since Cara's explosion outside the plane. He should probably be more worried about himself than anyone else. He'd get people killed if he didn't pull his own shit together.

"It's my fault," Michael said, joining them at the command post and giving Chamuel an out. *"I got this one,"* he added silently. Chamuel was grateful for the diversionary tactic.

Isaac gave them an ice-cold frown and drummed his fingers on the table next to the computer. "If you gentlemen are done sparring, I'd like to give you both your vector coordinates." Chamuel and Zeke reached into their pockets and handed over their cell phones.

Heavy boots sounded in the upstairs hallway right before Jade, Gabriel, and Raphael appeared at the top of the stairs. They were dressed in tight black jeans and fitted black T-shirts made for flying.

"Anything?" Isaac yelled up.

"No, mon," responded Jade with a shake of his head as he reached the bottom of the stairs; his long ponytail made of black braids swished from side to side with the gesture. "Just some random dark activity north of here by Napa, but it's not what we're looking for."

Raphael wiped a hand down his face and collapsed down onto the sofa. "Nothing notable between here and the Nevada border." He looked past

Chamuel's legs. "Hey, Gabe, grab me a bottle of water out of the fridge while you're over there."

"Bring enough for everyone." Isaac yelled over.

Gabriel grunted. "Guys, I only have two hands."

"Stop cryin' like a big baby," Jade said with a good-natured chuckle and headed toward the kitchen to help.

"Watch it, Jade." The rust-haired Guardian slammed the refrigerator door. "Or I'll clip your wings while you sleep."

"Tsk-tsk. What's the matter with you tonight? You have another midair collision with a turkey vulture?" Jade grabbed half the bottles out of Gabe's hands and headed back to the living room.

Jade handed Chamuel a bottle, and he gulped it down. It was just enough to hydrate him but not enough to make him need to piss mid-flight.

Isaac cleared his throat. "Michael, after Cham and Zeke return, I'll need you to take over for me at the command center while I fly with Raphael's guys." Then he eyed Raphael. "Your team's back on at midnight, so go get some rest. Hopefully, we don't need to do more than two 'rinse and repeat' cycles per team."

Chamuel tried to shake off his nasty mood. "Zeke, let's go."

"Ready when you are, Boss" he replied with a cocky grin.

"Give me my vectors, *I*," Chamuel said to Isaac.

Isaac returned the phone into Chamuel's outstretched hand. "Keep the blue blob within the purple lines and you're good to go."

Chamuel took a quick look at his flight plan and shoved the phone back into his pocket. He and Zeke took the stairs two at a time.

"Can I watch you guys take off?" Michael asked.

Chamuel stopped and shrugged. "Be my guest."

They passed Cara's room on the way to the roof stairs. Zeke burst out through the door onto the deck. Chamuel halted outside the door and turned back to Michael. He couldn't help it; he had to ask, hoping to conceal his desperation.

"How's she doing, Michael?"

Michael stared deep into Chamuel's eyes before reaching out to squeeze his forearm, and in a sympathetic voice said, *"About the same as you, my friend. Fly safe. I'll make sure she's prepared for later."*

A lump formed in his throat and he nodded before he joined Zeke at the far edge of the deck.

"I'll go first," said Zeke. "See you back here in an hour." Given the narrowness of the deck and their wingspan, taking off one at a time was easier.

Simon stepped back as Zeke's wings slipped out through the hidden slits in his shirt and unfurled with a muted *whoosh*, filling the space between them. The white, downy brilliance was only slightly less blinding in the dark than in broad daylight. Appearing soft and silky, Nephilim wings are actually made up of thousands of feathers of differing sizes, loft, and textures layered on top of a powerful bone-and-membrane understructure. Some feathers were as soft as silk, others as sharp as knives.

Zeke's plumage arched high above him as he poised for flight. He gave one good shake before his huge body crouched and he leapt into the air, vanishing before Chamuel's eyes as he cloaked.

Pushing thoughts of Cara from his mind, Chamuel followed suit, heading south with the intent of finding their Trinity's Center Stone as fast as possible.

Chapter 49

San Francisco. Safe House. Monday, March 31, 2:10 a.m. PDT

CARA LAY IN BED wide-awake, thinking about Simon as Sienna slept soundly next to her. As angry as Cara was, maybe Sienna was right, maybe she needed to hear Simon out. Not that she expected him to have an acceptable answer. Thinking back to all the time they'd spent together, she never detecting him lying to her about anything. Quite the opposite. There had been nothing but truth in his words. Then again, lying by omission wasn't something her training covered.

Her anger flared again when she realized he had to have known that . . .

What was he thinking?

Thanks to him, not more than two weeks into her training and she'd already broken the sacred rule: love not your Guardian.

Yet . . . she couldn't ignore the electricity that passed between them, setting her heart in motion and putting her back into an impossible situation.

Carefully peeling back the covers, she snuck out of bed. Closing the door softly behind her, she padded her way down to the cavernous, open living room.

She recognized Isaac's blond brush cut camped out on one of the modern sofas, manning the Guardian command post by hovering over a computer on the coffee table. He looked up as she entered the room.

"Is Simon back from his patrol yet?" she asked.

His ice-blue eyes drilled into her, displeasure written all over his face. "He just went downstairs for a shower and some sleep."

She bristled. She was in no mood for anyone else's judgment. In her book, she was the injured party here.

"Thanks," she mumbled and turned toward the staircase. This probably wasn't the best time for a discussion, but it definitely wasn't the worst, and it might possibly be the only time they'd have before the rescue.

"I wouldn't do that if I were you," Isaac said.

Cara's shoulders tensed. "Lucky for you, you aren't me," she snapped and continued down to Simon's room.

She let Simon's energy guide her to the right door. Her hand hesitated for a split second before she knocked softly. A familiar, deep male voice spoke from inside.

"Come in."

She doubted he was expecting her, but shame on him if he hadn't detected her coming. Taking a deep breath, she twisted the knob and walked in.

He stood frozen like a deer caught in headlights, holding his shirt but still clothed from the waist down. His face shed the impassible mask he'd worn since she'd confronted him at the airport. Emotions flooded his features, transforming him back into the man she recognized . . . the man she loved.

"Cara . . . " he said breathily.

As much as she hated to admit it, one look at him stole the air from her lungs. His hair lay in loose waves around his shoulders, framing his handsome face. But her eyes were drawn immediately to the hard muscles of his chest . . . and to the red tattoo on his pectoral with the Guardianship crest and his sigil.

Words wouldn't come as she battled down a scream of frustration. Had she so much as glimpsed the tattoo the night she'd had dinner at his apartment, he would've had a lot of explaining to do.

But still she had trouble looking away. His skin looked as smooth and silky as it had felt under her fingertips, every muscle clearly defined down to the six-pack abs and the ridges of his hips that disappeared into the top of his black pants. He was more beautiful half-naked than he was fully clothed, making her even angrier.

She wanted him, and she couldn't have him. The injustice of it infuriated her, and it was all his fault. Balling her fists at her sides, she paced like a caged tiger.

Simon swallowed and tried again. "Cara, you shouldn't be here," he said softly.

She'd been prepared to hear him out, but her anger consumed her, paving the way for her feelings of heartbreak and loss. *"Shouldn't be here?"* she said sarcastically, her eyes boring into him. "You're damn straight *I shouldn't be here.*"

He cringed like he'd been struck.

"You know what I'm the most angry about?" she asked, shaking her clenched fist. "The fact that I've spent the last nine years of my life in love with a man I could never have. You were the first person who made me forget . . . who gave me hope. You let me fall in love with you." Her face reddened, and she pointed her finger at him. "You . . . the only person on this damn *planet* who I'm forbidden to have! Why would you do that?" Her voice escalated until tears of frustration betrayed her, spilling over and streaming down her face.

She hadn't meant to cry, but was helpless to stop herself once the words were said and she realized the root of her anger. It wasn't so much that he'd concealed his identity from her, which was bad enough, but rather he'd stolen her chance for happiness. She couldn't live through another Kai situation. She deserved a man of her own to love who wasn't forbidden to her.

He stepped toward her, and she abruptly stepped back. "Stay away from me."

Simon wore a mask of pain, his eyes beseeching her to listen. "Cara, I wanted to tell you. I planned on telling you Friday night before Constantina called. This lie has been eating me up from the inside since we met." He drew in a breath, and his gaze grew brighter. "I fell in love with you the moment I caught you in my arms, and I've been agonizing about what to do ever since."

Cara's heart lurched at his admission. Then, with crystalline clarity, something hit her. *He. Would. Never. Age.* Sniffling, she asked, "When did Calliope die?"

He looked confused. "Why does that matter?"

"Tell me!"

His eyes dimmed, and he replied quietly, "December, 1889."

Her anger reared back and struck a second time. He'd given her no options in this relationship. He'd denied her free will and stolen her happiness.

Her hands clasped her head as she stalked back and forth on the carpet. "How could this relationship have ever worked? When I'm ninety years old, you'll be a young two-hundred-something and look like a fresh thirty-two! People will think I'm your great-grandmother. It's impossible, it's all impossible."

Stopping mid-pace, she looked at him. "Is it Simon? Or should I be calling you Chamuel? Is Simon even your name? I feel so manipulated!"

Cara watched the hurt register on Simon's face before he spoke in a low voice. "Everything I've told you, everything I feel for you, is real and true. My warrior name is Chamuel, but my name is Simon. I'm a man as much as I'm Nephilim. I'm the man who gave you his love. I *am* Simon. For you, I'll always *be* Simon."

When he looked at her, she could see the unshed tears threatening to overflow from his eyes. "I would've given everything I had to be with you, and that's a lot for a Nephil and a Guardian in my position."

Squeezing the shirt in his hand, he shook it at her as a tear broke free and rolled down his cheek. "Do you even know what that means? I am facing one hundred years in prison for just kissing you. I'm sorry if that sacrifice wasn't worthy enough of your love. And maybe you're right. Maybe this should've never happened."

She stood, shocked and immobile, her tears now frozen in her eyes.

Prison for one hundred years? She hadn't known that was the punishment. Her heart nearly cracked in half.

"You need to leave now, Cara," he said and turned, walking into the bathroom and closing the door behind him. When she heard the water turn on in the shower, she left. Shame over her selfishness engulfed her. Blinded by tears, she ran.

Chamuel locked the bathroom door behind him and turned on the water, refusing to let her rip away another shred of his dignity. He leaned against the bathroom wall, his legs no longer able to support his weight. Sliding down into a sitting position on the floor, he rested his head in his hands. He knew Cara was angry, but he'd held out hope that maybe they could forget their problems after they rescued Kai and had some time to breathe.

Unable to hold back any longer, his body was wracked with uncontrollable sobs as he hugged his knees to his chest. Hot tears splashed down onto his arms. He'd cried only twice since Calliope's death, both times since he'd met Cara.

She didn't just reject him because he'd hidden his identity. Worse, she'd rejected him as a man because of his Nephilim blood. That was something he'd never expected. Didn't she understand the punishment he'd have to endure for violating the law? He'd have to relinquish his wings *after* he spent one hundred years in prison. Her human life would have long since ended while he would continue to live in shame for centuries.

How could I have been so stupid?

Her words shattered his hopes. The pain was unbearable, as if his heart had been ripped from his chest. He couldn't believe how much she'd hurt him. His stomach clenched violently. Lunging forward, he made it to the toilet just in time to throw up his last meal.

Collapsing back into a seated position, he wiped his mouth with the back of his hand. With a deep breath, he hoisted himself up and shed the rest of his clothes. His body and soul naked, he walked into the hot shower, wishing he could wash away the pain inside him as easily as he could wash himself clean on the outside.

Maybe it's for the best, he thought, trying to take comfort from the warm water cascading over his body. But he didn't really believe it. What he believed was that he'd screwed up royally on too many levels to count.

Chapter 50

CARA THREW OPEN the door of the roof deck and ran outside, her sobs echoing in the dark. Not wanting to wake Sienna from her Xanax-induced sleep, she'd bypassed her room and come straight upstairs.

Fog slowly rolled in, muting the twinkling lights on the Golden Gate Bridge in front of her already tear-blurred vision. She leaned against the glass railing, wishing she'd never gone to Simon's room, wishing she'd never gotten a taste of a love she thought she could have.

She shivered in the chilly night air. The temperature had dropped sharply from earlier.

"Need a shoulder to cry on?"

Cara froze. Her head jerked around to pinpoint the voice in the darkness.

The orange end of a cigarette glowed at the far end of the deck, punching a hole in the night, shimmering and crackling as the smoker inhaled.

"Who's there?"

"Why don't you come on over and find out," he teased. "I promise I don't bite... hard, anyway." He chuckled at his own joke. When she hesitated, he added warmly, "Just kidding. Come over and keep me company. I'm just relaxing over a beer and a smoke after my patrol with Chamuel."

She hugged herself tightly, sorry she hadn't grabbed a sweater in her haste, and wandered over toward the glow of the cigarette. As she drew closer, the angle of the light inside the deck's bathroom window illuminated the man sitting astride one of the chaise lounges, his legs spread wide and his boots touching the deck.

Zeke patted the lounge next to him. "Have a seat."

She sat, pulling her legs up underneath her.

He rested his elbows on his knees as he smoked. He was shirtless like Simon

272

had been earlier, and his dark hair wafted in the light breeze, hanging loosely around his tattooed shoulders. He had a red tattoo similar to Simon's on his rippled chest among all the other ink on his arms and torso.

"Aren't you cold?" she asked, squeezing her gooseflesh-covered arms tighter.

He glanced at her with a rakish smile. "Nope. I don't feel heat or cold like you do. I'd give you my shirt, but it's covered in bug splatter." He winked and his smile grew wider. "If you weren't Cham's girlfriend, I'd offer to warm you up."

Her cheeks flushed. "I'm not his girlfriend," she said, adding in her head, *anymore.*

"Semantics," he said with a smirk. "Either way, if I lay so much as a finger on you, Cham will hack it off and feed it to me."

He pulled the towel from behind his back that Sienna had left there and handed it to her. "Here, wrap this around you. It should help."

Cara nestled inside the towel. It was warm to the touch and did the trick in chasing away the cold.

Picking up a bottle of beer from the other side of the lounge chair, he tipped it at her. "Want one? They're in the fridge under the bar next me."

She rubbed her eyes with the back of her hand, ridding her cheeks of any residual dampness. "Tempting, but no, thanks."

He took a long slug from the bottle. "You don't know what you're missing."

Eyeing his cigarette, she said, "I'm surprised you smoke."

He held out the cigarette in front of him and contemplated it. "I know. Bad habit. I blame it on one of my old girlfriends. She turned me on to it after sex. At least I don't have to worry about getting cancer."

Cara couldn't contain her surprise. She'd just made a sweeping assumption that Nephilim were somehow above human vices.

"A Nephil girlfriend?"

His face scrunched, and he looked at her like she had two heads. "What? Are you, kidding? In suburban Connecticut? There are only, like, fifty Nephil females in my entire class, and most of them live somewhere in Europe, Asia, or South America. Not to mention, they were snapped up long ago as mates by the older guys. No, to answer your question. A human girlfriend."

He threw his butt on the deck and ground it out under the heel of his boot.

Taken aback, Cara said, "I thought the Nephilim stuck to their own kind."

He scoffed. "Yeah, if they want to stay celibate. Speaking of . . . The sun and the moon must rise and set on you for Cham to have broken his celibacy and violate the only sacred law we have."

Cara flushed with the mention of Simon's name. "He's celibate?"

With a sideways smile and a raised eyebrow, he said, "Don't know. You tell me."

Her face grew even hotter, and she shrunk inside the towel.

"Um . . . Based on your reaction, I guess he still is. Let's just put it this way: he hasn't laid a lip on anyone in longer than I've been alive. As far as I know, he's been celibate as far back as the flipping Victorian era. Lots of pent-up demand there." He chuckled.

Cara wasn't sure if she should be offended by his comments or not. He sure was irreverent. If anything, she found it refreshing. Plus, she started to understand just how much more Simon had at stake than she did and how much more he'd risked. Her anger started to melt away and she realized how self-centered she'd been. True, he'd lied to her, but more and more she started to believe it was because he wanted to be with her and not that he intentionally set out to hurt her.

"Tell me about. . . " His Guardian name stuck in her throat. ". . . Chamuel."

Zeke lit another cigarette and took a long drag. "He's good people, Cham. I've known him my whole life. I'd say he's like a brother, but he's more like a father. Both he and Isaac." He sat up and leaned forward. "Can I just ask a question here?"

"Sure."

"Why the heck would you pick a Nephil, older than dust, when you could have one in his sexual prime, like me?" he asked, sweeping his hands down his sides.

She laughed at his mock earnestness. "I can't believe you just asked me that."

He chuckled warmly and relaxed, leaning back, stretching his legs out on the chaise, and crossing his boots at the ankles. "Made you laugh, though," he said with a sweet smile and took another drag.

"Just be careful not to offer yourself like that in front of my friend Sienna," Cara warned. "She might take you up on it."

He released a loud snort. "I doubt it. She's got her sights set on your Messenger."

Cara sighed. "I wouldn't hold my breath. I've given up. They nearly shed each other's blood a dozen times over the last three days. I'm getting tired of body-blocking for them."

"Don't be so sure. Twenty minutes in a dark closet would be life altering for those two if they'd just get out of their own way." Zeke took a last drag and tossed the butt over the side of the deck.

The thought of Michael and Sienna in a closet brought a wide smile to her face. She had to admit talking to Zeke helped, even if she felt like she was hanging out with someone's hot younger brother.

"Don't take this the wrong way, but you look about seventeen. I'm having trouble thinking of you as more than jailbait."

His eyes flashed. "Hey, I'll have you know that I shaved forty years off my driver's license to match my perceived age."

She smirked. "So, do tell. How old are you?"

He turned his head on the cushion and suppressed a grin. "Don't you know it's impolite to ask a guy's age?"

"Yeah, right. That's my line."

"Sixty-three, if you really want to know."

He looked great, although young, for his age. She'd give him that.

"You were telling me about Chamuel . . . "

He held up his beer. "You sure you don't want one?"

She shook her head.

"Listen, Cara. I might be a smartass and act like an immature idiot, but I'm not stupid. He loves you, and Isaac almost kicked his ass on the plane because of it. Believe him, Cara. And please don't hurt him. He deserves better than he's allowed himself. He's never stepped over the line for anything or anyone before. Give him a chance."

Cara swallowed and bit her lip to keep from crying. She let out a nervous laugh, and brushed her finger under her eye to trap an escaped tear. "I don't know how to get past this, Zeke. We exchanged words before I came up here. He probably hates me now."

"Apologize and *make* it work." Zeke sat up and swung his legs over the lounge to face her. "I'll admit, you screwed the pooch when you outted him like that at the airport. Isaac will have to report him, but I won't. As far as anyone knows, I saw nothing and I know nothing. The law is stupid. If you love each other, you should be together."

She hugged the towel more tightly around her. She had to make this right. But when? How?

"I think Isaac hates me too."

"Nah. His bark is worse than his bite. Don't let his frosty exterior fool you. He inherited it from his mother. She's the angel of snow storms. That said, he's Cham's best friend and super protective of him. They've been tight since Calliope and Mina died."

Cara's head popped up. "Mina? Who's Mina?"

Zeke cringed and lifted his beer. "One bottle and I'm spilling everyone's secrets . . . "

"Who's Mina?" she asked again, her heart suddenly pounding in anticipation.

He swore under his breath and took a deep breath followed by a long slog of beer. "Mina was the Soul Seeker in his last Trinity. She was killed the night Calliope died. The Dark Ones used Calliope to divert Cham's attention away from Mina and they killed her. He never forgave himself for their deaths. It's the reason he took a voluntary vow of celibacy."

Cara's heart dropped, and she covered her mouth with her hand to catch her gasp. She squeezed her eyes shut, shoving down the bile rising in her throat.

Zeke cleared his throat. "While I'm airing everyone's dirty laundry, if you haven't figured it out yet, Calliope was Isaac's sister."

His words slapped her in the face. What an idiot she'd been. What a selfish, stupid idiot. Simon—Chamuel—took a chance on her and she'd failed him—badly and inexcusably.

THUD!

Cara flinched at the noise.

Sun stumbled and collapsed in a heap on the other side of the deck.

"Sun!" Zeke moved in a blur across the deck and lifted the Guardian to his feet. Cara popped up and stumbled on one of the chairs before she found her footing and made her way over.

Sun's chest heaved, sucking in breath as he draped his arm around Zeke to stand. He tried to speak, his lips forming shapes but no sound came out.

"Calm down. It's okay," Zeke said evenly.

"F–found . . . in . . . warehouse," Sun sputtered through gasps. "Found . . . Dr. Solomon."

Excitement ripped through Cara. He'd found Kai!

"Cara," Zeke said sharply, straining under Sun's dead weight. "Go down and tell the others and have someone bring up food and water. I'll wait up here."

Cara nodded, dropping the towel as she ran for the door. She screamed over her telepathic link. *"Simon! Michael! Sun found Kai!"*

Chapter 51

Menlo Park. Monday, March 31, 3:30 a.m. PDT

CARA CLUTCHED HER ARMS tightly and stared at the back of Michael's head from the backseat of the Escalade as Simon drove, breaking land speed records. Zeke sat next to her with his eyes closed and his arms folded across his chest, pretending to sleep.

"Meet us at the closest rendezvous point . . . " Simon said into the Bluetooth headset.

Two rendezvous points had been set up, one for the three Guardian warrior teams and a closer location for the Guardian rescue teams who would need to carry non-Nephilim charges in or out. The Guardian warrior teams would fly the distance to the closer rendezvous point where Simon was currently headed.

Cara looked down at her black uniform, which Raphael had given her. She hadn't questioned how they'd found one small enough. He'd also offered her a small blessed dagger, like the one Michael had used to train her, but she'd refused it. She might have rethought her decision if she'd known it might have come in handy to cut the tension in the car.

Other than the rigidity in Simon's shoulders, there wasn't any evidence of their earlier encounter. His energy had disappeared completely, like he'd dropped an iron shield around himself to keep her out. Not that she blamed him.

She could barely look at him after what she'd said—and after her discussion with Zeke. Her emotions tore at her, now knowing how much she'd hurt Simon and how much he'd risked to be with her. Still, she couldn't fully deny her anger. She couldn't deny her love either, but that would have to wait until after they rescued Kai. For tonight, their safety was tied to the strength of their Trinity, and they couldn't afford any weak links—his or hers.

When they arrived, Simon pulled the SUV into the shadows.

He stared straight ahead at the windshield. "Zeke, Michael, can you step outside for a minute?"

Zeke glanced at her in the dark, and lightly poked her leg before he got out of the backseat.

Her anxiety flared. Being alone with Simon wasn't high on her list of things to do right now. She'd successfully managed to avoid doing just that from the time she'd made her announcement about Sun's discovery. She couldn't handle any more confrontation, not when they were so close to rescuing Kai. Part of her wanted to spill her guts and just tell him she loved him to disarm him, but another said he deserved a more thought-out apology and declaration of her feelings.

He turned off the ignition, and the dim overhead light went on.

One blue eye caught her gaze in the rearview mirror, and he cleared his throat. Apparently, she wasn't the only one doing the avoiding . . .

"Can I count on you tonight?" he asked evenly.

His question unnerved her. Any thoughts of a quick apology disappeared. "Yes. Can I count on you? I can't even feel your energy right now."

"This isn't just about us, Cara," he snapped, slamming his hand down on the steering wheel. "The life of every person going in there tonight is on me." Both eyes now visible in the rearview mirror, flashing an angry blue. "I've made enough mistakes for one week, and I can't afford to make any more."

Tears welled, blurring her vision. Before she could stop herself, she asked, "So, I'm a mistake now?"

His shoulders slumped, and he turned in the seat to look at her. His face crumpled, losing some of its anger. He shook his head. "Don't put words into my mouth. I just need to know I can rely on our Trinity . . . that I can rely on you."

"So I don't end up like Mina?" she whispered, her lip quivering.

A look of shock and pain washed over his face, and his eyes shone like she'd never seen before. "Who told you about Mina?" he asked softly.

Suddenly, it struck her with the force of a high-speed train. She could die tonight like Mina. He could die tonight trying to protect her. Kai could die tonight if she failed.

Out of nowhere, her lungs heaved and the SUV caved in around her.

No air. I'm not getting any air. Her eyesight closed to pinpricks, and she clawed at the door handle. She rolled out of the SUV. Landing on her feet, she sucked in the cool night air, trying to mine it for oxygen. And then, her legs took off, and she ran blindly away into the darkness.

"*Cara!*" Michael screamed silently.

"*I've got it,*" Simon growled in her head.

Whoosh! Two massive arms hooked under her armpits and lifted her straight up into the air. Wind whipped through her hair before her body was pressed up and sheltered by a warm, muscular chest. Air rushed under her, reminding her of an amusement park ride gone off the rails.

"*What the hell was that about?*" Simon asked, positioning her crossways underneath his body. His wings flapped above them.

THUNK! His feet hit the flat asphalt roof of one of the low warehouses further away in the complex, and he set her down. Leaning over her, he rested his hands on his knees and breathed heavily, his brilliant white wings aloft behind him.

Cara's eyes popped wide. His wingspan had to be at least eighteen feet. Even in the dark, it was dazzling. Then he straightened up, and in a blink of an eye, his wings furled and disappeared behind him.

The adrenaline rush hit her immediately, freeing up her breathing, her oxygen no longer held hostage by her panic. She could barely speak from a combination of her acute ordeal and the shock and awe of flying in his arms.

"I . . . couldn't breathe . . . panic attack . . . like the day in the subway when I first saw you . . . Have to get my mind off of it."

Simon's brow softened and he lunged over, taking her into his arms. His lips crushed down on top of hers, exploring and tasting her until the anxiety drained from her body. Her body reacted instantly, circling his lean waist with her arms and pulling his pelvis tightly against her belly. A shock of heat filled and tightened her core. She hadn't realized how much she'd wanted to touch him until she cried out in relief.

His fingers cupped the sides of her head, holding her in place against his lips. She broke the kiss, breathless. "They can't see us, can they?"

His eyes blazed with blue fire, and his voice was husky. "Cloaked." He covered her lips again with his, and deepened the kiss until her lungs screamed for air in a good way.

Slowly, he pulled away. "Why didn't you tell me?" he whispered, holding her against the hard curves of his pectorals.

She laid her ear against his beating heart and inhaled his musky scent mixed with citrus. "I've had the attacks under control for years until that day in the subway. This is the first one since then." She brought her hand up to caress his cheek. "I'm sorry for what I said before. I truly didn't mean to hurt you. Know that I'll protect you with my life in there."

"I would expect no less." He tucked her head under his chin and kissed her hair. "I won't let you end up like Mina. I promise it on *my* life," he said with a faint hint of his accent.

Before she could utter the words stuck to the tip of her tongue, he stepped away.

"We need to go, Cara. We'll talk about everything later when it's more appropriate." He looked over the edge of the building and beckoned her with his hand.

Fear tore down her spine. "We're not jumping are we?"

A wicked grin touched his lips. "Payback's a bitch." He snatched her into his arms and leapt off the roof. She screamed the entire five seconds it took to hit the ground softly.

She punched him the arm when they landed, her face beet red. "Don't ever do that again!"

He eyed her warily. "Then don't run off like a scared rabbit. Time's a wastin'."

They walked the five minutes back to join the others, Cara's lips still plump from their kiss. Simon instantly engrossed himself in finalizing last-minute tactical details with Isaac and Raphael, who had arrived while they were gone.

Cara went to join Zeke and Michael by the SUV.

"Are you okay?" Michael asked with concern in his eyes.

She gave him a sheepish look and nodded.

Zeke smirked at her, giving her a knowing look when Michael's back was turned.

Within a couple of minutes, the soft landings of the remaining Guardians could be heard just outside their line of sight. Men walked into view, wings retracted and ready for battle. When they'd all arrived, Simon called her over with Michael and Zeke.

"Cara, we need you to help us find Kai within Achanelech's lair in order to finalize our logistics," said Simon.

"I'm ready. What would you like me to do?" That would be the easy part. She'd been attuned to Kai's energy ever since she'd accepted her Calling.

"Focus on the warehouse and give us a quick energy read, specifically reaching out for Kai," he said.

Cara thought for a moment on the best approach and settled on a technique Constantina had suggested which would strengthen her abilities.

"Simon, Michael, join hands with me. I want to leverage the full energy of our Trinity," she said, extending her hands toward both men.

Resting her hands inside theirs, they daisy-chained together allowing Cara to use them as conduits. Reaching out slowly, she pulled energy down through all of them. The effect was both immediate and jolting as the Flow filled her and fully opened her third eye.

Eyes closed, she pushed outward with her mind. "Based on the black energy, I'm counting well over a hundred soulless entities on the main level. They seem to be gathered on the north side of building, probably in a big room. Kai's not on that level."

Cara followed her third eye deeper into the building until she honed in on him. Excitement shot through her. "I feel him. He's in the center of the building, one floor below. He's alone."

She dove deeper into the subterranean structure. "Underneath, another level down, I feel energy similar to Kai's, probably Sara. I feel others . . . like Simon. Nephilim. They have varying levels of strength. Some are injured or near death."

Emotions rippled through the Guardians when they heard their brethren were among the captives. Cara could hear their telepathic chatter, their voices overlapping each other as they all spoke at once.

"Sun, didn't you feel them?" Gabe growled.

"I only felt the soulless," replied Sun defensively.

"Maybe Ishmael's with them," said Isaac.

"Who do you think is down there?" Christian asked.

Still holding her hand and Michael's, Simon joined the conversation aloud. "That's one of the reasons we'll be wearing the listening devices to communicate. There's something preventing our natural form of communication."

He dropped Cara's hand, and the Guardian chatter stopped abruptly.

"I'm surprised, and thankful, that Cara picked them up, even if we couldn't. Yet, I felt them when she did." He started to pace.

"Simon?" Cara spoke up behind him as a hypothesis formed in her mind.

He turned. "What is it, Cara?"

"As soon as you let go of my hand, I stopped hearing the Guardians in my head. I think between us . . . " Her finger moved in a triangular motion between him, Michael, and herself. "When we link all our gifts, we create new ones."

Simon froze mid-step. "You could hear us speak behind our veil of silence? That's our own Guardian frequency."

"Yes. Everyone started speaking at once when I mentioned the Nephilim."

Michael chimed in. "I could hear them too."

Cara released a tense breath. "There's more. I saw something else the moment Simon dropped my hand. There's evil I don't recognize. Two ice-cold spots close to where the Nephilim are being held. Not your garden variety form of energy. Whatever it is has a much different footprint than the soulless or any other being I've encountered."

Simon looked at her intently. "Is the energy static or does it move?"

Using Michael as a conduit, Cara held both of his hands and did another quick sweep of all the floors. "They've moved to Kai's floor," she said nervously.

Simon nodded. "Okay, that gives me a few ideas. Thank you."

He turned back to the team. "This is as much as we have to go on. Follow me and Raphael, and I'll run through logistics one last time with each team."

Cara stayed behind with Michael. A wave of exhaustion hit her, and her knees buckled.

"Whoa, you okay?" Michael's strong arms caught her, and he pulled her into his chest.

She shook off the dizziness. "Sorry. Channeling that much energy takes a bit out of me. I'll be fine, I promise. I just need a couple of minutes." She took a deep breath and stood firmly again on her own. Constantina told her over time she'd build up more tolerance, but the use of her gift would always come with a price.

At this point, she was ready to get in there and get Kai out.

Slowly, the teams disappeared, one by one, toward the warehouse. When all the teams were deployed, Simon and Zeke approached her and Michael.

Simon's face was serious and ready for battle. "Are you both ready?"

Cara ignored the butterflies in her stomach and nodded.

"Cara, I'll take you, and Zeke will take Michael."

Simon turned to Zeke and tapped his ear underneath his flowing hair. "Zeke, hook up our veils as soon as you get there so I can give you the update from the teams inside."

"You got it." Then he grinned at Michael and said, "Nephilim Air Flight 201, now departing. All aboard." Zeke hooked his arm around Michael, and they disappeared from sight.

Simon put his arm around Cara and then drew her into the warmth of his body. He tipped her head up and cradled her jaw gently in his hand.

"Before you ask, we're cloaked," he said softly. He passed his thumb gently over her bottom lip and held her gaze within the blue pools of his eyes. His lips descended on hers with a hungry desperation as if he were kissing her for the very last time. Melting into him, she inhaled his scent, wanting to lose herself in the firm contours of his body. Weakness returned to her knees with the intensity of his kiss. The tenderness combined with the passion of it left her breathless. It made her want to cry. She recognized a note of finality wrapped inside his kiss.

"Time to go," he whispered, turning her in his arms.

Positioning her for flight, he pulled her securely into his chest with one of his arms crossed above her breasts and the other low on her hips. His wings unfurled and billowed out behind him with a sound similar to sails filling with air. He crouched low then launched them up into the sky with a powerful flap of his wings. Air rushed up under her and they were aloft, gliding up into the night sky.

Chapter 52

CONSTANTINA LET HERSELF into the now-quiet safe house. Her party was due to arrive any minute. Raphael's call hadn't been enough to summon her old friend, but at her request, he'd been more than happy to assist. He'd even arranged the use of this residence—that of his current charge—as another favor to her, in exchange for the one she'd bestowed on him.

The doorbell rang and the roar of Harley-Davidson motorcycles grew louder, building and filling the air as they approached from the distance. She smiled.

The Avenging Angel's Biker Club had arrived.

Constantina glided down to open the door. A tall and burly, yet attractive, Hispanic man with a shock of dark hair stood in the threshold wearing biker leathers and a smile. Her eyes lit up the moment she saw Angel Benitez.

"Benedictine, it's been a long time, dear one. How is retirement treating you?" She extended her arm to his shoulder, in the traditional Guardian greeting. He did the same. Although he went by his human identity, Angel Benitez, she still called him by his proper angelic name.

"Eae, so good to see you." He captured her small body in a big squeeze of a hug. "I figured this was Guardian business when I got a message from Raphael. But you know I'd only do this for you. Must be something big to take you out of hiding."

She smiled and blushed. "Much has happened since we've worked together last. You don't like the name Constantina?" Only a fair few still called her by her proper angelic name, and he was one of them. Opposite of the Guardianship, Council rules dictated that the Angelorum use their given names during each human lifetime as a sign of respect for their human form. New names are picked each time they are born, but they sometimes repeated their favorites.

His white smile glowed. "You'll always be Eae to me."

"It's noisy outside. How many members came?"

Angel paused, as if mentally calculating the number. "We're about one hundred strong. You got yourself into some bad shit, señorita. I figured you needed the muscle."

She tapped her ear. "Would you mind dropping a veil of silence to avoid unwanted attention?"

He snapped his fingers. "Anything for you, angel." A moment later the street outside went silent.

They ascended the stairs to the living room.

He reached out to pat Constantina on the shoulder. "I appreciate you taking care of Brett in Connecticut. Little brother vanished, and by the time Adela called me, he was already on a plane—the little bastard," Angel said with affection.

Angel had been watching Brett since he was ten years old, though Brett was none the wiser to Angel's true identity. To Brett, Angel was a good friend whom he rode with as part of the bike club. Constantina hadn't been directly behind Angel's assignment, but indirectly, she knew all about it.

Her lips turned up in a smile. "Isaac was more than happy to assign one of his Guardians at my request and, in return, I thank you for arranging the use of Brett's home in his absence."

"*Da nada.* He's used to renting it out if he's gone a while. He's got another month or so before he's done with his tour." Angel stood with his heavy boots on the floor and looked at Constantina's velvet cloak. "I hope you have something to ride in."

She eyed him with a sly smile and a tilt of her head. "What do you think?" Without a word, she slipped off her cloak, revealing a black Guardian outfit complete with weapons belt underneath. Constantina, in her angelic form, was the Angel Who Thwarts Demons.

Angel gave her a crooked smile. "Well, that's good. Just right for a demon slayer."

"I understand Cara, our Soul Seeker, made contact with your charge Brett." Exactly as Constantina had intended . . .

"Really?" He shook his head and smiled broadly at her. "You're already ahead in this celestial game of chess we're playing, aren't you?"

She gave him a knowing lift of her eyebrow. "Maybe for one move, but I take nothing for granted."

He clapped his hands together in anticipation and gave her another white-toothed grin. "Señorita, let's get this show on the road. I'll leave my ride here. You'll be more comfortable on Brett's Harley."

She followed him down to the garage, eager to join Chamuel and the others.

They would need the backup, and she couldn't afford to be late. Way too much was riding on all of their success.

Retrieving the extra helmet and motorcycle jacket Brett had stashed in the locker at the bottom of the stairs, Angel handed them to Constantina. The stainless-steel garage door ascended to reveal a street packed with bikers.

Angel hopped on the bike first and started it—the engine rumbled to life beneath him, sounding much louder in the open garage. He motioned for Constantina to get on. She swung her leg over nimbly and wrapped her arms around his waist. Angel rolled the bike out and signaled for Paco, his second-in-command, to follow him.

Angel took off, the rest of the club getting into formation behind him. He lifted the veil of silence and they roared out of San Francisco, heading straight for Menlo Park. Hopefully, they would arrive before it was too late.

Chapter 53

Menlo Park. Monday, March 31, 3:55 a.m. PDT

WITH A SOFT THUD, their feet hit the ground thirty yards away from the two-story warehouse. Michael and Zeke had already landed, and from what Cara could tell, Zeke was heading straight toward them.

Simon whispered a reply in the angelic language to the undetectable voices speaking to him through his earpiece.

Either that or he's talking to himself, she thought.

A moment later Zeke and Michael appeared as their veils connected when Zeke's hand touched Simon's forearm.

"We need to use the side door around the corner. Isaac's team disabled the alarms there and on the staircases," Simon whispered.

Whispering seems redundant, Cara thought, since no one could see or hear them.

"We'll go first and give an all clear," Zeke said.

Simon said something unintelligible to whoever was listening on the other end then looked back at Zeke. "Good. Next checkpoint is inside."

"See ya there." Zeke dropped his hand, and he and Michael disappeared. Cara sensed them move out ahead.

Her stomach clenched with the thought of entering the building. As much as she wanted to save Kai, she couldn't shake the dread plaguing her. Looking around, she saw only a few cars in front. The place gave off a deceptive air of desertion yet she could sense the army of soulless inside. What she didn't know was whether or not they were workers or assassins, since Achanelech employed both. Raphael had confirmed earlier that an actual business was run from this location.

Floodlights mounted on the building illuminated the entrances, leaving the remaining perimeter in darkness. When they were close enough, Simon snugged them up to the side of the building, and they crept along the outer wall. The damp smell of misty rain hung in the cool night air.

As they rounded the corner, she gasped and jerked back. Two men stood guard with automatic weapons.

Simon shoved her behind him, covering her with his body. "Don't move," he said. Cloaking couldn't protect them from a bullet.

Her heart pounded, and she poked her head around his elbow in time to see Michael, ninja-like, silently appear behind the man on the left. He sunk into an offensive stance and struck. He grabbed the man's arm from behind and with lighting speed twisted it back at an unnatural angle. The man screamed and dropped his gun. As the second man aimed his weapon in Michael's direction, Zeke appeared and stabbed him in the chest with a dagger so bright, Cara had to cover her eyes with her hand.

She heard a sound that reminded her of sugar pouring out of a five-pound bag. She uncovered her eyes, and they grew wide. She had expected the man to be crumpled in a bloody heap on the ground. Instead, a pile of black sand lay on the cement.

Zeke spun around and landed the sword in Michael's target. This time, Cara watched the body disintegrate in a blaze, leaving a second pile of black sand.

Zeke looked at the large guns and hesitated, then shrugged and tossed them behind the bushes. Then he threw his arm around Michael, and they disappeared. The door inched open, seemingly unassisted.

Cara rubbed her eyes to reset her vision. "What happened?"

"The soulless disintegrate when we use an angelic weapon—less of a mess. It works the same with demons, except they turn into black ash."

"I thought they were human?" her voice squeaked.

"They *were* . . . Once they lose their soul, they transform and become susceptible to our weapons."

"Why didn't they take the guns?"

"We can't cloak guns, only blessed weapons like your dagger."

Cara decided not to mention she'd left the dagger behind and any further questions she had were cut off when Michael poked his head out of the door. Locking in on their energy, he looked in their direction and beckoned them inside with a wave of his hand.

Simon whispered again in the angelic language then stood intently listening to the response. "Let's go. The teams inside had no idea about the guards. They must've shown up after the entrance was disarmed."

As soon as Cara stepped through the door, the unmistakable taste of tar attacked her tongue. The place was filled with evil.

She clung to Simon as they worked their way around the first floor with Zeke and Michael. Style and flair were definitely not part of the business model for the Dark Ones. The place had about as much charm as an old garage with its gray cinder-block walls and worn industrial carpeting. Offices lined the perimeter. A cafeteria, a large amphitheater, and a cavernous warehouse filled the remainder of the first floor.

Red dots of light pointed downward from the security cameras. Cara breathed a sigh of relief when they passed by undetected.

They worked their way inward to where Kai was being held below them. After-hours security lights lit their path as they searched.

As they drew closer, Cara sensed Simon listening to his earpiece before he reached out toward Zeke and Michael's energy.

He connected the two veils. "The staircase is around the corner to the right. Raphael and his team have already passed the lab and are on their way down to the prison to find Sara and the Nephilim. They disarmed the motion sensors on the cameras on their way."

Simon moved them ahead, separating the veils and shutting down communication. Zeke and Michael followed.

"Where is everyone?" Cara asked, unsettled by the eerie silence. "It's too quiet." For all the bodies located inside the building, shouldn't they at least hear someone milling around?

He pulled her to a stop. "We didn't want to worry you before, but we suspect this is a trap. You still have a choice. I can take you out."

Great. Just great, she thought as her gut tightened. She blew out a breath. "No, I'm in."

"Atta girl." He squeezed her shoulder. "I'm sorry. I should've told you sooner. I don't want to keep anything else from you."

"Thanks, I appreciate that," she said sincerely.

Within minutes, they found the stairwell and carefully entered. Gray metal stairs led the way down. Pushing her nerves aside, Cara tuned to Kai's vibration. By the time they exited below, she knew where to find him.

It was almost too easy.

This is a bad idea, she thought, sensing the trap closing around her.

Zeke uncloaked and suddenly appeared with Michael. Hovering over the electric lock, Zeke placed a device next to the keypad and punched in a series of numbers.

The lock popped and released a second before a deluge of blackness assaulted Cara's senses, and the soulless flooded the hallway from both directions.

Chapter 54

Le Feu's Warehouse. Monday, March 31, 3:55 a.m. PDT

ZEKE UNCLIPPED two empty hilts from his belt that instantly blazed to life with blades of blinding light.

"Michael! Keep Cara safe!" Simon roughly shoved them both through the door into the lab, pulling it shut behind them.

Cara stumbled into the darkness, her heart pounding. She sensed Kai on the other side of the room.

"Kai?" she whispered. "Can you hear me? It's Cara."

The room remained silent while the melee echoed outside in the hallway. Cara said a little prayer for Simon's and Zeke's safety.

Lights burst on, revealing a large laboratory. Cara had to squint to shield her eyes from the sudden brightness.

Across the room stood Kai, wearing a white lab coat. A tattooed, dark-haired thug wearing leather held a knife to his throat.

Cara gasped, and her heart jumped into her mouth. She hadn't picked up any soulless in the room, and she still didn't. She could kick herself for missing a plain vanilla human.

Kai's normally handsome face was pale and gaunt, his eyes staring intently behind her. A split second later, a pair of meaty hands grabbed her roughly by the shoulders. Michael cursed next to her as he was grabbed too.

She wrinkled her nose at the sweet, overpowering smell clinging to the man behind her.

The tattooed thug sneered. "Well, well, looks like your little friend came to rescue you after all, Doc."

"Who are you, and what do you want?" Cara asked through gritted teeth, feeling like a cliché in a bad action movie.

"She speaks. Our master, Le Feu, would like to have a word with you . . . personally."

Cara's blood ran cold. *Achanelech was Le Feu?* How had she not made that connection?

The dream. The knife. She'd been right. She hadn't saved Kai's life last year; she'd just delayed the inevitable. Le Feu still planned to kill Kai. The realization took her breath away.

A body hit the outside of the door with a loud thump, followed by a blood-curdling scream.

"Michael?" she prompted silently.

"Waiting for an opening," came his terse reply.

"Le Feu wants me. Let him go," Cara said, indicating with her head toward Kai.

Jerking Kai backward, the thug said, "I have a better idea. Why don't I slit his throat, and we'll all watch him bleed to death."

Cara flinched. *Think, think, think!*

Her nose twitched from the floral notes of the fragrance wafting off her attacker, and she let out a violent sneeze.

Before Cara could recover, Kai wedged his hand between his throat and the attacker's arm, creating some space before head-butting him with skull-clattering force. Next, he delivered a swift karate chop to the guy's groin right before his elbow smashed back up into his face. Tattoo let out an agonizing wail and collapsed to the ground.

Nice work, Kai! Cara thought, torn between shock and admiration.

Next to her, Michael had turned into a whirl of motion, releasing deep grunts with every blow. The guy holding Michael screamed when a bone snapped loudly in one of his appendages, reducing him to a heap on the floor.

Michael turned to the man holding Cara and attacked him before he could react.

Cara managed to stumble away from her attacker while Michael fought him. Unlike the man Michael had already taken out, this one appeared to have some martial arts training.

"Kai!" she shouted as she saw Tattoo lunge for Kai's legs. Kai hit the floor with a hard clunk. Tattoo pummeled Kai with his fists while Kai did his best to block the punches from his position on the floor.

"And this is for punching me in the nuts!" Tattoo croaked, reaching down to return the favor.

Cara dove onto his back, hooking her arm around his neck and squeezing with all her might. No way she'd let him make Kai a eunuch on her watch.

"Bitch!" Tattoo gasped, clawing at her arm before he reached up and grabbed a fistful of her hair. Cara saw stars, and her eyes watered as he pulled.

A scream tore from her throat, but it ended abruptly when Tattoo flipped her onto her back, knocking the wind out of her. A nice-sized clump of auburn hair hung from his fingers. Tossing the strands away, he straddled her and locked his hands around her throat.

"If we had more time, I'd teach you to show a little respect," he leered, strings of saliva stretching between his lips. He planted his thumbs into her throat.

She caught the panicked look in Michael's eye as he spotted her with Tattoo. His opponent seized the opening and swept Michael's legs out from under him.

She wasn't about to let this scumbag kill her. She'd thank Michael later for teaching her fifty ways to break out of a choke hold since the demon attack. Clamping her chin down, she shifted her hip underneath her, ready to monkey paw him off of her, when the door burst open with a battle cry.

Two powerful hands grasped him around the chest from above, ripping him off of her.

Suddenly airborne, Tattoo flew, flailing ten feet across a table, sending lab equipment crashing to the ground. He fell in a crumpled pile on the other side on top of the equipment.

Simon dove after him, and Cara heard the sound of his fists viciously connecting with Tattoo's flesh—screams accompanied the sickening crunch of cartilage.

Cara cringed and crawled over to Kai. "Are you okay?" she asked, rubbing her neck.

He sat up and shook himself. Then he hooked his arm around her and pulled her close. "Thank God you're okay."

The warm, familiar scent of him greeted her through the smell of a few too many days without a shower. She hugged him back and helped him to his feet. Glancing over his wounds, she determined that other than a few bruises, he'd be fine.

A few more *hi-yas*, and Michael was the only one left standing among the two men who'd attacked them inside the door. He looked like he'd barely broken a sweat or dislodged a hair from its perfectly mussed style, while both men lay in broken mounds at his feet.

Simon reappeared, wiping his bloody hands on his black pants. "We need to go. Zeke's outside. Everyone stay behind me." He strode for the exit.

"Did you guys get rid of all the soulless yourselves?" Cara asked, incredulous, hurrying after him.

"No. Isaac's team dropped in. I told Zeke to send them on when they were done."

Kai followed her and Simon while Michael brought up the rear.

Simon cracked open the door into the now-silent hallway.

"Zeke," he whispered.

More silence. Black sand covered the floor outside.

The iciness hit Cara right as Simon's head whipped around.

"Sphinx," he uttered a moment before he was snatched off his feet by an enormous, not-quite-human-looking man.

Zeke appeared, wrapped inside the arm of its twin with his feet dangling off the ground. Unable to speak due to the baseball mitt–sized hand covering his mouth, frustration filled his angry scowl. The tight embrace prevented Simon and Zeke from unfurling their wings, rendering them immobile.

Before Cara could react, more rough-looking soulless men appeared, grabbing her, Kai, and Michael. Her heart sank.

The twin holding Simon spoke. "If you fight us, your Nephilim will die." Its hollow, cold voice matched the inhuman quality of its appearance.

Simon ground his teeth. His face reflected the same frustration as Zeke's.

Naively, Cara never expected there to be a force stronger than Simon.

"Come with us," said the other Sphinx in the same hollow voice as his twin. He led the way upstairs with a pissed-off and helpless Zeke in his arms. Cara, Michael, and Kai were dragged behind by their respective goons while the other twin brought up the rear with Simon.

As they marched in silence, Cara hoped the other teams had gotten an earful. Outwardly terrified, she wasn't as alarmed as she thought she should've been. Whether it was due to the prophecy and the fact she needed to stay alive, or too much faith in Simon's team—she didn't care, she'd take it.

Thinking about her conversation with Michael earlier in the lab, she tried her Trinity's telepathic link. *"Michael, can you hear me?"* She waited for a response . . . nothing. Again, but this time to Simon, *"Simon, can you hear me?"* Nothing.

A voice spoke but not one she expected. *"Cara, it's Kai. How are you doing that?"*

"Kai, you can hear me?" Now isn't that an interesting twist, thought Cara with excitement.

"Yup. I heard you in the lab talking to that guy Michael. He wanted an opening, I gave him one. For the record, this is pretty friggin' weird. Who're these people you're with?"

She tried to suppress a smile. *"They're friends, and their job is to get you out of here alive."*

"Le Feu is real, and he wants to kill you," Kai said without preamble.

"I know. I picked up the name when that tattooed nut job said it, which means you're still in danger too."

"They have Sara. She's in the dungeon with someone named Ishmael and ten of his brothers."

"How'd you find that out?" That would explain the Nephilim she'd sensed back at the rendezvous point.

"Yesterday. I thought I was losing it when Ishmael spoke to me in the lab, just like we're talking now. He said he could only speak with me when the twins, Chaos and Destruction, weren't close by," Kai said.

"The Sphinx twins?"

"Yeah."

So it wasn't *something*, but *someone* blocking the Nephilim and Trinity communication. She wondered how she was able to speak to Kai with them so near. A puzzle for her to solve later. In the meantime, she'd bet money that the Sphinx were the ones nabbing the missing Nephilim.

"Cara, did you get the notes I sent you?" He asked with a sense of urgency.

"No, I've moved. Don't ask, long story. They're probably in my mailbox as we speak. Mel mentioned them. That's what they want?"

"Yeah. Mel is one of them," he blurted. *"She came with them yesterday to see me. She's been spying on me since I took Tom's job. I can't believe she would do this to me . . . to our family—"*

"Don't panic. Things aren't what they seem. She was unknowingly possessed by a demon. Simon cast it out. With some recovery time, she'll be fine. Promise me you won't give up on her." Cara knew all too well how Kai could write someone off. This would be hard enough for Melanie to accept, but losing Kai too would be simply unfair.

They arrived at the large set of double doors leading into the Amphitheatre.

The Sphinx twin holding Zeke stepped aside. Fingers dug into Cara's upper arm and propelled her ahead into the Amphitheatre.

Soulless filled the room; their blackness sucked at Cara's energy the deeper she went inside, and the taste of tar thickened on her tongue, making her want to gag.

On the stage below, a sharply dressed man and an attractive, raven-haired woman sat in two regal-looking high-backed thrones on a dais.

Cara's heart lurched.

She recognized him . . . It was the man with the V-shaped scar from the subway.

Chapter 55

Le Feu's Warehouse. Monday, March 31, 4:20 a.m. PDT

"THAT'S LE FEU *on the stage with Emily, the Foundation rep from Forrester,*" Kai said to Cara. She'd never seen her before.

"Well done." Le Feu's voice boomed from the dais, his greeting ominous rather than welcoming. "I see we have our Angelorum guests and our trusted scientist. They're just in time for the . . . festivities."

Cara hairs prickled on the back of her neck. Black tendrils of energy curled around her like a couple of boa constrictors. One by one, her party was shuttled into the theater, the doors slamming shut behind them.

She stumbled as her goon manhandled her down the stairs. When she regained her footing, Kai was shoved roughly ahead of her.

A whimpering sounded from the other side of the curtain behind the dais made Cara's stomach clench. A minion pushed aside the heavy fabric to reveal Kai's daughter Sara, who was tied flat to a wooden platform that was rolled out onto the stage.

"Sara!" Kai screamed, struggling to escape his captor.

"Daddy!" she screamed back, her small limbs wriggling against her bindings.

"Dr. Solomon, unless you'd like me to kill your daughter to shut her up, I'd suggest you both be quiet," said Le Feu.

Sara cried softly, not saying another word while Kai stood pale and immobile.

Without warning, melodic music reverberated within Cara and the voice from her Calling whispered a singular message in the angelic language. Though she didn't understand the words, her body reacted on an instinctual level, filling with confidence, strength, and resolve. A moment later, the music was gone—and she knew what she had to do.

Determined to fight to her last breath if necessary, Cara reached down inside herself and drew on her well of protective energy. She cast it out in bright, sparkling rain to cover not only herself, but also the rest of her party.

"I see that you've had a very good teacher," Le Feu said. His gaze was uncomfortably warm as it touched her.

"I still do," she said coldly, thinking of Constantina and wishing she were here. But right now, they'd have to work with what they had, and she'd do her best to buy them some time.

Cara narrowed her eyes at him. "Why are you so interested . . . in *me*?"

"Don't play with me, girl, or overestimate your strength." He rose from his chair on the dais and glared at her. "You're but a pawn in an angelic game of chess, albeit the winning piece."

She heard an accent similar to Constantina's. "And, what's that supposed to mean, exactly? This time in English," she jabbed, surprised at her own boldness.

He fired a burst of sizzling air at her. It snapped over her skin, burning her, until she dropped a veil of protection around herself, wishing it worked on physical weapons too.

"Maybe your education hasn't been as thorough as I initially thought. Let me take some time to correct that. It's not as if you have anywhere to go. Can I at least make the assumption that you know who we are?"

"Yes, a bunch of pathetic, wingless, fallen angels, known as the Dark Ones. You're the servants of the Morning Star who use soulless humans as muscle. Am I close?"

She heard a low growl behind her. Fingers tightened on her upper arms and the goon shook her roughly from behind.

"Cara, tone it down. Are you trying to get us killed?" Kai's voice yelled in her head.

"Trust me," was all she gave him back.

Le Feu's eyes bulged. "I will fry you from the inside out for your disrespect!"

She raised her eyebrows in mock innocence. "I thought you had a story to tell?"

He let out a low hiss and began pacing on the stage, using his jewel-topped cane as he walked, his free hand tucked elegantly into his pants pocket. "Hmm, interesting that you mention the Morning Star. He's the one who's so deeply interested in you. To me, you're nothing more than a snack for one of my demons," he leered.

"You're correct about one thing," he continued. "We were cast down to this damned rock. Stuck here, really. What is it they say? 'Better to rule in Hell, or in this case—on earth—than to serve in Heaven' . . . or rot in one of its prisons. As with everything, it's what you make of it. But I digress . . . "

He moved closer to her, his fiery energy singeing her. "Rather than leave well enough alone, some of His pesky Hosts were permitted to follow us down and form the Angelorum. Yet, He gave them the advantage of a small, self-created army of Nephilim. Of course, we've created an army of our own, as you see around you." He swept his hand in front of him then gave a gracious nod to Emily. "Thanks to my lovely consort, Emanelech, we have the Sphinx, her personal ice minions. They've proven very effective against the Nephilim. I only wished we had more."

Le Feu resumed pacing. "We've coexisted for over two thousand years, sharing the same small . . . space. The prophecy says there will be, pardon the pun, a fight 'til the death, between us, casting the others back to where they respectively belong and allowing the other party the freedom to rule, so on and so forth. Your birth, little one, indicated that the prophecy has begun. You're the First of the Twelve who will lead us all into battle. I suspect that's why the Morning Star is so anxious to . . . speak with you. In the meantime, we've been doing a bit of work to strengthen our position."

He turned to Kai. "Thanks to Dr. Solomon here, we now have the ability to create our own Nephilim using a genetically engineered vaccine that he has prepared for us. But let me add, he's not the only scientist who's been working on this project. If his formula fails, there will be others. In the interim, he alone provided us with the perfect bait to trap you." He chortled.

A woman's voice came from the back of the Amphitheatre. "I see the sin of pride still drives you, Achanelech, but you shouldn't congratulate yourself just yet."

Cara's heart soared when she looked up to see Constantina at the top of the stairs, her blonde hair pulled tight into a ponytail and a sword in her hand. Cara hadn't sensed her enter.

Le Feu's head shot up and he glared. "Eae, the Angel Who Thwarts Demons. It's been a long time. To what do I owe this pleasure?"

Cara had never thought to ask Constantina if that had always been her name. Like Simon, it appeared that she also had an angelic name.

"Not long enough apparently, and I rarely bring pleasure to demons."

"Must you always be so . . . *literal*," he said, looking at her with disdain.

"I think you mean *honest*," she replied.

"Since we are being *honest*, lose any children lately?" His snide reply was incongruous to the maelstrom of heated energy that surrounded him. His hand twitched on the top of his cane.

Cara silently gasped. *Constantina lost a child?*

Constantina's small shoulders tensed, her grip tightening on her sword and her eyes boring into him with ice-pick precision. "Maybe I should ask you the same question."

His face reddened, and his tongue darted out of his lips to hiss at her. "Unlessss you have an army behind you, Eae, I doubt even you can take me on by yourself, especially given the fact that these five are, shall we say, incapacitated." He made a sweeping gesture toward where Cara and the others stood captive. "Not to mention a roomful of my minions."

Constantina gave him a tight smile. "Why does it always have to come down to violence with you? There are other ways."

She started down the steps.

"Stop!" Le Feu said, bolting across the stage. "Unless you want me to spill the precious blood of your First right now."

"We both know that would be unwise, don't we?" Constantina spoke with an air of authority, but there was something else.

Constantina and Le Feu know something I don't know, Cara thought.

Le Feu glared with black fire in his eyes. "There's one thing you're right about, Eae—there are other ways."

As he spoke, Cara noticed a subtle movement behind the curtain, and her body tensed. Her attention shifted back to Le Feu and the evil grin spreading across his face.

"Dr. Solomon, I'll give you a choice," he said, pulling up on the jewel that topped his cane and removing the serrated dagger hidden inside. "You can either choose Cara or Sara. Funny, the similarity of those names. Are their lives equally as interchangeable?"

Cara gasped, and she saw Kai pale next to her.

Kai looked at Cara, horrified. "He can't ask me to make that choice."

"Oh, but I just did," he said, standing over Sara with the dagger. He placed the tip on her little cheek, drawing a drop of blood. The whimpering from the stage grew louder.

Le Feu's face darkened. "Choose, Dr. Solomon."

Kai's face was panic-stricken. *"I can't choose,"* he whispered through their telepathic link.

"Choose you daughter, Kai," Cara replied softly. "You must."

The man holding Cara put a knife to her throat, setting off a fruitless tussle between Simon and the Sphinx.

Out of the corner of her eye, she noticed the curtain move again. If she planned to do something, she'd better do it now. She had nothing to lose.

Her heart raced, and she dipped into her training, grasping the man's knife arm and twisting into him. Ripping a page from Kai's book, she kneed him in the groin as she pulled his arm back and forced him the ground with a shriek of pain. She had trouble keeping the smirk off her face when she sunk her fingers into the pressure point on his neck, rendering him unconscious. Michael was a very good teacher indeed.

"Stupid girl," said Le Feu, flinging the dagger he'd been pointing at Sara.

Time slowed, and a scream tore from Cara's lungs as she watched the dagger travel end-over-end toward Kai. Still restrained by the thug holding him, his eyes widened and fixed on the knife.

Without a second thought, Cara launched herself between Kai and the knife at the exact moment the curtain opened and Nephilim, wings aloft, stormed the stage.

Gabriel suddenly appeared with a blazing dagger behind Kai and his captor.

Behind her, Simon let out a piercing wail, "NO!"

The agony of the knife tore into her side before she fell into a crumpled heap on the floor.

"Cara!" Kai yelled, running over to her.

From Cara's vantage point on the floor, she could see his shoes so she knew he was still standing, which meant she'd been successful. She'd saved him. He knelt beside her.

"I love you, Kai . . . " she whispered to him as everything went black.

Chapter 56

BURSTING THROUGH the doors from behind the stage, more than a hundred angel-like beings with white wings swarmed the room.

Kai strained against the man holding him, watching in stunned horror as Cara flew through the air between him and the jewel-topped knife.

A piercing wail sounded from the big blond guy Cara called Simon as he attempted to struggle out of the Sphinx's stranglehold.

The knife struck Cara, and her body collapsed in a mound, her blood flowing rapidly around the hilt of the knife.

The man restraining Kai cried out, and his grip loosened enough for Kai to twist away. A huge red-haired guy stood with a blade over Kai's captor.

In a white blur of wings barely visible to the eye, Kai saw a coffee-skinned angel with long black braids pluck Sara up off the stage and fly away with her to what he could only hope was safety. He decided to have faith in Cara and her friends.

The battle raged ruthlessly around him. The room filled with white wings, the flash of blinding swords, screams, and the sound of sand hitting the floor.

"Cara!" he yelled as he dropped to his knees next to her.

"I love you, Kai . . ." she whispered.

His heart squeezed painfully when her eyes shut and she went still.

Never had Kai been so torn. There was nothing worse that he could think of than having to choose between two people he loved. Even though he'd been saved from making the choice, he had to act to make sure the end result wasn't the same. His mind shifted into crisis mode.

Two large men with swords suddenly appeared out of thin air behind the twin holding Simon. Driving their weapons home, they freed him. In two long strides Simon was next to Kai and dropped down alongside him. He pulled Cara into his lap, cradling her in his arms.

Michael and six large men in black with blinding weapons surrounded the three of them, forming a circle to protect them from the fray.

Kai could see the agony and powerlessness written on Simon's face as he rocked her gently in his arms while blood drained from her side.

Kai made a split-second decision. He removed the syringe from his sock that he'd smuggled out of the lab. Shrugging out of his lab coat, he shoved it at Simon.

"Here. Take this to stop the bleeding. Put pressure on the wound."

The fine, aerosol mist of blood on her lips led Kai to believe the knife had pierced a lung. He leaned down, put his ear to her chest, and confirmed his hypothesis. But the rapid escape of blood indicated her lung wasn't the only injury. He had no way of knowing what other organs had been hit.

"Give me access to her chest," Kai demanded. Simon positioned her on his lap so her arms were out of the way.

Kai brought his hand down with force, jamming the syringe into her heart to give him the fastest delivery of the vaccine into her bloodstream. He calculated the healing rate. If she could just hang on for three to five minutes, the vaccine should work and would save her. But he needed to remove the knife to prevent her tissue from healing around it.

Simon's body was coiled for action; he was looking at Kai in tense silence, as if waiting on Kai's instruction.

Kai locked his gaze on him. "On my count, remove the knife on three. Put pressure on the wound. You understand?" Kai needed to keep his hands free to perform CPR if needed.

Simon nodded stoically.

"One, two, three!"

Grasping the jeweled hilt firmly with one hand while prepared to apply pressure with the other, Simon slid the knife out in one swift tug.

Kai held her wrist, feeling for a pulse—it was very weak. He touched his ear to her heart, monitoring the faint beat. In that moment, he did something he never used to do, but had done quite a bit in the last week—he prayed.

He kept his head on her chest. His blood ran cold when her heartbeat went silent.

"Put her down flat!" he yelled at Simon, who moved her onto the floor in front of him with lighting speed, terror in his eyes.

Kai performed CPR on Cara with single-minded focus.

I will not let you die. I will not let you die. Cara, please don't leave us, please don't leave me. I'm so sorry.

He counted off his compressions and filled her good lung with air. Brushing the perspiration from his brow and the coppery taste of her blood from his lips with his sleeve, he kept going, ignoring the rivulets of sweat running down his sides under his shirt.

Come back, Cara! Please don't leave me.

Her normally pale skin grew even whiter, her dark eyelashes resting in delicate crescents on her cheeks. He vowed not to stop until she came back or he died of exhaustion.

Mindlessly, he counted, compressed, and blew breath into her blood-covered lips. He checked his watch—over four minutes. It felt like an eternity.

Please, God, don't let Cara die. Help me save her. Don't leave me, Cara . . . I love you, too. I'm so sorry. Kai's eyes watered and his vision blurred.

The blackness receded and Cara found herself surrounded in a warm and loving light, wanting to embrace it.

"Cara, dear, welcome . . . " A young woman stepped out of the light.

"Grandma, is that you?" she said, overwhelmed with the same love she'd had when she was a child of four.

The woman smiled and took her hands in hers. Grandmother Hannah looked as she did in the wedding picture her father kept on the mantle in their Summit home.

"Yes, my dear. What a lovely woman you've become. I'm so proud of you—we all are."

"Is this Heaven?" Cara asked, looking into the bright mist, elated and surrounded by love.

Hannah gave her a coy look. "Close, but not quite. We're just outside. Once you pass through the gates, there's no going back."

Cara looked down, and she saw herself lying next to Simon while Kai performed CPR on her. Their love pulled at her from below.

Bashfully, she looked at her Grandmother. "I should return. They need me."

Hannah smiled warmly. "Yes, they do. Your time hasn't come yet to return into the light. But before you go, there are two things you need to know. The first thing is that your soul chose this important journey, so trust in yourself and who you are to guide you. The second thing is that another holds a piece of your soul, which you gave to him willingly. You're destined to be rejoined. He's the key to your self-discovery. Look down and see him."

Cara gazed down. A part of her soul, a glistening seed, lay within Simon next to his heart. Her gaze shifted to Kai, and she saw that she was connected to him, too, only differently. Theirs was a debt, now repaid, sealing their loyalty one to the other.

Her grandmother drew her in for a hug. "I love you, Cara. Godspeed, my dear."

"I love you too."

"We'll meet again."

Cara closed her eyes, allowing herself to be sucked backward into the blackness.

Cara's breath brushed against Kai's cheek. Relief exploded out of every pore in his body, and he wiped his face with the back of his hand.

"She's back," Kai said, exhausted and soaked.

Simon's shoulders slumped and he expelled a deep breath. His face, still drained of color, carried the haunted look of a man who had escaped disaster.

Kai glanced at his watch again. They were beyond the five-minute point, and the bleeding had slowed to the point of almost stopping.

"You need to get her out of here, and I need to find my daughter," said Kai.

Simon touched his ear and gave him a weak smile. "Your daughter has already been taken to safety. She's waiting for you at the rendezvous point."

Kai shuddered with relief. "I'd hoped you'd say that. Thank you."

"Thank you for saving Cara. I couldn't have continued living if anything had happened to her." Sincere gratitude was written in Simon's eyes.

Kai nodded. "I feel the same way." He looked at Simon and saw his love for Cara shine through as he looked at her. A pang of jealousy slammed into his chest. Cara had never told him she was dating someone new or that she was in love.

Michael broke into the circle. "Kai, Simon, the place is going to blow in about ten minutes. We need to make tracks, now."

Kai looked down at the bloody knife. Rather than leaving it behind, he wiped the blade on his discarded lab coat and stuck it in his belt. He'd keep it as a reminder of what he'd almost lost.

The fighting outside their protective circle had ended, leaving the floor covered in thick black sand. Sword-wielding men with white wings milled around the packed room, but there was no sign of Le Feu, Emily, or the Sphinx twins.

Simon gently picked up Cara, who was unconscious but breathing.

"Zeke," Simon yelled over to a large, dark-haired guy who looked like he was barely old enough to drink. "Take Kai."

"You got it."

A guy with a short, blond, military haircut showed up. "Cham, I'll take Michael."

Simon nodded with pain in his eyes. "Thanks." Then to everyone, "Let's go."

A couple of minutes later, Kai breathed in the night air for the first time in almost a week.

"OK, dude, here's how we do this," Zeke said and provided a quick explanation of his "ride."

"Don't be bummed if you barf. A lot of people do the first time."

Kai's stomach dropped upon takeoff, and the next thing he knew, his body was pressed up into Zeke's body. They flew at a dizzying speed away from the building. Air raced underneath him, brushing his face with dampness. The ride was rougher than any dreams he'd ever had of flying, but, at least he didn't vomit. If anything, he found it exhilarating.

Dawn was breaking and there were over a hundred men on motorcycles waiting when they landed a few minutes later at the rendezvous point farther away in the warehouse complex. Kai saw Sara sitting on one in the lap of the mixed-race man with the long black braids who had snatched her from the stage, his wings no longer visible. She turned and saw him.

"Daddy!"

The man placed her on the ground, and she set off running straight for him.

Kai swept her up into his arms, overwhelmed and thankful. "Hi, honey. I'm so glad you're okay." He peppered her face with kisses and squeezed her tight.

"Daddy, stop squeezing so hard. I can't breathe."

"I'm sorry. I'm just so glad to see you."

"I know," she said. "Angels protected me until you could save me." She turned back and pointed. "Jade let me sit with him on a motorcycle until you got here."

Simon landed with Cara in his arms and approached the SUV where the woman called Eae waited.

Kai followed with Sara perched on his hip.

"She's injured," Simon explained. "Kai saved her. He said she'll recover well from here. Please take her to the Angelorum clinic. We'll join you later."

Kai spoke up. "I'm not sure how long it will take before she returns to consciousness. Probably best to give her a sedative and keep her out for a couple of hours to help her heal."

Constantina placed a hand on his arm and Simon's. A peaceful wave rolled through Kai and he relaxed. "We'll take her there immediately, dear ones. Ishmael and the rescued Nephilim have been taken there already, as well as the injured," she said.

Simon placed Cara gently onto the backseat, and kissed her forehead.

Kai accompanied Simon to meet briefly with the team leaders. The one called Raphael introduced them both to Angel Benitez, aka Benedictine, the leader of the Avenging Angel's. Simon and the other team leaders arranged to meet back at some Marina District location to debrief. Then he and Kai jumped into the nearest SUV.

Kai kept Sara securely in his arms in front with him, refusing to let her go even though she would've been safer in the back seat.

"I'll drop you off at the clinic on the way," Simon said, his face unreadable.

Kai nodded.

The roar of motorcycles led the way, followed by their motorcade of SUVs.

In the rearview mirror, Kai watched as the warehouse exploded, rising up into a mushroom cloud of fire against the early-morning sky and erasing everything left behind.

Chapter 57

CHAMUEL SAT NEXT TO Cara and held her hand as she lay pale and small in the hospital bed. He brought her hand to his mouth and brushed his lips over her knuckles, closing his eyes to savor the softness of her skin.

Kai had come in earlier to take a blood sample to monitor changes in Cara's body as a result of the vaccine. When the door opened behind him, Chamuel expected Kai, not Constantina.

"My son, how are you faring?" she asked softly, placing her hand gently on his shoulder.

It had been a long time since she'd acknowledged him as her progeny, and the connection felt good. Even though she'd given birth to him in a prior incarnation, she retained her memories of him and of all her other children.

He clasped the small hand she had laid on his shoulder in his free hand. "Mother, I trust that you understand what's transpired?"

"Yes, my love. Isaac told me. Do you love this woman?"

"With all my heart," he replied.

"You know the consequences."

Simon turned to look at her. Pain and sincerity shone in his eyes. "I would give anything . . . " He cleared his throat. "I would give my life for hers, but that may not be enough . . . "

"I believe you. You've grown since Mina and Calliope's deaths. If she feels the same . . . well, we shall see."

"You must release me from this Trinity. Let me go before she wakes up," he said anxiously, turning in the chair to meet her eye to eye. "Put Isaac in my place. He's the only one I trust to guard her. You can take me to the Tribunal. I'm prepared to throw myself at their mercy and stand trial."

"Chamuel, if you love her, why would you choose to run from her?"

He rose to his feet and scrubbed his hand over his face to erase the look of anguish written there. "Mother, don't you understand? I've compromised the safety of my Trinity. I couldn't save her. If Kai hadn't been there, she'd be dead right now, and I would've lost not only another Soul Seeker, but the First of the

Holy Twelve." The memory of her almost dying in his arms wrecked him. He'd gladly smash his own heart into shards just to keep her safe.

Constantina seemed to anticipate his request. "We must all make our own choices as well as take accountability for them. I think you should wait until she wakes."

He wanted to scream in frustration. "Didn't you hear me? I failed her."

Constantina shook her head and said patiently, "Please sit back down."

He did as he was told.

"My dear son, don't confuse Cara's fate with your own. Did you happen to think that perhaps your failure was exactly the thing that needed to happen in order for her to fulfill her destiny and for you both to end up in each other's arms? There are no coincidences, Chamuel. Look closely, and you'll see."

He sometimes forgot how kind and wise she was, and how much he loved her even when she berated him as his parent.

"In my opinion, you'd be wiser to wait and face the Tribunal with Cara at your side," she concluded.

After what Cara had said to him last night, he wasn't so sure. Quite the opposite—he was convinced she'd never fully accept him as a Nephilim or agree to be his mate. He'd kissed her on the roof to both ease her anxiety and to see if she'd let him. The last kiss, before he took her into his arms, was to say good-bye. By then, he'd already decided to ask for his release after the rescue. Truth be told, he'd been prepared for her to push him away, but her passion and willingness had surprised him.

In the unlikely event he'd be fortunate enough to end up with a suspended sentence, he vowed to put as much distance between them as possible in order to keep her safe and to give her back the chance to find a human man to bestow the happiness he'd so boldly taken from her.

Unshed tears glistened in his eyes. "Please, just let me go. I only came here to see her one last time."

"Chamuel, you were born with free will, far be it from me to interfere. I've already given you my opinion. You're free to go, if that's your wish. But if you leave, you leave behind your chance for redemption. I'll try to help, but you'll be at the mercy of the Tribunal."

He could tell she was disappointed in him, but not as disappointed as he was in himself.

"Redemption isn't meant for someone like me . . . " he said softly and lowered his head. A tear fell from his eye.

She laid her cheek on the top of his head and stroked his hair. "That is where you're wrong, my sweet and loving son," she whispered, her breath warm and comforting. "The reason I named you Chamuel, dear one, is because your fate is tied to matters of the heart. You deserve love. You've paid too much already in this lifetime. I hope you'll reconsider and have a little faith in our Cara."

She released him and headed toward the door.

Wrapped up in his own worries, he'd almost forgotten to acknowledge what he'd learned on his mission.

"Mother," he said, and her hand stopped as it reached for the doorknob. "I'm sorry to hear of the loss of your daughter, my sister Hope. I didn't know."

She smiled sadly. "Thank you on her behalf. Her sacrifice paved the way for the success of your Trinity. Honor her well. Journey forth in peace and love, Chamuel."

She left the room without waiting for his response.

Chapter 58

San Francisco. Angelorum Clinic. Monday, March 31, 8:30 a.m. PDT

CARA SWAM THROUGH the darkness toward the surface of her consciousness. The beeping of her heart monitor grew stronger as light broke through the blackness in tiny pinholes. Was she looking at the stars in the night sky?

"Cara. Cara, wake up," urged a masculine voice.

Kai, she thought, continuing to fight against the blanket of unconsciousness still wrapped around her.

"Her vitals look good," he said.

Her eyes fluttered and eventually opened a crack, only to be assaulted by the fluorescent ceiling lights.

"Bright," she said through parched lips. The inside of her mouth felt as if it had been bathed in sand.

"She's awake," a female voice said. "Turn off the lights over her bed."

Cara slowly opened her eyes and saw familiar faces. Michael, Sienna, Kai, and a woman doctor, based on the white coat, crowded around her bed.

"What happened?" she asked and turned to Kai. "You're okay?"

Kai's eyes glimmered with emotion, and he grabbed her hand. "Yes, Sara and I—you were amazing."

"I don't remember anything." Her mind was a blurry mess. The last thing she remembered was speaking with Kai telepathically on their way to meet Le Feu. From there, it was a foggy jumble.

"Don't worry, you will at some point," Kai said and squeezed her hand. "We almost lost you."

Sienna piped up. "Kai, you're too modest." She leaned over Cara with red-rimmed eyes and whispered, "Kai saved your life, Carissima. You scared us half to death. Please don't do that again."

Michael stood behind Sienna, his hand protectively on her back. When she straightened herself up, she leaned back into him, taking comfort against his body. The corner of Cara's mouth tipped up in a smile seeing them together like that. She'd dig into that one later.

Cara looked around. The one person she needed to see immediately was missing. "Is Simon here?"

An awkward silence gripped the room.

Michael cleared his throat. "He was here before you woke up, but he's been called away."

Cara caught the bitter taste of the lie as it passed over her tongue.

"He didn't just get 'called away,' did he?"

Michael bowed his head, released a breath, and opted for the truth. "He left. He petitioned Constantina to relieve him of his post."

Michael's words triggered something primal within her, like her soul had been cleaved in two.

"No!" She wailed, and the air left her lungs. She reached for the handrail and pulled herself up. He couldn't be gone! She needed to tell him she loved him. She needed him to stay and never leave her.

"What're you doing?" Michael asked with alarm and stepped around Sienna.

"I have to find him. He needs to know that I'm sorry and—" She stopped as a wave of dizziness seized her. She looked into the concerned faces of her friends, and she realized that she loved them all, but without Simon, her heart and soul would never be complete.

"Shh." Michael gently pushed her back down into a prone position.

"Is Constantina here?" she asked.

"She'll be here later. Why don't you rest." Michael glanced over at the doctor whose nametag read DR. JESSICA STONE. He nodded at her, and she adjusted Cara's IV.

Cara relaxed and drifted off to sleep.

Loud voices and the squeaky wheels of a hospital cart cut through Cara's drug-induced haze. She wasn't sure how long she'd been out. Then Simon's energy hit her. Fuzzy dreams of angels fighting. Pain. Simon . . . Something was wrong. He was weak.

Before she could react, sleep pulled her back under.

Cara bolted upright in bed, aware that more time had passed since she'd sensed him. Her head swam at the sudden change. She'd been removed from the heart monitor. Only one IV bag for hydration remained tethered next to the bed. She grabbed the tall, mobile trolley with the bag and used it as a crutch to swing her legs over the side of the bed.

I have to heal Simon, she thought, her heart hammering.

Michael walked in. "Are you all right? I sensed your distress."

She tried to stand, her eyes wild. "Where's Simon? What happened?"

Michael took a deep breath and placed his arms on her shoulders, lowering her back onto the bed. "I'll tell you. Just sit."

He sat in the chair next to her bed. "He joined Raphael's team to look for a second hideaway that Ishmael told us about. He was attacked in the air. One of his wings was torn and he took a nasty fall. He's in surgery right now."

Cara sighed. At least Michael told her the truth this time.

"Will he be all right?"

"They're optimistic," was all he said.

"I need to see him as soon as he's out of surgery. Michael, I made such a huge mistake." Her eyes spilled over. "I love him so much I can hardly breathe. He needs to know that. He needs to know that I'm sorry and that I love him."

Michael leaned over and hugged her tightly. "It'll be okay," he said softly, "I promise."

"Can I speak with Constantina?"

"She's here. I'll send her in when she's finished with Dr. Stone. Hang in there."

Before he reached the door, she asked, "Michael. Um . . . things better with you and Sienna?"

His shoulders stiffened. "Let's just say we've reached a truce and leave it at that," he said softly without turning. Cara sighed, hoping for more, but she'd take whatever small steps they made—to use Zeke's words—to get to twenty minutes in a dark closet.

He left, closing the door behind him.

Fifteen minutes passed while Cara waited. By then, her strength had surged, and she felt absolutely energetic, enough to go for a run. She was halfway in the closet to retrieve her clothes when Constantina entered.

"You're looking well, Cara, dear," she said with a warm smile. "Apparently, the vaccine has accelerated your healing beyond even your own powers."

"What do you mean?" she asked, grabbing the clothes Sienna had left behind for her—a pair of jeans and the clingy top Sienna liked so much. Leave it to Sienna to choose a shirt meant to peddle Cara's "breast-ware," as she liked to call it.

"Your Kai. He injected you with the vaccine as you lay dying from a knife wound in Chamuel's arms. We thought we'd lost you. Since we're unsure of how the vaccine will change your body chemistry, we're studying you closely for the effects. In the meantime, you're healed." Her smile widened. "And, one of the mysteries of your Trinity has been answered. Angelis, our High Council leader, and I had found it odd that you showed up as a Nephilim in your Trinity Stone when we knew you were human."

Cara didn't want to rain on Constantina's parade, but Trinity business could wait. Cara had one goal. "Can we talk about that later? I need to speak with you about Sim—Chamuel . . . " She sat on the bed and glanced at her hands.

"Chamuel is my Simon," she whispered, tears threatening to return as she spoke the words. "I know it's forbidden to be with my Guardian, but I didn't know until we were on our way to San Francisco. I need to know if he's actually going to jail for one hundred years for kissing me, and if there's anything I can do to stop it . . . I want to have a chance for us to be together." She looked up, holding her breath.

"I've heard the tale of you and my son."

Cara's jaw dropped. "Your *son*? Simon is your *son*?" She hadn't seen that one coming.

"Yes. From a prior incarnation," Constantina said with a coy smile. "But I didn't know he was your Simon until Isaac informed me. My question is this, Cara—what would you sacrifice to be with him?"

Without hesitation, she replied, "Everything that I have, including my life if that would save him." She wrapped her arms around herself, trying to find comfort.

"The ultimate gift is the sacrifice of one's life for another," Constantina said. "When asked the same question, he gave the same answer."

"He said that?" Cara's heart leapt, and her head snapped up.

"Yes, he did," Constantina replied with a nod of her head. "Would you be willing to spend the next three hundred years by his side?"

"Huh? What do you mean? I'd be lucky to give him the next sixty years, if he'll have me after what I said to him."

Constantina beamed at her. "Not so, my dear. According to Dr. Solomon, the vaccine was made to mimic the longevity of the Nephilim. You now have Nephilim DNA in your body, minus the genes to generate a pair of wings, that is."

Cara blinked, trying to process Constantina's words. "I'm going to live as long as Simon?"

"We believe so," she replied, "which is why I believe you should petition the High Council to sanction your bond. I know you'll have at least one vote, if you'll have him, that is."

Cara's heart soared, and she hopped off the bed. "Yes, yes! A thousand times yes! Can we go to see him?"

Constantina eyed her hospital gown. "May I suggest a change of clothes first?"

Cara poked her head into Simon's room. His energy was near normal now. He lay unconscious, wearing a hospital gown, with a sheet pulled up to his waist. His dark, golden hair, free of the tie that normally held it back, fanned out around his handsome sleeping face. His beautiful wings, white as snow, were folded on either side of him, the left one swathed in bandages midway down.

She gasped when she saw his wings up close in the light. Feathers of all sizes shimmered in a dazzling array of subtle texture. Unable to wait another second, she went to him. She reached out to touch the glittering feathers to see if they felt as incredibly soft as they looked. Delight filled her as she ran her fingertips over their soft, silky texture, melting at their beauty.

She sat on the edge of the bed next to his folded wing and took his large hand in hers.

From the doorway, Constantina said, "I'll give you some time alone with him. I'm sure he'll be pleased to see you when he wakes." The door clicked shut behind her.

Cara cradled his warm skin next to her cheek then pressed his fingers to her lips and kissed them. His face held an unexpected, youthful innocence in sleep, very different from the commanding Guardian of her Trinity. His full lips parted, and his eyelashes lay in golden fans against his smooth cheeks.

She ached to talk to him . . . even though he wasn't awake.

"Simon, it's me, Cara," she said softly, squeezing his hand in hers. "I'm so glad you'll be okay. I don't know what I'd do if anything happened to you. I'm so sorry for what I said and how I've treated you. It wasn't fair of me to judge you as I did." She paused, a lump forming in her throat. "I wanted to tell you on the roof . . . I love you, Simon . . . I don't want to live without you. I want you to stay as my Guardian. Can you ever forgive me?"

Taking advantage of his sleeping state, a wicked smile suddenly touched her lips. She ran her fingers lightly over his forearm, tracing his veins. "You know, the day I first saw you in the subway I thought you were some Greek god. You're the sexiest man I've ever laid eyes on. Every time I look at you I want to—"

"Take your clothes off?" A smile formed on his lips as he replied, his eyes still closed.

Startled, she blushed. "How long have you been awake?"

Opening one eye, he turned his head toward her and chuckled. "Since you walked in."

She tsk-tsked him and gave him a little pinch.

"Ouch! That wasn't very nice coming from someone who's seeking forgiveness," he said, rubbing the red mark on his arm.

Her pique forgotten, she gazed at him with love in her eyes. "I'm sorry. Can you forgive me? I know—and understand—how much you've risked being with me, how much you sacrificed to take that chance. It's me that's unworthy." She cupped her hand to his cheek.

He lifted it to his lips and kissed her palm. "I forgive you," he whispered. Then with a mischievous glint in his eye, he rolled sideways.

She let out a girly squeal as he scooped her up on top of him. She stretched out along the length of his body, her hair cascading around their faces, giving them a curtain of privacy. His strong arms surrounded her like warm pillars.

Her face only inches from his, she locked her eyes on the blue radiance below her, and whispered, "I love you, Simon. Promise you won't leave me." She lowered her lips onto the softness of his. His arms flexed around her, and he kissed her with an insatiable passion that made her toes curl.

Low moans rose from both of their throats. He took no quarter as he drank her in and explored every part of her mouth with sensuous hunger. Familiar electricity woke up her entire body with a jolting awareness. He reacted equally underneath her, and there was nothing more in the world she wanted than to lose herself with him inside her.

They came up for air, breathing hard. His hand caressed her cheek. "I love you, Cara. I promise on my life, I won't leave you."

"Make love to me, Simon," she breathed, her voice husky. The feel of him so close was too much for her handle. She wanted him with so much certainty, she physically ached for him.

He tucked a strand of hair behind her ear; his half-lidded eyes blazed with desire. "I want you more than I want to breathe right now, but I'm . . . "

The door opened, and Isaac strode inside, stopping only when he noticed Cara.

" . . . *expecting Isaac.*" He finished in her head, giving her an apologetic look.

Isaac's icy-blue eyes widened in surprise. "Sorry, Cham. I expected you to be alone." He swept his pointed finger between her and Simon then crossed his arms over his chest. "Let me guess. Change in plans?"

Cara gingerly crawled off Simon and sat on the edge of the bed as he rolled onto his side and positioned his wing to hide the evidence of his arousal under the thin sheet.

"Yup. Change in plans. See you at the Tribunal."

Isaac passed a hand over his face and smirked. "That was the shortest Trinity assignment in Angelorum history."

Cara's head jerked around. "Isaac was going to take over for you?"

Simon shrugged. "Was . . . "

Shaking his head, Isaac headed for the door and snickered. "I'm going to pretend I never saw you. You two lovebirds have fun while you can, but don't get too cozy. This place is crawling with people who want to see you both."

The door closed, and Simon pulled her back against him. His arms encircled her, and he kissed the top of her head. She wanted to scream in frustration. Her hormones were all dressed up with no place to go.

"One more promise," he whispered into her hair. "The first moment we're guaranteed a couple hours of privacy, I'll make love to you until we're both too exhausted to move. I won't be satisfied with anything less for our first time together."

A thrill shot through her, and her heart skipped a beat. She smiled. "Deal."

Chapter 59

AFTER CARA'S ATTENDANT left her room, she spread out on the bed and tried reading a book, wishing time would move faster. Restless, she shifted and let out an exasperated breath, unable to find a comfortable position. The last couple of days had been filled with a large dose of hurry-up-and-wait. It would be still another few hours before she and Simon were brought together to face the High Council.

Constantina had briefed them on the expectations and procedures of the Council during their plane journey, and Cara had been less than pleased to learn she and Simon would remain in isolation until after the Tribunal hearing. With the exception of a Council-assigned attendant, they would see no one else. If the outcome fell in their favor, Cara would see Simon again. Otherwise, they may never spend another moment alone. Her heart squeezed in agony at the thought.

She kept wondering what Simon was doing and if he missed her much as she missed him. Her stomach fluttered with both apprehension and excitement. As tempting as it was, while they were within the Sanctuary complex, they were prohibited from using their telepathic link. Cara enjoyed a good challenge, so they'd hatched a plan on the plane to get around it. No one said they couldn't send energy pulses. But that only worked when they were in the same room.

Tossing the book on the bed, Cara gave up and lifted herself off the bed to pace. Her confinement made her feel like a prisoner, rather than a witness. Simon was the one standing trial. Other than a mere glimpse of the secret underground city when she'd arrived, she hadn't seen anything but marble hallways within the Council's section of the complex and this room. Granted, it had all the amenities of a fine hotel, but she was anxious to see the city. From a quick glance, it looked like a cross between the Emerald City from the *Wizard of Oz* and a European village, all underneath a city-size dome of rock.

She crossed her arms over her chest, and wandered around the short length of the room. Even Michael being here would've helped. She stopped and smiled. During their flight from San Francisco, Cara had noticed the truce continue between Michael and Sienna and prayed they would get their "twenty minutes" someday. When the private jet had touched down in Westchester, it had been sad to see them go with Chloe and Zeke, but better in order for her and Simon to prepare for the Tribunal with Constantina and Isaac.

A knock at her chamber door startled her. She wasn't expecting anyone. Cara opened it a crack to find Constantina on the other side.

"Cara, there's someone here who wants to see you," she said.

"I thought I wasn't allowed visitors?"

Constantina smiled. "We made an exception."

"Who is it?"

"Why don't you come with me and find out?" Constantina didn't need to ask twice. Short of Attila the Hun, Cara would gladly talk to anyone to escape the room.

Latching the door behind her, she followed Constantina through the two-story, windowless hallway and down one level along a massive, circular central staircase. Cara didn't bother pressing her. It would be easier breaking into Fort Knox to steal gold bars than getting Constantina to tell her anything.

They stopped at a large doorway in the Sanctuary wing off the main hall. Cara didn't know what to expect beyond the large ornate door in front of her.

"Go in. Your guest is waiting." Constantina pushed open the door and ushered Cara through it, closing her inside.

Cara stood in a vast, white-walled gallery. Works of art covered the walls. Then she spotted him in profile across the room, dressed in white as he admired one of the paintings.

This is the place! she thought. This was the dream she'd had of Kai after her birthday!

Kai turned to see her, and without thinking, they closed the distance between them until they were locked in an embrace.

Cara had been disappointed that she hadn't spent more time with Kai before she left San Francisco. Between sorting out his family issues, and studying the effects of the vaccine on her DNA, his hands were full. But he'd promised he'd visit her soon. In the end, she was okay with it since larger issues loomed. For one, the pressing date with the Tribunal, and for another, recovering her memory and finding out what was coming next.

Happiness gushed through her. She hadn't known he'd be visiting this soon.

Cara hugged him tightly, and her body melted with relief into his. The warm scent of him mixed with the white birch of the Calvin Klein Escape cologne he'd worn since college, when she'd given him his first bottle.

Kai moved first. Clasping his hands on her shoulders, he held her out far enough to see her face. "I'm sorry I had to leave so soon after the rescue."

She pulled him back into her arms. "It's okay. I understand. Thank you for saving me."

"Cara, you were the one who saved me and Sara. I don't know what I would have done if either of you had died," he whispered in her ear, his arms flexed firmly around her.

Her mouth turned up in a smile. "How are Melanie and Sara?"

"They're fine, thanks to you and rest of the crew." He pulled away and shook his head. "I had to come. I realized that I owed you a big apology . . . " Closing his eyes, his hand covered his mouth for a moment. His eyes glistened when he opened them, and words tumbled out of his lips. "I'm so sorry I doubted your loyalty. I never meant to hurt you like that. When I thought I'd lost you, I knew what happened between us back in college was my fault. I know you didn't cheat on me. I let my issues get in the way. I know I caused us both pain. Will you ever forgive me for being such an idiot?" Longing filled his eyes as he waited for her answer.

Her heart ached and rejoiced at the same time. Like Kai, she knew something. She knew, finally, what it all meant. She understood why she'd been so drawn to him. Her soul finally recognized him for who and what he was—her Center Stone. Their souls were bonded through a mutual promise, which they both fulfilled. They'd saved each other in more ways than one.

Her eyes welled. "There's nothing to forgive. Everything turned out exactly as it should have . . . "

He pulled her back into an embrace, resting his face against her hair. "I love you, Cara. Thank you for always being there for me."

At that, her tears brimmed over and trailed down her cheeks. She hugged him even harder. She'd waited forever to hear he'd forgiven her, and even though his forgiveness wouldn't lead to where she'd imagined so long ago, the words were just as healing. Because of Kai, she had a life and a chance at love.

"I love you too," she said.

"Simon's one lucky man." He kissed the side of her head.

She pulled away, brushing her fingers underneath her eyes. "Wish us luck. I have to get back. Are you staying for a while?"

"Not this time, but I'll be back. Constantina offered me a job."

"*Really?*" Cara eyebrows shot up.

He grinned. "Someone I care about needs a personal physician, and the Angelorum needs a lead researcher on Nephilim DNA. I believe I'm uniquely qualified."

Cara couldn't stop the wide smile from bursting across her face, or stop herself from throwing her arms around him again. "Thank you."

His blue eyes twinkled. "Good luck. I'll see you soon."

She tasted the truth in his words and knew he meant it.

Chapter 60

CARA ENTERED the Tribunal chamber from the right. Lavender candles flickered on sconces flanking the door. The scent reminded her of Constantina. Her heart skipped a beat as she watched Simon's large frame fill the doorway from the left. Dressed by their Council attendants, they wore identical sandals and the white ceremonial robes of a law violation hearing. Simon's eyes lit up and the corner of his mouth lifted as soon as he saw her. He silently sent her a little pulse of energy, which she returned, but it did little to quell the nervous fluttering in her stomach.

Cara's attendant held her back with the gentle pressure of her hand, and Simon's did the same while Isaac, dressed similarly, was led from the center of the room. He walked by and gave her a sad smile. Her heart sunk as she thought of her outburst outside the plane in Connecticut, wishing she could take it back. When the door closed behind Isaac, she and Simon were ushered into the center of the floor to take their places. They were left alone, standing side-by-side to face the High Council. Close enough to touch, but prohibited from doing so. Simon's energy warmed her side.

Cara clasped her hands tightly together in front of her, and forced herself to stand with her backbone rigid in an effort to calm her nerves.

The room reflected the quiet serenity of a church. Set up like a small courtroom, the rectangular space held seating for spectators behind them. From an elevated boxed enclosure one floor up in front of them, the Council members gazed down at them from the twelve seats within it. Constantina was seated to the far right. One level lower and currently unoccupied, an ornately carved octagonal pulpit jutted out into the center of the room. Murals covered the walls, reminding Cara of the paintings on the ceiling of the meeting room at the penthouse.

Angelis, the Council leader, with his short, gray-peppered hair, cleared his throat and spoke from his seat. "Before I ask either of you to present, we'd like to share some events selected from the Flow."

Cara's stomach clenched, recalling her discussion with Constantina. Like a giant cosmic video recorder, the Flow stored every moment of history on earth.

God, this can't be good.

The lights dimmed and a 3-D, life-sized holographic film sprung to life in the open air above their heads. In the scene, she lay cradled on Simon's lap, unconscious, after the demon attack in her apartment. His large hand hovered over her face next to a lock of her hair; he had a look of wonder in his eyes.

Cara's breath caught in her throat. She never knew this happened, and it warmed her to see it.

The image faded, replaced by another until the 3-D moments flashed by in a continuous stream: Simon's arms securely around her after catching her as she fell in Raphael's; Simon's hand creating the looping script of the note inviting her to dinner; her hand in his over the dinner table at Raphael's; their first explosive kiss at the jazz lounge; standing in his arms viewing the Rubens at the Met; her head tucked under his chin as he told her about Calliope; their kiss outside the Standard Grill; her exposure of him at the Westchester airport. Every time they'd been together was played for everyone to experience. Her vision blurred, and she bit her lip to keep it from quivering as hope drained out of her.

How will Simon ever be pardoned for this? The bitter lemon taste of fear in Simon's energy reflected hers. Wishing she had a tissue, she brushed away her escaping tears with her fingers, and clasped her hands back together.

When the clips ended, Angelis cleared his throat. "Cara Collins, you may go first." Simon's energy pulsed at her. She wanted more than anything to reach out and touch him. She wrung her hands to remove the sweat from her palms and suppressed the urge to scream.

"What can I say? You've seen it all," she whispered. When Constantina had coached her, she hadn't mentioned the possibility of a moving picture show.

Angelis's voice was kind. "Those are only snippets; they cannot possibly tell the full story. The Flow is not privy to your thoughts or intent, my dear. That's what you must tell us."

Cara nodded and swallowed, then proceeded to tell her side of the story, sticking to thoughts, feelings, and intent.

Simon presented his side next in the same manner.

After they finished pleading their case, they were taken to separate sanctuary antechambers while the Council debated their fate behind closed doors.

Two of the most painstaking hours of Cara's life passed—sitting alone with only her fear to keep her company—before she and Simon were led back onto the floor of the Tribunal chamber to hear to the verdict.

She couldn't avoid seeing the slump of his shoulders or miss the concern in his eyes and his energy when she entered.

The Council members filed into the chamber from above and took their seats in the boxed enclosure, while Angelis stepped down and stood inside the low center pulpit. He unrolled a parchment scroll and cleared his throat.

"I address you both: Cara Collins, Soul Seeker of the Collins Trinity and First of the Holy Twelve; and Chamuel, Son of Eae, and Guardian of the Collins Trinity.

"You have been called forth today to address a violation of Angelorum Law. The law in question prohibits romantic involvement between Trinity members. More specifically, it prohibits the assigned Nephil Guardian from pursuing a romantic attachment with the human Soul Seeker or Messenger within the Trinity. The purpose of the law is to prevent attachments that create biased judgment and jeopardize the success of the mission and the safety of the Trinity members. The history of the Angelorum is rife with Trinity mission failures and dead members to support the need for such a law. Every failure gives the Dark Ones more power to tip the balance.

"The oath of the Trinity Guardians requires them to put the needs of the Trinity before their own, since their purpose is singular to our world. They are created to protect and defend. In order to do that effectively, they are given humanity and human emotions, rendering them fully capable of falling into the trappings of romantic love.

"To prove guilt, we examine intent, which can start with a look or a caress. Though not all intent is acted upon, the line for judgment starts with a kiss."

Ice water rushed through Cara's veins as she thought of the clips from the Flow. She'd hoped Simon had exaggerated when he said he could be sentenced to one hundred years in prison for just kissing her.

"Punishment for the violation of this law is as follows: revocation of membership within the Guardianship; forfeiture of the benefits associated with the post of Guardian; removal of the Guardianship Mark; mandatory separation from Trinity members; one hundred years of mandatory imprisonment within Sanctuary complex without visitation; at the conclusion of the imprisonment, removal of the Nephilim wings."

Each punishment layered on top of the next drove the air slowly from Cara's lungs until the crushing weight of Angelis's words settled fully in her chest. She struggled for oxygen in ragged gasps.

Can't breathe! Cara's fingers clawed at her throat, unable to get enough air. Woozy, her vision narrowed and the horizon flipped. Her eyes rolled back in her head, and her knees turned to jelly underneath her. Strong fingers gripped her upper arms as her world turned pitch-black.

"Cara? Can you hear me, dear one?" Constantina's worry-laced blue eyes stared down at her. Cara had been carried to the sofa in the antechamber outside of the Tribunal chamber. They were alone.

Sobs ripped from her lungs until she hiccupped. Constantina pulled her into her arms, and smoothed her hair back, soothing her. "Shh."

"I can't lose him like that," she choked out. Then she whimpered, "Please don't let that happen." The back of her hand was wet with tears.

Constantina's lavender scent caressed her. She leaned over and kissed Cara on the forehead. "Shh. The verdict has not yet been read. Have some faith, dear one." Removing some tissues from her Council robe, she handed them to Cara. "Take a minute then rejoin us in the Tribunal."

Cara shook as she sat up and blew her nose. Dabbing her eyes, she said, "I love him, Constantina. I can't do this without him."

Constantina nodded and smiled kindly. "I know." She moved to leave.

"Why me, Constantina?" Cara blurted, caving in to the self-doubt eating away at her. "Why was I chosen to be the First of the Holy Twelve? I may not be the best choice. My anxiety makes me . . . weak."

The petite woman returned to her, and placed her hand over Cara's heart. "The answer's right here. When I said to have some faith, I also meant in yourself."

With a parting smile, her robe swept over the threshold as she left, and the door shut behind her.

Cara hoped she wouldn't let them down in the end. Giving her eyes a final wipe, she took a deep breath and opened the door to the chamber.

Simon's chest heaved and his crystal-blue eyes filled with support as she walked toward him. She gave him a wan smile before stepping in next to him and facing the Council.

"Welcome back, Miss Collins," Angelis said, dipping his head in greeting. "May we proceed?"

Her cheeks flushed. "Yes."

"All right, then. We, the Council, believe this case is not a simple violation. As such, we have come to a decision based on the guidance given within the Trinity Stones."

Cara stood straighter, wondering if that was better or worse. She'd take Constantina's advice and have faith. Angelis paused, looking between her and Simon, before settling his gaze on her. She swallowed and clamped her hands together until her knuckles turned white.

"The Trinity Stones revealed that you, Cara Collins, have been destined to be with one of your own kind since birth."

A shudder passed over Cara. Technically, she and Simon weren't born the same kind. Again she ached to touch him, but she didn't dare. He stood ramrod straight next to her, facing forward, his apprehension reflected in his energy.

Angelis rolled the scroll forward and continued reading. "The anomaly within your Trinity Stone revealed you as a Nephil." He glanced at her briefly. "Something that hadn't been true until quite recently, as I understand it. As such, your destiny shows you bonded with a fellow Nephil."

She released a sigh of relief and heard Simon do the same.

Lowering the scroll, Angelis looked at them seriously.

"Chamuel, Son of Eae, would you willingly bond with the Nephil, Cara Collins?"

"Yes," Simon said, his deep voice cracking. An unexpected thrill and hint of hope traveled through her.

Angelis pressed his lips together and turned to Cara. "And you, Cara Collins, would you willingly bond with Chamuel, Son of Eae?"

"Yes," she said evenly, though she wanted to shout it at the top of her lungs.

Angelis gave a small nod and continued. "From the beginning, it was clear to the Council that in order for the Twelve to succeed, we, the Council, would be challenged to allow a few rules to be broken. In this case, Chamuel, not Cara, violated the law."

From the corner of her eye Cara saw Simon dip his head.

Angelis looked at Simon. "Look up, Chamuel. We all have destinies, and within yours you were called to break the law to be with Cara. That, in itself, takes a certain amount of courage. One of our Council members, the one who is now known as Constantina, who birthed you in another life, chose you for this role. She has spoken on your behalf. In addition, we heard testimony from Isaac, Son of Heiglot. We would be breaking our own rules if we were to orchestrate or interfere with destiny. Ultimately, you were free to make your own choices. This was clearly your choice and your destiny."

Cara sensed Simon's energy take a positive turn.

"After much deliberation over the nuances of our own laws, we've decided not to deliver the traditional punishment to Chamuel for breaking this law. With that said, this violation cannot go unpunished." Angelis took a long pause. "Chamuel, Son of Eae, we, the Council, hereby remove you as the Guardian of the Collins Trinity, and place you on furlough from the Guardianship until further notice."

Simon's energy flagged. Cara tightened her spine to compensate for the weakness in her knees. She chanted to herself: *Breathe. Inhale. Exhale.*

Constantina stood up and descended the staircase to stand next to Angelis in the pulpit. He handed her the scroll. "Dear ones, Angelis has agreed to let me deliver the remaining verdict." She smiled at Simon. "Chamuel, my son, you will retain your Guardianship Mark and membership, since it is expected you will someday return. As for mandatory imprisonment . . . "

Cara stood perfectly still, her legs and lungs paralyzed.

"The Council unanimously voted and agreed to accept your self-imposed celibacy, which lasted well over one hundred years, in lieu of mandatory imprisonment. We believe you've paid enough. Furthermore, we have chosen to sanctify your bond with Cara. The strength of your love and the mutual willingness of your sacrifice have proven you both worthy."

Air rushed from Cara's lungs in relief, and her pulse quickened with expectation. Zeke hadn't exaggerated; he *had* been celibate since Calliope died.

Constantina rolled up the scroll and turned to Cara. "Is that acceptable, dear one?"

She nodded vigorously, too excited to speak.

"My son, there's one more thing. The Trinity Stones have revealed you as the Second of the Holy Twelve."

A gasp sounded alongside of her. Not caring if she broke protocol, her head snapped to the side to look at Simon. His jaw hung slack.

"We will also share with you that there'll be a need for those attached to the Twelve to draw their power from love. Unfortunately, this also may be an innate vulnerability for you all against the Dark Ones."

Before Cara could stop herself, her hand flew up.

"Yes, Cara? You may speak," Constantina said.

"But . . . but . . . I thought the Twelve all belonged to a Trinity . . . "

A smile spread across Constantina's face, and she winked. "I don't recall mentioning that in any of our lessons . . . Do you?"

Constantina handed the scroll back to Angelis, and stepped back. Angelis smiled at them. "We, the Council, bless you to journey forth in peace and love. This hearing is adjourned."

Cara stood, incredulous. Simon's energy spiked next to her before he reached over and took her hand in his.

Catching Cara's eye, Constantina gave her a nod.

Cara smiled broadly and bowed her head in thanks. She turned to look again at Simon, her eyes locking on the crystal-blue pools of the man she loved. Her soul filled with joy.

"Let's go," he whispered, clutching her hand for dear life. He led her from the Tribunal chamber. When they were far enough away, one smile from Simon, and they set off running.

Chapter 61

France. Angelorum Sanctuary. Friday, April 4, 7:00 p.m. GMT +1

FIVE MINUTES LATER, Simon threw open the door to his room.

Cara tried to catch her breath through her laughter. As soon as the door shut, Simon lifted her into his arms and swung her in a circle. She felt weightless in his arms, exhilarated by the freedom and feeling of flying. It matched how her heart had soared when the Council delivered the verdict.

"Whoo-hoo!" His eyes positively glowed with joy. After a few dizzying circles, he gently placed her down on her feet.

"I can't believe it!" Cara said, her arms encircling his neck, still pressed up against his white robe. She grew serious. "Are you okay with the verdict? You're not my Guardian anymore."

He shrugged. "I didn't have to relinquish any of my power, and I can keep you safer as one of the Twelve. I can live with it."

She batted her eyes at him seductively. "Hmm. In that case . . . I'm thinking of a certain promise made in your hospital room . . . "

He kissed her tenderly. "Hold that thought. I have something for you," he said, beaming at her. Then he scooped his arms under her legs and raised her up and against his chest. He carried her in two strides to a chair in the sitting area.

"Wait there."

She kicked off her ceremonial sandals, anxious to be rid of them, hoping her robe would soon follow.

He disappeared into the walk-in closet, reemerging a couple of minutes later with a small antique ring box cradled in his palm. Dropping onto one knee, he cracked open the box to reveal a stunning antique engagement ring.

Her hand flew to her chest, and she gasped.

A large, cushion-cut diamond surrounded by sapphires in a platinum filigree setting sat poised within the velvet-lined box.

He gazed up into her eyes. "This was Constantina's from her last incarnation. She thought you'd like it."

"It's so beautiful," she whispered breathlessly.

Sadness tugged at the corners of his mouth, and he bowed his head. "Cara, I know you said in front of the Tribunal you'd willingly bond with me, but that's not the same as me asking you. I want to ask . . . more than anything in the world."

Cara's heart beat faster. "Then what's the matter?"

He raised his head slowly, pain blazing in his eyes. "I'm sure Constantina already told you that as a Nephilim I can't give you a child." He swallowed. "I'll understand if you refuse . . . if you want to wait to marry a human man."

His willingness to sacrifice his happiness for hers touched her deeply, reaffirming why she loved him. For all she knew, the vaccine may have rendered her sterile, making it a moot point anyway. But she'd take alive and childless over dead any day.

Her eyes filled, and she gently cupped her hand to his cheek. "I know we can't have children, but that's not what's important to me. It's *you* I want."

He kissed her palm and searched her eyes. "In that case, Cara Collins, would you agree to wed and become my bonded Nephil mate?"

She brushed away a tear. "Yes."

She couldn't believe the number of twists and turns her life had taken since her birthday. Never did she expect to find the man she'd marry and to finally move past Kai. Being with Simon satisfied her soul in a way that no one before him ever could, and there wasn't anyplace she'd rather be than with him.

He gently took her hand and slipped the ring onto her finger. Looking into her eyes, he said, "I'm honored by your acceptance."

Cara's throat tightened. "I can't believe I almost lost you."

He brushed a strand of her hair away from her face. "You're my destiny. I love you more than words." Leaning over, he kissed her, and the now-familiar electricity and excitement shot through her. He deepened the kiss, unleashing the heat they'd bottled up at the hospital.

Before she knew it, he'd swept her up into his arms and carried her to the bed.

"Now, I believe I owe you a night of exhausting passion . . . " He lay down next her and nibbled on her lip.

"Mmm. Promises, promises," she said and unbuttoned his robe to reveal nothing but boxer shorts covering his skin underneath. Her mouth fell open and she sat up. "You're practically naked under there!"

He chuckled deeply and shrugged. "I slipped on the boxers while I was in the closet getting your ring. I was told not to wear anything underneath."

Cara thought about the slip, bra, and panties she wore underneath her robe, and wondered why he was told to go naked. "Who told you that?"

"My attendant," he said innocently, his eyes big blue marbles.

She narrowed hers at him. "Who attended to you?"

He batted his eyelashes and gave her a mischievous grin. "A woman."

Cara flushed at the thought of someone else gazing at the man she loved. "What woman? Another woman saw you naked?"

He laughed in a deep, rich baritone, rolling onto his back. "She's definitely seen me naked, since she was the one who birthed me."

"Constantina," Cara said flatly and pinched him on the arm for teasing her. "That was mean."

Still laughing, he grabbed her and rolled her on top of him, placing a kiss on her nose. Her hair cascaded around them.

"Take her gesture as confidence in the outcome of the Tribunal. She was readying me as an offering to you, knowing this was where we'd end up if we were exonerated."

Cara's eyebrows shot up. "Are you saying Constantina served up her son—naked—on a proverbial platter?" Heat rushed through her at the thought of Constantina asking him to go naked underneath his robe.

His smile crinkled the corners of his eyes. "She's nothing if not pragmatic and direct."

Cara stared down at him and chuckled. "Yes, there is that. She's a woman after my own heart."

Then he narrowed his eyes at her. "I believe you were in the middle of disrobing me."

"Yes, I believe I was," she said in a throaty voice. "But first . . . " Reaching underneath his head, she freed his hair and combed her fingers through the thick golden waves. Cupping his head in her hands, she pulled him up to her lips and kissed him with abandon.

His fingers traveled down the curve of her spine before grasping her hips and pressing her close. With a small rotation of her hips, she ground into him. A low moan rumbled from his throat as his neck arched back, his hands pushing into the small of her back. Without warning, he traded places with her and she was suddenly underneath him. He knelt over her, all hard ripples and soft skin. This time, she admired his Guardianship Mark, tracing her fingers over the red lines of his tattoo.

"If I have to wait another second, I might lose my mind," he breathed, leaning down and kissing her deeply while adeptly removing his robe and tossing it to the floor.

Hovering above her, he separated the two halves of her robe. Gently pulling her up to sit in front of him, he slid the white cotton garment off her shoulders and cast it onto the floor. Burying his nose in the delicate skin at the base of her neck, he inhaled before his tongue left a sizzling kiss in its place. His hair brushed over her in feather-like touches as he explored her neck, sending a shiver down her back.

A moan rose from her throat, and she swayed into him, her body igniting with desire. All she wanted was to lose herself in his touch. Lifting the hem of her slip, he peeled it off of her and discarded it into the pile, leaving her in her bra and panties.

Slowly, he lowered her onto the bed.

With one hand he reached around to unclasp her bra. Gripped by a sudden bout of butterflies, she grasped his forearm.

"Wait . . . " she whispered. "I'm a little nervous . . . it's been a while." Five years to be exact since she'd been naked in front of a man.

He stroked her hair with the back of his free hand. "Would it make you feel better to know that I'm nervous too?" he asked softly.

She nodded shyly.

"As the Council pointed out, this is the first time for me in over one hundred years." Regardless of hearing it during the Tribunal, his admission still moved her.

Cara removed her hand from his forearm and gave him a come-hither smile. "I believe you were disrobing me?"

"I believe I was." His eyes brightened, and he finished unclasping her bra, releasing her full breasts. With one toss, it was gone. Hooking his thumbs under her panties, he slid them off and threw them aside. Once she was naked in front of him, his eyes lit up like she was a present he'd just unwrapped.

"You're even more beautiful than I'd imagined," he whispered with reverence. He trailed his fingers lightly down her neck and over her chest, passing his thumbs lightly over her breasts. Her nipples hardened under his touch. He rolled the hard peaks between his fingertips until her core pulsed with need.

Cara closed her eyes and cried out, her back lifting up to meet him. Any residual shyness fled the moment he laid his fingers on her. Her body awakened and yearned for more. Like a person denied water in the desert, she wanted to drink until her thirst was quenched.

With a low growl, his mouth came down on her breasts, hot and needy as he sucked and pulled at her sensitive peaks, grazing them gently with his teeth. He groaned deep in his throat as he worked her touch-starved body.

She wound her fingers in his hair as he set her skin on fire with his skilled tongue. Moving lower, he kissed her navel, his mouth blazing a trail of gentle nips and kisses over her stomach and along her hipbones. Grasping her thighs, he opened them, giving himself full access to her. Already swollen and ready for him, even the air touching her there made her twitch.

She'd waited for what felt like an eternity to be with him. It wouldn't take much to send her over the edge.

With heavy lids, he gazed up at her, his powerful arms resting over her legs. "I've dreamt of tasting you since the night we met," he said in a deep, husky whisper.

"Please . . . do it . . . now," she said breathily, her heart racing. Right then, she needed him more than she needed oxygen.

She cried out the moment the hot tip of his tongue connected with the sweet, plump nub in her cleft. Her fingers dug into the hard muscles of his shoulders as he teased and tasted her. Licking and probing just enough to drive up the pressure inside her, he pushed her to the sweet brink of orgasm.

"You're so ready for me, my love," he said just before sliding one of his thick fingers down along her wet folds. When he reached her opening, he sunk one finger, then another into the heat inside her. "So beautiful . . . "

A scream of ecstasy ripped from her lungs, and her body pulsed around him as his fingers penetrated her deeply, in and out, touching her in crevices she didn't know existed. He rested his head on her inner thigh, keeping her opened with his fingers, until the waves of her orgasm subsided.

Just as she regained her breath, his tongue darted back to her sweet spot, and he resumed his exploration deep inside her. A second orgasm gripped her, jolting her off the bed, her fingers clasping the bed covers.

"Simon!" she screamed as he drank her wetness. When her body finally stopped shaking, he crawled up to lay next to her.

"So . . . incredible," she said, lacing her fingers in his and kissing his knuckles. He'd reduced her to a boneless, panting mess, leaving her amazed at the ease with which he'd been able to make her body sing.

"Consider that a small taste of what's to come." He nuzzled her neck. "I promised you neither of us would be able to move afterward . . . and I always keep my promises."

"Can't wait . . . for the main . . . course," she said, gasping and eyeing his black boxers.

"We have all night." He took her into his arms and kissed her, the faint smell of her on his lips.

She gave herself a moment to recover, and then propped herself up on her elbow. "There's only one thing left between us," she said with a coy look, her fingers traveling to his waistband and inching them down ever so slowly.

An amused smile touched his lips. "Are you sure you are ready for the big reveal? I warn you, Nephilim tend to be a little bigger than your average human male."

Cara's breath caught. She'd already figured that part out having touched him a couple of times, but that didn't stop her from being intrigued—and a little apprehensive.

"Don't worry." He caressed her shoulder. "We're well trained from adolescence. Sensual Pleasures is required coursework for all Nephilim before they enter the Guardianship, with advanced electives offered afterward."

Cara was only half surprised, knowing the Angelorum and their pragmatism. If what he'd just done was any indication, she was one lucky woman. She looked at him modestly. "How advanced did you get in your studies?"

"Very." He winked.

That was good enough for her. Without hesitation, she pulled his boxers down the rest of the way, releasing him in all his uncircumcised glory. He was totally hairless, his skin smooth and pink. True to his word, his size was extra generous by anyone's standards.

Simon rose to his knees and knelt before her like a piece of living sculpture. *Michelangelo's work has nothing on him*, she thought.

"Oh my . . . you're truly breathtaking." Cara couldn't help but stare, caught between wanting to drink in his beauty and devour him. Overcome with longing, she moved up onto her knees to get closer.

"I'm yours, my love. Claim me." He placed her hand on his chest, inviting her to explore him. Heat rushed through her veins.

She started with his face, gently dancing her fingertips down along his cheek, her lips meeting his skin and kissing a trail following her fingers, down along his jaw, and then up to his lips. She kissed him deeply, running her fingers through his golden hair, cradling the back of his head in her hands. When their lips parted, his eyes were dark with desire.

She moved her lips lower to the warmth of his neck, breathing in his clean and citrusy smell. Taking her time, she explored him, allowing the gentle electricity between them to wash over her, making her heart beat faster.

He let out a soft groan, his fingers caressing her bare shoulders as he steadied himself.

Pulling back slightly, she ran her hands across his broad shoulders and over the muscles of his chest, taking in the smoothness of his skin under her fingertips. Her hands traveled around to the hard ripples of his back, and then down and over his backside.

As she experienced Simon, it struck her that the root of her desire for him stemmed from the strength of his heart and his tender soul. His physical attributes, while undeniable, were mere icing on the cake. And what a delicious cake . . .

Unable to resist, her hand circled the thick length of him and her fingers glided up the smooth skin in a firm stroke. He thickened even more against her palm.

His fingers tightened on her shoulders, and a hiss escaped through his teeth.

"Not yet . . . please," he whispered hoarsely and shut his eyes.

Unable to resist the hard, masculine beauty grasped in her palm and the gorgeous glistening head calling her name, she slowly lowered her mouth to heed its call, hoping he'd forgive her.

Chapter 62

France. Angelorum Sanctuary. Friday, April 4, 8:30 p.m. GMT +1

Simon's eyes rolled back in his head behind his closed eyelids, his groin tightening almost painfully with the need for release. His heart pounded with the rhythm of a freight train careening down the tracks. If she stroked him even one more time, he was not sure what would happen, and all bets were off if her fingers grazed his sensitive head. He'd had to pinch himself twice while his tongue explored her to tone down his own excitement.

The taste of her had been like ambrosia to his senses.

He wanted her more than anything he could ever remember wanting. Her body was soft and deliciously pliable, as much as a Nephilim-born woman, easing his concerns about hurting her.

Her fingers hadn't moved, but they were still wrapped around his throbbing length.

Taking a deep breath, he opened his eyes just as her hot mouth engulfed his tip, and the sensation shot straight to his brain. A scream ripped from his throat as her tongue bathed him in white-hot ecstasy. His hands clamped her shoulders as his sack contracted, turning his balls into two hard limes as his length kicked up in her palm, expanding to capacity in her mouth.

"Please, not yet . . ." he croaked. With every shred of willpower he had, he gently removed himself from the heaven inside her mouth. "Feels . . . too good."

"I couldn't help it. You looked so delicious," she said, licking her wet lips, her wide, green eyes meeting his as she rose back onto her knees. She caressed his face, her finger touching his lip before she kissed him. Tucking a piece of his hair behind his ear, she pulled him to her.

Her tongue explored his mouth with powerful need. Circling his arms around her waist, he pulled her closer, his erection trapped between them. Her naked, creamy skin against his was sheer bliss.

"Make love to me, Simon," she said in a sultry whisper, her eyes at half-mast.

"With pleasure." He laid her back onto the bedcovers and savored the view of her. Although desperate to bury his length inside her, he held back. He needed to assure her readiness for his size by giving her more pleasure first.

Cara was his first fully human woman. She was more delicate than a Nephil woman, with narrow hips and a delicate bone structure. If he caused her any pain, he wouldn't be able to continue . . . in many ways. He'd be shattered.

Leaning over her, his hands caressed the full, round globes of her breasts, and he thumbed her beautiful pink buds, gently rolling the tips between his fingers. They begged for his tongue.

Cara threw her arms above her head and moaned beneath him. Her moans connected with something innate within him, and his mouth immediately found one of her nipples while his fingers kept the other one ready. Swirling his tongue around the sensitive peak, he sucked and pulled, dancing from one tip to the other until she writhed underneath him.

"Please . . . Simon," she begged with a moan, jutting her hips up to try to meet him.

"Let me taste you again first," he whispered and grazed his fingers down over her belly to the triangle of soft, curly hair the color of autumn leaves at the juncture of her thighs. The feel of it against his fingertips fascinated him. Genetically hairless, Nephilim had nothing like it.

He moved down to the slice of Heaven that lay between her open legs. Parting her wet folds, he plunged his tongue into her. She cried out, arching up into him as he massaged the tender stem of her sex, careful not to cross the threshold from pleasure to pain. His tongue replaced his finger on her nub, while he slipped two fingers back into her. Using his training, he found all of her most intimate pleasure spots. Reading her micro-reactions, he mapped them out and committed them to memory for later when he'd pleasure her with his thick shaft.

"Simon!" she cried and buried her hands in his hair as her body pulsed around him, milking his fingers with the intensity of her orgasm.

He grappled with his own control as he pleasured her, his body ripe for release. His movements created just enough friction between the bedcovers for his erection to move his foreskin over the ridge of his head, driving him wild.

His hands cradled the cheeks of her backside as his mouth drank at her opening, swallowing her essence as she bucked in the throes of pleasure. Her scent triggered a powerful déjà vu . . . wildflowers. Something having to do with wildflowers. Suddenly, the sensation of her was powerfully familiar. It had to be soul recognition. Had to be . . .

One final test. He slipped a third finger into her. She accepted it easily, her body still riding the wave of forceful pulsations.

"Simon . . . now. I want you . . . now," she gasped, pulling up on his biceps, her eyes insistent.

He split her legs wider and positioned his body over hers. His erection kicked up against his stomach. He was ready for her. More ready than he cared to admit.

She looked up at him with deep desire in her eyes and wrapped her legs around his hips, opening the most intimate part of herself to him. The pink glistening folds sent out a siren's call, inviting him inside. He positioned his tip at her entrance.

With a deep intake of breath, he pushed inside, his head sinking into her hot wetness, sending a shock wave through him. His lips parted in a silent scream, and he pushed in deeper. She clasped him like a fitted glove.

She moaned loudly underneath him and winced. Fear shot through him, and he started to pull out.

"I'm not hurting you, am I?" he asked.

Her eyes blazed, and in one movement she dug her nails into his backside and pulled him into her. His eyes burst wide open as he sunk in up to the hilt. The velvet friction inside her set his nerve endings crackling in sweet overload.

"Cara . . . " he growled.

"Simon," she gasped as she reached up to caress his cheek.

Releasing a breath filled with relief, he rolled his hips and moved inside her. The feel of her almost brought tears to his eyes. He started gently for a few strokes, the pressure low in his pelvis already unbearable. He rocked in and out, the muscles of his abs bunching with each thrust. Picking up his rhythm, he pushed deeper with each stroke, seeking out her pleasure spots along the way. Her swollen nub rubbed over his length with every stroke.

Leaning in, he kissed her deeply. She met him, her tongue rising up to meet his. Balancing on one arm, he held her in place against him, his hand supporting the small of her back. Her nails traveled up the length of his back from his backside. A shiver rippled through him. She moaned in rhythm with his thrusts.

He increased his tempo, and Cara moved in tandem with him. Every stroke he made held the heat of his passion and his absolute wonder at being with her, while the tight embrace of her sex worked to unleash the powerful release threatening to explode out of him. But he'd die before denying her a perfect first experience.

"Oh . . . Simon!" Her body arched up into him, her fingers digging deep into the cheeks of his backside. Her hot, moist heat seized him in a snug, pulsating grip, milking his hard length.

His vision blurred, and he threw his head back. His heart pounded so hard he could hear the blood hammering through his eardrums. Rocking his hips fast and hard, he stroked her with deep, penetrating thrusts.

Out of nowhere, her hand reached around and grabbed his sack. She squeezed him with gentle pressure, his balls jerked, and he bellowed. His senses exploded with the strength of his orgasm as he erupted deep within her. His length pulsated wildly inside her, and his bones turned to jelly as he rode the tide of his release.

Still joined and buried deep, he rolled them over and collapsed on the mattress. Her strained breaths joined his as she lay stretched out on his heaving chest.

Her green eyes looked at him, heavy and satisfied. "That . . . was beyond incredible." Her lips met his briefly, before she laid her head against his pounding heart.

Holding her in his arms, their skin was fused from head to toe; she was like heaven around him, a deliciously perfect fit. She eased the restlessness he'd been living with for over a century, and she'd been worth the wait. He looked forward to making love to her for the rest of his life. He was truly happy for the first time in more years than he could count.

He stroked her hair as she lay with her arms draped around him from her vantage point on his chest. "I love you," he whispered.

She raised her head, and touched his face with her fingers. "I love you too."

Maybe Constantina was right, maybe he did deserve redemption. Because of her, he was finally free and ready to stand by Cara's side.

He ran his hands down Cara's back, keeping her body melded into his. He thought back to the déjà vu he had earlier. He had to know if he was right. Hopefully, she wasn't too tired to indulge him.

Pulling her up, he pressed his forehead to hers. "The night I caught you in my arms, I experienced what we call 'soul recognition.' At first, I didn't think it was possible. But now I'm convinced I was right. I think that's what drove me to break my oath and why the Council let us off so easy. Are you willing to help me answer that question?"

With love in her eyes, she said, "Just tell me what I have to do."

Chapter 63

AFTER A QUICK clean-up, Simon carried Cara's limp and satisfied body back to bed. Crawling up onto his knees, he knelt over her.

Cara's scalp started to tingle. "What does soul recognition mean, exactly? Is it like finding a soul mate?" She understood the concept in terms of Kai as her Center Stone, and in her heart-of-hearts she'd always believed in the concept of soul mates.

His eyes took on a radiance. "Close. It means our souls may already know each other. This time, we can join our energy while we make love and allow our souls to touch. The experience will be the closest we can come to the veil that separates Heaven and Earth."

She wasn't sure how it could be any better than what she'd just experienced with him. She could say honestly that her body had responded in ways she'd never imagined. Simon found nerve endings she didn't know existed and elicited sensations she'd never dreamed of feeling.

He reached out his hand, palm up, and she placed her hand in his.

"You think we've met before?" she asked.

"More. I think we've loved before."

A shudder traveled through her. His words reverberated in her brain, and she accepted it as a possibility. "How do we do this?"

"Let me call my power first," he said, kissing her hand and then releasing it.

"What kind of power?" She didn't know Simon could call power of any kind.

"The power of my angelic side," he said and closed his eyes.

A glowing light filled him, spreading out until he was surrounded by a white light that radiated from his skin and illuminated his face and eyes. His wings unfurled with blinding brilliance behind him. She squinted and gasped at his beauty.

He positioned himself over her. "Put your hands on my shoulders, then call your energy. I want to keep my hands free."

With a deep breath, she called down her Pillar of Power. The energy rocked her as it entered the top of her head and shot through her hands and into Simon. Instantly surrounding them, her light eclipsed his. She had to close her eyes against the brightness.

His lips touched hers, and the sensation knocked her back. A breeze engulfed her, carrying her swiftly into a current and transporting her someplace else—like when Constantina had shared visions with her . . .

High-pitched laughter filled with joy rang in her ears. Opening her eyes to locate the sound, she realized she was the source of the joyous noise as she ran headlong through a meadow of wildflowers in every color with the clear, blue sky above. Running swiftly, she tried to avoid the nettles as her white tunic billowed around her legs.

"You can't outrun me forever," said a teasing, masculine voice behind her, which only fueled her happiness and elicited even more bliss-filled giggles. Her heart was so light, happy tears formed in her eyes.

She wanted to be caught, but she delighted in not making the catching too easy. The thought of spending the afternoon making love to him in the meadow made her heart burst with joy. There were so few days like this when they could escape from their duties and languish in each other's arms. But today was special. He would be leaving Heaven tomorrow on his next earthly assignment, and it would be a long time before they could be together again. So, she wanted to make today memorable for them both.

Of course, their separation would pass more quickly for her. Time had less meaning here. She needed more time to find a suitable soul to fill her post before her rebirth, still in the planning stages. She wanted to be highly selective in her choice, knowing the importance of both the post she held and what lay just beyond the horizon. Darkness threatened entrance through Heaven's Gate.

Strong arms encircled her from behind, lifting her off her feet.

"I have you," he whispered in her ear.

Her joyful laughter continued as she turned to face him and threw her arms around his neck. The energy of his soul burned brightly across her eyes, his beauty undeniable.

She recognized him immediately . . . but his name wasn't Simon then.

"You do have me. Forever," she said before his lips came down hungrily on hers, his arms encircling her tightly and melting her into a pool of warmth within his embrace.

His hands traveled over her, seemingly unable to get enough. He broke away, the desire in his eyes said he was no longer able to wait. Lifting her tunic over her head, he cast it aside then quickly removed his own. They stood naked and radiant. Sweeping her up into his arms, he lowered her onto a bed made of their clothing and crushed wildflowers before he collapsed down next to her. The sun warmed them as they lay.

He hovered over her, propped up on his elbows, touching her face with his fingertips. She lost herself in the pull of the love in his eyes, the color of the blue sky above them. Her body craved to couple with him, wanting nothing more than his powerful arms around her and him inside her.

He smiled, and positioned himself between her thighs. Her laughter mixed with tears, and she wrapped her legs around him, pulling him down closer to her. His muscles tensed and he slid into her.

She cried out in ecstasy, her senses reeling with the exquisite feel of him thrusting inside her. Her heart exploded with the perfection of the moment. Birds chirped in the background, and the hum of heavenly music resounded in her head as he made love to her for the last time in their meadow.

When she opened her eyes, he stared down at her, smiling lovingly with delight in his eyes despite his tears streaming freely down his cheeks.

"Promise you'll find me?" he asked, looking for reassurance.

"I promise on my soul I'll find you. I'll love you forever and a day," she said, caressing his cheek. Touching her chest over her heart, two of her fingers melted into her skin, disappearing. A moment later they reappeared holding a small pearl between them.

Holding it up to show him first, she pressed the pearl into his skin over his heart until it disappeared.

"Now there's a part of my soul inside you, so you can be sure I'll find you."

His mouth found hers again, exploring every inch of it with his tongue. His arms squeezed her more tightly, and he increased his rhythm inside her.

Her body shattered into a million pieces of pure sensation. Her eyes fluttered shut the moment he threw back his head and bellowed out her name. And then her cries joined his and she drowned in a wave of pure, unbridled rapture.

Cara screamed out, the rapture traveling back with her. She opened her eyes to see Simon smiling above her, his eyes wet.

Her senses returned and she could feel Simon, here and now, inside her, joined with her.

"Did you see the vision?" she whispered.

He nodded. "You kept your promise," he whispered back.

Smiling, she brushed a piece of his blond hair back behind his ear. "Forever and a day, my love."

Her heart leapt when she recognized the glow in his crystal-blue eyes. His mouth hungrily took hers. She flexed her legs, already wrapped around his hips, and pulled him in deeper. Cupping his face in her hands, she locked her eyes on his.

"Make love to me, and don't ever stop."

"With pleasure." His arms tightened around her, and he thrust deep. "I love you, Cara," he whispered and then showed her how much, taking her home.

Chapter 64

"WHAT CAN I DO to convince you to come back to bed?" Simon asked in a deep, sexy growl.

Cara put her brush down and glanced away from the mirror at Simon, grinning. "You're insatiable, you know that?" In a half-hearted attempt to avoid encouraging him further, she'd dressed in one of his T-shirts to cover up.

He eyed her with a mischievous smile from where he lay naked on the bed, propped up on his elbow. "I have over a century of celibacy to make up for . . . "

She chuckled and resumed brushing her hair. "I think we've made a lot of progress over the last few days, don't you?"

As far as she was concerned, she'd put a nice dent in her own five-year celibacy run. Not to mention, one hundred twenty-five years of celibacy—to be exact—hadn't hindered Simon, given the mind-blowing sex they'd had and the arsenal of Sensual Pleasures techniques he'd shared with her. Very advanced, indeed.

A soft knock sounded on the door.

Cara cleared her throat and pointed at him. His lips turned down in a frown, and he grabbed the sheet to cover himself.

Cara opened the door a crack to find Constantina.

"There's something I want you to see before you and Chamuel depart," she said.

To celebrate their freedom, she and Simon had decided to take a couple of weeks off and visit their favorite places, starting with Monaco. They planned on staying in a vacation home owned by one of Simon's fellow Guardians, followed by a trip to the Grand Canyon. When they'd spoken to Constantina about it the day before, she'd encouraged them to go. According to the Trinity Stones, they'd have a small respite before needing to jump back into the fray and gather the rest of the Twelve.

Cara gave her a sheepish look. "Give me five minutes?"

She nodded. "Of course, dear one. I'll wait for you down the hall."

Cara quietly shut the door, and Simon came up behind her, enveloping her in his arms. "So, what does Constantina want at this early hour?" he asked, nibbling on her earlobe and sending a shiver through her.

She sighed and relaxed into the length of his naked body. Being this close to him offered her both security and the thrill of wanting to crawl inside him. She turned around to face him and planted a warm kiss on his mouth.

"I only asked for five minutes. If you continue to stand this close to me looking this delicious, my chances of leaving this room are slim to none."

"Until later?" he cocked his eyebrow.

"You can count on it. In the meantime, I suggest . . . clothes, lots and lots of clothes."

She released a breath and drank in the rear view of his firm, naked body as he strolled to the bathroom. After he disappeared through the doorway, she discarded the T-shirt she wore and pulled on some clothes. Form-fitting black slacks, a clingy T-shirt, and pair of low-heeled sandals did the trick.

"I'm going for a workout and then to pick up the keys to the villa from Yves," said Simon from inside the bathroom. "Do you mind leaving before lunch?"

"Sounds perfect to me," she said.

He poked his head out the door. "Another kiss before you go?" he asked expectantly.

Meeting him halfway, she wrapped her arms around his neck under his hair and touched her lips to his, quickly slipping him her tongue in promise. He cupped her backside and moaned in response.

"I love you," she said with a satisfied smile.

"I love you too." He bestowed a kiss on the top of her head. "You'd better go. You don't want to keep Constantina waiting."

Constantina stood next to a wide-eyed Cara as they stared into the Trinity Pool. Constantina trained the magnifier on the Trinity Stones that made up the Holy Twelve and stepped aside to show Cara. The Pool, filled with the smooth, triangular stones marking each Trinity, moved in a kaleidoscope of colors before them. Each stone sparkled, shimmered, and pulsed.

Cara drew in a breath. "They're dizzying to watch. How do you know what they're telling you?"

Constantina placed her small hand on Cara's shoulder. "When you're ready, they'll reveal their secrets to you too. But, with their secrets comes knowledge, and in turn, great responsibility. Like Semyaza and his Watchers before us, there will always be the lure to share too much. Good is a choice, but temptation always lies close even for us. One of the reasons we reside within the Sanctuary walls and maintain our distance is to help us to resist the appeal of power that our borrowed humanity affords us. We're not immune to sin, and we can still fall." The face of one of her fellow Council members flashed through her mind. *One of us may have already slipped.*

Frowning, Cara asked, "Why are you showing me these now?"

"I've been remiss in your education, as Achanelech so bluntly pointed out. I need to explain some things to you, Cara." Constantina saw the look of distress in Cara's eyes.

"I still don't remember much from that night."

"I know, dear one. But you will at some point soon. The most important piece is that our encounter with Achanelech was only the opening salvo. Lucifer is anxious to get you in his clutches, and we must protect you. There's much more to come. You're the most important piece in this puzzle, but without Chamuel and the others, you won't succeed. We must gather them and ease them all into their knowledge as time and destiny dictates. Our work begins again soon."

Cara stood watching her, ready for her to say something else.

No need to burden her now, Constantina thought, having a sudden change of heart. She just smiled. "Enjoy your time with Chamuel . . . I mean Simon. Journey forth in peace in love, Cara."

It would take time for Constantina not to stumble on her son's name. Not renouncing his birth name, he'd said, just adding a new one since to Cara, he would always be Simon.

"And you, Constantina."

Constantina stayed behind as Cara exited through the door at the end of the catwalk above. She stared back at the cluster of the Twelve in the Pool. The Collins Trinity Stone had broken; its broken piece still attached to the cluster. She smiled. Another shift had also occurred, just as she'd anticipated. Their next move would be to gather the Wanderer's children.

Her smile broadened when she glanced at the broken stone even further down in the cluster . . . the impossible had just become possible.

Epilogue

Hell. Sunday, April 6.

ACHANELECH, unable to move, cracked open a swollen eye to survey the blackened lump of flesh lying in a heap next to him. He knew he looked no better. They'd been dumped, like demon garbage.

Agony tore through him in unending waves of fire, and he wished hard for an oblivious death, anything to escape the pain and infernal wailing of souls writhing in torment outside their cell. As much as he didn't want to move, he had to know if he was now truly alone.

He forced his charred, clawed digit to inch across the tar-covered floor to reach Emanelech. Her hair had burned away, leaving behind the dragon-like shape of her demon form. Her leathery skin had burned to flaky black ash.

The pain in his throat was no better or worse than the rest of him. "Em," he said in their native hellspeak. The effort made him feel as though he'd swallowed knives.

Something fluttered on the black mound, and his demon heart palpitated. There it was: a slice of blue—her eye, not her demon eye, but her human eye. "Acchie . . ." It was barely a whisper over the horrific noise surrounding them. "I hurt, Acchie." Her eye fluttered shut.

"Don't leave me, Em." A shot of pain ripped through his dead heart, exceeding the suffering of his flesh.

"Can't . . ."

"Please," he begged. He didn't understand how he'd ended up here in such utter despair. But he knew he couldn't survive it without Emanelech at his side.

"Miss . . . home," she whispered, this time not in hellspeak, but in words.

Their Master had done a number on them for their screwup with that Soul Seeker. They'd almost gotten her killed before she escaped, and Lucifer had been less than thrilled with their performance. He'd shown his displeasure . . . for what seemed like an eternity. They'd never be able to survive in this state topside.

His clawed finger caressed the ash of her arm, bits flaking off under his touch. "Where, *ma chèrie*? Le France?" he asked in a harsh croak, his throat not fit for speech.

"No . . . Heav . . . "

If he could have paled at her words, he would have. Did he really hear her correctly? She had to be delirious from her punishment.

Terror gripped him. It was forbidden to ever mention that place—the "H" word—in Hell.

"Em, no. Don't ssspeak," he hissed, his forked tongue flicking between his teeth. "We'll never get out of here if you do."

Her eye opened in a slit. "Redemp . . . "

Redemption. Achanelech wanted to choke her into silence before she had them condemned to a permanent residence in Lucifer's wailing wall.

Anger bubbled through his veins like red-hot lava. There would never be redemption for them. Ever. In the meantime, he had a score to settle. Eae would pay for all she'd done to him. He'd been patiently waiting for her mate Leo to descend from his heavenly perch for over a century, but he'd wait no longer. Vengeance would be his, now that he knew she had more to lose.

The sigil on the back of his neck pulsed into action, and their cell filled with the inky black haze of his children. He thought with irony about his demons. As Semyaza and his Watchers languished in unending darkness since the time of Noah, he'd been commanding the disembodied spirits of their Nephilim spawn for just as long. And here they were to do his bidding.

Master . . . Master . . . Master . . . Their voices spoke to him, one by one, in the language of Hell.

"Take us home," he whispered back, misery filling his plea.

Readers, thank you for sharing the world of the Angelorum!
Cara and crew return in *The Wanderer's Children*
Coming in Fall 2014
To learn more, visit: www.wandererschildren.com

Turn the page for a SNEAK PEEK!

Los Angeles. Beverly Wilshire Hotel. Saturday, May 11, 11:00 a.m. PDT.

WHAP!

Brett King cracked open one eye and groaned. His skull threatened to split in half if he so much as blinked. Everything above his shoulders hurt down to his hair follicles. Silk sheets caressed his body on the monster-sized bed at the Beverly Wilshire. The good news: he was in a bed. The bad news: he didn't remember how he'd gotten there.

A hand came down a second time on his ass. *Whap!*

"You're welcome."

"What the hell?" Brett turned over to protect his backside, and spun his head in the direction of a familiar, pissed-off female voice. The movement sent a shooting pain straight into his cortex, and stars danced in front of his eyes.

Roxy sat Indian style next to him like an irate pixie, her arms crossed over her chest. One of his stylishly ripped T-shirts covered her petite body. Python scales inked a trail up one side of her collarbone, looped around her neck, and came back down the other side, disappearing into the T-shirt. Her kohl-rimmed blue eyes stared at him, the rest of her makeup long gone. Her short cap of black hair stuck up in angry spikes, and a small row of hoop earrings crawled up the curve of her left ear like a silver caterpillar. Roxy was a force to be reckoned when he was fully awake; he couldn't imagine what he was in for after being woken up from a drunken sleep.

"Why are you hitting me? And why are you in my bed wearing my clothes?" he croaked, his voice ragged. Thankfully, he didn't have to sing again for at least a week. The moment after he asked the question, he could feel the color drain from his face. Lifting the covers, he peeked down to see if he was still wearing his underwear.

Roxy rolled her eyes and shoved him. "Oh, for crissakes, King! Your virtue is safe with me. Even you couldn't tempt me to go straight. I'm wearing your fucking shirt, you moron, because you vomited all over me on our way up to the room last night."

No wonder his mouth tasted like an acidic jock strap. He stuck his head under the pillow and wrapped it down around his ears. "Stop yelling, Rox, or my head will explode."

She reached over and poked him. "So, I'll say it again. You're welcome."

Every time she touched him, pain shot through his cranium. He blew out an exasperated breath and looked at her with daggers in his eyes. "Okay, thank you. Now, tell me for what, and stop poking me. It hurts."

Arching a brow, she smirked. "You really don't remember, do you?"

"If I remembered, I wouldn't be asking," he mumbled, resting his cheek against the cool mattress, wishing for an ice pack to dull the pain in his head.

Leaning back on her elbows she straightened her bare legs, crossing them at the ankles. A look of wicked delight lit up her face. "Well, let me start by saying that you sure know how to end a tour with a bang."

Brett and his band King Metaljam had done their penultimate concert in Los Angeles the night before, capping off their nine-month tour. Technically, they still had one more date in New York to make up for a prior cancellation.

"Rox, if I'd ended the tour with a bang, I'd be enjoying some post-coital bliss with Rachel right now instead of waking up next to my lesbian best friend." He'd known Roxy since their sophomore year at the University of Southern California, right before he dropped out and the band hit it big. Not only was she his best friend, she was also his publicist and doubled as his stylist.

"Ha! Like *that* was going to happen after you and Rachel traded drinks in the face last night. Truth is, she's a bitch, and you're better off without her." Roxy gave him a self-satisfied smile.

His face twisted into a scowl. "Thanks. Tell me what you really think." His heart sunk for a moment as the memory slowly returned. His ten-month relationship with his model-actress girlfriend Rachel had shown signs of strain the closer the tour came to ending. He had high hopes when they'd first met, but as time passed he was less sure which she loved more: him, or his money and rock star status. He hungered to find someone with whom he could escape the plastic reality of the limelight when he wasn't working. Disappointment filled him when he realized Rachel would never be that person.

He'd already consumed five drinks too many by the time they'd gotten into an argument about taking a vacation when the tour ended. All he wanted to do was return home to San Francisco, relax, and enjoy some privacy. The conversation ended with him calling Rachel a gold digger, and her telling him to fuck off, punctuated by her flinging a drink in his face. Without thinking, he tossed the remainder of his drink back at her.

He groaned. "Uhhh. Is that all?"

Roxy smirked and pushed her finger into the sensitive skin of his cheek. "Not. Even. Remotely."

Pain jolted through his face, and he pounded the bed with his fist. "Ow! What the hell?"

"Lucky for you, I saved your pretty, surfer-boy face after Randy's first punch."

Punch? What punch? Why would his bass player want to beat the crap out of him?

Brett knit his brow. "Why did Randy hit me in the face?" Then he added, "And don't call me 'surfer-boy,' you know I hate that." He bristled at her derogatory use of the term. So he was blond and he surfed, so what? She liked to say the only two things separating him from being a bad-ass rock star and a surfer was a pair of black leather pants and the fact that he didn't own a puka bead necklace.

Roxy circled her neck, cracked it, and then gave him a mischievous smile. "That would have to do with me saving you from the two harlots who planned to take you upstairs and bear your bastard children nine months from now."

He looked at her in pained disgust. "What?"

Tilting her head, she said, "Yup. It happened after the fight with Rachel."

Shit, how much did I drink last night? Ironically, he was the lead singer in a rock band and could have any woman he wanted—or two—but he abhorred one-night stands. Strangely enough, he preferred monogamy. Less complicated that way. He caught more than his fair share of abuse for that from the band, but he didn't care.

"So what does that have to do with Randy popping me in the face?"

She covered her mouth with her hand and chuckled. "One of them was his wife."

His gut clenched, and he suddenly felt sick. "Oh, fuck me." He buried his head back underneath the pillow. That's it, no more alcohol until further notice. How he could stray so far from his own sense of civilized behavior, he didn't know. It had been a long time since he'd felt like this much of a jackass.

"I'm afraid to ask, but anything else?" Peeking out from under the pillow, he braced himself for Roxy's reply.

She gave him a sour look. "Yeah, and you owe me big time for this one. I held your hair back while you lost the other half of your stomach in the toilet last night."

"Ugh." He groaned from inside his pillow cave. "Thanks, Rox."

She crawled off the bed. "Now go take a shower—you stink. I'll check to see if you created any more PR disasters last night."

"What would I do without you to prop up my ego?" Slowly, he sat up, the silk sheets slipping down around his waist. He caught a whiff of what she meant. She was right. He reeked.

Roxy scrolled through the e-mail on her iPhone and snorted. "You don't need me to prop up your ego when more woman than you can count would willingly drop to their knees and blow you." She turned and wiggled her eyebrows at him. "Oh, and don't forget, number eight on this year's hottest bachelor countdown."

Brett rolled his eyes. How could he forget? Roxy reminded him every chance she had. She'd submitted him for consideration via a friend of hers at a well-known publication. The photo shoot had been painful. He'd spent hours, half-naked in nothing but leather pants, locked in poses under hot lights. The experience gave him a new respect for models.

Frowning at her, he grumbled. "Come on, Rox. You know me better than that. That's not what I'm about. I'd rather have something meaningful."

"Meaningful, huh?" She cocked a brow at him. "Then why did you check under the sheets before when you thought maybe we'd slept together?"

He gave her a wounded look. "It could've happened. It's not like it hasn't before," he said defensively, leaning back against the headboard. He'd lost his virginity to Roxy back in college, and she'd seen him naked probably as many times as any of the woman he'd ever dated.

Her expression softened. She came over to him and put her arms around his neck. "We were nineteen, King. I hadn't come out yet." Leaning over, she kissed his forehead. "You're such a girl when it comes to women. It's one of the things I love about you. But I'm serious, go take a shower. You smell like ass." She pushed away from him.

"Fine. I can take a not-so-subtle hint." He swung his legs over the side of the bed, and shuffled off in the direction of the bathroom.

Roxy ran in ahead of him and snatched her black leather dress from where it hung on a hook next to one of the fluffy white robes and headed for the door.

"Now that I know you're safe and not going to die by choking on your own puke, I'm heading back to my room. Be ready in forty minutes. I've scheduled an interview for us at noon."

The door closed with a *thunk* on her way out. Brett squeezed his eyes shut and whimpered, not only from the pain in his head but also at the thought of seeing anyone before tomorrow.

Brett slept for most of the flight. Forty minutes after Roxy had left his room at the Beverly Wilshire, he'd sat in a limo dressed in jeans, a T-shirt, and boots with his hair pulled back in a wet ponytail and hidden under an LA Dodgers baseball cap, heading for LAX.

Halfway through his shower he'd realized that he needed to disappear until the last concert date. Granted, this wouldn't be the first time he'd slipped away during the tour. The last time was two months ago when he'd reached a saturation point and snuck off for a long weekend.

He'd texted Roxy after he left the hotel: HAD TO JET, SORRY ABOUT THE INTERVIEW. SEE YOU IN NYC. Then he turned off his phone to escape the tirade he knew would follow.

Almost to his destination, he stared out the first class window and listened to his iPod with his cap pulled down around his ears, trying to maintain a low profile.

Where he planned to go, he wouldn't have to fight off any fans.

When he had called his Aunt Adela, she happened to be in Paris on business. She kindly reminded him that he had an open invitation to stay at her place in Connecticut—his one safe haven—anytime. She even called ahead to have the house stocked with food. It was perfect.

Another thought hit him, and the corners of his mouth turned up in a smile. Taking out his phone, he scrolled through his contacts until he found the name he was looking for . . .

Cara Collins.

Methinks it's time to collect on that breakfast, he thought, arching his brow.

Acknowledgments

IT TAKES A VILLAGE. Thank you to my critique partner, Joanie Sorensen; my writer critique friends (Deborah, Cindy, Jenni, and Kisa); the "cross-stitch" beta reading crew (Marilyn, Pat, Lesley, and Eileen); and my progression of editors, most recently, Zetta Brown. Without them, this book would have never been published.

Did You Know?

ANXIETY DISORDERS are the most common mental illnesses in the United States, affecting forty million adults (18 percent of the population) age eighteen and older. Panic disorder alone affects six million people annually; women are twice as likely to be affected as men.

I should know—I was one of them.

Anxiety disorders also affect one in eight children, and the average age of onset is eleven years old. Anxiety disorders are highly treatable, yet only about one-third of those suffering receive treatment.

To learn more:

American Depression and Anxiety Association:
http://www.adaa.org/about-adaa/press-room/facts-statistics

National Institute of Mental Health:
http://www.nimh.nih.gov/statistics/1anyanx_adult.shtml

About the Author

photo © Leo O'Connor

By day, L. G. O'Connor is a corporate executive in a Fortune 250 company. By night, she's a writer of adult Urban Fantasy, Paranormal Romance, and Contemporary Romance who lives in Northern New Jersey. She lives a life of adventure, navigating her way through dog toys and soccer balls and loaning herself out for the occasional decorating project. When she's feeling particularly brave—she enters the kitchen.

For access to special perks, discounted rates on print books for Book Clubs and Book Club Packages, and signed printed copies:
Visit my website and blog: www.lgoconnor.com

Also, find me here:
www.Facebook.com/lgoconnor1
https://twitter.com/lgoconnor1
www.TrinityStones.com
Goodreads

If you enjoyed this book, I would greatly appreciate it if you would spread the word. You can help other readers find this book in these ways:

RECOMMEND it to family, friends, online forums, discussion groups, book clubs.
REVIEW it on Amazon, Goodreads, or any other review site.
LEND it to anyone who loves Urban Fantasy and Paranormal Romance.

SELECTED TITLES FROM SHE WRITES PRESS

She Writes Press is an independent publishing company
founded to serve women writers everywhere.
Visit us at www.shewritespress.com.

Watchdogs by Patricia Watts.
$16.95, 978-1-938314-34-6

When journalist Julia Wilkes returns to the town where her career got its start, she is forced to face some old ghosts—and some new enemies.

In the Shadow of Lies: An Oliver Wright Mystery Novel by M. A. Adler.
$16.95, 978-1-938314-82-7.

As World War II comes to a close, homicide detective Oliver Wright returns home—only to find himself caught up in the investigation of a complicated murder case rife with racial tensions.

Water On the Moon by Jean P. Moore.
$16.95, 978-1-938314-61-2.

When her home is destroyed in a freak accident, Lidia Raven, a divorced mother of two, is plunged into a mystery that involves her entire family.

Clear Lake by Nan Fink Gefen
$16.95, 978-1-938314-40-7

When psychotherapist Rebecca Lev's father dies under suspicious circumstances, she becomes obsessed with discovering what happened to him.

Fire & Water by Betsy Graziani Fasbinder
$16.95, 978-1-938314-14-8

Kate Murphy has always played by the rules—but when she meets charismatic artist Jake Bloom, she's forced to navigate the treacherous territory of passionate love, friendship, and family devotion.

Shanghai Love by Layne Wong
$16.95, 978-1-938314-18-6

The enthralling story of an unlikely romance between a Chinese herbalist and a Jewish refugee in Shanghai during World War II.

CPSIA information can be obtained at www.ICGtesting.com
Printed in the USA
BVOW07s1219250315

393182BV00001B/1/P

9 781938 314841